THE SOMETHING ABOUT HER

OPPOSITES ATTRACT BOOK FOUR

RACHEL HIGGINSON

Copy Editing by Amy Donnelly of Alchemy and Words
Cover Design by Zach Higginson

 Created with Vellum

OTHER ROMANCES BY RACHEL HIGGINSON

The Five Stages of Falling in Love

Every Wrong Reason

Trailer Park Heart

Bet on Us (Bet on Love Series)

Bet on Me (Bet on Love Series)

The Opposite of You (Opposites Attract Series)

The Difference Between Us (Opposites Attract Series)

The Problem with Him (Opposites Attract Series)

FOLLOW RACHEL

Keep up with Rachel on her Newsletter

Connect with Rachel on her Facebook Page

Follow Rachel on Twitter and Instagram

To Sam,
My favorite Conversation Starter,
So glad to call you a friend.
Thanks for writing your number on the
Back of a picture of your kids.
You always know how to make the
Best first impression.

ONE

WHEN I WAS A LITTLE GIRL, I collected personalities. For me, becoming someone else was an art form and a secret challenge, like a competition with myself that I always won. The less I was myself, the easier it was to blend into the different social situations I was forced to experience.

And the longer I lived, the more I realized most experiences were of the horrific and traumatic variety. Or at least the experiences that left the biggest mark. The longest scar.

But I relied on those alternate personalities, my chameleon ability to blend in so seamlessly. That collection of personalities had saved me over and over again. It was the one constant thing I could rely on when I was a kid. And it had followed me into adulthood as I navigated the rough waters of living and working and struggling to breathe through everything.

For my dad, I dressed up in princess gowns and greeted grown-ups with handshakes and tiny curtsies. I tolerated the late-night business meetings he dragged me to by pretending I loved to sit and stare at walls for hours. I smiled at his balding, middle-aged friends that had more money than was good for them and pretended their uninvited wandering hands on my butt didn't bother me. I played the perfect daughter. While he played the negligent self-absorbed father.

For my mom, I wore party dresses and high heels and laughed at all the bawdy jokes I didn't understand. I played off her bad decisions and supported her unhealthy addiction to my dad. I skipped homework so we could hang out with her wild friends. I didn't mention the school plays she forgot or the ballet recitals I had to skip because she wanted to drive to the beach for the weekend. I was the best friend in her life, not her child. And she loved me more than anything else on the planet. The feeling was mutual, even if the hard truth of our relationship was only remembered by me.

At school, I got straight As and answered every question when called on. I was on student council and the senior class vice president. I tutored. I was the basketball team captain. Like every teenager, I stole my mom's cheap liquor and my dad's cash paid for all our shenanigans. I said yes to everything. Boys and parties and drugs. A life of endless fun and zero responsibilities. Even when I wanted to say no.

And when I did say no, nobody listened. I had said yes too many times to be taken seriously. I played my party girl role too well.

I played all my parts too well.

Dillon Baptiste, the girl everyone liked because she was the girl no one knew.

Not really.

By the time I graduated high school, I'd lived a hundred different personalities for a thousand different people. And I hated who I pretended to be.

Because they weren't me.

The worst part was, I didn't even know who I was.

Still don't.

Depression hit hard those first few years after school. I lacked direction because I didn't have a purpose. And I didn't have a purpose because I didn't know what I wanted. And I didn't know what I wanted because I had no idea who I was or how to even figure that out.

And then my dad got sick.

There wasn't a therapist in the world who could have untangled the mess my mind became. My thoughts were overrun, watching a man I equal parts loved and hated, succumb to a disease he couldn't pay to go away.

Those were dark, dark years.

Ezra had shown up because he cared about his father. Like a white knight in gleaming armor, he rode into our broken mess ready to fix everything—including me.

Maybe especially me.

Our dad was too sick for Ezra to help. But I wasn't totally irredeemable. I, at least, had my health.

And so he'd started the slow, arduous process of pulling me out of the black abyss I'd let myself fall into. I didn't latch onto him like I had every other person in my life. I studied him. I learned from him. And eventually, I tried to become him.

Not literally, of course.

I liked his mannerisms. He was detached. So effortlessly aloof. He didn't come from money, but he walked into my world like he was meant to be there. He looked down on everyone except me. He was intolerant of incompetence and bullshit and knew how to get what he wanted.

More importantly, he knew *what* he wanted.

I was enamored with this new older brother of mine that selflessly took care of other people without letting them touch him in return.

I wanted his... armor.

Ezra already had a life before he walked into mine. He loved food. It started with his friend Killian and their foster mom Jo—his small, trustworthy tribe, the only people he let in. And I experienced them at their most open and candid when they were creating and making good food.

Later, Elena showed up. I had hated her from the beginning, but too afraid to push my new brother away, I had kept my mouth shut. When he married her, he'd disappeared for a while. They had a restaurant to open. They had a new life to start. There wasn't room for a spoiled brat of a half-sister that was lost in grief and confusion and couldn't name one thing she actually wanted for herself.

I had parties to fall back on and a long list of contacts willing to help me forget what it was like to have someone care about me, someone who liked me because I was me.

I picked up my cache of personalities and dove back into a dark, depressing world that would show me the real meaning of rock bottom. Glitz and glam and money and parties and all the other beautiful nothings that filled up those years of my life came with a price—a price I had to pay with my soul.

I thought I was broken before... I had no clue. I thought I was wrecked and ruined and lost... I learned quickly that those words had sharp, lethal teeth and when aptly applied, sunk into flesh until they found bone. And then they did not let go. They left me bloody and broken and... alone.

Eventually Ezra came back, only this time he brought cooking with him. Not just food and good meals, but the art of it. The business of it.

And he saved me a second time.

I'd stolen more of him then. Out of necessity this time. Out of the need to cushion my survival and paint a picture of my reality that was something other than the truth.

I'd been desperate for purpose by this point. Greedy for anything that wouldn't make me feel so... empty. So very wrong.

Violated.

When Ezra introduced me to cooking—real, heartfelt, blood and guts cooking—I absorbed everything he offered. It wasn't mine to begin with, but somehow, surrounded by fire and heat and spice, I found myself.

In the middle of a kitchen, covered in sweat and grease, I discovered who I was.

It was the greatest gift Ezra could have ever given to me. It was a gift I couldn't even explain to him without confessing the mismatched, messed up rest of me, and even then he would only ever see the surface. Of me. He would only ever see my mistakes. He would stop seeing the pretty sister he loved so dearly and find the ugly, distorted train wreck instead.

I kept those puzzle pieces hidden, even while I let cooking refine my soul—even while the heat healed me and the fire fed life back into my battered body. And I adopted one last personality to soften all the other hard edges. I became the girl that pretended everything was always fine and fun and wonderful. I created a second skin that seemed normal. And I decided to wear it for the rest of my life.

Ezra owned restaurants, so I got a culinary degree to work for him. It seemed consistent with this new personality. I knew it made logical sense to him. I knew I would never be able to explain all the intricate reasons for falling in love with food, but I also knew I wouldn't have to. I came from a food family. Food was my present. Food would always be my future.

And most of the time, I loved working for my brother.

But he'd gone too far this time.

Way too fucking far.

"This is too much," I whispered, struggling to breathe through the panic. My made-up personality was already slipping, but I was too flabbergasted to care.

My brother smiled at me from across the host stand of his most notorious restaurant, Bianca. "Happy birthday, Dillon."

"You're not serious." I whispered the words, hoping he would mistake them for surprise instead of the hissing viper I felt rising inside me. My birthday was two weeks ago. We'd already celebrated number twenty-seven. He'd given me a Joule sous vide for my apartment. This had to be a joke.

His grin widened—a rare and unusual sight to see him so happy. "I am. Serious."

"Ezra, I can't possibly—"

"I know what you're thinking," he rushed to say. "But you're a perfect fit for this kitchen. And the staff here has been running the place on their own for over a year. They're here to help you make the transition."

"I'm barely out of school. I haven't even been at Lilou for two years yet." The growly edge of my voice didn't dissuade him at all. If anything, his eyes got that glint in them that told me he wasn't going to back down. Not now. Not ever. I swallowed the lump in my throat put there by dread, frustration, and large amounts of fear. "I wouldn't know the first thing about running this restaurant. I thought you wanted to save her? Not run her into the ground!"

"You're not going to run her into the ground," he countered patiently.

"Fine. I'll do something worse. Set her on fire. Blow her up. Send her to the freaking moon." Hysteria clawed up my throat and jumped out of my mouth. "Ezra, I'm not qualified for this restaurant! Are you crazy?"

His smile finally fell, revealing his signature frown. "Dillon, are you? This is an opportunity of a lifetime."

I resisted the urge to roll my eyes. "Yeah, an opportunity to watch my career go up in flames. And I'll never forgive you if you fire me. Which is bound to happen, since I'm not qualified for this job. And then we'll be estranged. Do you want to be estranged?"

"You'll do fine—"

"I'm not a good enough chef for Bianca, Ezra. I don't want her. At least not yet."

His eyebrows scrunched together in defeat. "I can't wait any longer. Bianca needs a leader. And I want you. If I give her to someone else, they won't only stand-in. I'll find the best chef I can get my hands on. If you don't take her now, she might never be yours."

"Ezra, goddamnit. Let me get my feet beneath me before you start handing out jobs like this."

He shook his head. "I wish I could."

The kitchen door swung open and our friends burst out into the dining room. "Congratulations!" they shouted in unison.

I resisted the urge to cry.

Molly and Vera walked out, both hands laden with balloons. Kaya held a ridiculously expensive bottle of champagne. Wyatt walked beside her holding a stark white chef's hat in his hand, marked with Bianca's lily emblem. Killian followed behind all of them, pushing a cart with a monstrosity of a cake on it.

I blinked at the frosted eyesore. *Congratulations Chef Dillon.*

"Is that from Costco?"

The lot of them burst into laughter. Explanations of time constraints and nobody knew who exactly was in charge of it and what kind of cake did I like anyway were shouted back and forth.

It was hard not to smile when my friends filled this space and laughter rang through the air. It was hard not to take in the elegant décor and open design and the Bianca's eyes, the mural that Molly had painted so perfectly on the long wall, and not want to make this place mine. It was even harder to remember Bianca's sullied reputation and the difficulties she'd been through over the last several years and not want to bring her back to life.

I wanted this place.

I wanted her more than I wanted my next breath.

But what Ezra failed to see was that I just wasn't good enough for her.

I was a newbie. Green at best. Hopelessly ignorant in my worst moments. I was still navigating waters of not even knowing what I didn't know.

Sure, I'd worked in kitchens since I started culinary school. I worked as the *maître d'* before that. My brother was a restaurant business genius. And my best friends were all chefs.

Just like most things in my picture-perfect life, I had the pedigree for this job. I just didn't have the experience. Or the ability. Or the fucking know-how. And how dare Ezra dangle this in front of me when he knew I'd have to turn it down.

"She doesn't want it." Ezra's sullen voice cut through the joy in the room and turned the atmosphere to ice.

God, he could be a true bastard when he wanted to be.

Killian was the first to speak. His disbelieving "What?" echoed through the room.

"She doesn't want Bianca. There's no reason to celebrate."

Every gaze in the room swiveled to me. They looked at me like I was crazy. And maybe I was for turning down this once in a lifetime opportunity, as Ezra had so articulately put it.

But I would have been crazier to take it.

Their reaction churned in my stomach and my chest burned with the desperation to please these people I loved so much. They knew me as *fine. Everything is fine. Everything is always fine.*

Their expressions reflected utter disbelief. It would make sense for me to take this job, to take my place among them.

Each of them owning or running their own kitchen. Each of them career-oriented and relentlessly driven. These were the best of the fine dining best in Durham. These were the influencers that shaped culinary culture in our part of the world.

And why wouldn't I want to join them in their quest to give the masses the best dining experience on the planet? Why wasn't I part of the Durham, North Carolina Food Revolution?

Why didn't I want to carve my name in the chopping block of who's who in the holy, almighty food-dom?

But it wasn't fair to compare me to them. Or even put my name in the same category.

They were experts at their craft.

And I was still learning from them.

How could I ever become one of them?

The room settled in tense silence. I opened my mouth to explain or excuse my answer or say something—anything—but nothing came out.

"We're still eating the cake though, right?"

Everyone in the room moved at the same time, our bodies in complete sync as we turned toward the voice that had broken the frozen tension in the room. Vann Delane leaned against the wall next to the in and out doors to the kitchen, his arms folded over his chest, his legs crossed at the ankles, his shoulders slouched casually.

"Are you serious?" Vera snapped at him.

He shrugged, his smooth chin jutting toward the metal cart with the white-frosted Costco cake on top of it. "I'm just saying, it's a good cake. We shouldn't let it go to waste."

I worked my jaw back and forth feeling irrationally furious with this veritable stranger in the room. Sure, everyone else was well acquainted with Vera's granola-loving brother. But I wasn't. And this was my party, damn it.

Er, my pity party.

He could take the cake and shove it down his biker shorts.

(Not that he was dressed in biker shorts now. Unless they were hidden beneath his slim-fitting maroon pants.)

Vera spoke up before I could voice my opinion out loud. "Since when do you eat cake?"

"Why wouldn't I eat cake?"

"It has sugar in it," Vera reminded him. "And gluten. It's jam-packed with gluten."

He had the audacity to look offended. "I'm not gluten free."

Vera raised her eyebrows.

He shrugged. "I avoid it when I can. But I'm not anti-gluten or anything. In fact, I rather appreciate it. In moderation of course."

Was this guy serious?

"The cake looks good," he continued. "I'm just saying, we shouldn't let it go to waste."

"Nobody's going to waste it," I snapped, unable to hold my

tongue any longer. I needed this awkward string of moments to end. I needed these people gone. And for the cake to go. And me too.

Ezra and I probably needed a deeper conversation about why I had to turn down his excessively generous offer. I would need to curl into a ball and cry at some point. And there would be an existential crisis mixed in somewhere. I could do none of those things with all these people—especially the cake-obsessed moron in the corner—standing there taking up space.

Vann pushed off the wall and dropped his hands to his narrow hips. "I'll get the plates," he said, like it was the most brilliant idea in the world.

As soon as Vann disappeared back into the kitchen, my friends and brother snapped back to gape at me.

"Why don't you want to run Bianca?" Kaya demanded, eyebrows bunched together beneath her vibrant purple hair—a recent change for her. She'd called the new, vibrant pixie cut Boss Bitch. The entire package, including the new hair, suited her and Sarita perfectly.

"I do want Bianca," I answered patiently. "I'm just not ready for her yet." At their immediate protests, I held up a hand and tried to explain. "You guys, I've only been in a real kitchen a little over a year. I'm not qualified for this place. I'm barely competent enough to work for Wyatt."

"That's not true," Kaya insisted. She was my girl. My ride or die kitchen bitch. My sparkly vampire soulmate. And she was the most driven woman I had ever met. Of course, she wasn't going to understand my reluctance. She walked out of the womb ready to take on the world and cook five-star meals. "You're one of the finest chefs I know, D. Bianca would be lucky to have you."

"I would be lucky to have you," Ezra echoed. "Come on, Dillon. I'm so sick of high maintenance chefs that can't run my restaurants because their gigantic egos are in control and not their reason. Or their raw creativity. I need someone fresh. Young. Terrified of failing." He took a deep breath and let the full force of his puppy dog eyes work their magic. "I need you, sis."

There was a weighted pause before Killian said, "I think I'm offended."

"I think I am too," Wyatt added.

"That makes three of us," Kaya grumbled.

Vera leaned forward, tottering on the balls of her feet. "I've never worked for Ezra," she told no one in particular. "I turned him down actually."

"I'm not ready," I stated firmly.

Before anyone could argue, Vann stuck his head through the kitchen door and said, "I probably should have asked. But, where exactly are the plates?"

A collective annoyed sigh rippled through the room, but I saw the interruption as an escape. "Here. I can help you." Shouldering my way through my friends, I scurried after Vann for a moment of quiet.

As soon as I stepped inside the kitchen, I forgot my entire purpose for being there. I walked over to the nearest counter and carefully set my palms on the cool stainless steel. The lights were still off and the only sound filling the empty space was the buzz of the refrigeration units.

"Son of a bitch." I growled at my manicured nails. I closed my eyes against the spirit of this space, the living, breathing, tenacious something that inhabited this place and the chefs that worked here.

It seeped through my skin and caught fire in my blood. I took a breath, filling my lungs with the contagious hunger to stay here.

"I found these," Vann announced, interrupting my solitude.

I opened my eyes and found him standing on the other side of the island with a stack of dinner plates in his hand. My muscles tensed out of instinct, assuming he'd manage to drop and shatter them before he made it out the door.

Fear and anxiety and a jumble of idiotic hope tangled in my throat and I was unable to give him better instructions. "What is your obsession with cake anyway?"

Setting the plates on the counter with more finesse than I gave him credit for, he eyed me across the distance with something like arrogant insight. "It's why I came. Hell, it's why you came."

I shook my head, defiant and digging my heels in, set on my decision. My loose, wavy blonde hair dancing around my shoulders like Medusa's snakes. "It's not at all why I came. I had no idea any of this was going to happen. Ezra asked me to meet him here to get my advice on a possible new menu. The head chef offer was a total and complete surprise."

I got the feeling he resisted rolling his eyes when he said, "But you knew it was coming."

"Y-yeah, maybe," I conceded, not willing to lie. Ezra had been hinting around about this position since I graduated school. I had known he wanted to give me this restaurant for a long time. And lately I'd realized he wanted to give it to me sooner rather than later. But that didn't mean I knew he would do it today. Or even in the next five years. "But I was still surprised. I thought he'd at least give me a few years' experience before he thrust an EC of a lifetime in my face."

This time he gave into the eyeroll. "So be honest, you were never going to take the job. You should have told him from day one."

The fire inside me turned into a furious dragon. "Excuse me?"

"We're here for the cake," he repeated. "You and me both."

"What exactly are you saying?"

He pushed the plates to the center of the island and walked closer, dragging his hand over the cool metal surface. "I don't even know you and I can see this job isn't for you."

"And why is that?"

"It's hard work, for starters. And from what Vera says, the chef that takes over is going to have to be a badass both in the kitchen and in real life. This place needs someone to resuscitate it. Whip it into shape. You're too soft."

"Too soft?"

He smiled, but it was teasing... smug. "You're a good girl, Dillon.

Gentle. Delicate... Afraid to hurt anyone's feelings. This place would chew you up and spit you out. And you know that."

The hair on the back of my neck stood up and I could have sworn my nails stretched into talons. It was all I could do to keep from launching myself across the counter and wrapping my hands around his throat.

But I didn't.

I was a lady after all.

Which only doubled my desire to choke this man out since it went along exactly with his accusations.

"I'm not taking this job as a favor to my brother," I hissed, needing him to understand I wasn't any of the things he said I was. "If he'd have waited another year, or three, I would have been happy to accept the position. But, the hard facts are, I need more experience. It has nothing to do with how nice of a person I am."

He shot me a tightlipped smile. "That's a good line. I guess you need a good line though if you're going to have to feed it to yourself for the next thirty years."

He started to walk by me, but my hand shot out and I dug my finger into his bicep before he could get away. "And what the hell do you know?"

Turning his head to face me, he pierced me with gray eyes that were far too observant and volatile for my liking. "I know good girls." His explanation came out with notes of pure and unfiltered disgust. "And you Dillon Baptiste are a good girl to the core."

Pulling his arm from my slackening grasp, he left me alone in the kitchen with his words echoing in the air.

Now that I was alone with my thoughts and the abandoned stack of plates, I realized two things.

First, Vann Delane was a complete and total asshole and I was grateful I hadn't had to put up with his shit prior to today.

And second... he was right. These were excuses I would feed myself for the next thirty years. I knew Ezra was serious about hiring someone permanent. I knew he would search until he found someone suitable for this place—someone who would stick it out till the bitter end. Or at least for a good chunk of the next decade.

If I didn't take Bianca now, this opportunity might never cross my path again. We might crisscross through life, never aligning, never finding each other, never getting to work together.

I touched the edge of the plate on the top of the stack. Could I live with myself if I walked away today? Could I get over the disappointment of never running this kitchen?

For as long as I'd wanted to be a chef, Bianca had been the carrot I'd chased, dangling at the end of the stick. My gastronomic journey had led me to this exact moment.

Fine, I would have preferred it if this moment had happened a few years down the road. But that was no longer an option.

And Ezra believed in me. That counted for something right? It wasn't like he could fire me either. If he talked me into this position, he'd have to deal with the consequences.

Good or bad, we were in this together.

Plus, the staff had been running the kitchen without a captain for nearly a year. There was a rumor floating around that sometimes even Ezra filled in. If he could manage this kitchen without a formal education or any real experience, so could I. Right?

Also, my friends meant a lot in the decision-making process. The dining room was filled with competent chefs kicking culinary ass all over Durham. And those same superstar chefs believed in me. They'd come here to celebrate me.

So why was I getting in my own way?

Why was I shrugging off the same dream that had gotten me through countless grueling nights working for psychotic egomaniacs? Why was I abandoning the hope that had nursed me through ugly, horrible memories and a life I never wanted to return to? Why was I walking away from a gorgeous kitchen and stunning restaurant with a relatively wonderful reputation? Because I was afraid?

Why? Because I always picked the wrong thing.

For all my pedigree, I had terrible taste.

Six years of celibacy and years of memories I wanted desperately to forget were a testament to that.

I picked up the top plate, my fingers curling around the edges of white porcelain. Bringing the dish to my chest, I hugged it tightly to me, my heart thrumming against it.

Bianca was mine.

She belonged to me.

And I would be a fool to let her go to anyone else.

Spinning on the heel of my studded Sam Edelman bootie, I pushed through the in and out doors again and, still clutching the plate, announced. “I changed my mind. I want Bianca.”

TWO

"THAT WAS QUICK." My brother was huddled together with Killian and Wyatt, no doubt trying to figure out a way to do just that —change my mind.

"I thought about it," I explained, ignoring the sickening feeling of nerves as they flooded my body, "and I realized this really is a chance of a lifetime. I'm worried if I let it go now, I'll be walking away from the dream I've had since I started out."

"I'll always have a place for you—"

"I know you will," I assured Ezra, cutting him off. "But I want Bianca. I have always wanted Bianca. Besides, I'm holding all of you accountable to make sure I don't screw this up."

"You're going to be amazing," Vera assured me at the same time Kaya said, "We won't let you embarrass yourself, don't worry."

I hoped the truth was somewhere in the middle.

There was a flurry of congratulations and a confused Molly asking if she could take the plate I still clutched in my death grip. Someone brought out the correct dessert plates and somebody else cut the cake and handed me a piece.

Champagne popped and laughter followed. I never saw Vann

again. Apparently, he split before the cake was actually cut. *Ha! Sucker.*

I thought about him in those perfectly tailored maroon pants that should have seemed too effeminate on him and instead gave him the sense that he had great style for a single guy. Paired with his long sleeve cream Henley and a pair of expensive throwback Nikes, his look was well put together.

And that annoyed me for some reason.

I wanted him to smell like hemp oil and have a secret beer gut. He'd hurt my feelings in the kitchen. He'd trampled on my dreams and mocked me. He'd done the one thing I found to be totally and utterly unforgivable—he hadn't taken me seriously.

"I didn't realize your brother was such a dick," I told Vera as we stacked plates after the cake had been poked at, complained about, and inevitably devoured.

"Who? Vann?"

I gave her a look. "Do you have another brother?"

She laughed and twirled the engagement ring on her finger. "No. Just the one brother." She cleared her throat uncomfortably. I realized I'd offended her.

"Oh, no. I've made you mad. I'm sorry, Vera! I was just joking. I definitely didn't mean that he was—"

"Oh, gosh," she cut me off. "Please stop apologizing. He's totally a dick. Especially to people he doesn't know. When he first opened his bike business, my dad and I would make bets on the kind of complaints he was bound to get. He's just... really smart. And I think that makes him a gigantic douchebag sometimes. Also, he's super cheap. And his frugality comes across as asshole-ish. And honestly, he's terrible at dating. Like the worst. I can't remember the last time he's been on a second date. Girls flee from his presence. Er, not at first, obviously. He manages to get them to go out with him. But as soon as they've ordered drinks, they start sending emergency texts and SOSs to anyone who will answer their cries for rescue."

I couldn't help but laugh at her brother's expense. "But you're so wonderful," I told her.

She beamed at me. "I know."

"It's why he's still single then? Women are terrified of him?"

She rolled her eyes. "Yes. And he keeps dating nice girls. They're no good for him. He needs someone with tenacity. The kind of girl that won't get chewed up and spit out before they've gotten to second base. I tell him all the time to stop dating good girls. Find someone with a police record or something. Or at least a misdemeanor. But does he listen to me? No. No he does not."

"Good luck to him then," I muttered beneath my breath. *I know good girls*, he'd said to me. *And you, Dillon Baptiste, are a good girl to the core.*

I chewed on my bottom lip and let the insult wash over me again. He wasn't just saying I wasn't a good enough chef for Bianca, he was telling me I wasn't good enough for him either.

Well, fuck you, Vann Delane.

I'm awesome.

And more than qualified for Bianca.

And way better than anyone you've dated before.

So, take that.

Fighting the urge to cover my face with my hands and scream, I shot Vera a wobbly smile and turned my attention back to the remnants of cake scattering the cart. "I need to grab something to wipe this down with."

"I'll get it!" she volunteered, stepping back toward the kitchen. "This is your celebration. Relax for now. You'll be working your tail off soon."

Too soon, I thought, but I kept my mouth shut.

Wyatt bumped my shoulder with his as soon as Vera was gone. "I'm going to need your formal two-week notice in writing, if you don't mind."

"You're kidding."

"Afraid not," he sighed. "But you see, it's not me. My boss is a real stickler for the rules. He's going to require a handwritten letter, no less than five thousand words, with an additional essay on the value of market price fresh fish versus shipping in stock from a conglomerate."

"You're so full of shit," I told him.

He grinned at me. "It's funny because you think I'm joking."

I rolled my eyes. "Then I guess you're just going to have to keep me. No job in the world is worth all that."

His head tipped back and he let out a bark of laughter. "Willing to give up your fancy new position so easily? I thought you had more moxie than that, Baptiste."

That was a compliment coming from him. His girlfriend and my best friend on the entire planet, Kaya, had the most moxie of any female I'd ever known. I was on the other side of the spectrum.

No moxie. No grit. I was completely squish from the inside out.

Lifting a shoulder in a casual shrug, I told him, "This isn't about moxie. This is self-preservation."

He smiled and it lit him up from the inside out. Several months ago, Wyatt was nothing but my terrifying boss I tried to avoid entirely. Luckily for me, he had it bad for Kaya, which meant my mistakes in the kitchen usually went unnoticed. Still, he was the kind of boss that evoked fear and trembling on the regular.

Since he'd started dating Kaya, I'd gotten to know him in a different capacity. True, he was still a total hard-ass at Lilou, my current place of employment, but outside of those whitewashed walls, he was kind and generous, even funny.

We'd become true friends. That was another reason to leave Lilou. Now that I knew his bark was bigger than his bite, I'd stopped taking him seriously when he started shouting and pounding on things. My obstinance was causing quite the dissension in the ranks.

When Kaya left to run Sarita, I was promoted to sous chef, second in command. So, when I rolled my eyes at Wyatt's antics, the rest of the staff felt it was okay to roll their eyes at Wyatt.

It was so not okay to roll eyes at Wyatt.

"You'll be good for him," he told me. "Ezra, I mean. He listens to you. He respects your opinion. And I'm afraid your only chance of getting Bianca back where she needs to be is ignoring every damn thing your brother has to say. He's right about most things in life, I'll give him that, but his restaurant philosophies are dated. I've had to fight for autonomy. Killian left to find it. Kaya isn't asking for permission, she's just doing whatever the hell she wants. You're going to have to find your own way with him. But you're going to have to do something to revive this place. And Ezra has no clue what that is."

"The eyes were a good choice," I said, defending my brother. "The mural brought life to this place."

His lips twisted in a smirk. "Molly's idea. And she told him to butt out while she did her thing too. Like I said, he's super smart with money. But he doesn't know shit about what it's going to take to get this restaurant back on top. That's up to you, Dillon. Make this restaurant your own. Give her your feel. Your style. Your... something special. She'll bounce back naturally."

Fresh panic swirled through me. "What if I don't have a style? What if I don't even know how to go about getting one?"

His smile softened and his eyes warmed. "I've seen you in the kitchen. I've watched you lead. I know you don't think you're qualified for this, but there are ten other chefs at Lilou that have been cooking decades longer than you and can't do what you do. There is something incredibly special about the gentle way you handle food. You love it in a way that is rare."

Emotion clogged my throat and I blinked back tears. "Aw shucks, Chef."

He playfully punched me in the bicep. "Call me if you need anything, yeah?"

"Okay."

"I mean that," he reiterated, shooting my brother an annoyed look. "Kaya and I have your back. This isn't going to be easy. You know that. But that doesn't mean it's not going to be the best damn ride of your life."

I sucked in my bottom lip and sunk my teeth into it. He was right about that. Right about all of it.

"Seriously, thanks, Wyatt." He nodded in acknowledgment and another thought dawned on me. "Wait, who are you going to get to replace me?"

His expression hardened and he glanced desperately at the ceiling. "Hell if I know. I merely mentioned the idea to Benny and he already shot me down. Nobody wants that job."

"Yeah, well, nobody wanted this job either, but look, Ezra found a sucker. I'm sure you'll find a sucker too."

He snorted. "I guess we'll see about that."

"I guess we'll see about all of this. Maybe don't fill the position too quickly. I might need to come crawling back."

The others joined us before he could assure me for the millionth time that I'd be fine. That was a good thing. I knew I wouldn't be fine. I wouldn't even be close to fine. I didn't need any more false assurances that I'd be great at a job that was entirely out of my league.

I wasn't going to be great at it.

I wasn't even going to be okay at it.

Holy shit, what did I just sign up for?

THREE

THE FOLLOWING MORNING, I woke up with a splitting headache. I rolled over and buried my face in my pillow, willing my body to go back to sleep. The sun wasn't even awake yet, why was I?

This was one of those rare traits I'd inherited from my father. Ezra was the same way. As a whole, the Baptiste family were terrible sleepers. Driven by insane work goals and the need to conquer the known world, we woke up ready for battle.

I usually enjoyed waking up early. Even if I had a late shift the night before, I preferred to be up and at 'em. But today, my head felt like someone had split my skull in two with a chisel and my entire body ached. Another hour of sleep would've helped.

My phone beeped with an incoming text. And then my email started to buzz. I'd dealt with migraines my entire life. This wasn't a terrible one compared to some of the other ones I'd had in the past, but it was enough to make me want to stay in bed for the rest of the day.

Okay, to be honest last night's surprise ambush to take over Bianca was the real reason I wanted to hide inside my three-bedroom loft with my blackout curtains drawn and Netflix rolling for the rest of forever and ever amen. The migraine was a byproduct of my recently imposed head chef position and all the stress that came with it.

Groaning into my plush pillow, I blindly reached for my phone, patting the nightstand until I nearly knocked it to the floor. It started ringing just as I grabbed it.

Without bothering to look at the number, I pushed it against my ear and croaked a garbled, "Hello."

There was a beat of hesitation before my mom said, "Dillon? Is that you?"

Rolling over, I faced the curtains that hadn't been fully drawn last night. A glimmer of early morning light slipped between the opening. Downtown was just on the other side of those dark curtains. The city would be waking up soon. Trucks would start delivering their goods to nearby businesses. Men and women with briefcases and suits would start dotting the sidewalks as they trudged their way from nearby parking garages to their high-rise office buildings. A man with a pushcart of coffee, fresh fruit, and savory hand pies would appear on my corner—like an angel sent to earth every morning, winning over humanity one delicious, flaky, buttery crust at a time.

I loved living in the middle of Durham city life. I loved the hustle and bustle. I loved my expensive loft that overlooked the high rises and gritty streets and was way too big for just little old me. I loved the doorman that let me double park and helped me with groceries because I kept him fully stocked with leftovers from Lilou and chocolate croissants I made every weekend.

Waking up in my giant, king-sized bed with my down comforter and ten pillows in this city I loved so very much was the best way I could imagine a morning. And it eased some of my fears concerning Bianca.

Not much. But some.

My headache pulsed at my temples, reminding me that there was still plenty to fret over.

"Hi, Mom," I told the woman on the other end of the phone. "You're up super early. Is everything okay?"

I said the Baptistes had the early morning bug. Not my mom. She could easily sleep till noon and not even notice. The woman was a total night owl. All my life, I'd hear her moving around at all hours of the night. I always had to rouse her to eat lunch the next day.

"Is it early there?" She sounded distracted. "I forgot about the time change."

I scrunched my eyes closed and searched for the missing information. My mom lived in Durham. If it was early for me, it would be early for her. "Where are you?"

"Dillon, I told you. Tony and I are spending the summer in Paris."

"You did not tell me that."

She sighed, thoughtful. "Yes, I did. Of course, I did."

I blinked at my curtains. "I think I would have remembered you were spending the next three months in France."

"Maybe you're right." She laughed at herself. "Sorry, darling. Tony and I are spending the summer in France touring. We'll be home by Thanksgiving."

That was more than just the summer, but I rarely argued logistics with my mom. "You're going to miss Killian's wedding."

I heard a smack on the other end and knew she'd slapped her hand over her forehead—a trait we shared. "Oh, I totally forgot they moved the wedding up."

"It's because Vera's knocked up." I tsked conspiratorially, totally joking.

"Shotgun wedding then," my mom teased in return. "I always knew if Killian were to get married, someone was going to have to be held at gunpoint. Although, honestly I always thought it would be that girl." She took a breath. If I didn't have a migraine, I would have cut her off before she could speak again. But the pain in my head was throwing me off my game. "You know, I always thought he would fall in love with you, Dilly Bar. I was so surprised when you told me he'd met someone else."

I bit back a groan, we'd had this conversation at least one thousand times. Maybe more. Even before Vera showed up, I'd constantly had to remind her that nothing would ever happen with Killian and me. We were like brother and sister. Sure, I looked up to him. I respected him. I was going to totally take advantage of his offer to help with my transition to Bianca. But romantically we were about as compatible as a kitten and a stampeding elephant.

I was the kitten in this scenario.

Obvi.

"Mom, Vera is amazing for Killian. She can handle all his... bullying. They're basically the most perfect couple that has ever existed." She made a sound in the back of her throat so I quickly added, "After you and Tony, of course."

I could hear her smile all the way from France. "You're too sweet, baby."

Laughing at her easy retreat, I rolled on my back and adjusted to the pain shooting through my head. I needed some drugs. Fast. Which meant, I would need to disentangle myself from a conversation that could go on for the next four hours.

My mom and I only chatted on the phone about once a week, but we texted constantly. Both of us hated talking on the phone, but we made an exception for each other. And then we'd spend all day catching up, telling each other everything going on—except when she was headed to France for months at a time.

Okay, we told each other everything we could remember. I usually remembered more than she did.

Cynthia Troy had been flighty her entire life and she was only getting worse. I loved her easy-going personality and ability to laugh at herself. But her forgetfulness was only getting worse the older she got.

At least she had Tony now. They'd married three years ago after dating for the same length of time, both second marriages with grown children. Mom only had me, but Tony had four kids that lived all over the country.

They'd known each other almost my entire life. Tony had been one of my dad's investment partners. But it wasn't until after Dad died that the sparks had flown—they'd accidentally reconnected at a little wine shop where they were both bottle of the month members. He was a very successful investment banker and my mom loved money. It was a match made in heaven.

Luckily, Tony had turned out to be a great guy, even after working with my dad for so long, and I was thrilled my mom had finally met a man that loved her so completely.

I'd grown up watching her put up with my dad's shit. Once he'd died, she'd gone into a tragic cycle of meeting, dating, and dumping countless losers. For a short period of time, I'd followed in her footsteps. We'd both broken free around the same time. But for different reasons.

She'd gone on to find her happily ever after. I'd spent six years avoiding men completely and wishing they'd feel the same way about me. Now I just prayed I wouldn't have to wait until I was fifty-seven to meet my soulmate.

"Please, please, please don't make me wait another thirty years," I whispered to the ceiling, hoping the powers that be could hear my plea.

I knew I wouldn't be as fortunate as my mom if I had to wait that long. I was barely getting out of my twenties without Botox. In another three decades, I might be a cautionary tale of plastic surgery gone wrong.

The kitchen was not a kind place of employment for people like me, who preferred clear skin over the alternative, and clean hair over greasy and straggly. Cooking in a hot kitchen was not conducive for those things.

"I'm glad to hear you're safe in Paris," I told her. I could hear Tony in the background, reminding her about reservations.

"I guess I have to go," she pouted. "The slave driver is summoning me."

"Have a good time. And keep in mind I'm ridiculously jealous and now I won't be able to enjoy my day at all."

She laughed and I pictured her tossing her long blonde hair over her shoulder so she could tug on her earring like she did when she thought something was truly funny. "Yeah, right, Ms. Head Chef. I'm sure your life is so terrible right now."

I groaned in response. I'd texted her last night to share the news, somewhere between being excited for the position and absolutely terrified.

"Oh, stop that. This is a dream come true. Your brother spoils you rotten."

That was true. "It's already given me a headache and I haven't started yet."

"Take some medicine before it turns into a migraine," she instructed. "And then drink a glass of champagne. You'll feel better."

It was pointless suggesting I shouldn't drink alcohol this early in the morning with a handful of pills. But I let it go. She knew that. She just wasn't thinking about her words.

"Love you, Mama."

"Love you too, Dilly Bar. I'll call you later."

We both knew that was a lie, but she probably meant it at the moment.

After hanging up my phone, I stumbled to the kitchen, following her advice. At least to search for the ibuprofen.

I skipped the champagne.

For now.

I chased the drugs with a full glass of water and a few crackers to keep from getting nauseous. Then I dragged myself to the shower and turned it on as hot as I could stand it.

The heavy stream of water washed away some of the tightness in my shoulder blades and across the back of my neck. I worked through my daily shower routine and then stood under the pelting water until my fingers were prunes and the medicine kicked in.

By the time I'd finished dealing with my thick head of blonde beachy waves and applied some eyeliner and mascara, my phone had really woken up.

I'd missed texts from friends in the industry, congratulating me on my new gig. News traveled super-fast between kitchens. We loved gossip as much as we loved cooking.

My email box was filling up quickly too. I'd also missed calls from Kaya, Vera, Wyatt and Ezra.

Good grief.

I texted the first three and dialed my brother.

"Thanks again," he said, sounding wide awake and chipper. "I can't tell you how much I appreciate you stepping into that kitchen."

"Good morning to you too." I sounded significantly less poised. Unless this hoarse, croaky man-voice thing I had going on was poised.

He ignored me. "You're the best, you know that right?"

"I am aware," I teased, sighing for good measure.

"Good."

I smiled at my unmade bed. "I'm not starting until Sunday though. We're clear on that, right?"

"Sunday..."

"I want one last shift at Lilou," I reminded him. "And I want a weekend before I become head chef and never get another vacation day again. One last hoorah before I sell my soul to saving your ass."

He barked out a laugh. "Is that what you're doing?"

I didn't say anything. He knew that was what I was doing.

As sous chef at Lilou, I still got nights off. Sure, I worked almost every day. And night. And Wyatt basically couldn't run his kitchen without me. But I did occasionally get a night off.

I wouldn't get the same luxury at Bianca. Especially not in the beginning as I attempted to undo all the damage the last year and a half had inflicted on her.

He groaned, reminding me of how I talked to my mom this morning. "All right, fine. I guess I can cover for you until then."

"And I still want off for all the wedding stuff. Don't forget about that."

"Right," he agreed quickly. Too quickly. "The wedding."

"And the rehearsal dinner," I reminded him. "And the bachelorette party."

"I don't know if I can swing—"

"Ezra. You promised."

"I don't think I promised."

"I think I quit."

"Excuse me?"

I sighed, realizing this was how it was always going to be working for him. He was impossible. How Molly ever put up with him was an unsolved mystery. "I quit. I can't work under these conditions."

"These conditions? You haven't even started at Bianca! That's the whole point!"

"Then you should have hired me after the festivities. Those events are nonnegotiable."

He cursed under his breath, a word he didn't usually say in front of me. You know, because he was the big brother and I was the delicate little sister. Cue eye roll. "You're a ballbuster, you know that?"

My smile was real when I quipped, "Learned from the best."

"Hmph."

"Love you, Ez."

"I hate it when you call me that." He sighed and added, "Love you too, sis."

We hung up and I tossed my phone on the bed, the sick feeling of panic curling through me once again. It was hard to say if Ezra had called as a big brother checking up on his little sister, or if he'd called as the boss protecting his investment.

He was like that. As much as I loved him and looked up to him, he was also a cutthroat restaurateur that wanted to be the best in the city.

I didn't quite have such lofty goals.

Yes, I wanted to be good at what I did. But mostly I just loved to cook. I loved food. I loved creating. I loved turning something so simple into an artform. I loved getting lost in the focus it took. When I cooked, it was just me and the food. Nothing else mattered. Not who I was. Or where I came from. Or how much money I had in my bank accounts. All that mattered was that I had the ability to turn seemingly random ingredients into a beautiful, cherished experience for someone else.

I didn't have lofty ambitions like the rest of my friends. I wasn't even competitive. I just wanted purpose and redemption and the gift of toiling at something I so wholly loved.

My headache pulsed back to life at my temples.

This wasn't going to end well.

By the time I got to Lilou four hours later for prep, I was a weepy, hysterical mess. I sniffled as I put my black chef jacket on for the last time and stepped into the already crowded kitchen.

The staff that was there turned around and started clapping for me. Their expressions were proud and sappy and so encouraging. They stood there cheering me on as I if I had won some great championship.

I lost it. Tears poured down my face and I hid behind my hands, embarrassed by my emotion.

"She's sad to leave," Wyatt announced to my peers, "because she knows the White Witch can never compete with us."

He was partially right, but I couldn't let him know that. Today I was his second in command. Tomorrow, we would be big competition.

Wiping my tears away with the back of my hands, I released a shaky laugh. "I'm crying *for* you," I told him. "You're never going to find someone dumb enough to replace me."

He scowled at the laughter that followed. "It's not funny," he growled at them. "True, but not funny."

"Poor Wyatt," I empathized. "His sous chefs keep running away."

A glint appeared in his dark eyes and he surveyed the kitchen. "They run away to run their own kitchens. Seems like this position is a pretty great stepping stone for those of you serious about your careers."

His words were a crafty ploy disguised as a challenge. He might murder the next sous chef to abandon him.

Okay, maybe not murder, but at least kidnap and force to continue working for him under duress.

The kitchen avoided looking directly at him. I saw Benny back away into the pantry. Hiding my smile, I said, "Everybody don't volunteer at once."

He glared at me. "A competition then."

Why was he looking at me?

"Dillon's taking lead tonight."

"Wait, what?"

"She needs some practice for her fancy new job and we're going to give it to her. And at the end of the night, she's going to pick one of you to step up."

"Wyatt, you're not serious."

He winked at me. "That person will be sous. Final answer. Unless of course I don't like her pick, then she'll choose someone else."

I punched him in the bicep. "Are you crazy?"

He rubbed his arm and looked totally affronted. I rolled my eyes because I didn't realize he'd been hiding rocks for muscles under his jacket. My hand hurt way more than his arm.

"You need practice, Dillon. I'm happy to give it to you."

"Did Ezra put you up to this?"

He laughed maniacally. "I just thought it up. Pretty great, huh?"

Butterflies rioted in my gut. Sure, he'd put me in charge before, but not for the entire night. I was relatively new to the position. Kaya had only quit a few months ago.

I couldn't do this.

Oh, shit, I had to do this! On a nightly basis.

Maybe if I puked in here, they would have to shut down for the night and I could get out of Wyatt's trial by fire.

He leaned in, probably noticing the panic and greenish hue of my skin. "You can do this, Dillon. You got the chops. Stop doubting yourself."

"Nepotism," I hissed at him. "Ezra is a nepotist. That's the only reason he asked me to take over Bianca. He's crazy with nepotism."

His eyes narrowed. "He saw real, raw talent in you and was smart enough to snatch it up. Don't doubt yourself, Chef. Tonight, is just like any other night. Be precise. Be diligent. Be a fucking badass. You have dinner service to prepare for."

I swallowed around the fist-sized lump in my throat and let his words of encouragement sink into my skin. He was right—I was doubting myself. Big time. But now wasn't the time for that. I needed to put on my big girl panties and step into the role I had already accepted.

Besides, tonight would be like learning to ride a bike with training wheels on. Wyatt would be here to save my ass should anything go awry. And I already knew this menu. I could cook most of these dishes blindfolded.

"Okay," I whispered. "But you're going to have to fill in for me."

He wrinkled his nose. "All right." Glancing over his shoulder, he added. "I should probably go stop Benny from running away." He looked back at me, dropping his voice so no one else could hear him although they were all watching us. "You know he's the first choice, yeah?"

I suppressed a smile and nodded. Poor, poor Benny. There weren't enough head chef positions in the world to make working for Wyatt worth it.

Oh, god. Was I going to be that impossible too? Was I going to walk into Bianca and turn into a total egomaniac who thought I ruled the world with my spatula in one hand and my toque crown atop my head?

I guess we'd find out tonight.

FOUR

TWELVE HOURS LATER, the rush of a successful night at the helm of Lilou had me feeling like the queen of the world. I got how easy it was to let the power go to your head. I felt the buzz of victory in my blood and the thrum of perfection in my chest.

I hadn't just run service well, I'd nailed it.

Okay, fine, it helped that Wyatt was there to cook things perfectly before they even got to me. In fact, the entire kitchen had been especially on top of things tonight. I liked to believe they were cooking their asses off for my last night.

But then I realized they cooked to perfection every night. This was the well-oiled machine amazing chefs had molded them into. First Killian, and then Wyatt.

They were five-star ninjas. Service went smoothly. There weren't mistakes. There weren't oopsies. There weren't even slightly overdone pieces of meat. There was only flawless execution.

It gave me hope for Bianca. Could I do this in my own kitchen? Could we run this effortlessly? Could we be this efficient? This faultless?

Of course we could.

It wasn't even that hard.

Er, it hadn't been tonight.

I supposed Sunday at Bianca would be the real test. This time when my stomach flipped though, it was with anticipation, not dread. Tonight, had been, honest to God, fun—one of the most thrilling nights of my life. And the idea of living like this for the rest of my life filled me with bubbly excitement.

The rest of the staff had slowly filtered out. They'd hugged me, said goodbye, and made me promise to come back and visit as they left.

Wyatt walked into the kitchen from the dining room, carrying three fluted glasses and another bottle of ridiculously expensive champagne. His raised eyebrow was full of mischief.

"Is that for *moi*?"

He tilted his head toward Benny. "And my new sous chef."

Benny the Brick, as I liked to call him, was built like a linebacker. Big, bulky muscles for days. His shaved head and tough demeanor gave him the "I used to work for the mob" look that intimidated most everyone at first. Until you got to know him and realized he was a big old softy.

And kind of lazy.

He loved cooking, but he didn't want the responsibility of sous chef. The man ran from anything that required more than his hourly-employee shifts. He didn't want a salary that would force him to work more hours than he was technically getting paid for—even if it also came with a gigantic raise.

He also didn't like to be the bad guy. He was too worried about everyone liking him to enjoy the idea of being upper management.

Too bad for him he was fantastic at his job. With Kaya gone and me leaving, there was no way Wyatt was going to let him get away with slumming it any longer.

It was sous chef or no chef.

"I blame you for this," he said to me as he made his way over from one of the cooktops. "This is all your fault."

Grinning at him, I accepted the full glass of champagne from Wyatt and held it up in the air. "You're welcome."

He grumbled something profane under his breath while Wyatt passed him his drink.

"To chefs that can cook like fucking gods," Wyatt toasted.

My smile stretched as we clinked glasses and tasted greatness from a bottle. "God, that's good."

Benny finally loosed a smile too. "That is pretty damn incredible."

Wyatt shrugged. "I found it in Ezra's office." At our stunned expressions, he quickly added, "Don't tell him."

"He was probably saving that for his wedding night or something."

Wyatt's cheeks turned a pinkish hue. "I hadn't thought about that." He took another long drink and then poured more into his glass. "Shit."

"Your secret's safe with me," I assured him.

"Me too," Benny agreed. "But mainly because I don't want to die. I like breathing."

I leaned forward, unable to wipe the goofy grin off my face. "Especially now that you have your fancy new job."

He pursed his lips together and shook his head. "On second thought..."

"Don't be a weenie," I laughed. "It's time to step up and take the bull by the horns." I tilted my head toward my former boss and said, "Wyatt being the bull in this scenario."

The big, muscly marshmallow looked at Wyatt and grimaced. "I'm not a weenie."

"She's right," Wyatt agreed. "You're a weenie."

"I'm not. I just don't want to work for you."

Wyatt gave him a quizzical look. "You already work for me."

"Yeah, but not like that," Benny insisted. "I don't want to ruin our friendship, bro."

Wyatt's confused look did not go away and I couldn't help but laugh. This was a bromance thing? Who would have guessed?

"He can be an asshole," I shared with Benny. "The important thing to remember is that he doesn't really mean what he says when he's in the kitchen. Just think of him as being temporarily possessed and you'll be able to forgive him in the morning."

Wyatt's insulted expression made me want to laugh again so I took another drink of champagne. I felt tipsy, despite having only had a few sips of alcohol. I realized it was the kitchen high. And it was amazing. It was why I went to culinary school. Why I sacrificed a life as a socialite—even though I had plenty of money to live on—to work my ass off in a blazing hot kitchen night after night. It was the reason I had taken Ezra's offer even though I knew I wasn't ready for this job.

I was chasing and would forever be chasing this feeling.

"I'll try to remember that," Benny murmured. "This isn't Wyatt. This is Evil Wyatt. Wyatt isn't a total asshole. Evil Wyatt is a total asshole."

"There you go," I encouraged. "Now you're getting the hang of it."

"You guys are the assholes," Wyatt grumbled.

Benny and I shared a conspiratorial smile and clinked glasses again. "This has been a ride," I told them, hopping up on one of the counters and leaning back on my free hand. "I'll miss this place."

"And we'll miss you," Wyatt said sincerely. "Bianca's a lucky bitch."

I smiled, knowing the champagne and lack of eating dinner during my crazy, busy shift was going to my head. "Maybe she is."

Wyatt's phone chirped and he set his glass down to pull it from his pocket. "It's my woman," he told us, apparently channeling his inner caveman. Putting the phone to his ear, he said, "Hey babe, just finishing up?"

I looked up at the clock to see that it was after midnight. Sarita, where Kaya ran the kitchen, was open later than Lilou, so she would still have to clean up and shut down. I knew Wyatt stopped by after we were finished so he could help her get her kitchen in order and they drove home together.

A strange pain stabbed inside my chest. I took another sip of champagne hoping it would go away.

Loneliness.

That was the name of it. A feeling I was altogether familiar with, and one that had been showing up more often than usual lately.

I blamed all the love happening around me. It was like Cupid was rampaging through Durham intent on making everyone I knew fall in love.

Meanwhile, I was still over here with a full-on candle vigil for the death of any possibility of love in my life. *Um, no thanks! I'm good. And single. And good with being single.*

Liar, liar, my pained heart crooned.

It had been fine when Killian fell in love with Vera. I mean, had there ever been a more perfect couple on the planet? And love had totally changed Killian, making him a way more tolerable human.

And then there was Ezra. Obviously, I had been beyond thrilled for my brother to have found a woman that wasn't the total worst. After his long list of crazy exes, I was so completely happy for him. And Molly was just the best. I couldn't have asked for a better sister-in-law.

But honestly, who would have guessed that Ezra would have found true love before me?

Not me.

Or him.

Or anybody that knew us.

Ezra had been the one to make all the obvious dating mistakes. I had been the one lucky enough to have only needed to make one mistake. If lucky meant tragically unlucky.

Spotting losers was easy, when I said no to everyone.

Okay, that wasn't entirely true. I sometimes went on first dates. Er, or enough first dates that people assumed I was a dating machine.

But, I had a strict catch and release policy, promising myself that as soon as I found a guy worth keeping around, I wouldn't let him go. I would recognize a good thing when I found it.

But lately, I'd been questioning my ability to recognize even half-decent men.

Either my standards were significantly lowering or my options were drying up.

I mean, even my mom had found true love.

And now Wyatt and Kaya? It was too much.

I was officially the third wheel. That didn't mean I would stop tossing back the fish the second I'd gotten a free meal and a couple of drinks out of them.

Watching Wyatt talk to my best friend with a big, stupid grin on his face killed whatever good mood the night had put me in. Bringing the expensive champagne to my lips, I tipped my head back and finished the glass.

"I think I'm going to get going." I faked a yawn until it turned into a real one. "I'm beat."

Benny was staring into his champagne glass like it was a crystal ball with hidden answers to all his life questions. "Oh, yeah? I guess this is goodbye then."

His sarcastic comment pulled a smile from me. "Don't be so fatalistic, Benjamin. We'll see each other again."

He made a face that made me realize how little we would see each other from now on. Another pang of sorrow punched through me.

"Oh, hey." He snapped his fingers at me. "A buddy of mine saw a picture of us from the other week, when we went out for your birthday. He asked if you were single and if he could get your number."

My sad feelings were immediately replaced with a confusing mix of piqued curiosity and crippling dread. "Uh... what's he like?"

"My friend?"

"The guy that wants my number. Is he awful?"

He gave me a look that said he didn't have awful friends. But what did he know anyway? Guys were nose-blind to their buddies. "He's good people, Dillon. I think you'd like him."

"What's his name?"

"Matt." When it was clear I was waiting for more, he added. "Matt Brennan."

I filed away the information so I could stalk him online later. "What does Matt Brennan do for a living?"

"He's a pastry chef. I've known him since school. He works at Fifi's."

I pursed my lips together. It wasn't that I disliked pastry chefs as a whole… I just didn't like that they thought we did the same thing. They worked in quiet kitchens under zero pressure. At least, compared to our kind of pressure. Sure, they had standards of perfection too. But it was not the same.

Still, Matt Brennan was a good name. And I had just been mourning my single status seconds ago.

Plus, it had been a long time since I'd been on a date. And I preferred everything to be fine. And normal. And for people to see that I was making an effort at the whole dating thing.

Even if I wasn't.

"Is he cocky?"

He rolled his eyes at my question. "He's cool, Baptiste. It's just a text. You don't have to answer it."

"What I'm hearing is that you don't want to let him down."

He made a face at getting called out. "He thought you were hot! Take the compliment."

Was it a compliment? Or was Matt Brennan just desperate to find a girl outside of his usual stock pond? Stalking your friend's Facebook account for pictures of women you hadn't met before felt desperate to me. And weird. Still, I heard myself say, "Okay, fine. You can give him my number."

He made a gleeful sound. "Aw, you're going to make him so happy. You can thank me for the love connection later."

I set the champagne glass down, deciding this was Wyatt and

Benny's kitchen now, they could deal with the dirty dishes. Without giving a formal goodbye to my former coworker and boss, I made my way toward the back exit, waving at Benny and Wyatt as I went.

For all my warm fuzzies for this kitchen, I found myself leaving it way faster than I had planned. I thought I would savor the walk out, take in the gleaming glory one more time. By the time I stepped into the night air, I was shocked that it was over—that my time at Lilou had come to a close.

I breathed in the balmy night air and shed my chef jacket before I started sweating. My car was in the employee lot not far from here, but I realized too late that I'd walked out alone.

I usually waited for Wyatt or Benny to walk me to my car.

The lot was well lit and my car was parked under a streetlight, but I still didn't like being out here alone. Fear skittered over my bare arms, sending chills down my spine. I hurried to my car, Lilou fading into the background as I hunted for my car keys. Which was when I realized that I'd left one of the overhead lights on accidentally. It was barely flickering in the dark night, a telltale sign it was just about out of juice.

I didn't even remember clicking the light on. But the evidence that I had at some point today was right in front of me. Damn.

My baby, er car, was ridiculously fast and breathlessly beautiful. She was my absolute pride and joy. Ezra thought he was hot stuff because of his sleek Alfa Romeo, but we both knew mine was the superior automotive vehicle.

His was the economy version of fast. Mine was the real deal.

I mean, Ezra's Alfa was fine. It ticked a lot of boxes for a lot of people. But mine was hands down just better in every way.

Faster.

Nicer.

Prettier.

Pricier.

The total package.

Porsche 911, candy apple red. Hard top, of course, because I wasn't a total douche. And perfect in absolutely every way.

But now she wasn't going to start because I'd stupidly left the lights on.

You'd think, after all the bells and whistles she'd come with, she'd also be equipped with a tiny robot that turned off lights when their driver happened to forget.

The car automatically unlocked as I got closer. I slid into the driver's seat and wrapped my hands around the leather steering wheel. I switched on the ignition and waited for the revving purr of the engine rumbling to life.

She groaned. She sputtered. She made a sound that in a human would have been considered a hacking cough. I stopped trying to get her to do what I knew she couldn't right now.

Damn. I turned back to Lilou, knowing Wyatt and Benny would help me. The parking lot was really dark though. And I didn't love the idea of walking back to the restaurant alone.

It wasn't that far, my rational mind reasoned.

But far enough, my past hissed into the quiet solitude of the car.

I found that I didn't want to leave the safety of my driver's seat though. I preferred the silence here. The loneliness. The isolation.

Dropping my forehead on the steering wheel, I attempted to start her again. She went through the whole dramatic inability to start all over again.

"You don't want to leave either," I murmured, finding tears pricking the corners of my eyes. "I don't blame you. I liked it here too." Tears wet my cheeks and I had to sniffle quickly to keep snot from dripping over my lips. "But I'm sure we'll like the next place too. Maybe. Eventually... If they don't fire us first."

I sucked in a shaky breath, readying to let out a full-blown sob when a knock at my driver's side window had me jumping out of my seat and screaming at the top of my lungs.

When I gathered my wits and enough courage to identify the intruder, I saw that it was Vera's brother standing outside.

Vann Delane.

Not a serial killer. Not a rapist. Not a mugger.

Just Vann Delane.

Quickly wiping at my soggy cheeks with the backs of my hands, I tried the automatic window button first before I remembered the whole car was dead. Pushing open the door, I leaned my head out and faced him. "Yes?"

"I didn't mean to scare you," he said. "I thought I heard a cat in significant need of assistance. And found your car instead."

I pursed my lips together, wondering if he realized the insult he'd just delivered or if it was a total accident.

My Porsche 911 was not a kitten.

Nor did she sound like one.

She was a regal lioness and she could bite your head off if I let her.

Deciding he was just obtuse and not intentionally rude, I said, "My battery died. Apparently, I left the overhead light on all day."

Vann stepped back and glanced across the parking lot toward his bicycle shop, Cycle Life. "Bummer."

Letting out a trembling breath, I looked down at my hands and shrugged. "It's fine. I'll get Wyatt or Benny to jump me."

"Are they still here?" he asked, nodding toward Lilou.

"Yeah, we just closed down." That comment sparked a thought and I found myself planting one leg on the pavement and leaning further outside so I could get a look at him. "What are you doing here? I didn't think your shop kept evening hours."

His brows furrowed at my observation. "Uh, I don't usually. I forgot my laptop earlier." He ran a hand through his hair. "I couldn't sleep," he added, filling in the obvious blanks in his story. "So, I thought I would work. But then my computer was here... Anyway, once I'd come all the way here, I decided to do some things in the shop."

I glanced down at his outfit as I disentangled myself from the curved bucket seat and stood. He had on a gray hoodie over a plain white V-neck t-shirt and gray and white plaid pajama pants. He looked like a Gap ad.

His pajamas fit his preppy style in every way. It was strange to seem him like this though. Flip-flops on his feet, his long toes peeking out beneath tattered hems. Admittedly, I didn't know him that well, but I'd seen him enough times that I knew this wasn't a side of him that many people knew—unkempt, undressed, unpolished.

It made me feel... intrusive. Like I'd walked in on a private moment. But he was the one that had come out to check on me.

"Gotcha," I murmured. "Anyway, uh, thanks for checking on me."

His eyes drifted over my wide-leg black pants and tight black tee. I brushed hair out of my face, nervous beneath his perusal. I couldn't imagine why though. This was what I wore to work every day—unless the wide leg trousers were replaced with velvety leggings. What I was wearing made sense—unlike Mr. Bananas in pajamas over there.

"I could jump you," he blurted, as if he hadn't meant to. "I mean, if that's all you need."

I blinked at him, taking in his stubbled jaw and his perfectly arched cheekbones. A Gap ad would be lucky to get this guy. He had all of Vera's beauty but the masculine version of it. "Um, how?"

It was his turn to be confused. "What do you mean?"

"How will you jump me?"

He looked back at his shop and I got the distinct impression he wished he was back there—away from me. "With my car?" His offer sounded like a question. He turned back to face me, punching me in the gut with the judgment burning his gray eyes. "Unless this thing isn't like normal cars? Maybe you need a spaceship to jump it? Moon juice or something."

"Moon juice?" I hid a smile behind my palm. "Uh, sure. No spaceship required. I'd be grateful for a jump." I rested my hand against my throat and willed him to ignore the dirty joke hanging in the air between us.

Maybe I'd been hanging out with Kaya too much, but I expected him to shout, "That's what she said!" at the top of his lungs.

"Uh, okay. Sure. Let me just go..." he nodded his head toward the parking lot across the street, apparently too mature for easy humor. "I'll be right back."

"O-okay."

I watched him cross the street without using the crosswalk. At this time of night there wasn't anyone around, so he just jogged right through the middle of downtown. It was a strange feeling observing a person break the law who I distinctly got the feeling never broke the law.

The side door of Lilou opened and shut and Benny and Wyatt walked into the parking lot, laughing and cracking jokes about Wyatt being Benny's boss. They noticed me immediately, but I explained that Vann planned to jump me.

"I bet he did," Benny teased.

There it was. Maybe it wasn't Kaya. Maybe it was working in a kitchen—we were all perverted deviants.

Purposefully ignoring his full meaning, I ran a hand over the top of Veronica and said, "Who could blame him? A chance to get down and dirty with this beauty doesn't come around very often."

Benny laughed while Wyatt texted Kaya, telling her he wanted to wait for my car to get going. "Yeah, yeah, moneybags. We get it. You have a cool car."

I glanced at Benny's souped-up Nissan and wrinkled my nose. "Psht. You're one to talk."

He stuck his tongue out at me, then moved out of the way so Vann could pull his Jeep next to mine. The three of us gaped at him as he jumped down from the cab.

"What?" he asked, noticing our open mouths.

"Nothing," Wyatt answered quickly. "I guess I just thought you drove something like a Prius."

"I thought you rode a bike," I blurted.

He looked at the three of us, shrugging one shoulder. "Nope. I have a real car." The irritation in his voice rang through the night air. "It's kind of hard to ride a bike to work in the winter. Also, I'm normal. Every chef I know thinks I go home to a treehouse in the middle of the woods and live off the land. But the truth is, I'm a normal guy. I live in an apartment. I eat sugary cereal and I drive a car."

Sugary cereal? How did that prove he was normal?

"I'm going to get going," Benny said interrupting the awkward short silence. He saluted us before running off like a coward.

Wyatt glanced at his phone. I knew he wanted to get to Kaya, which only endeared him to me more. But I needed backup here. I couldn't be left alone with Vann Delane and his crusade to prove how normal he was to everyone.

My mouth didn't get the message apparently and I heard myself offer, "If you need to get going, Wyatt... you can."

He looked up from his phone and said, "Yeah?"

"Sure, I think we have this covered?" I looked to Vann who nodded in response.

"Can you pop your hood?"

Was that a yes to my question? I looked back to Wyatt. "Worst case scenario, I'll call a tow truck and uber home. I'm not far." Wyatt started to protest and care for my friend overcame the concern for myself. "Go, seriously! I'll be fine."

He glanced nervously at Vann. "All right, but only if you're sure."

"I'm sure."

"The hood?" Vann asked, his irritation back loud and clear.

I waved Wyatt off. "We'll talk later. I'll have questions I'm sure."

Wyatt said his goodbyes, but I barely heard them as I leaned inside my car and pulled the trunk lever. To Vann, I said, "The battery is in the trunk." The trunk opened with ease and I heard Vann's sharp intake of breath.

Nervous something was seriously wrong, I hurried to where he stood surveying the clever casing. "Is something wrong?"

He looked up at me, awe glinting in his gray eyes. "You drive a nice car."

His compliment nearly knocked me off my feet. I mean, it *was* a good engine. He was right in saying that. It was just strange to hear him admit something positive. "You like cars?" I guessed, surprised again.

"I grew up working on cars with my dad," he explained. Leaning forward to clamp the jumper cables in place, he continued, "He worked a lot, so it was pretty much the only thing we ever did together. It's still one of our favorite things."

I turned and looked at his Jeep again. It was an older version, one that the entire top came off. It looked like it had fresh paint though. And new wheels. In fact, the whole thing gleamed in grayish blue.

"It's a 1959," he explained, catching my ogling. "I just finished restoring her."

Her. He'd called his car a her. Something so simple shouldn't have made me like him more, but it did for some silly reason.

"I'm impressed," I told him. "I figured you preferred two wheels to four."

He looked up at me from between our two cars, a befuddled look on his face. "Just because you cook for a living, does that mean you want to cook for every meal? Or do you sometimes go out to eat? Maybe even to restaurants that don't carry your specialty?"

"All right, I get your point," I conceded. "I don't always want to cook."

"I love my bikes," he added. "But riding one to work at one in the morning seemed exhausting." I smiled unexpectedly and stared at him, working on a witty comeback. "Do you mind starting mine?" He tossed his car keys at me before I could decline.

Catching them reflexively, I followed his bidding. We awkwardly stood there until we thought Veronica had gotten enough juice to get going. After another ten minutes, we'd gotten her juiced to the point that I felt confident enough to go our separate ways.

I stepped out of my car after coaxing her to life. Vann rolled down his window, but didn't step out of his car. It wasn't like I expected him to come around and give me a hug or anything, I just hated feeling like I was this big inconvenience to him.

I stepped up on the footboard and rested my elbows on his window frame. "Hey, thanks for your help."

His smile was the biggest I'd seen tonight. "I should have known you drove something like this."

My feelings of gratitude shriveled into bitter raisins. "Do you mean, this amazing?"

He leaned toward me as if telling me a secret. "This pretentious."

I scowled at him, hoping he felt the force of my fury. "I don't know why you think you know me," I snapped at him. "You don't know anything about me."

Sitting up and away from me, he shrugged that one shoulder again. "Money. You have a lot of money."

"So that makes me... snobby?" He didn't know pretentious. I could introduce him to a world of truly pretentious assholes that would sneer him under the carpet. But I wouldn't do that to him. Because no matter what he thought of me, I didn't think I was better than him. Nicer, sure. Kinder, obviously. More gracious and full of class and poise? Duh. But not better.

He released an impatient puff of air. "Forget I said anything, okay? I'm happy to help. Really." He shifted the car into reverse.

Hopping off the sideboard, I stepped back, deciding whether to let him have it or let him go. "You know, you keep assuming these things about me. You're the most judgmental person I've ever met, Vann Delane."

He smiled patiently, like my insults were adorable but meaningless, and I had never wanted to punch something more than I did in that minute.

"I would let the engine run for a while," he offered, as if he hadn't just insulted me completely. "Drive around for a bit or something."

He started to back up but not before I shot back, "And I would try sleeping again if I were you. You might wake up a nicer person."

If he heard me, he didn't acknowledge anything I said. I watched him drive across the street again and park at Cycle Life. His door opened and I all but threw myself into my Porsche, desperate to get out of the parking lot before he saw me standing there like a total serial killer, maniacally planning his demise.

"He did help you," I told myself as I drove home, ignoring his advice to keep the engine running for as long as possible. I could get help in the morning if I needed to. It was more important to defy Vann Delane than anything else at this moment in my life. "So he can't be all bad."

Pretentious.

Nope.

Nuh-uh.

He was all bad.

Poor Vera, she didn't even know her brother was the devil.

FIVE

SUNDAY MORNING, I pulled into Bianca's tiny backlot with butterflies waging civil war in my stomach. My last night at Lilou had filled me with a kind of hopeful anticipation for what life at Bianca could be. But reality reminded me that it was going to be a long time before I got there.

There being a confident head chef at a successful five-star restaurant.

Tonight, I was starting here. Here being an insecure, flailing, green wannabe chef at a struggling, mediocre restaurant.

Jesus, take the wheel.

Ezra met me on the other side of the door wearing a smile and an obvious look of relief. "You're here."

"Did you think I'd mutiny?"

He let out a nervous laugh, betraying the truth. "I'm just glad to see you."

"I wouldn't have run away without giving you enough notice to fill in for me," I told him. "I owe you that at least."

His happy expression turned sour. "Thanks, I think."

I looked around the kitchen, worrying about the state of it. It was nothing like Lilou. So there went my shaky hopes of turning this place around by tomorrow. Okay, I didn't think I could do that. But there was this small part of me that had held out hope that revival wouldn't take that long or be that hard. Seeing the kitchen from the head chef position sent disappointment crashing through me.

The cooktops were greasy. The shelves under the stainless steel counters were messy and cluttered. I was afraid of what I'd find in the coolers.

"Check your phone early tomorrow," I told him. "Just in case."

I felt his frown follow me around the room as I inspected everything before the rest of the staff arrived.

"Do you want to go over the menu?" he asked as I opened one of the dishwashers and found it full. I wanted to growl. Didn't they know to put everything away so it didn't sit in there, collecting a funky smell and water stains all night?

"Um, maybe?" There was a roll of knives next to the glasses that someone had forgotten to take home. I tugged it open and found them smudged and not properly cared for. "I might start in here though, before everyone arrives." I looked back at Ezra. "When do they start to show up?"

He glanced at his watch. "Two or three? I can't remember."

"Is that enough time to prep for dinner service?"

"They do a lot of it the night before," he said. "So, it's ready to go when they get in."

I ground my teeth together and bit back the urge to scold him. Of course, my brother, the efficient business man, would prep everything the night before. That would make sense to him. He wouldn't notice the difference in freshness from the night before versus the day of.

For as much as he prided himself on his ability to cook, he didn't know the first thing about running a kitchen. Which was fine, when he hired excellent chefs to do the dirty work for him. But right now, I wanted to pull my hair out.

"How long has Bianca been without a head chef?"

"Over a year," he said. "I've had chefs filling in throughout though. She hasn't been completely rudderless. I've stepped in too. Whenever I could."

I restrained the eye roll that so wanted to happen. "Okay. Yeah, I better start in here. When the rest of the staff arrives, I'll come out and talk about the menu."

"Are you sure you're okay in here?" he asked, sounding doubtful.

"If I'm not, I'll come find you."

"Can I help?"

I held up a new rag I'd pulled from an open box full of them. "Not unless you want to get dirty."

"You think this kitchen is dirty?"

I decided that lying to my brother wasn't going to do any good. He needed to hear the truth. He needed to face reality—that he never should have waited for me to get experience. He should have just hired the first mildly talented chef he could find.

A first year home-ec student would have been better at this point.

"This place is filthy," I told him honestly. "I'm surprised you don't have a rat problem yet."

He swallowed roughly, working his Adam's apple up and down. "Are you serious?"

"Your staff has been slacking off in a major way, Ezra. This kitchen is a travesty."

He rubbed his hand over his jaw, clearly having no idea it had gotten this bad. They'd probably been doing just enough that Ezra thought it was clean.

Or maybe they had never had the direction that they needed to know what acceptable standard in the food service industry was.

I supposed if their last boss was a total bum, then they probably didn't know how a kitchen should look.

I was going to tell myself that until I believed it.

A sick feeling twisted through me. I'd wanted to ease into this job, take my time, slowly come to terms with the position I had accepted. I did not want to come in like a wrecking ball and dictator the shit out of my staff right out of the gate.

But apparently, my wishes didn't come true.

Because this kind of negligence required some dictatorship asap.

I realized for the millionth time how lucky I had been to have Wyatt as my first real boss. He'd been diligent with how to take care of a kitchen. And he'd required us to do the same. It was a lot of awful work a lot of the time, but it taught us habits that would be beneficial forever.

Ezra stood there stewing for a few more minutes and then stalked off into the main body of the restaurant. I didn't know where he was going or when he'd be back, but it didn't matter. I had work to do.

I took off my chef jacket and hat, realizing now it had been silly to wear them to start with, and got to work. I scrubbed. I cleaned. I organized. I dug into the coolers and made sense of them, throwing out a ridiculous amount of rotten food.

By the time I paused to grab a drink of water, I needed a shower and a glass of wine. And yet there was still more to do—but I'd decided to let the staff deal with it.

Whenever they decided to show up.

I wondered if I should find my brother and walk him through all that I had done. But there was something I wanted to do first before I talked logistics with him.

Picking up my hat and coat off a freshly shined counter, I walked to the back of the building, to the tiny office that would be mine.

In Ezra's kitchens, all four of them, there were two offices. One office for him and one for the executive chef. He didn't need an one in every building for himself, but it was a kindness for his head chefs, so he wouldn't be in their way.

When I was in culinary school and Killian had been the head chef of Lilou, Ezra had kept his main office of operations there. After Killian left and out of managerial necessity, he'd moved to Bianca. But lately, I knew he was working from home more and more.

Because Molly also worked from home. For him.

He'd told me once it was more efficient for them to work together.

I'd countered by telling him that was because they were so close to a bed.

Hey, he'd still offered me the job!

Sister perks.

The space was quiet with the restaurant still empty. I flicked on the light and it buzzed to life overhead. There were no windows in this room and it was barely big enough for a desk, chair, tall bookshelf, and a filing cabinet.

A newer computer sat on the desk, the keyboard covered in loose papers and handwritten notes. It would take some time to go through everything and figure out my own system, but I finally felt the reality of the job settling over me.

This was my restaurant now. I was in charge. This would be the place I made or trashed my name.

Oh, how I wanted next year's who's who lists to include Dillon Baptiste as Durham's up and coming wunderkind. The hunger to be known for culinary greatness burned through me, slow and smoldering, new dreams only now awakening.

Until this moment I had been happy to live in someone else's shadow, supporting their hopes and dreams. But this office, this kitchen, had birthed a need to be something so much greater than support staff.

My happy-go-lucky-*fine* personality started to slip. I didn't want to be fine. I didn't even want to be normal. I wanted greatness and notoriety and to be known for my ingenuity. I wanted to stand out. I wanted to be wholly dedicated and committed and eccentrically weird like only incredible people were.

But my old ways had a strong hold on my soul. The new feelings bumped into years and years of hiding. Into years and years and years of chameleon personalities that slipped into place whenever necessary. I breathed in and I was normal again. Safe again.

Afraid again.

I walked behind the desk and sat down. The leather chair creaked beneath my weight and rolled into the wall. I wrapped my fingers around the edge of the desk and centered myself. Those new feelings burst to life again, stronger this time, tougher.

Power vibrated through my fingertips and my mind spun with the heady feeling of decisions waiting to be made. Closing my eyes, I let my guard drop and the sensation of stepping into myself took deeper root.

I loosed a smile and whispered a prayer of hope. Yes, this was scary. No, I wasn't ready or prepared. But dang, this was going to be a ride.

The outside door opened and from my vantage point, I could see two chefs walk into the newly cleaned space. They noticed the fresh, sanitary environment immediately. I could hear them commenting on how clean it looked because they hadn't noticed me yet.

Wanting to make a good first impression, I ignored the pterodactyl-size butterflies flapping prehistoric wings in my belly, quickly threw on my jacket without buttoning it, and met them in the center of the kitchen.

When they turned at my footsteps, I smiled demurely and said, "Hi, I'm Dillon Baptiste, the new head chef."

They turned to stare at me, sizing me up with shrewd, bulletproof gazes. A man and a woman, they both looked older than me. Although the woman was older than the man by maybe ten years or more. And they both seemed to have more experience.

Okay, you couldn't tell who had more experience just by looking at them. But they had a confident air about them. A surety I lacked. And a hardness in their eyes when they looked at me, like they were obviously so much better than me, like I was a toddler compared to their maturity.

But what did I know? The whole culinary adventure could be a mid-life crisis for each of them.

"Hi," the woman said in return. She had fiery red hair and pretty freckles from one side of her face to the other. Her face was totally bare of makeup and a bandana was tied around her neck. She looked tough. It wasn't just the fresh face and glint in her eyes. It was something her whole body wore like a flashing sign. She was thick and solid, the kind of woman I could easily imagine in a prison kitchen. "I'm Ashlynn Young," she continued, as terse and straightforward as I expected. With a nod of her head in his direction, she added, "This is Blaze Ferrand. We're the sous chefs."

Giving them a wobbly smile, I held out my hand and doubted myself. It was a sickening feeling, and the emotional switch from proud and energized to insecure and fearful made bile rise in my throat.

I should have told them I hadn't decided on sous chefs yet. I should have inferred that I might be bringing my own sous chef with me. I definitely shouldn't have accepted their verbal claim on the position and changed the subject.

But that was exactly what I did. When they finally returned my handshake with limp versions of their own, I said, "Nice to officially meet you. Ezra has told me so much about you already. I feel like we're old friends."

They did not laugh or smile. They nodded their heads absently and avoided eye contact.

Damn.

So much for winning over the staff with my charming smile and connections to the boss.

"Where is Mr. Baptiste?" Ashlynn asked. "We didn't realize we'd have to work with you already."

Blaze, who was much younger than Ashlynn, but still older than me, had taken to staring at me with his arms crossed over his chest. He wasn't a bad looking guy. Certainly, more friendly looking at first than Ashlynn with all her mob-mom vibe happening. But I didn't like how he hadn't spoken yet. His attempts at intimidation felt childish at best, arrogant bullying at worst. And I hated that it was actually working! I wanted to crawl back inside my office and slam the door shut.

No wonder Ezra hadn't been able to entice anyone over here.

"He's out front," I told her. "Let's go find him."

I pushed between the two of them, desperate to get out of this awkward tension. I didn't know what I expected taking over this kitchen, but it hadn't been this. They were like toddlers that had gone without adult supervision for too long—spoiled, entitled, and angry for no reason.

And I was playing right into their temper tantrums, I realized.

I wanted to smack my hand over my forehead and scold myself. Instead, I whipped around, causing both of them to stumble to a stop before they slammed into me.

"I'm sorry," I told them, and then regretted apologizing and showing them any kind of weakness. Be strong, Dillon. Be the badass boss you know you can be. "I don't want to find him right now. He'll come find us in a little bit."

They blinked at me, totally thrown off by my change of plans. Not that they had softened any, but I could tell they didn't expect me to stand up and take charge.

"Before we get Ezra involved, I want to talk to you about clean kitchen habits. When I got here today, this place was a disaster. If the health inspector had happened to stop by, he would have written us up on a hundred different violations." Slight exaggeration, but I hoped they were getting the point. "I realize this place has been without solid leadership for a while, but that doesn't mean you all can slack off on every day duties."

They glared at me, clearly despising me for questioning their leadership. Blaze tilted forward on his toes, folding his arms over his chest, choosing to stare at the floor. Ashlynn poked her tongue into her cheek and raised her eyebrows as if waiting for me to retract my accusation.

Nerves bounced through me, bowling balls playing Ping-Pong in my skeleton. I pressed my legs together to keep my knees from knocking. Still, I needed to establish dominance.

Granted, I didn't come in here today to claim the alpha position, but I also couldn't let them think I was weak. Or underqualified for the position.

Even though I was both.

"I worked through what I could before you guys got here," I continued, "but I'm going to write up a checklist for us to use moving forward. Each station will be responsible for cleaning up after themselves. Together the work will be fast and efficient." I didn't really have a game plan as far as the checklist went, but we'd used one at Lilou. My plan was to adopt that one.

I thought they might have something to say about that. But they didn't. Ashlynn ground her teeth together and Blaze continued to stare at his feet.

"When does the rest of the staff arrive for prep?" I asked, keeping my voice polite and upbeat.

Ashlynn shrugged. "Soon."

"Do you have an official start time?"

She shrugged.

"That will change too," I said calmly. At Lilou we not only had detailed shifts, we arrived early for them. Wyatt ran his ship with the "if you're on time, you're late" philosophy. It looked like I would be adopting that one as well. I cleared my throat. "We're going to move prep work to the day of. I want everything fresh. Does Jo deliver produce here?"

Ashlynn stared at me. Blaze offered nothing.

I could ask Ezra later. I felt the fire of their hatred and decided I could ask Ezra now. "My plan tonight is to mostly observe," I told them. "I'll have the final say in all the dishes leaving the kitchen, but I'd like to see how you work."

Ashlynn rolled her eyes. Blaze finally looked up, but it was to give his coworker a disgusted look.

I cleared my throat for a second time. "I'm still familiarizing myself with Bianca's menu," I confessed, hoping that if I showed them some weakness, they would drop the Pitbull act. "I'll rely on you two a lot over the next few weeks. I appreciate your cooperation and support."

There was a heavy beat of silence and then Blaze finally spoke. "Are you done?"

My teeth clicked together at his lack of respect for me. Both of them should have addressed me as Chef. There should have been deference in their tones. There should have been reverence in their gazes.

Instead, nothing but contempt and resentment looked back at me.

I was in so far over my head. My hand reflexively wrapped around my throat as I struggled to breathe. Desperation to preserve whatever remained of my dignity around these people kicked in and I nodded as regally as possible. "You're dismissed," I told them.

As soon as they turned away, I spun on my heel and bolted from the kitchen like it was on fire. Hot tears pricked at the corners of my eyes, but I refused to let them fall. I refused to let my first day at my new job get to me.

My cheeks flushed as shame and embarrassment crawled up my sternum and dug into my chest. God, what was I thinking? Why had I agreed to this? Why had I let Ezra talk me into this?

A sour taste filled my mouth as I realized it hadn't been Ezra that finally convinced me to say yes, it had been my irritation with Vann Delane. His obvious disbelief in me had kicked at my pride. And in a misguided attempt to prove him wrong, I'd given Ezra false hope that I could handle this job.

If my first staff meeting was any indication of what I was capable of, I clearly couldn't handle this job. Or the people that worked for me.

I needed to cut my losses before it was too late. I could talk to Ezra before the rest of the staff got here. I wouldn't even have to miss another shift at Lilou. No doubt, Wyatt would let me come back. Benny would be thrilled to give up sous chef responsibilities.

It wasn't that I didn't want this job anymore. I did. Or I thought I did. But eventually. Not today. Today I was just straight up not qualified for it.

I wasn't a boss. I wasn't a badass. I wasn't the savior Bianca needed.

I would be the silver bullet that finally took her out for good.

Ezra was sitting at a table beneath the eyes Molly had painted, clicking away at his computer. I appreciated the space he'd given me to familiarize myself with the kitchen by working out here instead of in his office. The big brother gesture immediately softened my panicking, overly-emotional heart and I was able to slow my pace from a sprint to a stumbling walk before he noticed me.

He smiled when he saw my cautious approach. "Hey, I was just about to come find you. How's everything going so far?"

Horrible. Terrible. I want to quit. "Your sous chefs just showed up."

His brows furrowed together, but his proud grin stretched wider. "You mean *your* sous chefs just showed up."

Ugh, the pleased tone to his voice was like a donkey kick to the chest. "They're intense, aren't they?"

His expression sobered some and he regarded me carefully as I took the seat across from him. "Maybe, but they're also really good. You'll appreciate how hard they work every night. You'll like them once you get to know them."

I chewed on my bottom lip, deciding on how to tell him that I didn't want to get to know them. I didn't even want to see how they cooked in the kitchen tonight. I just wanted to run away and never come back.

But before I could say a word, Ezra let out a sigh filled with a hundred years of grief and pain and disappointment. "God, I wish our dad could see us." The comment was so out of nowhere that I couldn't control my facial spasm. He laughed at my utter shock. "We did it, Dillon. Don't you see that? He didn't think we'd be anything but spoiled trust fund babies. And yet here we are. We turned his money into successful careers. Doesn't it make you so incredibly proud?"

I tried to swallow around the jumbled "I quit!" sticking in my throat. "You turned your trust fund into a successful career. I'm, uh, still figuring my shit out."

His thousand-watt smile reappeared. "Dillon, come on! I know Bianca is struggling right now. But you're the EC of a fucking five-star restaurant. Own that. Be proud of what you've accomplished."

I swatted his compliment out of the air with a swoosh of my hand before it could land anywhere near me. "I've accomplished nepotism. I don't have the reputation for this, Ezra. This isn't mine to claim."

He rolled his eyes. "Stop looking at this like I did you some huge favor. You're the one that's bailing me out!"

"Oh, come on—"

"Seriously, woman. You don't think I did my research? You think you only got this because you're my sister. Give me some credit, I'm not a total moron."

"What do you mean?"

"I went to Killian. I asked him to evaluate you. I interrogated Wyatt and Kaya until they blocked my number. Hell, I cross-examined the entire kitchen at Lilou. I made Vera go on secret spy missions and test your skills. This wasn't a whim, Dillon. This was a well-researched, high-level vetting process that you passed."

My procession line of excuses dropped to my stomach like a stone. I caught myself on the table, barely comprehending his words. "What?"

He gave me that look, the one he'd been giving me my entire adult life. The one that said he knew better and I should just believe him because we both knew he was right and I was wrong.

"You're saving me, Dillon. Not the other way around." He leaned forward, dropping his voice. "And just in the nick of time too." Giving the dining room a furtive look, he cleared his voice and admitted, "Between the two of us, things have been getting bad enough here that I have been considering closing her doors."

I gasped for air, feeling the weight and pressure of exactly what he'd brought me in to do. "Are you serious?"

"She's hemorrhaging cash. I've had to dip into the other restaurants' profits to keep her afloat. And the reviews that have been coming out about her lately have been bad. I've done what damage control I can. I've put off as many critics as possible. But I'm risking her reputation and the publics' interest." He reached across the table and squeezed my hand. "I need you, Dillon. I know it's not fair to ask so much from you. But it has to be you. Not just because you're my sister, but because you're the exact profile I need to rescue Bianca's reputation. Fresh, new to the scene, up and coming. If anybody can save her, it's you. I know it." His smile was self-deprecating, apologetic, "I'm betting everything on you."

I tried to smile, but it fell flat. How could I walk away after a rousing speech like that? Plus, he'd brought Dad into it. If there was ever a challenge I loved to win, it was one where my asshole dad was involved.

"Say something," he pleaded, his eyes as scared and nervous as the first day I met him.

"I was just thinking," I started softly, struggling to put strength into my voice, "how Vera's odd pregnancy cravings now make sense. She wasn't craving deviled eggs with foie gras and lemongrass. Or candy stripe beets with stone-ground mustard aioli. She was testing me."

His head tipped back and the sound of his rich, full laugh was enough to bolster my courage—at least for tonight.

"She's kind of an evil genius, isn't she?"

"Totally."

"Want to go over the menu?"

I nodded, not knowing what else to say. I couldn't exactly walk out after all of that. I had to say, it was nice to hear that he actually believed in me and that I hadn't gotten the job based on blood relation alone.

Now if only I could believe in myself.

Ezra and I spent the next hour going over the menu and the consistently top-selling dishes. He talked to me briefly about his vision for future menus and invited me to share my opinions.

By the time I walked back to the kitchen, my spirits were momentarily boosted thanks to his utterly genuine faith in me.

But that was where my hope crashed and burned. Because behind those swinging in and out doors, the kitchen was practically mutinous. Blaze and Ashlynn had spread their bad attitude to the rest of the small staff.

Or maybe they hadn't needed to spread it. Maybe it came naturally to these people.

Either way, it was the worst night I had ever spent in a kitchen. It was worse than my first night at Lilou. It was worse than my finals at school. It was worse than the first time I'd taken over for Wyatt and happened to have a period migraine and a blister on my heel the size of a fist.

Nobody listened to me. I might as well have just kept my mouth shut the entire night, because it didn't matter what I said or who I said it to. Orders came in and the kitchen filled them. Without acknowledging me. Without taking my suggestions. Without accepting my criticisms.

By the end of the night I was so utterly defeated, I didn't even bother to go over cleaning projects. I let them leave and did what I could myself.

I stumbled into bed close to 3:00 a.m. and cried myself to sleep, still wearing my tank and white work pants. I promised myself tomorrow would be better, but not even my usually gullible heart could believe the lie.

This was the hardest thing I would ever do.

But I would do it for Ezra.

Even if it killed my reputation.

Even if he had to close the restaurant anyway.

I couldn't let him down. I couldn't walk away. I wouldn't let his dreams die because I was too afraid of some hard work.

SIX

I PARKED Veronica in Lilou's front lot and made sure she was locked before hurrying around to the side door. I pulled on the handle, expecting it to cooperate. It didn't. I frowned at the time on my cellphone.

Where was Wyatt?

He was supposed to be here. He was supposed to solve all my problems. He was supposed to listen to them too. Admittedly, I was an hour earlier than usual open, but I had wanted to talk to him before I had to be at Bianca.

I should have texted him to let him know I was stopping by. Argh. Why didn't I text him?

And why hadn't I reached out to Kaya first? Or Vera? Or Killian?

Oh, I knew that answer. I didn't want them to give me false hope. They were my actual friends—which meant they wanted to see me succeed. And that made them awesome.

But right now, I needed truth. And Wyatt was the most honest person I had ever met.

Granted, his honesty was of the brutal variety. But I had girded my loins and readied my abused heart for this conversation.

Also, after a full week of emotional, verbal and that one-time physical abuse when I'd gotten in the way of a service tray on its way out of the kitchen, I was pretty sure I could handle anything at this point.

Wyatt's open criticism might even feel wonderful right now. At this point, I wouldn't be surprised.

My attempts at taking complete control of Bianca had crashed and burned every single night. And not for lack of trying.

I'd been firm. I'd been tough. I'd been a downright asshole. I'd been kind and sweet and gentle. I'd been professional. I'd been a raving lunatic. I'd even thrown in a night of being a complete basket case, hoping the rapidly switching back and forth between manic and sane would confuse them long enough to get them to listen.

Nothing had worked.

Just when I had started to make progress in some areas—for instance, I'd finally convinced the servers to let me inspect the dishes before they left the kitchen—another problem would come up. The dishwashers would take ridiculously long breaks and our dishes piled up until I had to serve dessert on dinner plates and appetizers on dessert plates to keep food moving out of the kitchen. Or when I'd finally convinced the cook in charge of risotto to let me show him my technique, the cook in charge of protein had decided to overcook every single thing.

Ezra had forgotten to mention that I needed to order desserts every few days from our pastry chef. And not one member of the staff had offered the information when we'd started to run low. Consequently, we'd gone one entire night of service with only vanilla bean ice cream available.

God, I was fucking this up so badly.

I needed advice. Or a mentor. Or goddamn Mr. Miyagi.

And the worst part, the very worst part, was how proud Ezra was of me. He texted me often to say it. He would stop in the kitchen during dinner service just to give me a smile and a thumbs up. He thought because I hadn't burned the place to the ground yet, I was doing a phenomenal job.

The truth was I was going prematurely gray and currently growing a boat-sized ulcer.

Jogging to the front of the building, I tried those doors. They didn't open. I jogged back to the side door and tried it again. Then I kicked it when it didn't budge.

Momentarily losing my mind, I grabbed the handle and violently tugged on it. It wouldn't move, but that didn't stop me from trying.

"Just freaking open!" I shouted at it as I lost my grip completely and flew backwards, arms flailing in a desperate attempt to catch myself from landing on my ass.

Bracing myself for impact, I lost my breath in surprise as strong hands managed to catch me around the waist before I bit it on the concrete.

"Whoa," a rumbly, masculine voice breathed into my ear, sounding as though he were settling a frightened horse. "Careful."

Vann.

Vann Delane.

Only upon hearing his whispered voice as it ran across my bare skin did it occur to me how completely crazy I had been acting. I managed to get my feet underneath me and stand up straight, pulling away from his saving grasp.

I tugged my fitted white tee down at my waist where it had ridden up when he caught me. Putting on my most sophisticated air of professionalism, I turned around to face him. "Thank you," I told him evenly.

"Are you okay?" He was amused, like he couldn't believe I was trying to pull this off without admitting my looney behavior.

I glanced at the side door to Lilou again. God, what I wouldn't give to get in there right now. I realized it wasn't even about Wyatt anymore. I just wanted to be inside Lilou's safe, familiar doors. I wanted to smell that kitchen again, stand inside her, run my fingers over the smooth stainless steel and be home again.

Tears brimmed against my bottom lashes. I kept my attention on the door so Vann couldn't see. "Not really," I admitted, knowing it was futile to try to play this off. "I, uh, I need to talk to Wyatt."

"Is it an emergency?" Vann asked rationally. "I could call him for you."

"I have his number," I snapped, brushing away a stray tear with the back of my hand. "I just... argh." I cleared my throat. "To be honest, I'm kind of desperate to get inside Lilou. I've been working at Bianca all week and it's been... difficult. I just wanted to be somewhere familiar."

"I thought you were a robber."

The laughter in his voice immediately dried up my tears. "What?"

"I saw this crazed lunatic yanking on the doors from across the street and I honestly thought you were trying to break in. I ran over here ready to..."

He had put his hand over his mouth and looked away, prompting me to ask, "Ready to what?"

"Detain you," he confessed on shaky breath. He was clearly trying not to lose it. "I was going to tackle you to the ground citizen's arrest style and call the cops."

A laugh bubbled up inside me at the ridiculousness of this moment. My emotional instability got the best of me and I pictured Vann launching into a tackle to keep me from breaking the heavy metal door down with my bare fists and another laugh exploded out of me. "Oh, my god," I gasped. "You must have thought I was a total psycho!"

"Deranged homeless person to be exact." His laughter rumbled in the air, like thunder before a spring storm. "I was prepared to buy you a meal if you needed it. But I was definitely going to call the police."

I wiped away tears that were from laughter this time. "I am deranged. This is so embarrassing."

"I'm just glad I don't have to wrestle a crazy person and call the cops at the same time. On the way over, I realized I should have called them first and then tried to stop the intruder."

Giving him an exasperated look, I said, "Thank God you didn't! That's all I need. The staff at Lilou arriving just in time to witness me getting shoved into the back of a squad car."

He snickered again, unable to stop himself. "And then your brother would have had to come bail you out."

We laughed hysterically all over again. I doubled over, barely making sound as I imagined explaining to Ezra that I wasn't trying to break in, I just wanted to smell Lilou one last time. He would have had me committed for sure.

"Ugh," I groaned, remembering my beef with Vann and sobering some. "You were right. I'm not cut out for executive chef. Look what it's done to me! Total strangers are having to tackle me in alleys to keep me from breaking and entering. Oh, my god, what am I even doing with my life?"

"I'm not a total stranger," he reminded me, sounding offended. There was a beat of silence where I didn't know what to say after I'd blurted so much and he clearly didn't know what to say in response to any of my issues. But then he asked, "So you took the job at Bianca?"

I gestured at my white shirt and wide-leg pants, as if he would know the difference between Ezra's restaurants and their uniforms. "Against my better judgment... yep. I did." His gray eyes were intense this morning, lasering into me with that penetrating focus of his. I turned to stare at his shop across the street. "But I'm in way over my head. My brother thinks I can save his sinking ship, but I'm pretty confident I'm just drowning us faster."

"Are you not a good chef?" I flinched at his bluntness. "I'm sure Vera could help—"

"It's not that," I snapped, bristling at his assumption. I wasn't great at bragging about myself, but there was something about this guy that forced my fighting spirit to surface. "I'm a fine chef. I was top of my class. Wyatt promoted me to sous chef the second Kaya left. My friends all gave extremely high recommendations for Ezra to hire me at Bianca."

"Okay, then what's the problem?"

He irritated me with how unruffled he was by me. He wasn't at all charmed by my looks or money or car. I didn't know if he knew how much money I had, but I was Ezra's sister, so that should tell him something. And he didn't seem to notice when I grumped at him. It was like nothing phased this guy. He was completely unfazed.

Which only bugged me even more.

"The staff," I blurted, questioning my sanity all over again for confiding in this guy. "They hate me."

He weighed my words. I could feel his analytical energy from where I stood. "You don't seem like the kind of person to shy away from a challenge. If they hate you, make them like you."

"I don't think that's going to work," I pouted. I'd tried that already. And about a hundred other tactics. "They don't listen to me. I'm there in the kitchen, telling them what to do and they just... collectively ignore me. It's like I'm a ghost they can't see." I cleared my throat of the bitterness burning hot. "They don't want to see."

"Hmm..."

"And I don't want to go to my brother," I explained, answering the question he hadn't asked. "I don't want to be that person. The girl that can't fight her battles, so I run to my brother every time someone does something I don't like. They already don't think I'm qualified for the position and that Ezra gave me the job out of pity. If I get him involved, that's just proving their point. I will never get their approval then."

I knew he'd heard everything I'd said, but he was quiet for so long that I turned to look at him, curious of his expression. He stood there in fitted khaki pants and an army green short-sleeved button up, his arms folded across his chest, showing off his toned biceps. His hair had been recently trimmed short, just barely longer on top. His temple had lines shaved into the side. Trendy, but edgy for his usually polished look. His angular face was scrunched in thought and his eyebrows were drawn together over his nose.

I lost my breath, suddenly realizing how striking this man was. I mean, I'd always known he wasn't an ugly guy, but this feeling of... attraction was new. He'd been this familiar stranger until this moment, this very one. I'd recognized his face before. I didn't hate looking at him. But he was a guy I had never cared to get to know before now.

Not that I necessarily wanted to get to know him now... it was just different. I kind of, sort of, knew him. Or if I didn't know him, he wasn't a total stranger anymore, as he'd just pointed out.

He'd convinced me to take the Bianca job. He'd started my car for me the other night. And now he was listening to my job problems.

We weren't friends. But we weren't...acquaintances only either.

"They don't listen to you at all?" he asked thoughtfully.

"No. None of them. I've barely convinced the servers I'm the one in charge. The kitchen staff is completely feral."

He lifted his gaze and gave me the full force of his stormy gray eyes. If I was a lesser woman I would have fainted. Or at least had to fan my face.

"Fire someone," he said.

I shook my hair out, afraid I'd been so distracted by his face I'd misheard him. "What?"

"Fire someone. Tonight. The first time someone doesn't listen to you or talks back or ignores you, fire them."

His advice was so completely out of left field to me that I had trouble processing it. It was like he'd spoken a foreign language. "Your solution to getting the staff to respect and listen to me, is to fire someone? Just like that? Just walk in the door and make someone leave?"

"These aren't your people, right?" At my look of continued confusion, he clarified, "You didn't hire them? They came with the restaurant?"

"Right. Ezra hired them. Or the chef before me. I just stepped into the position with the current staff in place."

"Okay, so they have no reason to be loyal to you. You're the outsider, not them. And my guess is that you're younger than all of them too?" I nodded, hating every second of his honest assessment. "Less experienced?"

I shrugged, not wanting to admit this part. "It's impossible to say." His gaze hardened, expecting the truth. "But most likely, yeah. I'm relatively new to the game."

"And even though you have the chops for this job, they likely assume you only got it because of your brother." When I started to protest, he reminded me, "You said so yourself."

"Okay, yeah."

"Fire someone. The first time someone talks shit, cut their ass loose."

"I get the lesson, but don't you think that's a little harsh?"

He shrugged. "Honestly, depending on how hostile this work environment is, you might have to keep firing people."

Laughing at the lunacy of his suggestion, I decided I wasn't the only one on the brink of insanity today. "You're suggesting I handle dinner service all by myself every night?"

"I'm suggesting you do what it takes to get this kitchen, your kitchen, under control. You clearly can't keep working like this. And you shouldn't have to. You're the boss."

His rousing speech was delivered with such conviction that I couldn't help but repeat, "I'm the boss," as if saying it for the first time ever.

"You're the boss," he repeated. "Is this how a normal chef takeover happens? You walk in to someone else's kitchen and have to convince them to listen to you?"

I thought about his question and shrugged. "Not always. Sometimes EC's bring their own sous chefs. More often, they promote from within so the staff already respects the new leadership. I have never been a head chef before so I don't have a sous to bring with me and I'm obviously not being promoted from within."

"You have no choice," he pointed out. "You're going to have to fire someone."

I wiggled, feeling uncomfortable with the idea. "I don't know."

"I mean, you could fire them all and start from scratch. I'm sure you have friends in the industry that would be willing to come work for you."

Chewing on his words, I realized that to get people I knew to come work for me, I'd have to poach them from my friends. That wasn't an option.

And starting from scratch wasn't an option either—not if I wanted to turn Bianca around in a reasonable amount of time. I needed people in the kitchen that knew what they were doing, that already believed in her mission and wanted what was best for her. I needed people that gave a hell about the restaurant, but also listened to me.

"God, I feel sick," I mumbled, slowly accepting that his suggestion made sense. Fire someone? Me? That would take guts. So many guts.

Who did I think I was? Gordon Ramsay? I never yelled at people. I convinced them to be my friend and then got them to do what I wanted by respectfully asking them to do their job. It wasn't in me to walk into a hostile work space and take away someone's livelihood just to get everyone to wake up and pay attention.

"Can I hire them back?" I asked him.

His chin jerked in surprise. "What do you mean?"

"You know, make my point, fire someone. And then once they've all realized I'm serious, let the fired person come back to work again?"

He shook his head slowly, as if still trying to process my question. "That defeats the entire purpose of trying to get them to respect you."

He was right, but I obviously couldn't tell him that—his ego was big enough already.

"So, you're saying... just walk in there and fire the first person that doesn't listen to me?"

"Or talks back or rolls his eyes or breathes in a way that you don't like. But yeah, that's the general idea."

"And as soon as I ruin that one person's life, everyone else will magically listen and follow orders?"

"You're not ruining anyone's life. You're doing your job. Just like these idiots working for you should be doing their job. They're ruining their lives by being entitled assholes. You're the boss. Regardless of how you got the job or whether or not they believe you deserve it, you're. The. Boss. Which means they follow protocol or they find a different job. Have any of them given you the impression they're looking for other work?"

I thought seriously about his question. Had they? They'd been consistently late all week. They'd been consistently negligent and disobedient and willfully obtuse. But they'd shown up every single day without fail.

That gave me the impression they didn't want a different job, they just didn't want me at their current job.

But if I started firing people willy-nilly, they might change their mind.

Truthfully, I hated what was happening right now. I also couldn't man the kitchen alone.

"Have you ever used this tactic?" I asked him, hoping he would give me an honest answer.

He was silent for a few seconds before admitting, "I've never had to. My employees have always respected me."

His words burned through me, ripping fresh wounds open even wider. "Oh."

"That said," he continued, "I have dealt with others not taking me seriously. I know what it's like to be young in business. It's hard to get anyone to take you seriously, but especially your peers. Sometimes people behave the way they're supposed to and things go the way they're supposed to go. And sometimes you have to force your way in the door and carve out your own place. It's not the fun way to do things, but it's worth it." He held my gaze. "If you love what you do, it's worth it."

The burn he'd set off inside me turned into a consuming fire driven by desire and a conviction I didn't even know I had. I wanted this job. More than anything I had ever wanted in my life.

To be fair, I had lived a mostly charmed existence and I had never had to want for much. In a materialistic way. Regardless, I knew how to work. I wouldn't think too hard about how this was the first real thing I wanted and couldn't easily have.

Liar—my heart whispered. *You wanted your dad to love you. How did that turn out?*

You wanted your early twenties to end differently than they did.

I didn't know if I'd ever recover from those years.

Ignoring the painful reminder that not everything I ever wanted was handed to me on a silver platter, I mentally built an armor of grit and steel. I had goddamn moxie. "You're right," I told him.

His lips twitched with what could only be described as an almost smile. I ignored how charming the expression was on his usually grumpy mug. "What was that?"

Rolling my eyes so he knew I didn't enjoy repeating myself, I said, "You're right. If I want them to pay attention to me, I have to go in guns blazing. I can't let them bully me. I have to take this bull by the horns and fucking ride it."

"Whoa, there were a lot of metaphors in there." When I glared at him, he loosed a cocky grin. I retaliated with a harsher glare. "But I think you get the point." Job apparently finished, he started to back away toward the street and the shop he'd left unmanned for the last twenty minutes. "If I go back to work, you're not going to try to throw a brick through the window or something are you?"

I pressed my lips together to keep from smiling. "I don't need inside anymore."

His smile softened, punching me right in the girly bits with the sweetness of it. "Good luck, Baptiste. Don't leave too much carnage tonight. Remember, you can't run that kitchen alone."

"I'm calling you in for backup should things go awry. If you can't cook, you can at least be my character witness when the cops question what happened." He laughed at my joke and it left me with a heady feeling of triumph. I remembered my manners at the very last second. "Uh, thanks, Vann."

He waved me off like it was no big deal. And maybe it wasn't. Maybe he wasn't being kind and considerate like I'd painted him in my mind. Maybe he was only talking a crazy lady down from the ledge.

It didn't matter now. No matter the reason he'd chosen, it was advice I needed. It was advice I was going to use.

I would have to find the courage between now and three hours from now to do it. I could fire someone. I could.

At least I hoped I could.

For a split second, I thought about sticking around and waiting for Wyatt or going to Ezra to ask what he thought. Shaking those wild thoughts out of my head, I jogged back to my car and slid into the driver's seat again.

There was no point. Vann had given good advice and I found I was anxious to see what happened.

SEVEN

BY THE TIME I'd driven across town to Bianca, I had lost the positive attitude I claimed after talking to Vann. I walked into Bianca feeling freshly defeated.

It took some kind of special determination to fire someone, to take away their hopes and dreams and kick them out on the streets. And, honestly, I didn't think I had it in me.

Then what are you doing here? a small voice whispered inside me.

It was a valid question. One that I took a few minutes to ponder.

Ignoring the staff that had managed to be on time today, I trudged back to my office and threw my purse on the desk. What was I doing here?

If I couldn't do something as simple as get my kitchen to follow me, why was I here?

What did I want?

I mean, really want?

Was it to be handed an easy job and given my career? Or was it to carve out a name for myself in the industry through blood, sweat and tears?

Was I going to give up because it wasn't easy?

Or was I going to dig in my heels and force people to do as I asked?

The answer was obvious.

The door to this job might have been opened for me, but nobody was going to hand me a legacy on a silver platter.

"Enough of this inner dialogue bullshit," I whispered to no one.

Spinning around, I buttoned my chef jacket and stomped back into the kitchen. I decided this was it. I'd had enough. There were decisions that had to be made for tonight and I was done pussyfooting around. But I also wasn't ready to start firing people left and right.

That would have to play out naturally, I decided. And hopefully, going into my second week at Bianca, it wouldn't have to come to that.

I pulled down the clipboard from where it hung next to a cooler and started to go over the schedule. Checking people off the list as they slowly walked in for their shifts and prep work, I started to feel carefully optimistic.

Everyone managed to walk in close to ten. Granted, it was ten-forty-five and Ashlynn, the head sous chef and second in command was only just strolling through the door, but a quarter to eleven was a big improvement over last week.

She glared at me, per usual, as she shrugged on her jacket and started buttoning it. I held her stare, not backing down.

"Now that we're all here," I addressed the room in my most commanding voice, "we can start." I pulled the pen I'd used to secure my hair in a makeshift bun and started going down the list, assigning stations and prep tasks.

"A few final things," I told them, struggling to keep their attention. "We're out of the duck for our duck confit." A murmur of disapproval rippled through the ranks. This was a popular dish at Bianca, one of the staples, and I hadn't ordered enough. It was my mistake, but I was still learning the kitchen. "Instead, we're going to do a strip steak and duck fat frites with a mango and watermelon chutney."

"You can't do that," Ashlynn said, speaking up for the first time that day and speaking to me for the first time in two days.

Stunned by the vehemence in her voice, I asked, "Can't do what?"

"You can't just change the menu day of," she snapped, folding her arms over her chest. "That's tacky."

My body snapped to attention at her insult, standing straight and flexing every muscle. "It's not tacky," I corrected her. "It's a solution."

"We wouldn't need a solution, if you wouldn't have created a problem." She wasn't wrong, but that wasn't the way to speak to your boss either. "Now you've put us in a bad situation and want us to fix it by making shit up on the fly? This is ridiculous."

I took a steadying breath, trying not to let my anger get the best of me. I decided to reason with the logical part of her brain, hoping to help her understand. "This isn't a difficult dish. I'll go over it with you today, we'll prep the chutney ahead of time and we'll use the fat already prepared for the duck to make the frites. I think it will be a great addition to tonight's service."

If she would have kept her mouth shut, I would have been able to move on. Or at the very least, she could have asked to speak to me in private. But she was too angry and too bitter to think clearly. Or that was what I told myself after she growled, "This is fucking bullshit," in a whiny, high-pitched voice I had to believe was an imitation of what I was supposed to sound like.

And that was the final straw.

God, I hated that Vann was right again. And I hated that it was Ashlynn of all people. In a mostly male-dominated space, I was not in a hurry to fire one of my only female employees.

But that was too far. And she'd questioned my authority blatantly in front of the entire staff.

Honestly, she left me no choice.

Before I could overthink it or let my soft, squishy heart get in the way, I shouted, "That's it! You're fired."

The room froze in place. Ten pairs of eyes stared at me. It was hard to know if they took me seriously enough to even heed my order. It was just as likely Ashlynn would ignore me entirely and keep working through service. Then I would have to call Ezra in here.

Or the cops.

Meanwhile, it took everything in me not to drop my face into my hands and groan.

Or reach out, grab her hand and apologize.

Instead, I steeled my resolve and glared at her, not backing down.

The entire room flinched when she finally spoke. "What did you say?"

I leaned forward, planting my hands on the counter to get eye level with her. "I'm done with your disrespect, Ashlynn. Now you're questioning me in front of the staff and refusing to follow orders. You are fired."

"You can't fire me," she argued, sounding slightly hysterical.

"I just did."

"You're not even the fucking boss!" she railed, her voice taking a demonic pitch that managed to be high and low at the same time.

I thought I would break down the second she questioned my decision, but I found it easier to remain calm the more crazed she became—especially because after all this she still hadn't learned to respect me. "I am the boss," I assured her, rather serenely if I did say so myself. "And you are fired."

"You childish bitch!" she shouted. "You're a fucking toddler! An infant! You can't just come in here to my restaurant and pitch a fit every time you don't like something. News flash, we don't like you, but you don't see us acting like babies." She turned to Blaze, fomenting, "This is unbelievable. Fucking unbelievable."

There was this part of me that hated what I had just done, the can of worms I'd just opened. I wanted to shove my words back in my mouth and swallow them. I wanted to apologize and tell her I didn't mean it. I wanted to run away and not have to come back here and deal with these people and this responsibility and Ezra's expectations of me.

And why couldn't it have been Blaze? Why of all people, was I forced to fire the only woman on shift today? Not only that, she had the most seniority. I was basically firing the only other person capable of running this kitchen without me.

But most of me, all the important parts, knew that I'd made the right decision—especially after her reaction. It was the wise decision. Vann had been right. I had to assert my dominance. I had to show my people I meant business.

And, most importantly, I needed to purge this place of bad juju.

This atmosphere was toxic. And the longer I let it fester, the more people were poisoned. Ashlynn had to go. It was obvious now.

"This isn't your restaurant," I told her calmly, with almost no tremble in my voice. "It's mine. And if I say you don't work here anymore, you don't. Get your knives. Get whatever else is yours. And leave."

"You won't survive dinner service tonight without me," she hissed, spittle flying with her fiercely punctuated words. "You need me. You can't run shit without me."

Now I was just irritated. "This is one of the most capable kitchens in the city. Look around, Ashlynn, they've never needed you. They don't need me. They've kept this place functional for months. I'd venture to say they'll hardly notice you're gone."

Her face wrinkled in frustration. She knew I was right. She knew the staff had been operating without leadership for a long time and they could continue to operate well without leadership if they had to.

True, the menu wouldn't change, and the quality of cooking would diminish, but these people weren't idiots. They just needed the right leadership.

And it clearly couldn't be found in Ashlynn.

I wondered if that was why Ezra had never promoted from within, if he'd known she was a total headcase from the start.

Taking in the rest of the staff, now still as corpses and just as quiet, I raised challenging eyebrows and spoke to the entire staff, "Unless you're willing to follow my lead and respect my position, leave now. If you want to continue cooking in this kitchen, you better turn it around. You better learn to listen to me. If not? This is your opportunity to walk out. I'll even write you a letter of recommendation as long as you don't insult me on the way out." A snicker broke through the silence, but I didn't catch who it originated from. "I'm serious," I assured them. "If you don't want to cook for me, if you're offended by my age or my family or my looks or whatever the hell else, leave. Save me the headache and go now. Because understand that if I have to listen to any more of that 'She doesn't deserve to be here' shit, I will toss you. I don't care what you think. I don't care if you have an opinion on how I got here or if you don't know how I got here or even if you know who I am right now. The point is, I'm here to cook good food—really good food. I'm tired of Lilou and Sarita getting all the glory. I'm over losing to them. And the Chophouse. And the May Bistro. And whoever else. This is one of the best kitchen's in the city. We're going to start acting like it."

I clamped my mouth shut and waited. Running through my speech, I realized there were probably ten other things I should have said, but it was too late now. They either stuck with me or left.

There was a good chance there would be a mutiny.

God, how desperately I wanted to chew my bottom lip until it was raw and bloody, but I refrained. It was more important to maintain the illusion of control than to snap and let them all know I was out of my damn mind for taking advice from a bike shop owner I didn't even like.

Oh, my god, what had I done?

To my surprise nobody moved. In fact, they seemed to settle into more permanent postures. Blaze spread his legs apart and crossed his arms over his chest—the universal signal for, you can't make me leave.

Okay, maybe it wasn't universal, but I read his intention clearly.

The rest of the kitchen followed suit, nobody even acknowledging Ashlynn anymore.

She picked up the message too. "Are you serious?" she demanded. "After all we've been through?" She turned to her fellow sous chef. "I expected this behavior from you," she snarled at him. "You've wanted my job for three years. You can fucking have it. Good luck to you."

He didn't turn his head or look at her, but I felt his attention shift to her for just long enough to say, "Don't forget why you're leaving, Ashlynn. This wasn't your choice. She fired you."

I glanced to my left and watched the line of men nod their heads in agreement. Same thing was happening on my right.

"I was going to Red Oak. You know that," she argued weakly.

I nearly laughed at her lateral move to the city's oldest steak house. If she thought that was going to be an easier work environment, she was in for a rude awakening. The head chef there, Trent Shepherd, was one of the meanest chefs by reputation. Total and complete egomaniac and asshole.

Nobody else moved to help her or walk her out. They just stood and waited for her to leave.

The better side of my humanity kicked in and I started to worry about her. Had I screwed her from getting another job? Had I taken away her hopes and dreams completely and ensured she wouldn't get another position as respectable as Bianca? Had I ruined her career completely?

But then she leaned forward and spit on the ground in front of my feet. The gloopy mucous dripped through the no-slip mats between the quarter-size holes.

"Classy," I murmured in a poisonous tone.

She stepped back, grabbing her roll of knives from the countertop behind her. Taking a step toward the door, she lifted her chin in the air and said, "I can't wait to watch you drown."

I didn't have a comeback for that. She might be right. I didn't know if asking her to leave would expedite that coming to fruition, but I knew it wouldn't help. She was a good chef most days, but possessed a venomous attitude that was corroding her from the inside out.

"Your coat," a steely voice demanded from behind me.

My shoulders instantly rose at the sound of Ezra's voice. He was pissed. Beyond pissed. This calm, cold voice was his most angry.

And I didn't know if it was directed at me or at Ashlynn.

Ashlynn had the insight to look cowed. "M-my coat?"

"From what I understand, you don't work here anymore," Ezra deadpanned, his chilling tone sending an icy wind through the kitchen. "Leave your coat."

Her teeth ground together as she considered her options. Ezra wasn't just siding with me, he was sticking up for me, taking her down off her high horse and reminding her who she used to work for.

Her jaw clenched so hard, I thought she might break a tooth. Then she slammed her knives down and started to rip open the buttons.

I couldn't help but wonder if she had ever been proud to work here. By her attitude and total negligence for authority, I would assume no. But she'd been here since Bianca opened five years ago. She'd survived under Marcel, who had been a total nightmare to work for from what I had heard. She'd run the ship after Marcel had left and she'd tried to transition under me.

Did she start with this attitude? Or had the volatility of her time here broken her down?

Would it break me down too?

Or would I break the rest of the staff eventually?

Ugh, why was being the boss so damn hard?

Holding Ezra's glare this time, instead of mine, Ashlynn tore off her coat, held it up in the air with one finger and then dropped it on the ground. "Fuck you too," she snarled before storming out of the building.

As soon as the door closed behind her, I let out an explosive breath, not caring if it made me look weak in front of the rest of the staff. Geez, that was intense.

Ezra's strong hand came down on my shoulder, squeezing tightly. "I'm proud of you, Dillon."

At his words of affirmation, hot tears sprung to my eyes. I was two seconds from losing it completely. Lifting my chin high and gathering whatever dignity I could muster, I addressed the room. "I'm sorry you had to witness that, but I hope we can move forward professionally, doing what's best for Bianca. If any of you have questions or concerns about my leadership, please come talk to me. In private." I pulled away from Ezra's hand, stopping myself from sprinting to hide behind closed doors. "I will be back in a few minutes to discuss my menu changes for tonight. For now, why don't you... start prep like usual?"

I didn't wait for their replies or even for them to acknowledge my order. Instead, I walked briskly back to my office, Ezra hot on my heels.

When we were safely inside, I gently shut the door behind him and then threw myself into his arms, sobbing against his shoulder. "I'm sorry!" I sniffled, turning my head so I didn't cover his crisp, white button-up in tears and makeup.

His hand landed on my back, safe and secure and so like the big brother I loved. "For what?" His voice was full of careful amusement.

I didn't even know what I was apologizing for. Or if it was necessarily directed at Ezra. Maybe I'd meant it for Ashlynn, but he was the closest human.

Rather than admit I didn't know what I meant, I said, "That was crazy. She is crazy." I sucked in another shaky breath. "What an awful way to start a Monday."

He chuckled at the truth in my words. "I have to be honest though, I was hoping you'd can her. She made life hell around here."

I pulled back, resisting the urge to punch him. "What? You knew she was a nightmare and left it up to me to fire her?"

He shrugged, like he hadn't really thought it all the way through yet. "I couldn't have kept Bianca open without her," he admitted. "That's why it was so important you took this job."

Glaring at my brother with all the fire and brimstone I was capable of, I said, "You thought you'd bring me in so I could do your dirty work?"

His eyes bugged innocently. "I thought I'd hire a real EC so I could finally get rid of her."

A knock at the door saved his life. I had just decided to strangle him.

He opened it and let Blaze poke his head in. He addressed me. "There's a delivery."

I smiled at him and hoped it didn't look totally deranged. "Thank you."

After he'd walked away, I turned back to Ezra. "You deal with it. I need a few minutes by myself."

"You did the right thing," he assured me. "I'm proud of you."

All I could do was roll my eyes and say, "Next time, warn me when you know something like this is going to happen."

"I didn't think I—"

"What if I would have quit instead?" I asked him, cutting him off before he could offer a lame excuse. "What if I would have just walked out?" My point hit home and he shut his mouth. I repeated myself, slower and with more conviction than I knew I was capable of. "Next time warn me."

When I was finally alone in my office, I dropped my face into my hands and growled. I sat there for a few minutes, until all the blood had rushed to my face and I knew my fingers were going to leave marks.

I expected tears to fall, or gush, or just show up for a pathetic little pity party, but nothing came. My eyes remained dry and slowly, gradually, the adrenaline left my body and I began to find myself again in the midst of panic and anger and the feeling that I still didn't know what I was doing.

I picked up my phone, ignoring my motives, and searched the internet for the Cycle Life phone number. I'd pushed the call button before I could even absorb the store hours and pressed it to my ear.

Nibbling on my thumbnail, I waited for someone to pick up.

Vann answered only a few seconds later. "Cycle Life."

My throat dried out, at a loss of what to say after his crisp greeting on the other end. If anybody's voice matched their personality and style so perfectly, it was Vann.

He managed to make me picture him in slim fit pants and a button up short sleeve top—his uniform—with two words.

"Is Vann around?" I had to ask the question. If I admitted I knew it was him just by the sound of his voice, I would sound like a creeper.

"This is Vann," he answered easily.

"This is Dillon," I told him. And then realized I didn't have a game plan. Or even a vague idea why I'd called this man. "Er, Dillon Baptiste."

"Hi, Dillon."

Ignoring the confusion in his tone, I pushed valiantly forward. "I was just calling to..." Good grief, what was I calling to do? "To..." Make something up, Dillon! "To..." It's now or never, say something! "Thank you for your advice. I took it."

His confusion evolved into disbelief. "You took it? You mean already? You already fired someone?"

I licked dry lips and questioned my decision all over again. "You did say the next time someone talked back."

He laughed, the sound of it rumbling across the distance separating us. "I underestimated you, Baptiste."

I bit my bottom lip and then bolted forward in my seat, boldness filling my body. "Twice."

"What's that?"

"You've underestimated me twice now," I told him. "First with the job. Now with this."

There was a heavy beat of silence before he admitted, "You're right."

I smiled. I couldn't help it. Although it didn't sound like a compliment, it somehow was. Coming from this man that was so arrogant and so full of himself and so usually... right, it was high praise.

"Anyway, thank you," I repeated, needing him to know I really did appreciate his guidance. And the time he took to talk me off the ledge. "It was truth I needed to hear."

"Your problems are over then? Smooth sailing from here on out?"

A bark of a laugh escaped me. "Hardly. But I'm hoping firing that one will at least make things a little better."

"It will," he assured me. "Especially if you keep listening to me."

I found myself smiling at my desk, looking like a total loon. "Is that right?" Where had that throaty voice come from? Was I flirting? With Vann Delane? "Guess, I better ask you for more advice then."

His voice did the same thing as mine—took on that smooth, sexy quality, dropping low and husky. "Guess you better."

Blaze knocked again, sticking his head in my office before I had a chance to hang up with Vann. I shot out of my chair, standing, fumbling with the cell at my ear.

Get it together, Dillon. You're a grown woman. Talking to a grown man. Be an adult.

"We need you, Chef," Blaze said.

It was the first time he had addressed me as Chef and I was immediately floored by the weightiness of hearing that one word.

Oh, my god, I was the boss.

This was my restaurant.

And damn did it feel good to hear someone call me Chef.

"I'll be right there," I told Blaze. To Vann, I said, "Duty calls."

"Let me know if you fire anyone else today," he teased.

I laughed, unable to help myself. Who was this guy? "You'll be the first to know."

"Bye, Dillon," he murmured.

My stomach flipped at the familiar way he said my name. "Bye, Vann."

I hung up the phone and dropped it inside my desk drawer. I had a kitchen to run. I couldn't be thinking about Vann Delane and his surprisingly good advice. Or his shockingly cute butt.

Slapping a hand over my mouth to hide my smile, I walked back to the kitchen, pushed up my sleeves and got to work.

EIGHT

I WAS FIFTEEN MINUTES EARLY, because I hated being late to anything—especially dates. I hated that awkward feeling of waiting around for the other person to show, so I never wanted anyone else to wait because of me.

And yet, by being early, what had I made sure would happen? I would be sitting at this trendy little coffee bar all by my lonesome while I waited for Matt Brennan the pastry chef to show.

True to his word, Benny had passed my name along to his friend Matt, who had reached out shortly after. We'd spent the last two weeks exchanging texts and had finally found a free Saturday morning to meet for coffee.

It hadn't been easy. Our schedules were totally opposite. When Matt got off work, somewhere in the middle of the afternoon, after a good twelve-hour shift, I was well in the middle of prep. And when I got off work, in the early hours of the morning, he was only hours away from waking up and heading in. Basically, if this casual conversation turned into an actual relationship, we would get to spend about four hours together every day. In the middle of the night.

So, coffee this morning sounded promising.

Still, it was hard to find a guy that understood the number of hours I had to work without questioning them. Matt understood the chef life. He lived it himself. Sure, logistically it would be difficult to spend real time together. But theoretically, we were already on common ground.

Right? At least that was what my eternally optimistic heart was trying to tell me.

Matt worked for an up and coming bakery that he swore was *the* place to get baked goods in Durham. Ezra used a pastry chef he'd worked with for years, so I didn't know too much about the bakery scene, to be honest.

Pastries were outside my area of expertise—except for chocolate croissants, which were basically my favorite thing on the planet. Admittedly, I didn't pay too much attention, other than to know if what my kitchen was putting out was good or not.

Nothing at Bianca was made in house. We cut pieces and plated them with all the pizazz to let you think we knew what we were doing. But nobody on my staff could recreate the magic Ezra's girl managed.

I fidgeted in my seat and took a sip of my cooling latte. I shouldn't have ordered so soon because now it was getting cold while I waited for Matt to arrive. But I preferred to pay for my own drinks, another reason I showed up early. Everything was better when I was in complete control of my beverages.

Taking in the dark browns and hunter greens of this cool spot, I couldn't help but applaud his choice of meeting place. As far as first dates went, this was an excellent choice.

Not that I went on a lot of first dates. Or even met guys alone in public. But I was trying this whole take-charge-attitude thing at work and I was hoping I could apply some of it to the rest of my life and work out some of this heavy shit that always followed me around. If for no other reason, at least I could add a fun coffeeshop to my life.

I wanted to come back here with my laptop and work on Bianca's fall menu. I would curl up in one of the round booths by the back windows and dream up the most delicious food Durham had ever seen. Plus, this place was more than just its décor. Their coffee was excellent.

Even lukewarm.

Dinking around on my phone while I waited for Matt to arrive, I confirmed my participation in Vera's bachelorette party the following week and answered a few emails. Nerves swam around my stomach, jumping off high dives and executing synchronized swimming competitions.

The last few guys I'd loosely dated had been more of the same—setups by well-intentioned friends. Loosely dated might be an overstatement. Basically, we shared the most awkward, stilted meal in blind date history, and I ran away before they could ask for a second chance.

It had been years since I'd dated a guy that captured my interest. During high school, I'd been forced to run in Durham's prep school circle thanks to my good old dad. The boys I'd met during those pretentious years were the stuff of nightmares. When they could manage to not assume you were going to sleep with them three minutes after meeting them, I found them boring and unambitious.

Sure, they wanted to make money, but there was no sacrifice there. No real drive. And why would there be when daddy had already carved a path for them. All they had to do was walk forward into the planned future their trust fund paid for.

Not that I had any room to talk when it came to trust funds.

Which led me to the next segment of dating—men after my money.

To be honest, that was partially my fault. After high school, when my dad had died and I'd inherited full access to the money he'd left me, I'd gone a little... wild. I could hardly complain about the guys attracted to the cash I was throwing around, when I was pretty much making it rain every single night.

That had been a dark, dark time. I'd been lost in grief and confusion and this world that I couldn't navigate without my dad's guidance. I'd started to self-medicate with drugs, alcohol, and the party scene.

It had worked for a while. I hadn't had to think about what an asshole my dad had been and the guilt I felt for missing him anyway. And I hadn't had to think about what I was going to do with my life or what I wanted to do with it or what was even my purpose on this planet. The crowd I'd run in had everything I needed to numb out—especially men willing to help me.

Or take what they wanted without my permission.

When the partying ended in the worst possible way, I'd spiraled into depression. There were no men there. There were no people there at all. It was just me, my regrets, and my self-hatred.

And an ample amount of fear-induced panic attacks.

Culinary school had pulled me out of the worst of those hopeless days because it taught me how to work for something. It showed me that work, especially work I loved, could be way more effective in helping me move on from the hard parts of my past than partying ever could.

I could never overcome my sadness during those wild days. Or shake loose the feeling of being isolated. Depressed. More alone than ever.

Food showed me how to feel amazing at the end of a hard night. Fulfilled. Empowered. Exhausted.

But it had also led to the next stage of dating—the one that didn't exist because I was so freaking busy all the time.

The one I liked to call self-ordered celibacy. And I was happy here. I was happy alone. Mostly happy anyway. I was at least happy that I'd removed the fear from my life.

Most of the fear anyway.

Did I even want to settle down? That was the big question.

Full disclosure, I was a million miles away from wanting kids and the whole domestic thing. But I was starting to notice how completely alone I was. I wanted someone to text at the end of a hard day. I wanted someone to bring to Christmas dinner at my mom's house. I wanted the flippy feeling in my stomach and the giddiness that came after answering a particular phone call. I wanted to get rid of the pang in my chest every time I thought about my happy friends or the random people holding hands while they walked around a grocery store together.

Watching my brother turn so completely upside down for Molly had been the most adorable thing ever. And Killian and Vera. Now Wyatt and Kaya.

I couldn't help it. I wanted what they had. I just didn't have the time to go through all the hoops to get there. Or the tenacity to survive it.

Ten minutes later, the coffee shop door opened, and Matt Brennan walked inside. At least Matt Brennan's profile picture walked in.

I'd been doing this long enough. I couldn't rule out a cat-phishing scenario just yet. Guess I'd hope for the best.

Standing up from behind the tiny table, I lifted a hand in hello. "Matt, hey."

His eyes swept over my low-cut olive jumpsuit and distressed cream cardigan and lit with approval. I'd worn my hair down for the first time in weeks and it suddenly felt too hot on my back and shoulders. I struggled against the urge to tug at my top and cover myself more fully, I gave in a moment later, wishing I'd been more conservative with my outfit choice. And then I scolded myself for letting my past fears intrude on this moment. I loved my outfit. I looked amazing. Who cared what he thought? Pulling my hair over my shoulder, I reached out. "So nice to meet in person."

He took my hand and pulled me into a hug. My thigh jostled the table as I jerked against him. "We're closer than handshakes, aren't we?"

No. No we were not. My entire body bristled at the surprise contact and I had to breathe slowly through my nose to keep from bolting.

God, I hoped this guy was just overly friendly with zero ability to recognize social cues. Because otherwise my knee was going to find its way to his balls uninvited.

Generally, hugs didn't bother me. In fact, my friends would probably consider me a hugger. But this felt forced and awkward. Pressured. I would have preferred the handshake—and even that seemed generous.

Laughing awkwardly, I pulled away and took extra care not to bump the table again as I sat down. "I hope you don't mind, I got here early, so I already grabbed a drink."

He frowned at the mug on the table. "I was going to get that for you."

No apology for being late? No acknowledgment that I had put some effort into making this as easy for him as possible? Laughing off his comment, I said, "It's no big deal. Like I said, I was early."

His eyebrows lifted, a lightbulb turning on inside his head. "You're one of those people, huh?"

"What people?"

"Type A. You know, always on time, bossy, do things for yourself."

Uh... I wasn't even sure how to respond to his list of barely veiled insults. "I am a boss... if that's what you mean."

He sunk down into the seat across from me. "That's right. I keep forgetting you're the EC. That's cool."

My lips turned up to form a smile, apparently pleased at his compliment. "Yeah, it's been... uh, interesting. I mean, I love the job. But it's been a difficult transition."

Matt was a good-looking guy. Tall and big-boned with the warmest chocolate eyes and a few days' worth of scruff gave him an adorably disheveled look. Like a teddy bear. The last couple guys I'd dated were the kind of men totally obsessed with their looks. They spent half their day at the gym or staring in the mirror, which was fine. I just wanted someone that didn't care so much about their appearance.

Matt seemed like a good balance.

"How so?" he asked as he looked toward the counter.

Did he want to get a cup of coffee? He could totally get something. I would wait... He looked back at me and smiled. "The staff, mostly," I told him. "They haven't been the most receptive kitchen in the world." I lifted my gaze to his, my heart squeezing tightly at the memory. "I've already had to fire someone. It's killed me the last couple weeks."

His lips pressed together in a frown. "Are you serious?"

I laid my hand across my eyes. "I know. I'm horrible."

"Hard-ass," he chuckled. "You're a boss bitch."

"No, I'm not! That's the thing. I'm a total pushover. I can't even believe I did it."

He gave me a look that had me flushing from the inside out. It was a look that said he didn't believe me. "I don't think pushovers fire people in the first week. Sounds like you're kind of a tyrant."

Was this his idea of flirting? This wasn't as fun as when we'd joked over text.

Or maybe I was the only one joking when we'd texted. It was hard to say when you'd never spoken to someone in person before.

I smiled, but it was wobbly and unsure. Shaking my head, I said, "Not really. I just, uh, I want the restaurant to survive. It's had a difficult year."

"Which restaurant?"

"Bianca."

His eyes lit with recognition. "Oh, that's right. I forgot you told me that." Disappointment spiraled through me that he couldn't seem to remember the minimal information we'd exchanged texting. But it grew to a tsunami of what the hell am I doing here when he said, "I've heard some bad things about that place. I think it's..." he made a swirling motion with his finger, pointing at the ground. I didn't know exactly what he meant by it, but I interpreted it to mean circling the drain to its death. "You sure that was a good career move? Hitching your wagon to a burning building?"

I took a sip of my cooled coffee, holding it tightly so he couldn't see my hands trembling with anger and frustration. "My brother owns it," I snapped, hoping that would put things into perspective for him. "He asked me to step in and help him save it."

He sat back in his chair, his legs sprawling wide. "Ah," he laughed. "Now I get it."

Leaning forward, I tried to stay calm. "Get what?"

He waved his hand at me again. "The job. Why you got the job."

"You'll need to be more specific." Oh, how I wished my coffee was still hot. That would have been a much more satisfying sizzle when I dumped it on his lap.

"Bianca sat without a head chef for how long? Nobody wanted that place. You're saving your brother's ass. I think it's admirable."

His explanation was just generous enough for me to retract my claws.

But then he added, "It also explains why you got the job."

My jaw dropped as everything attractive about him turned to dust. He stood up without saying another word and walked to the counter. No excuse me for a second. And no explanation why he just walked away. He just left.

Had he not totally insulted my career and family seconds ago, I would have excused his social awkwardness as quirky and tried to convince myself it was cute. Maybe even charming.

But now I just wanted to do the same thing to him and get up and leave. Without an explanation.

Unfortunately, I was raised with manners.

Instead of storming out, I gazed out the big picture window to my right and admired this artsy section of Durham. It was near the farmer's market where Jo sold her produce. If I could wrap this up fast enough, I might make it over there before it closed.

I needed to talk to her about Bianca and I needed a few things for my apartment. Currently I was living off salted tomatoes and beef jerky scrambled eggs.

The eggs tasted better than they sounded.

Matt sat again, a plate clattering to the table. "Have you eaten?"

A peace offering of pastries sat between us. Maybe this morning could be salvaged after all.

"Is this for us to share?" I asked, eyeing a chocolate croissant that was making my mouth water.

"No, I got it for myself." The dripping sarcasm in his voice was not attractive. He laughed at his own joke while I just stared at him and tried to get over my hurt ego. "Of course this is for us to share. I made this." I must have made a funny face, because he explained. "This is from the bakery I manage. We sell here."

"Oh!" That made more sense. I picked up the butter knife on the table and cut the croissant in half, not willing to reveal my true and eternal affection for these babies yet. I didn't always trust my reason when it came to chocolate croissants. Better he didn't know how vulnerable I was around them just in case he used them against me to grab a second date. "It looks amazing. Where do you work again?"

"The Green Patisserie," he said. "It's all right. The owner is a total bitch, but it's pretty well known around town."

I swallowed my croissant, surprised at how dry it was. Where was the chocolate? Or the butter? Unforgivable. Also, I didn't like how many times he'd used the word bitch when it came to women in the short time we'd been sitting here. I tried to steer him back to neutral ground. "I'm still learning the food scene here. I went to CAI for school."

"Oh, really?" he asked, a disgusted note to his voice. "That's an interesting choice."

Did he have a problem with where I went to school too? Geez, this guy had a lot of opinions.

I took another sip of my coffee and tried to reason away his behavior. I could give him a break. Maybe I was just being sensitive. Maybe I'd let my own insecurities get in the way. Maybe he was perfectly cool, but also nervous?

"Where did you go to school?" I asked him, determined to let go of my building resentment of this guy and give this date a chance.

"Oh, just a little place called Le Petit Paris. It's like the best pastry school in America."

I hadn't heard of it. But again, I wasn't a pastry chef. "Oh... cool."

"Yeah, it's a big deal. I'm kind of disappointed with where I've landed. But I'm looking at this like a stepping stone for where I want to go. Have to build a resume somewhere, right?" His eyes narrowed slightly, before he added. "Well, you don't have to, but the rest of us do." Then he laughed loudly.

I let out a patient sigh and looked around the coffee shop for some options. Maybe the espresso machine would magically catch fire and I would have a reason to run out of here, waving my hands wildly and screaming at the top of my lungs. Maybe the bathroom would spontaneously flood, and it would turn into one of those save yourself scenarios. Maybe the apocalypse would start, and zombies would invade and I would finally get to try out all the sweet moves I'd learned from those self-defense classes and watching seasons of *Buffy the Vampire Slayer* on repeat for my entire life.

But alas, everything stayed perfectly normal. No spin, flip, stake-to-the-brain moves for me.

"Not everyone can be as lucky as me," I murmured, not feeling lucky at all. This guy had no idea how hard my job was. I'd told him I had to fire someone already, but that must not have clicked for him.

"That's for sure," he agreed, taking a big bite of the fruit tartlet, spitting crust as he did it.

The door opened, jingling the little bells hanging above. I glanced up, hoping for zombies. Instead, Vann Delane walked inside.

I dropped the remaining chocolate croissant on my lap.

He clocked me immediately. By his wide-eyed expression, I could tell he was as surprised to see me as I was to see him.

Damn.

Double damn.

Why did he always have to see me at my very worst?

Without realizing what I was doing, I leaned closer to Matt and laughed, like what he had just said was the most hilarious thing in the world. And not the worst.

Vann's eyebrows drew down in surprise. I waved at him. Very nonchalantly. Like I should win an award for how nonchalant that wave was.

Matt turned around to check out who my attention was on. "Do you know that dude?" he asked when he went in for another bite of tart.

"I'm good friends with his sister," I explained. Then I took a sip of coffee so I didn't have to look at either man.

Vann got in line to order coffee and I tried to salvage the conversation with Matt. "So... what do you want to do with your career then?"

"What do you mean?"

"You said where you work now is only a stepping stone. What's your ultimate goal?"

"To own my own place." Finally, something we could connect on! Not that I would ever own my own restaurant. But EC was close enough, right?

"That's exciting," I told him, feeling genuinely happy for him.

"Yeah, I'm just so sick of these hours. They're killing me."

Okay, wait a second. "Are there bakeries that work different hours?" I thought all bakers were up before dawn to get ready for that morning crowd? What was he going to do, sell donuts for supper?

Not a totally bad idea... but still.

"Sure," he said obviously. "I don't even know if I want to have a full bakery, you know? I've been thinking about cakes. Cakes seem easier. I could work when I wanted to work and sleep in. Still go out on the weekends. I just can't do this grind. It's killing my social life."

I nibbled my bottom lip, trying to decide what to say to that. In one sense, I got it. My job was killing my social life too. And these hours weren't for everybody. But... this was the life we chose. Er, I chose. I walked in with eyes wide open. I knew what I was getting myself into. I wanted this life.

Because my work meant something to me. It gave me a purpose bigger than anything else in this world. It fulfilled me. It gave me this great, big reason to wake up in the morning and the energy to survive the long, grueling days. Yes, it was hard. But hard wasn't a bad thing.

Although, I could admit it wasn't for everybody.

Maybe I was crazy.

And maybe my friends were all crazy too.

Honestly, I could have let it go. I didn't think Matt and I were going anywhere, but I wasn't going to hate him for wanting a life outside of his job, even if it didn't exactly endear me to him. But then he added, "Besides, I've gotten so many clients from this job right now. It would be so simple to start something on my own."

"You're going to poach your current clients? To start your new job?" The words just fell out of my mouth. And to be honest, they were not said in a kind voice. Honestly, my tone was pretty judgy.

And poor Matt felt the judgment hardcore.

His face took on an expression of total defensiveness. "Not like tomorrow. I'm talking the future. Like I said, I'm building my resume."

Without any regard for his current employer. Ugh, this guy was a total douche.

"Seems like a shitty way to do it."

"You're right. But firing people the first week you take over is totally cool."

"Are you serious?" God, this guy was a total asshole. The nervousness I'd felt earlier turned to ash and I felt sick to my stomach.

His jaw took on a stubborn quality and he shrugged his shoulders instead of verbally responding.

"I'm so glad to see you, Dillon."

Vann's presence looming over the table was a total surprise to both Matt and me. We turned to stare at him slowly, in unison. I'm sure I had a "what the hell" look written all over my face. And I couldn't have even predicted what Matt looked like. This could not be happening right now.

"You are?" I heard myself say.

He gave me a look that said, "Play along!" but I didn't know what I was playing along with.

"Uh, can we help you, man?" Matt demanded, not earning any points from me.

"Yeah, thanks, *man*." Vann smiled, showing his teeth. He turned back to me. "I was going to call you today, so it's nice I ran into you. Do you have a few minutes?" When I hesitated, he added, "I wanted to go over that thing we talked about the other day."

"That thing?" I heard myself ask. God, Dillon, be cooler.

"Come on," he ordered, not waiting for me to act more confused. He turned around and walked to a table on the other side of the restaurant.

I smiled apologetically at Matt and said, "I'll be back in a few."

"You're kidding, right?" He threw his hands to his sides in frustration.

"We work together," I explained, finally getting my act together.

He looked at Vann. "That guy's a chef?"

"Consultant," I clarified.

"I thought you said he was your best friend's brother?"

Getting up before he could ask any more questions, I grabbed my purse and cell phone and hurried across the coffee shop.

"Are you with him?" Vann asked in disbelief as I slid onto the seat across from him.

Without looking him in the eye, I answered, "Ish."

I felt his eyes narrow, even though I was fiddling with my purse. "What do you mean ish?"

Finally, I raised my gaze to meet his. "Blind date," I confessed, "Bad, terrible, horrible blind date."

His lips twitched in an almost smile. "That guy is a total asshole."

Sighing out the frustration that was the last half hour, I said, "Apparently, he thinks I'm the asshole."

Vann snorted, then took a sip of his coffee and spent the next two minutes glaring at Matt. "Then he's an idiot. No wonder he's single."

I laughed, surprised at his harsh assessment. "I'm single!"

He took another sip of coffee, hiding a full-blown smile behind it. "I am too, I guess."

I laughed more and it felt strange because it was the first time I had genuinely smiled all morning. But it wasn't my date who'd made me laugh. It was Vann.

"We're only single because those are our options," I told him, still laughing.

His eyes bugged, "You're telling me. I went to dinner with a girl last week who walks dogs for a living."

"That's a real job," I told him, unable to lose my smile.

"But," he added, holding up a finger, "only so she can pursue her dream of becoming an influencer." His eyes got bigger. "I had to google what that was, by the way."

My head tipped back, and I had to hold my stomach as I laughed harder than I had in weeks. "She'll probably be a millionaire by next year."

He rested his weight on his elbows, leaning toward me to admit. "The dogs were pretty cute."

Where had this sense of humor come from? "We're in the wrong professions, I think."

He shook his head. "My selfie game is tragic."

"It's all about the angles," I told him. "You have to know how to work them."

Picking his phone up off the table, he barely tilted it toward himself and asked, "I hear this is a good one."

"That's perfect as long as you want three double chins."

He rubbed his throat with his free hand. "Think it will help me get more dates?"

I smiled, nibbling on my bottom lip at the same time. "Yes?"

"Speaking of..." he murmured. "Here comes yours."

Matt huffed across the restaurant and straight past where we sat toward the bathroom. He gave me an impatient look as he brushed by and I couldn't help but want to jump into Vann's lap and ask him to save me.

He'd already saved me. Thinking about it, he was pretty much making a habit of saving me.

As soon as the bathroom door swung closed behind Matt, I grabbed my purse and stood up. "Now's my chance."

Vann glanced over his shoulder. "You're right." Before I could completely walk away though, he added, "By the way, I think firing that employee makes you a smart boss, not a bitch."

"Wha—?"

"I overheard him giving you a hard time. He's an idiot. Don't let him make you feel bad for doing the best thing for your business."

I blinked, feeling unexpected moisture pooling along my lashes. "Thank you."

The bathroom door made a creaking sound and we both jumped. "Run, Dillon."

I hurried from the coffee shop with a smile I was unable to stop—no thanks to my actual date.

NINE

"THE BRIDE HAS ARRIVED!" Kaya and I shouted from the booth we'd slipped into while waiting for the rest of the bridal party to join us.

Vera and Molly slid onto the seat across from us. Molly was dressed in black from head to toe as we had previously decided, and Vera wore a super cute turquoise ruffly top and black ripped skinny jeans. The sash we'd bought her was nowhere to be seen.

"You're not wearing white," Kaya protested the second they'd settled in their seats.

"And where's the 'Bridezilla' sash?"

Molly leaned forward with raised eyebrows and pursed lips, confiding, "She's been especially difficult today."

An insulted laugh bubbled out of Vera and she slapped Molly's shoulder. "Stop it." She looked at Kaya and me and explained. "I don't own anything white that fits right now. It was this top or a garbage bag. Who knew boobs could get this big!"

Molly rolled her eyes. "We all feel so sorry for you and your giant boobs." To us she added, "And she looked great in everything she tried on. She's just being high-maintenance."

"I guess we'll have to save our obnoxious sash for your bachelorette, Molls," Kaya said, grinning.

Molly's cheeks flamed red, making the prospect of parading her around Durham wearing a veil, a sash and a necklace made out of tiny penises that much more enticing!

Okay, she would probably fake her own death and run away to the Caymans before wearing penis jewelry anywhere, but it would be fun to watch her reaction when I pulled it out.

"I still think this should count as a double bachelorette," Molly argued. "I mean, we might as well, since we're both here and everything. Then we don't have to try to align schedules again."

To her point, it had been a nightmare trying to pick a night where all four of us could be together. The bridal brunch had been easier to plan, but even that was difficult now that Kaya had opened Sarita up to brunch on the weekends and Killian and Vera were getting closer and closer to opening.

"We're not doing that," Vera said vehemently. "You deserve your very own special night of embarrassment and debauchery."

Molly pulled a face. "Debauchery? Do I have to?"

Vera looked at Kaya and me expectantly. "One of us has to do debauchery. It obviously can't be me."

Molly rolled her eyes. "Why can't it be you?"

Vera pointed at her belly. "Um... pregnant. Remember? I can't expose the baby to debauched things. That would be irresponsible parenting."

"Uh, it can't be me," Molly repeated. "I might be pregnant."

The three of us bugged our eyes out at the same time. She pursed her lips together and shook her head, letting us know she wasn't serious. I let out a slow breath. I wasn't ready to be an aunt yet.

One baby at a time.

"Debauchery's off the table for me too," Kaya said with a wistful sigh. "The old ball and chain is surprisingly against it."

The three of them turned to me. Vera grinned. "That leaves you, Dillon. You're the only one left to debauch."

"Ha! I'm not debauching alone," I told them adamantly. "We debauch together or not at all."

They shrugged. Apparently, it was a not at all kind of night.

"There go my fun plans for strip clubs and lap dances," I told them—even though I wasn't serious. Our real schedule for the night included supper at a hole in the wall that supposedly served the best chips and guac in town—possibly the state. Also, possibly the entire world. Margaritas for those of us not with child and an in-house lime refresher for the preggo one. Then dessert, at another hole in the wall that served the best tiramisu in the universe and had an excellent selection of Prosecco. Then second dessert with coffee and added Baileys for those of us not baking a human, raspberry fried ice cream and in-house ice cream cookie sandwiches with mascarpone cream sauce. But first cocktails and apps at this adorable Americana hipster place, Craft, that was known for their excellent bartending and house-made appetizers.

Basically, unlike other bachelorettes I'd been to where we were in a secret contest to see who could eat the least and drink the most, this one was all about seeing who could gain the most weight from our never-ending progressive dinner.

Which is why I loved this group of friends the most. They were the friends I had been waiting for my entire life. My personal circle of soulmates that I had to search for and find, and then claim for my own.

My prep school friends were all trophy wives and cautionary tales. My culinary school friends excelled at passive aggressive competitions that belittled and soul-stripped.

These girls were real. Authentic. True blue soul sisters with zero agenda and one hundred percent support—all day every day.

I couldn't have picked better friends. Or a better bachelorette.

All Vera wanted to do was keep it small, chill and full of her favorite pregnancy cravings. Molly, Kaya and I were all over that.

"Good!" Vera exclaimed, clapping her hands. "Because I invited the boys!"

"What?" I screeched the word.

Vera's expression fell. "Was that not okay?"

I schooled my expression and swallowed the complaint I wanted to voice. "It's fine," I assured her. "Totally fine."

"Two fines," Kaya noted. "It's definitely not fine."

Bumping her with my shoulder, I tried to come up with an excuse, but nothing came to mind.

"Are you really upset?" Vera asked, looking crushed.

I reached across the table and grabbed her hand, squeezing it in mine. "I'm not upset at all. This night is about you. I want to do whatever you want to do."

Her eyes narrowed. "Dillon."

They were all staring at me with expectant expressions. The truth came out unintentionally because I loved these people too much to default to my usual borrowed personalities. I didn't have it in me to be *fine* with them. "It's hard, okay? It's hard being the third wheel. Or the..." I quickly counted the couples that would be here tonight. "Seventh wheel." I held up my hands. "I don't want to be the loser here without a boyfriend."

"I don't have a boyfriend. I have a fiancé." Molly said, in the most pretentious voice ever. She eyed Vera. "Do you have a boyfriend?"

She jutted out her chin and sniffed the air. With the snobbiest tone on the planet, she said, "I have a baby daddy."

I couldn't help but laugh. At least they meant well. "And I have a string of bad dates. During my most recent, I snuck out of the coffee shop while he went to the bathroom." At their dropped jaws and raised eyebrows, I admitted, "Not my finest moment."

"Was he skeezy?" Kaya asked.

"It was nine in the morning, so it wasn't like he tried to get all inappropriate. We just... didn't click."

"You've got to click," Molly agreed.

"And we texted fine," I continued. "But there was zero chemistry in person. I laughed more with Vann in the two minutes I spent with him than I did on the entire date."

"Vann?" Vera asked, but I felt the question resonate around the table.

The waiter chose that moment to finally stop by and grab our drink order. A white wine spritzer for Molly, a paloma for Kaya, a water with cucumber for Vera and my latest obsession—an Old Fashioned with Buffalo Trace. One extra cherry. Thank you very much.

I could do the champagne cocktails and froufrou drinks when pushed, but whiskey was my thing—American. Barrel-Aged. Twelve-year-old. Amen and amen.

We also ordered a charcuterie board, the house pickles, pretzels, and bar nuts in various shapes, sizes and flavors.

"Did you say Vann?" Vera repeated when we were alone again.

Had I said Vann?

Damn.

I told you I was terrible at blurting out the truth and nothing but the truth when it came to these four women that made up my inner circle.

"Oh, yeah, it was the strangest thing. He happened to walk in when I was on this date from hell and he ended up kind of saved me." They blinked at me, like I'd just explained the whole thing in Mandarin. "You know your brother." I waved my hand in the air, hoping I had recently acquired the magical skill of getting girls to skip over conversations about boys.

"Apparently, I don't know my brother," Vera drawled. "Please, tell me more about him. And you. And this date he saved you from."

"V, this night is about you! I feel like I'm taking up all the oxygen. Enough about my failed dating life. Let's celebrate your more successful one!"

Kaya leaned forward, planting her elbows on the table. "Nice try, blondie. But we want the goods. Give us the whole story."

I looked to Molly for some help. She held her hands up in defeat and said, "He's basically my brother too. I'm just as curious."

"Ugh."

"Spill it," Vera ordered.

So, I did. I started at the beginning when Benny asked me if he could set me up with Matt and ended with my escape from the worst coffee date in history when Matt went to the bathroom, leaving out all the important details about Vann's smile and his rival bad dating life and that this was the third time he'd saved me from an unfortunate end.

I thought they'd give me immediate input into the whole ordeal, but all three of them sat back in their seats and were basically quiet until the bartender dropped off our drinks a minute later.

"That was nice of him," Vera finally said.

"That's what I said. He saved me. It was nice."

"He's off nice girls," she added.

"I know. He told me."

Her face screwed up like a shrewd field mouse. "Does that bother you?"

I gave her the look of a confused spider monkey in return. "Why would it bother me?"

"You're a nice girl," she pointed out.

"But I don't want to date your brother."

Now she looked offended. I needed her to make up her damn mind.

Could I blame this mental whiplash on pregnancy?

Sure?

Maybe I'd ask Killian later since he was apparently joining us.

I chose response-neutrality. "Thank you. I think you're nice too, Vere."

Working extra hard to pull us out of awkward territory, Molly said, "Benny should know better. Where's the bro-awareness for his own posse. Come on, dude."

But at the same time, Kaya added, "Vann's coming tonight, isn't he?"

I wanted to roll my eyes, but I politely refrained. "Can I just remind y'all that Vann wasn't the point of the story. I was actually talking about my terrible luck with men. Thank you for rubbing it in my face."

They really hadn't offended me, but I had to do something to divert their attention.

Kaya's elbow nudged mine where it rested on the table. "I think you broke Vera's brain."

"Not true!" she defended immediately. "Pregnancy broke my brain. Dillon just surprised me. I didn't realize you knew each other."

"We don't," I assured her. "Not really. It was this awkward, chance meeting thing. It lasted all of fifteen minutes." Regrouping, I realized Vera needed something besides the facts. She needed me to weave her a story that would make sense in her hormone-addled brain. "We've run into each other enough that he recognized me. And then he overheard our conversation and basically just stepped in because even he could recognize how awful it was."

It was that very moment that Killian arrived, sliding in next to Vera at our table and squishing her against Molly. He grinned at Kaya and me. "Hey, ladies."

What a dork.

Before we could even respond, Ezra appeared, looking buttoned up and socially awkward as ever. Then Wyatt walked over from the bar, the exact opposite of Ezra—tattooed, loose and totally comfortable in every space. And then... the man of the hour. Vann.

He wore a version of what I had come to realize was every outfit for him complete with trendy sneakers. He trailed behind the other guys, in no rush.

I squeezed out of the booth so Wyatt could sit next to Kaya, but that only squashed me awkwardly between Ezra and the table and god, I just wanted to leave. Why had I opened my stupid mouth? Why were men here at all?

This was supposed to be a bachelorette party. The plan was to gorge ourselves on good food, unbutton our pants or skirts later and curl up on my gigantic leather couches and finish the night with Meg Ryan movies.

We'd all taken the weekend off to celebrate the union of two of our favorite people. We had all let other, less qualified people run our kitchens for the entire weekend. That meant Blaze was currently at Bianca, by himself. Without my supervision.

I needed alcohol to soothe my frayed nerves and give me the courage to get through this vacation weekend. And I needed my friends. And a fantastic time. And for them not to write a narrative of what was going on between Vann and me in their heads only for them to get their hopes up and then dashed to smithereens.

"Dillon," Ezra said, in that way of his that didn't include normal words like hello or hey or how's it going.

"Ezra," I returned formally. "You going to make it through this weekend?" He had been ordered by Killian, Vera, and Molly that he could not work, no matter what.

I could already see his hand twitching, desperate to check his phone. He wasn't going to last thirty minutes.

Not that I was any better.

Ezra eyed me seriously. "That depends. Is my restaurant going to make it through this weekend?"

Ha. Touché! I shrugged helplessly. "Hopefully?"

His glare sent me running back to the bar. I knocked my drink down as I went, fully aware that I'd just thrown back an Old Fashioned like a shot, which was basically sacrilege in the Bourbon community. But desperate times and all that. I tottered trying to walk in the tall heels I hadn't worn in months, maybe longer than that.

These red-soled beauties used to be my party girl go-to, but since finding a real purpose in life, I'd traded them in for sensible sneakers with Dr. Scholl inserts.

Sometimes I wore Crocs.

Oh, if only my high school friends could see me now.

"I think you owe me a drink," Vann's reserved voice suggested from beside me.

I hadn't realized he'd followed me over here. I side-eyed him while leaning forward on the bar and flashing some upper cleavage. It wasn't for Vann. It was so the bartender didn't make me wait twenty minutes before he noticed me.

Listen, I'm all about female empowerment and making a name for myself in my trade because of my talent and not my tatas. However, this was a packed bar and I wasn't above using my assets to get drinks faster than the huddle of frat guys at the other end.

He rested his elbow on the bar and turned his body to face mine. "Saving you is turning into a bad habit. I feel as though some compensation might even things out for us."

"Someone thinks highly of his accidental ability to be in the right place at the right time."

He let out a laugh that had an edge to it. "Maybe it's you with the knack to be in the wrong place at the wrong time. Have you ever thought about that?"

I had definitely thought about that. It seemed to be the entire direction of my life.

Instead of admitting that, I miraculously held the truth back and gave him a flirty smile. "Do you mean, like right now?" I walked past him and let my hand settle on his shoulder. Brushing over his shoulder blades and down his spine, I felt brave and bold and like the Old Fashioned I'd downed had seriously kicked in.

"Just kidding," I murmured near his ear.

He spun around as I continued walking. "Hey, now, what about that drink?"

I twisted around on my toes, letting my heels use the momentum of the slick wood floor to propel me like a ballerina. "I thought I'd give you the chance to save me again."

His mouth split in a surprised smile and he tipped his head back and laughed. "One time, Baptiste. Just this one time you've outsmarted me. Don't expect it to happen again."

"We'll see," I called before hurrying back to the table. If I had to be stuck with Vann all night because the other couples were lovesick puppies, at least we'd started getting along. There were some definite friendship vibes sparking back and forth between us.

Maybe even more than friendship.

Or I don't know, maybe it was just irritation mixed with a few drinks.

Regardless, the whole mysterious broody thing was equal parts sexy and frustrating.

True, I liked to believe I could do most things on my own without a man stopping by to change my tire or replace my lightbulbs. But there was something about the way he delivered his help that turned me to warm happy goo instead of fire and brimstone.

The way he looked at me didn't hurt either. Vann was shockingly open and honest. He said what he thought. And not everything he said was nice. But somehow, his blunt honesty was growing on me.

TEN

THREE HOURS LATER, we'd made it to dessert stop *numero uno.* I was happy I'd worn my stretchiest pair of leggings—thank you Costco!— and flowyest tunic because I needed them.

Tonight, had been like Thanksgiving, plus the entire holiday season, plus the day after Valentine's day when all the candy goes on super sale—combined. These friends of mine could *eat.*

And drink, to be honest.

I was already planning a double session of yoga classes in the morning, or I was going to look like the Kool-Aid Man for Vera's wedding in two days.

Realizing the weekend had only started and that I had to get through a decadent bridal brunch, the rehearsal dinner, plus the actual wedding reception, I couldn't help but groan.

"What's wrong?" Kaya asked from across the table, where she sat nestled against Wyatt, his tattooed arm wrapped securely around her.

"I'm going to gain three hundred pounds this weekend."

Molly raised her eyebrows. "I was thinking the same thing. I'm going to have to recommit to those damn spin classes or I'm never going to fit into my wedding dress."

"Spin class?" That sounded interesting. I had been thinking about joining the same gym as Molly and Vera for months, after my gym had gone bankrupt and closed their doors. I'd been dedicated to my favorite yoga studio since, but I knew I needed to mix in some cardio. My limbs were all stretch and flexibility, but there was more to life than being able to stand on your head for twenty minutes.

I loved the idea of having friends at my gym. Not that I could get Vera and Molly to work out with me often. But maybe after the baby I would be able to coax Vera into some low-stress Zumba or biking or something.

A cycle class was an entirely different side of Molly that I didn't even know existed.

She rolled her eyes. "Vera tricked me into going a while back. I quit after she got pregnant because... because basically it was the worst. But now that I've eaten my weight in salsa and fried food tonight, I have no choice."

"It's not that bad," Vann countered, pointing a stern finger at her. "You just like to complain."

She leaned forward, dropping her voice to a secretive tone. "Every time I get off that cursed bike," she explained, "I think it should buy me dinner. It gets way too familiar for a forty-five-minute class."

I couldn't help but snicker at her expense. She bugged her eyes out, letting me know she was serious.

"It is a tough class," Vera agreed. "But dang, it worked. I'd still be dragging Molly's lazy bones there every morning if pregnancy wasn't currently kicking my ass."

"Don't say that," Molly groaned. "I don't even need to go. I'm perfectly fine adding all five thousand calories from tonight to my body. I got a man." Ezra smiled at her adoringly, squeezing her hand in his. Until she finished by saying, "I can officially let myself go."

"Wait, what?" Ezra asked, causing us all to laugh harder.

When the laughter died down, Vann leaned closer to me, so his shoulder bumped against mine. "You don't eat like this all the time?"

"What do you mean?"

He shrugged, and when his arm settled it was touching mine more fully. "You guys are chefs. Good chefs. I would think this would be every day fare for you all."

"It's actually the opposite," I told him. "We're usually so busy cooking for other people, we're too tired to cook for ourselves."

"Or I am so sick of the food I'm cooking over and over that I can't even stomach the idea of eating it," Kaya added from across the table.

"True story," I agreed. "When you've looked at something approximately three hundred times in one night, it's significantly less appealing."

"Interesting," Vann said.

"Nights like these totally make up for it though," I told him. "You know, when you go out with your friends that have good taste and they want to literally eat everything and you're like, 'oh, I guess I do too.' I'm going to have a food hangover in the morning."

He smiled at me, but it was slightly peculiar—as if he was surprised he thought I was funny.

The waiter stopped by again and Killian ordered a round of limoncello for the table. We were at this kitschy little Italian place with a tiramisu that I was confident would be served in heaven. We'd been sipping Prosecco and negronis and now we were apparently moving on to dessert beverages.

Killian nuzzled his bearded face against Vera's neck, causing her to giggle. "Dance with me?" he asked. I couldn't actually hear him from where I sat at the other end of the table, but I read his lips and watched her cheeks flush.

They stood up a minute later, escaping to the small dance floor in the corner where three older couples swayed and two-stepped to big band music and the best of a Frank Sinatra cover band.

"That looks fun," Molly told Ezra. He took her hand and led her away.

I gave Kaya a look that said, "Don't leave me alone here with Vann!"

She raised her eyebrows and tilted her chin toward the dance floor. I shook my head no. Her eyebrows rose higher. I glared lasers at her. She kicked my shin under the table.

Then stupid Wyatt got involved. Taking Kaya's hand, he said, "If you're done having your stroke, would you like to dance?"

She smiled serenely at me. "I would love to."

I slumped against the booth side of the table while the two of them pranced off to the dance floor. "Traitor," I mumbled beneath my breath.

"That's kind of cliché," Vann murmured, sounding as irritated as I'd felt. "Don't you think?"

I turned to face him. "The dancing?"

"Sinatra, the couples, all of it. I find it repulsive."

I couldn't help but laugh. He never said what I expected him to say. "Agreed. They might as well be an advertisement for happily ever after."

"Or erectile dysfunction," Vann added.

On that note, I nearly choked on my spit. "What?"

"Haven't you ever noticed those commercials? They're all about selling an image like this. Couple goes to dinner with friends. Couple dances romantically. Couple falls into bed only to be interrupted by something unexpected. Don't worry, this blue pill works whenever you want it to work. Unless it works for longer than four hours. Then you should be concerned."

I snorted—that's how hard he'd made me laugh. I'd resorted to snorting. "What concerns me the most, is how much you know about them."

He hid his sheepish smile behind a sip of the cocktail I knew he didn't really enjoy. He'd been nursing it for the last thirty minutes and every time he took a sip, his nose wrinkled. "They're on all the time."

"Mm-hmm."

"Have you ever watched a football game? Or the news? Seriously, you can't not know about ED. It's everywhere."

"Apparently."

I had a thing for the look of complete outrage on his face. He didn't like to be misunderstood. And I knew that sometimes that came off as arrogant, but it was also kind of cute.

"I'm good down there," he insisted. "Everything works great." He made the okay symbol and clicked his tongue against his teeth. "I'm good to go."

Widening my eyes and looking completely shocked, I asked, "Is that a proposition?"

"Oh, my god, no!" He dropped his head into his hands. "There's something about you I have never liked. This might be it."

I smiled as I took another drink of the cocktail that I found delicious. "I don't know what you're talking about."

The waiter returned and dropped off the limoncellos. I settled them around the table and then drained my negroni.

Vann eyed his small fluted glass and nearly neon-yellow liqueur with great suspicion. "What is this?"

"It's lemon liqueur," I told him. "It's delicious. You'll love it."

"It doesn't look like anything I'd love. I'm more of a beer guy."

"Oh? I'm sure they have something on tap."

He shook his head again and it felt like a final decision had been made. "I already looked. They don't have anything I like."

"That high maintenance, huh?"

He let out an impatient sigh and then explained his stance on beer—which was extensive. He was into the small breweries that were popping up around Durham and inside Charlotte. He loved IPAs the best. New England style which apparently looked like orange juice. And he was majorly disappointed at the beer selection in all the places we'd been to tonight. Except for Craft. That was the only stop tonight that had won his approval.

He shrugged. "I'm not high maintenance, I just know what I like."

"I know what I like too and I'm going to be honest, this time you're wrong."

"About booze?"

I gave him a look and said, "Yes, about booze."

"Nope. Sorry. I'm right." He eyed the dainty glass of limoncello. "That looks sour, bitter, and persnickety."

My lips lifted in an amused smile. "Sounds like you're scared to date her." I nudged the glass toward him. "Good thing it's just a drink. Much less commitment this way."

He shook his head. "You're set on making me drink this."

I bounced up, tucking one knee beneath me and turning Vann's first encounter with limoncello into a spectator sport. "Personally, I don't think there's anything wrong with persnickety." I batted my lashes innocently for dramatic effect.

His gaze drifted over me, starting at my face, drinking in every detail, line and contour. Then it dipped lower, scanning over my bare shoulders, pausing at the dip of exposed cleavage that my favorite subtly scandalous lacy black tunic showed off, dropping lower and lower until even my ankles felt sexy. My stomach fluttered with surprised butterflies.

I found myself transfixed as his focus moved back to the liqueur. I held my breath as his long fingers wrapped around the delicate stem and in one fell swoop he tossed it back like a shot.

My lips parted in shock. "You're supposed to sip it!" I cried too late.

His face scrunched and twisted, his lips puckering in disgust. "Goddamn," he gasped on the other side of the glass.

I couldn't help it, I nearly collapsed on him from laughing too hard. I'd wanted to introduce him to a fun, new drink. Of course, it was going to taste awful if he glugged it in one big gulp.

"This was a prank?" he asked, eyeing me as I draped myself over him and tried to breathe through the laughter. "Are you pranking me?"

"I didn't know you'd drink it like that!" I insisted. "I meant for you to sip it." I sat up, my head buzzing from the booze and from the nearness of this man. I'd propped my elbow on his shoulder and felt the deliciously warm heat of his skin beneath the smooth material of his crisp button-up. "You did it wrong."

From this vantage, I was sitting just slightly taller than him, with my feet tucked beneath my butt, my heels discarded on the floor. He looked up at me, his gray eyes a brewing thunderstorm of unspoken thoughts. "You should have warned me."

I leaned closer, desperate for more of his heat, more of the way he was making me feel. "You didn't give me the chance!"

He watched me for a few moments. My skin tingled as his intense eyes simply took me in, studied me, tried to figure me out. "I was right."

"About what?"

"Sour. Bitter. Extremely persnickety."

Leaning away from him, I grabbed my drink and brought it back to his lips. "Try it again." He gave me an adorably stubborn look, pressing his lips together in refusal. "Sip it this time." When he still didn't move, I pulled out the big guns. Don't be a chicken was sitting on the tip of my tongue, but at the last second, I heard myself say, "Please?"

It worked. However, he took the glass from me so he could do it himself. After he had taken the most careful sip of all time, he handed the glass back to me. I took a sip myself, making sure this wasn't a terrible brand in general. The taste hit my tongue with the force of ten lemons, opening up my palate and making me pucker my lips in the best way.

"Hmm?" I asked, bugging him for an answer.

"It's definitely better in small doses," he admitted.

"Like our friendship," I teased.

He looked up at me and his eyes were crystal clear. Gray sea glass. The ocean at dawn. "Is that what we are? Friends?"

Nuzzling closer, I slid back to my butt, finding that I was now nearly tucked into his side. "I figure three life-saving events bridged the gap between strangers and friends."

He chuckled, the sound rumbling through his body. I had the strangest urge to mess up his hair. It seemed too tightly maintained, too perfectly quaffed. He wasn't this clean cut, preppy guy he pretended to be. He was dominant, in charge, fierce. He wasn't docile and restrained. He wasn't only sharp angles and pressed pants. He was in your face with his opinion and bossy and... hiding a serious sense of humor.

"No wonder I have so little friends. I haven't saved nearly enough lives."

I found myself laughing again. Had I ever laughed this much with a guy before? "I think you could just hang out at coffee shops and interrupt bad dates if you're in the market for more friends."

He nodded seriously. "Especially if that last douche of yours is involved. Did you hear from him again?"

"He texted to tell me how rude I was to leave him there. I tried to explain that I had a kitchen emergency, but he saw through me. Our mutual friend, Benny, texted later to scold me on my bad manners."

Vann snorted. "Did you tell Benny his friend was a total asshole?"

"I did, actually. In those exact words."

He smiled at me and I nearly lost my breath. It surprised me, full and wide and nothing I had ever seen before. This man that usually scowled and glowered and pondered and considered, but rarely ever smiled at anything. At least not in the short time I'd known him.

I found myself staring at his lips, taking in the happy expression as I tried to wrestle my pounding heart into neutral attraction.

He was a good-looking guy. Naturally, I would be enticed by his smile. He had these perfectly masculine features and tanned skin, topped off with pearly whites that only appeared when his full lips lifted in this sigh-inducing expression.

It was the logistics of being female that had me feeling like all the alcohol tonight had very suddenly caught up to me. My anatomy couldn't help but be totally smitten with his anatomy.

Plus, there were all those times he'd saved me stacking up in favor that this guy was hot.

But he was also Vera's brother. He was also a mostly, total stranger. He was also not right for me.

Okay, Dillon, my inner future-cat-lady asked impatiently, if he's not right for you, who is?

Someone who worked similar hours to me, I told the desperation. Someone who didn't think I was a total moron. Someone who...

Oh, who was I kidding? Fear curled around my lungs, tightening, choking, suffocating. Memories from six years ago threatened the happiness of the night. I didn't want a relationship.

I didn't even want male attention. Not really. Kind of, but not really.

The freshness of those early wounds had faded. The sharpness of the hurt and pain and fear had dulled. The fogginess of that night had never lifted. But still. Still.... Still...

Still. That damn smile.

It made me want to try again. It made me not want to give up on the male species as a whole.

It faltered when I had stared at his face for so long I'd made it awkward between us. He leaned forward, apparently a prisoner to the same pull that I was.

"Good," he murmured, but I'd forgotten what we were talking about. "You should be careful meeting up with assholes like that. I can't be at every bad date to rescue you."

I had to slightly shake my head to get back in the conversation game. "It's not a bad idea though," I told him, hardly recognizing the sultry tone to my voice. "Usually, I have to fake texts from my mom."

His smile returned. "What do you say?"

"That she was rushed to the emergency room," I admitted. "I'm a terrible person."

That sexy as hell smile reappeared. "At least you don't have to stick it out because you're the one paying for the meal."

"Damn, that sounds almost like reverse-sexism."

His gaze dropped to my lips again. "This is serious, Dillon. You can fake a bad text at any point during the date. It's my chivalrous duty to stick it out till the end of the night and pick up the tab. No matter how bad the night is going, I can't exactly run off in the middle of dinner and leave her with the check."

He had a point. "I've never thought about it like that before. Maybe I shouldn't be so quick to abandon coffee just because my date insults me and basically tells me I'm a horrible person."

This time his smile was accompanied by a deep laugh. My body came alive at the sound, tingles rushing through me, heat flooding my core. I wanted more and more and more of that sound and that amused look on his face.

And the best part? He agreed with me. "On second thought, he deserved to get stuck with the check."

I slapped my hand to my forehead and groaned. "Actually, I paid for my coffee that morning. He was running late and I was impatient for caffeine."

"That guy was the worst."

"You're saying you wouldn't have made me pay for my coffee?"

"Or made you wait," he added.

Just when I'd decided to kiss him—because honestly, could he be any more adorable?—our friends decided to ruin my entire life by returning to the table. Their laughter and the scraping of chairs had us jumping apart like we'd been caught in something too tawdry for public.

Glancing at Vera nervously, I was thankful to see she was draped over Killian, engaged in a private conversation. Ezra hadn't seemed to notice either. Or if he had, he didn't realize what he'd noticed. My poor, oblivious big brother.

I had just started to breathe easier when I caught Kaya's shrewd eye. She raised her eyebrows when our gazes clashed, tipping her head toward Vann.

I waved her away and grabbed for my limoncello glass.

She wasn't deterred. "What did we miss?" she asked loudly.

"Oh nothing," I laughed loudly—too loudly. "Vann and I were just swapping bad date stories."

Vera laughed and leaned forward, "He has plenty!"

"So does Dillon," Ezra added.

Kaya's eyes narrowed with a wicked challenge. "Why don't you share your most recent one."

She meant the one Vann and I were just talking about. She was being a brat. And nosey. And pushy! I kicked her under the table and said, "How about a toast instead?" I raised my glass to Killian and Vera. "To the happy couple. May every day be a reminder of why you fell in love."

"Aww!" Vera swooned, leaning her head on Killian's shoulder. He handed over his glass so she could have a sip of his limoncello, kissing her on the head in the sweetest way and basically making all my insides go gooey for them and love and things I was just realizing I might want after all.

I struggled to swallow my own drink, finding it difficult with the giant lump that had taken up residence there. God, why was it so hard to watch happy, lovesick people? They messed with my head in the worst way. I didn't even want a relationship. Or a permanent significant other. Or anything but to figure out how to run Bianca and not totally drown in all the responsibilities in my life I was wholly unqualified for.

Warm fingers touched my hand that was wrapped around the liqueur glass. Vann gently, slowly nudged my grip away from the liqueur. "May I?" he asked softly so the rest of the table didn't hear him. "That seemed like a toast I should participate in."

I let the glass go, turning my head so I could watch him take a drink. Just as the glass touched his lips, I leaned forward and murmured in his ear, "I know you love it, but remember... small sips."

It was more than half gone when he returned it to me. He leaned closer, his lips brushing my temple, his breath moving my hair around. "I have a feeling you're going to sell me on persnickety before this is over."

I shivered at the sound of his deep voice, at the feel of his lips against my skin, at this surprising feeling that something was happening between us. But what was that something?

Other than a terrible idea...

ELEVEN

I HURRIED into Bianca's kitchen, knowing it was going to set me back by a half hour, but unable to help myself. I couldn't just let her go unchecked for an entire weekend. That was crazy.

And I wasn't crazy.

Most days, I wasn't crazy.

Even though I felt like it this morning. After a night of no-debauchery, but plenty of drinking, I woke up two hours late! I didn't even remember hearing my alarm go off. Or hitting the snooze button. Or turning it off completely.

On any other day I'd woken up late, I could have skipped the shower, grabbed the dry shampoo and called it good. But, today was rehearsal dinner day. That's right. Nearly the entire day was designated to Vera and Killian and their wedding festivities.

We had a bridal luncheon planned in approximately fifteen minutes, then we were joining the men again at Salt, Vera and Killian's restaurant, where we were going to be making appetizers, desserts and some of the special items for tomorrow. Vera had wanted her big day to coincide with Salt's big day—which meant wedding prep would be their kitchen's inaugural firing up of all engines.

Luckily for the happy couple, they had so many handy friends who could help them semi-cater their own wedding.

Benny and a team of misfits they'd gathered from around the city were doing the heavy cooking for tomorrow's reception, but the future Mr. and Mrs. Quinn couldn't help but put their own culinary spin on their union.

It was adorable and a sweet gift for their guests. And I was looking forward to an afternoon of fun, cooking with the people I loved.

Then this evening, we would practice the walk through of the ceremony—held at the same restaurant. Concluding the night with more cooking as we prepared the supper for the rest of the wedding party, family, and the officiating pastor.

Just like last night, I had been looking forward to this day for a long time. I adored all the special touches the bride and groom had woven throughout their weekend. And I couldn't wait for the festivities today to start.

But first, I needed to sort my shit out. Part of me wished Ezra had waited with the whole forcing me into my dream job thing until after this weekend. That way I could have focused completely on Vera and the celebration without the stress and dread of knowing things could be totally blowing up at Bianca in my absence.

Although, after firing Ashlynn and struggling through the last couple weeks, barely surviving dinner service every night, I got it.

Ezra couldn't have waited.

Which only made me more nervous for how Blaze and the gang were holding up.

I was extremely happy to see the kitchen bustling with life and that prep work was in full swing when I stepped inside. At least they'd kept to my earlier schedule and were learning to be more meticulous about cleaning, maintaining, and prepping. Part of me had feared opening the door and finding the entire place empty.

Blaze jerked his chin in acknowledgment, his hands busy julienning onions. "Chef, I thought you had the weekend off."

"Just wanted to check on y'all." I walked over to where he was working, the prominent position in the kitchen. Did Blaze want this job too? Was he waiting for me to fail hard enough so he could swoop in and take it?

I didn't really know anything about him—only that he'd handled the transition better then his superior sous chef. But that didn't mean he had kinder feelings for me. It just meant he was better at playing this game... biding his time.

Picking up an onion, I started to peel away the papery outer layers, even though I knew he would prefer to use his knife and chop off the ends. He continued to slice, intently focusing on the root vegetable at his fingertips.

"We've done this a time or two without an EC. Feel free to enjoy the weekend without worrying about us." His tone was carefully masked with neutrality, but I sensed the frustration of feeling like I was micromanaging him.

I wondered about his motives for a second time since stepping inside the kitchen. Not that anyone enjoyed being micromanaged. That was a universally frustrating feeling.

"I realize," I told him. "It's more about me than you." He glanced up at me, an unspoken question flashing in his dark green gaze. Shrugging, I let him know more than I intended to tell him. "My first EC job... I'm not sure what all it entails yet, you know? I just needed to know that the building hadn't been hit by a wayward meteor in the middle of the night."

"You could have called," he added. "Or texted."

I shrugged again. "Seeing is believing." He fell quiet for a minute as another chef walked over to ask my opinion on how I wanted the beef bourguignon prepared tonight. I tried not to wrinkle my nose at the reminder of how outdated the menu was.

I made a groaning sound and stretched my arms behind my back. "God, this place needs an update."

Blaze snorted next to me. I couldn't tell if he agreed with me or not. "Good luck with that. We've tried. Ezra—Er, Mr. Baptiste—is resistant to change."

I smiled at him, showing my teeth. "That's why we won't ask." The idea grew wings inside my chest, jumping out of the nest of thought into a full-on game plan that could be the change that saved this ship. "On Monday, when I get back, be ready to brainstorm ideas."

He stopped chopping to give me a look. "You think he's going to let you mix up his menu? He credits the damn thing as the reason Bianca hasn't gone bankrupt yet."

"We're not going to ask his opinion," I told him conspiratorially. "When it comes to my brother, it's better to employ the whole 'it's better to ask for forgiveness than permission' game plan." I realized I'd just tipped my hand. If Blaze wanted me out, he could absolutely use this against me.

Not that it would do him a whole lot of good.

But if Ezra came back to me today or tomorrow forbidding me to change his menu, I would know where Blaze and I stood.

Blaze chuckled at my approach to getting what I want and said, "You're the boss."

That was true. I was the boss.

I stood there for several more minutes, watching the staff scurry back and forth, preparing for tonight's service. Aside from Ashlynn, they seemed to be a great group. They all knew what they were doing, and they didn't need a lot of instruction—or maybe that was my lack of experience, not knowing how to instruct them.

Letting out a slow breath, I decided not to worry about all the things I didn't know for today. I had plenty of time to worry about it on Monday when we revamped the menu and I had to help them transition.

After a few minutes, the tense silence from my sous chef got to me. "What kind of name is Blaze? It sounds like you should have been a stunt double or spy or something."

He smiled at the thin strips of onion on the cutting board in front of him. "My parents thought they were clever. My younger sister's name is Ember."

"I kind of like it actually," I told him. "Blaze and Ember. It's clever."

"Thank you."

He grabbed another onion and had the skin off for quick chopping in seconds. Cutting onions wasn't a job he needed to concern himself with. He was the boss while I was gone. He could have easily delegated this to anyone else.

"On second thought, it's a perfect name for a chef." I rolled it around in my mouth again before admitting, "Blaze Ferrand. You'll be Michelin starred before you know it."

He smiled without looking at me. "Maybe one day."

Now that the onions were out of the way, I took advantage, turning around and hopping up on the counter to sit so I could look at him.

"Loyalty." The word was out of my mouth before I knew what I was going to say. My voice had just enough edge to catch his attention. He set his knife to the side and looked up at me.

"What about it?"

"I want it," I explained. "Yours." He leaned forward on his hands, dropping his head and hunching his shoulders. I continued before he could deny me the one thing, the only thing, I wanted from him. "I know I haven't earned it. I realize you're looking at me like I got lucky, like I got the job because my brother is the owner, like I don't deserve to be where I am. And honestly, you might be right. But I would like the opportunity to prove myself before you totally write me off. I won't even get a chance to get this right if you're just waiting for me to quit. Or fail. Or worse. So, either I need your loyalty, or I need you to leave."

I knew both of us were surprised at the way I'd delivered my speech. I hadn't been tough or stern since I fired Ashlynn. If anything, I'd been overly nice and polite to make up for my egomaniac moment.

"I don't trust you." His honest admission was even more shocking than my ultimatum. "You haven't earned it yet."

Was that true? What was a reasonable expectation of this staff? Weighing his words, I realized he was right. I couldn't expect, after only a little while of working together and in a position that for all intents and purposes looked and felt and smelled like nepotism, for him to blindly trust me.

That didn't mean he couldn't respect me, listen to me, and get behind me. At least until I proved myself one way or the other.

"Fair enough," I told him. "Still want your loyalty."

His head cocked to the side as he regarded me openly. "All right. You can have my loyalty. Let's see what you do with it."

He wasn't going to make this easy on me.

Strangely, I was okay with that. I respected his careful, honest approach to our working relationship. I appreciated that he was upfront with me without being disrespectful or downright insolent. And I appreciated that he did a good job when I asked, even before he trusted me.

"Right now, I'm going to leave and let you be in charge." I smiled, hoping he would feel some levity.

His lips cracked in a barely-there smile. "Sounds good."

Jumping off the counter, I brushed a hand over my butt just in case an onion paper had decided to hitch a ride. "Thanks, Blaze. I appreciate you taking over so I can go to this wedding."

His smile was softer, friendlier. "Of course." Before I could walk away though, he added, "It was a good decision to fire Ashlynn. She'd been unhappy here for a long time. She might even thank you for it one day."

A surprised laugh bubbled out of me. "Highly unlikely."

He lifted a shoulder in a casual shrug. "Okay, you're probably right. Still a good decision."

"Thanks, Blaze."

"See you later, Chef."

I stopped a few others on my way out the door, feeling entirely too elated over hearing everyone call me Chef. By the time I reached my car, I was smiling like a loon and had the heady feeling I was leaving something that was actually mine.

Could I trust Blaze? Not yet. But I didn't distrust him either. Which was probably exactly how he felt about me. At least we were on the same page.

Leading Bianca felt impossible at this point. Changing the menu felt like the biggest mountain to climb. Breathing life back into her and restoring her to her former glory was daunting to say the least. But it felt easier with a staff by my side that would stay loyal to me—stand up for me and work their hardest alongside me.

Only time would tell if I'd be able to manage all this.

In the meantime? I had a bridal brunch to get to.

I WAS thirty minutes late by the time I got to the sweet little bistro for the bridal brunch. Molly and Kaya were already sipping mimosas and Vera had her water with cucumber in hand, a paper straw dangling from the corner of her mouth.

They'd grabbed a table outside on the patio, the sunshine warm and inviting. "Y'all look like a magazine ad," I told them as I took in their big shades and sun hats. Kaya had a cute bandana wrapped around her shorter style, making her look like a pinup girl from the fifties.

They struck poses as I slid through the wrought-iron gate to join them.

"Spill it," Vera demanded before I could sit down.

I blinked at my friends, hoping she wanted other information I could possibly have. Like Ezra's childhood secrets. Or my social security number.

"What's going on with my brother?"

Okay, so not my social security number then. "What do you

mean?" Pretending to have no idea what she was talking about would work, right? Sure. We'll go with that.

She leaned forward, slamming her water on the table. "Um, I mean that you were all over each other last night. And that he was looking at you with gaga eyes. I mean that you laughed at all his lame jokes. And when we came back from dancing, you were practically sitting in his lap."

"Oh, that."

She narrowed her eyes at me. "Yes, that."

"Vere, babe," I said in my most soothing voice, "let's not bother talking about me today. This weekend is all about you."

Kaya snorted. "That's an interesting tactic."

"Hey!" I glared at her. "You're supposed to be on my side."

Vera's head snapped toward her. "Don't back out now. We agreed this needed to be a three-pronged attack."

"You're attacking me?"

Kaya held up her hands in surrender. "Nobody's attacking anyone! Also, this weekend is all about Vera. And right now, she wants to know what's going on with you and her brother. I vote that you give her what she wants before she turns into bridezilla and bites your head off."

"If only we'd brought the sash," Molly added.

"Way to navigate those tricky waters," I told Kaya, my words dripping with sarcasm. "You should go into politics with that kind of dodge and dive."

Kaya smiled widely. "I know, right?"

Vera's attention turned back to me. "Kaya's on to something. I will bite your head off if you don't tell me what's going on."

"Nothing's going on," I told them quickly. At their annoyed looks, I added, "Seriously, nothing. We're just friends." I jumped forward in my seat, holding up a hand. "No, not even that! We're getting to know each other. We're becoming friends. And who can blame us when we're always thrust into these major couple situations and we're the only two people in the room not making out in the corner."

"Don't turn this around on us," Molly warned. "If anyone was making out in the corner last night, it was you and Vann."

"We've never made out," I said patiently. At Vera's pursed lips and wide eyes, I quickly added, "We've never even kissed. Seriously, we're friends. That's all."

Vera slumped in her seat. "Probably for the best. He's not the nicest guy when it comes to girls. I haven't even met one of his dates before. I don't think he's into the whole commitment thing."

I resented her implication that I needed commitment. "Who said I am? Just because we might have flirted last night, after copious amounts of carbs and cocktails, doesn't mean I'm ready to marry him. Keep your wedding cooties to yourself, Vere. He's funny. I like talking to him. That's it."

"He's not funny," she argued. "He's grumpy and responsible and the cheapest person you will ever meet."

I shrugged. "Okay."

The three of them leaned toward me, eyeing me shrewdly.

"You're like complete opposites," Kaya pointed out. "You're never grumpy and you're never responsible and you're the opposite of cheap."

I couldn't help but laugh at the truth in her words. "See? It would never work. Good thing there isn't anything going on between us! Can we move on now?"

"I suppose," Vera sighed. "But it would make me happy to see him settled down with someone I love."

"Maybe you could set him up with Jo," I suggested. "She's grumpy and responsible and cheap."

Kaya snorted. "Cheap as hell."

"Good grief, they're perfect for each other," Vera groaned.

We were all able to laugh about Vann after that and finally move on. We spent the rest of brunch drinking more cocktails and talking about details of the remaining weekend and all the exciting things Vera had going on in her life right now.

Sure, there was also a lot of stress attached to all the major life events converging at the same time—a wedding, a restaurant opening and a baby in five months. But they were the very best things she could have ever hoped for.

And I was so beyond happy for her and Killian. Life wasn't going to be easy going forward, but dang, it was going to be beautiful.

That pang lanced across my chest again, reminding me that some day I wanted this too. Not any day soon, I tried to maintain, but my old argument fell limp inside my head.

Who wouldn't want this? Vera made it look wonderful.

And so did Molly.

And so did Kaya.

When I was surrounded by all this love, it was hard not to notice it was missing from my own life.

But it was. It so was.

After brunch, we headed over to Salt. The place was a madhouse. There were people everywhere. Florists setting up for the wedding tomorrow. Last minute construction guys making sure everything was in working order. An electrician. A couple of plumbers. Landscapers out front and around the building.

In one corner of the restaurant, Ezra's maître d' was instructing a gaggle of waiters. And in the other corner, Vera's wedding planner and business manager were in the throes of a knockdown, drag out fight, each wielding a clipboard like it was a sword.

"This place is a circus," Molly noted as we sidestepped a painter speckled with white paint and wearing goggles, a mask hanging around his neck.

"Killian's been coordinating the final stages. I told him that it doesn't have to be perfect, but he's insistent that we're in excellent working order by tomorrow." She glanced back at us as she led us through the dining room and bared her teeth. "As long as we don't have to use port-a-potties I'll be happy."

"Working on that now, ma'am," a man in overalls called out as we walked by.

Vera stopped to talk to him, but the rest of us forged on, arms full of produce from Jo's and protein from Vera's favorite butcher. The men had been in charge of finding everything else on the extensive list.

Molly pushed through the kitchen door, then held it for Kaya and me. We were the first ones here and the competitive part of my soul rejoiced.

"We won!" I cheered.

"What did we win?" Molly asked, sounding totally confused.

Kaya got me. "We beat the boys."

Molly set her bags down on one of the gleaming countertops. "Was it a race?"

Kaya and I mumbled noncommittal maybes while we unpacked our sacks laden with the best produce money could buy. Wyatt and Killian tumbled in a few minutes later.

"Damn," Wyatt groaned.

Killian set paper sacks next to Molly's. "I told you we shouldn't have stopped for those burritos."

"Were we racing?" Molly clarified more sternly.

Poor, poor Molly. She wasn't a chef, so she didn't get it. Even though she technically worked in the restaurant business as part of Ezra's EFB Enterprises, she was the only person in her department. She didn't have anyone to prove herself to or beat.

The rest of us were pretty much in a life long race to see who was better than everyone else. Sure, we were all good friends and loved each other fiercely. We also wanted to win. We would always want to win.

It was who we were.

Ezra pushed through the doorway a minute later, Vann and Vera following close behind.

"I told you those burritos were a mistake," Ezra said to Killian.

"Not you too," Molly murmured, staring at her fiancé in horror.

My brother looked at his bride to be with the most clueless expression I'd ever seen. "What?"

She shook her head at him.

We had picked stations naturally. Killian and Vera next to each other, with Ezra close to Killian. Wyatt and Kaya close together, with me not far off. Molly and Vann stood in the middle of the room, not having a clue what to do with all this food.

"I didn't think you were coming till later," Vera said to Vann, her gaze darting to me for a split second.

He shrugged and hopped up onto one of the counters, pushing the stack of one hundred quail eggs to the side. "I didn't have anything else to do. Thought I'd see if you needed help."

"But you don't know how to cook," Vera reminded him.

He shrugged again, but never looked at me. I wondered why he was here too. But then again, Molly was hanging out all day and she couldn't cook worth a damn.

Actually, it was worse than that. She was a total disaster in the kitchen. We were playing it risky just by letting her in the building.

"I can chop or whatever," Vann said, defending himself. "Or time things." He rubbed a hand along his smooth jaw and added. "I'm also adequate at pouring liquid into measuring cups."

"Oh, I can do that too!" Molly added. "I can also chop. And time things."

"We have ourselves a couple of sous chefs, y'all." Vann finally looked at me, his gray eyes sparking with laughter and familiarity and something warm. God, he was especially good looking today in only a gray t-shirt and dark red shorts.

He saluted me. "We're here to serve."

Without looking away, I announced, "Then I call Vann."

"Wait just a second," Killian crowed from the other end of the kitchen. "Shouldn't Vera get first pick? It's her wedding day."

Busted. "Oh, it's just that... I thought since Molly is the maid of honor and all... you know..."

"Vann is my brother," Vera argued. "I should probably stick with family on this one."

"Hey!" Molly planted her hands on her hips. "That sounds like an insult."

Vera and I shared a guilty look.

Vann ticked his chin toward me. "It's okay, Vere, you don't have to spare my feelings. I know you want to be with Molly."

Vera's jaw unhinged, not expecting her brother to throw her under the bus. "Oh, uh, that's sweet of you. Er, thanks."

Molly shook her head. "I still feel no love here, people!"

Kaya tried to hide her snicker in Wyatt's shoulder, while the rest of us avoided Molly's gaze completely.

"You can help me," Ezra told her, his voice holding all the affection he felt for her. "I want you on my team."

Molly walked toward him, her shoulders still slumped. "Aren't you supposed to tell them how much better I've gotten? Last week I made that toast. Remember? I didn't even burn it."

"You didn't," Ezra agreed patiently. "You didn't even burn the toast."

That led the rest of us to dissolve into fits of laughter. Shortly after, Killian broke up the shenanigans and we got to work.

Even though this was a totally informal afternoon of cooking together, I still drank in every second of Killian's leadership and how he led so effortlessly. I needed these tools in my pocket. I needed to be able to command a kitchen—any kitchen—flawlessly.

I needed to inspire greatness just by walking in the room.

"There's something I need to tell you," Vann admitted to me after I'd pulled our ingredients over to our station.

I turned my head to look at him, drinking in his casual attire all over again. There was chemistry between us today, a gentle pop and sizzle that sparked all around us. "What's that?"

He leaned even closer, our cheeks briefly brushing as he moved toward my ear. "My kitchen experience basically involves making coffee and pouring a bowl of cereal. You might have been better off with Molly."

It was then, at that moment, in that sweet, secret smile and those sizzling gray eyes, that I realized I had a crush on Vann Delane.

An actual crush.

What was I fourteen?

Maybe. Because all I wanted to do was pull Kaya into the pantry and tell her all about it. I felt giddy and giggly just thinking about him. And standing this close was pure torture.

Okay, I wasn't fourteen. I didn't have the imagination I do now when I was fourteen.

When I had a crush back then, it stopped there. Maybe I pictured handholding. Maybe a kiss. Today, with Vann standing so close and smelling so good, all I could picture was pushing him down on the counter top and throwing my body on top of his. Or jumping him in the walk-in freezer and heating things up... if you know what I mean.

Oh, brother... now I was punning.

Clearing my throat, I stepped forward and tugged on his sleeve, my fingers brushing over his bicep. "Don't try to talk me out of this now. Hell or high water, we're in this together."

His gray eyes sparked with something electric, like flashes of lightning before a downpour. "All right then, Baptiste. Let's show 'em what we got."

TWELVE

SIXTEEN HOURS LATER, I woke up with a start—this was not my bed.

I opened my eyes. This was not my apartment. It took me a few groggy moments to remember where I was and what had happened.

A warm arm was wrapped around my waist, the body attached to it puffing soft snores into my tangled hair.

I carefully, quietly, gently slapped a hand over my eyes as I shame spiraled into an eternal abyss of broken memories.

It had started with the appetizers. Vann and I were charged with preparing egg dishes for thirty. That meant making the wasabi scotch eggs and burrata, which was this delicious peasant bread served with a yolky egg and mashed potato spread, accompanied by homemade apple butter.

There had also been alcohol involved.

Lots of alcohol.

A a flirty afternoon of teaching Vann basics in the kitchen was followed by a swoon-worthy practice ceremony where Vann got choked up when his sister walked down the aisle for the first time. And then a night of eating amazing food including, but not limited to our appetizers, plus popcorn chicken served on mini waffles while Vera claimed some kind of redemption I didn't understand, also oysters on the half shell with a to-die-for green chimichurri sauce. The main course was surf and turf. Scallops with sweet potato and roasted beets; short ribs over the creamiest polenta, fried octopus; shrimp and curried grits with shaved coconut and crushed pistachios; and pork belly sliders with pickled red onions and fried kale. All of it accompanied by crispy brussels sprouts, charred broccoli, and butternut squash hummus.

And don't get me started on dessert. Individual pots of chocolate pot de crème, apple pie bread pudding, and my favorite thing on the planet right now, affogato—rich, hot espresso poured over creamy caramel ice cream.

It was delicious. And filling. And I probably gained thirty-ish pounds. I drowned that horrible thought by drinking. Don't ask questions, it made sense at the time.

I drank a lot. Champagne, gin fizzes, Old Fashioneds, and I think at some point there were tequila shots. Probably Wyatt's doing.

And now I was wrapped naked in a man's arms, barely remembering how I got here.

PTSD crashed hard all around me. I'd been in situations like this before—waking up with a fuzzy recollection of the night before, sharing a bed with a virtual stranger. And then the last time... that last night when I'd woken up alone with no memory of the night before and no clothes on... God, I felt like puking just thinking about it.

Too chicken shit to turn around and risk waking up the mystery man next to me, I scrunched my eyes closed and tried to remember again what had happened.

The cooking.

The drinking.

The rehearsal.

The drinking.

The eating.

The more drinking.

The dancing.

Oh, god, the dancing.

That's when the shots had come out.

My gasp of realization burst out of my mouth like a gunshot through the silent room. The man to my left stirred, pulling me tighter against his solid body.

I let my imagination take form while I registered that the man behind me was fit, firm... fabulously muscled. His chest was a toned wall of masculinity, his forearm wrapped around my middle evidence of tanned, perfect skin. His tapered waist, tucked against my bum—we didn't need to think about how nice that felt right now.

Or ever.

Ahem.

Starting now.

I started back at the beginning of the night once more, hoping the more awake I became, the clearer my memories would become.

Vann and I cooking.

Vann and I drinking while cooking.

Vann and I walking down the aisle together, the first groomsman and bridesmaid of the group.

Vann and I sneaking glasses of champagne while Vera and Killian worked out the kinks of the ceremony.

Vann and I making flirty eyes through the meal, meeting up halfway through to congratulate each other on our excellent appetizers.

Vann and I hanging out at to the bar, laughing, talking, teasing.

Vann and I dancing.

Wyatt giving Vann and I shots of tequila.

Toasting the happy couple with more drinks.

More dancing. With Vann.

Vann. Oh my god, Vann. That's who I was with now. That's whose apartment I was in. That's whose arm was wrapped around my middle.

I slid to my stomach, grabbing a few inches of space between us and buried my face in the pillow.

Bad idea! It smelled like him.

Struggling to remember the dirtier details of the night, I found that I couldn't put them in the right order or give them any clarity. They were a mess of muddled memories. His hands around my waist, pulling me against his naked body. Tripping over my shorts as I tried to step out of them. My shoe abandoned in the hallway. Gasping for breath. In the best way. But that was the only, paper-thin memory I could grasp. The rest all flitted away, dried leaves in a brisk breeze.

Fuck.

I had to get out of here.

Good thing I was a total pro at the morning after—even if I was a little rusty after six years of celibacy. My hangover pressed down on my limbs, making them weak and heavy. Still, I managed to push into a partial plank and slip over the side of the bed without making a sound.

Of course, if Vann were to wake up, I would look like a hungover ninja with yesterday's makeup streaked all over my face.

Probably not the vision of loveliness he would be expecting.

Popping my head up, I looked for my cellphone on the nightstand, but it was nowhere to be seen. Crap.

I had a vague memory of using an Uber to get here. No worries, I could Uber home. I was an Uber pro.

Assuming I could find my phone.

To be honest, this was not the first time I'd army-crawled through a man's bedroom before the sun came up. I had a few wild years under my belt. Er, maybe more than a few.

Culinary school might as well have been a nunnery. I gave it all up. The boys. The partying. The binge drinking. The drugs. Especially the drugs. The random hookups with assholes.

The accepting drinks from assholes when origins were unknown.

Dropping my head to the wood flooring, I took a minute to collect myself. I hated thinking back on those days. I hated remembering the girl I used to be and the mistakes I made.

I had been a total and complete fool. And a mess. The worst part, was that when it all came crashing down, I wasn't even surprised. By that point it had felt inevitable.

My therapist assured me that it wasn't my fault. And that blaming myself for what happened was natural. But it also felt logical. If I put myself in stupid situations weren't stupid things bound to happen?

A wave of nausea washed over me. I swallowed quickly, the reverse action to puking. I'd read once that it was supposed to stop the mouth-tingling feeling and calm your stomach when in danger of retching.

Five full minutes of struggling to swallow with a mouth that felt stuffed with cotton balls, the sickening feeling passed. God, was I really here again? In this same, alcohol-soaked-morning-after hell?

I had promised myself, on my twenty-first birthday, that enough was enough. It was time to get my life together. It was time to never wake up with fear again. It was time to move on from all those things in my past that had fucked me up, and use them to make me into something great.

Which I mostly had.

Until tonight, when I'd jumped off the cliff of sanity and sobriety into the backsliding pits of party girl hell all over again.

Don't get me wrong, I loved to hang out with my friends and drink and have a good time. But I also liked to stay in complete control.

And nowhere in my game plan for a new and improved life had I included sleeping with my friend's brother.

Oh. My. God.

I grabbed stray pieces of my clothing off the floor as I moved quietly from the bedroom. But by the time I reached the kitchen near the front door, my bra was nowhere to be found.

No worries—I had more at home.

I covered my eyes again as I stifled a panic attack. Leaving my bra at a complete stranger's house when I snuck out was one thing. I would likely never run into them again. They could hang my underthings on their hookup shrine for all I cared. Or hand it off to a new girlfriend. Or burn it in effigy or whatever.

But leaving lingerie at a man's house I was going to have to see again, namely later today, was... awful.

Good grief, this whole thing was just dumb. Why? Why had I let things get this out of control?

It was that stupid crush, I realized. He'd been so charming lately. And helpful. And for a split second, I thought I needed someone to take care of me.

Or at least I wanted someone to.

It was just that... I was so tired of being the only one in charge of my life. Especially when I got it wrong so often.

Damn, there were so many important decisions to make and so many things to do and now I was in charge of a whole kitchen and Vann had been so wonderful when I'd needed him and... now I couldn't even remember last night! Why couldn't I remember? What had happened? What had... breathe, Dillon. Freaking breathe. A panic attack wasn't going to do anyone any favors right now.

I found my purse on the counter with my cellphone miraculously inside. There was even enough battery left to order an Uber.

Vann made a sleepy sound from the other room, causing me to jump out of my skin and glance toward his room. He was still in the very center of the bed, sleeping diagonally across it. One of his arms was splayed wide where I used to be and the other covered the top of his face. The sheet draped over his important bits, leaving the rest of his gloriously sculpted body on display. Dang, this guy took care of himself.

Those thoughts pulled my attention around the rest of the apartment. The design scheme was clearly male. The biggest TV I had ever seen took up one wall, between two ceiling-high windows, flanked by a stationary bike on one side and a treadmill on the other.

Along that same wall was a row of dumbbells. The L-shaped sectional in the middle of the room was a monstrosity of overstuffed worn leather. There was a novel on the coffee table with a bookmark sticking out of it.

God, that shouldn't have made me want to crawl back in bed with him, but it did.

Three different bikes hung on the wall closest to the door. They were mounted in an artistic way, but by the look of the beaten tires and beat-up frames, I could tell they were used.

And used often.

"Cycle life," I whispered to myself. "It really is a lifestyle."

The kitchen was more of the same health-nut practicality. An expensive blender nestled next to an air fryer and a giant Tupperware container full of homemade granola mix. A huge container of protein powder sat next to the sink.

Aside from his affinity for being healthy, I liked the way he'd set his place up. It felt more comfortable than mine—more homey.

He clearly used this place.

Er, obviously.

But I meant his home was lived in. He worked out here. He made meals here. He made messes.

My apartment was the stop along the way. I used my bed. And my shower. And sometimes I cooked a meal. I couldn't remember the last time I'd bothered with the TV though.

With my phone in one hand and my shoes in the other, I took a moment by the door to admire the apartment one more time and the man that lay cluelessly in bed.

He had been equally as drunk as me, right?

There would be an awkward moment tomorrow when we had to face each other and remember what had happened. I needed to make an appointment with my therapist stat. But then I'd be able to move on. *We'd* be able to move on.

Maybe he'd even bring me my bra.

Maybe we'd be able to laugh about it and swear off tequila shots with Wyatt. Never again.

Maybe we'd be able to part as friends.

I slipped out the front door, ignoring the pang of hope in my gut as I made my way down the stairwell to the ground floor. It mixed with nausea as despair followed quickly on its heels. Did I even want to be friends with Vann?

I certainly didn't not want to be friends with him.

My Uber driver didn't even look twice at me. He simply took off in the direction of my apartment. I was probably par for the course for pickups at this hour.

Five minutes later, I was at home and locked inside my apartment. I hadn't realized how close Vann and I lived to each other until now and it filled me with sadness all over again.

God, I was a mess of emotions. Not to mention that had been the first time I'd had sex since...

I went to my kitchen and grabbed a handful of pills for my headache and a glass of water. Taking them in one big swallow, I planted my hands on the counter and tried not to shame spiral any further.

Girls my age slept with guys. This was a totally normal thing. Especially after a night of drinking.

Oh, you know all about that, the evil side of my brain reminded me.

But this wasn't that, I argued back. This was harmless fun. This was mutual attraction. This was... consensual. My therapist would probably be proud of me.

She'd been suggesting I try it again for a while. And now here we were. I'd tried it again. And it only made me want to cry a lot—or pack up and take off for an empty island to live out the rest of my days as an eccentric hermit.

I planted my hands on the granite countertop and slumped my shoulders. A tear landed on the glossy counter. And then another one.

Before I could grab a handle on my emotions, I slid to the floor and curled into the fetal position, sobbing harder than I had the night of the incident six years ago.

Tears of joy and sadness, of survival and grief, of knowing I could still have sex and live to tell about it.

Of knowing I could still have wild, drunk sex without getting drugged and taken advantage of.

Of hating that it still killed me, that there were too many similarities from that last time and this new time for me to ever want to do it again.

Of realizing that the crush I'd had on Vann was officially dead.

When I'd purged myself of the heaviness of emotion and confusion, I found that I was cold and soberer than I wanted to be.

Would this ever get better?

Easier?

Would I ever move on?

Or was this who I was. The girl that slept around. The girl that partied her way through life because she didn't have to try.

The girl that got raped.

THIRTEEN

"WE WERE WONDERING if you'd show up today." Molly smiled at me as I slipped inside the bustling kitchen at Salt later that morning. She had a charcuterie board in her hands and a smirk on her face. "You okay?"

Hell no, I wasn't okay.

I smiled and stole an olive off the counter. An angry chef in a Sarita jacket scowled at me. "Perfectly fine."

She nodded her head toward the back office. "Come on, we're eating before the hair and makeup people arrive."

Folding my garment bag over my forearm, I weaved my way through the kitchen to the large office Vera and Killian had designed for two.

Since they were both owners and head chefs, their office was rather luxurious compared to mine. And today it was covered in all things bridal—including a glowing bride, Kaya the bridesmaid, and white tulle as far as the eye could see.

"There she is!" Vera grinned at me, her hands busy with tweezers and a magnifying mirror. "You're the last one to arrive. I was getting worried you forgot."

"Never!" I declared as I plunked myself on the nearest wingback chair. A sudden surge of panic swished around in my gut. Had I acted a complete fool last night? Did I embarrass myself? Did they see me leave with Vann?

"How do you look that good?" Kaya demanded, her hoarse voice giving away her own hungover state.

I smiled at her and fished around in my tote. Pulling out a bevy of skincare products, I tossed her the under-eye patches made with collagen, green tea, and magic. "Here, these help."

"Ooh!" Vera demanded, "Me next."

"I brought more." Scooting my chair over to Vera's huge desk, I dumped out my bag and started passing out products.

"Now I understand," Molly whispered in awe.

I blinked at her. "Understand what?"

"I used to think you were an alien," she admitted.

Kaya nodded enthusiastically, "It's because you're so pretty. And skinny. And basically, we hate your pretty, skinny guts on principle."

"Wha—?"

"Now I know your secret."

I rolled my eyes. "My expensive secret. But seriously, this stuff works. Natural beauty is all about a good skin care regimen."

"In other words, it's not natural at all?" Vera asked.

Smiling patiently at her, I said, "If I had been born during the middle ages, without my arsenal of retinol, I would have been the town hag."

Kaya threw the container of under eye patches back at me. "Not true!"

"Okay, fine," I sighed. "The town drunk."

They laughed at my self-deprecating humor.

"You weren't that bad," Vera assured me. When I gave her a look she added, "All of us were bad. Last night was fun!"

"Best rehearsal dinner ever," Kaya agreed.

"Did Vann get you home okay?"

I pretended not to know who she was talking to and focused on finding my favorite moisturizer—aptly named Drunk Elephant.

Boy, if I didn't relate to that.

"Hello?" Molly snapped her fingers in front of my face. "Is there something you'd like to tell us?"

"Who me?" I asked, all aflutter with confusion.

Vera rolled her eyes. "Yes, you. Did my brother get you home okay last night?" She waggled her eyebrows. "If you know what I mean."

"Oh, was it Vann who helped me home last night?" I cleared my throat and tried not to be annoyingly obvious. "My memory is kind of fuzzy, to be honest."

The three of them shared a look, before Kaya announced, "Come on, you guys were all over each other!"

My cheeks burned bright red. I could tell them what happened. I could fess up and ask them for help wading through these complicated waters.

But then I'd have to confess the other stuff too. And then they would tell their men. And one of those men was my brother. And another one was like a brother. And the third one was my old boss.

I would never be able to look at these people again if they knew.

Right now, I just wanted to keep my ducking and dodging to Vann and Vann only. At least he would be mostly out of my life after this weekend.

"Yes, you left with Vann last night," Vera assured me. "We were positive you were also going to wake up with Vann, *to be honest*."

Evading the upfront fishing from her comment, I shrugged and gave her a blank look. "Nope. I woke up in my bed this morning." That wasn't even a lie.

I'd woken up in my empty bed, in my big, empty apartment. There had been no awkward good mornings or shared breakfasts. There hadn't even been a confused text.

It was almost like last night hadn't happened and I'd only dreamed waking up next to Vann and sneaking out of his apartment.

My friends tried to hide their disappointed looks, unsuccessfully. Thankfully, five minutes later an army of hair and makeup professionals showed up and did their best work to make us glow, shine, and look anything but hungover.

It was impressive work. By the time I was dressed in my floor length blush gown with draped, off-the shoulder sleeves and a sweetheart neckline, I was legitimately impressed with the way I looked. My hair was pulled over my shoulder, somehow rocking a braid and loose curls and a crown of flowers at the same time. I looked like a hipster supermodel.

"Now this is magic," I told Kaya and Molly, who had similarly stunned looks on their gorgeous faces.

"I've never looked this pretty," Kaya declared. "Never." When her makeup artist started to disagree with her, Kaya shook her head and insisted, "Seriously, never. I'm usually rocking a bandana, no makeup and three pounds of duck fat. Wyatt isn't even going to recognize me."

I couldn't help but smile. She might be right. Not that she couldn't totally rock a bandana, no makeup, and three pounds of duck fat. Because she could. And she did every single night. But she was stunning in full makeup and with her purple hair in loose waves.

Vera finally turned around and stood up, stealing our actual breath. She was a goddess in her wedding dress. It had all the romantic vintage feels with a sheer lace overlay covered in floral appliques and layers of white beneath. The back was a wide, deep V, coming together in a long train of buttons that started at her lower back. The intricately detailed lace sleeves were held onto the very curve of her shoulders with clear tape. They were short sleeve and nearly bell-like, but so ridiculously flattering, I couldn't help but be jealous of her. The front was a low-cut V too, ending at her sternum and remaining tasteful but eye-catching. Her dark hair was styled similarly to mine only with flowers interwoven instead of the wreath I wore. And her makeup was all soft pinks and expertly placed highlights and she looked like a magazine ad—even with the smallest swell of her belly.

She was everything a bride was supposed to be. The perfect picture of hope and anticipation and eternal bliss. My heart ached with the desire to live this out one day. To have what she had. To love like she loved. To hope for what she hoped for.

My mind flashed with drunken half-images of sleeping with Vann. God, what a mistake. I wanted everything, and yet my nights were spent alone. Except for last night. And I can't even remember what happened.

At least not accurately.

Not that Vann was the usual brand of loser I managed to attract in the past. But he wasn't exactly my perfect eHarmony match either. Nor was he broadcasting interested vibes my way.

At least not in the wedding bells and prenup kind of way.

I chewed my lip, wondering if I would be the kind of girl to demand a prenup when it came down to it. I had a vast enough fortune that it would be smart to include one. And I wanted to be smart.

And wise.

And mature.

And a prenup definitely seemed like something a smart, wise, mature woman would get.

But I knew Ezra wasn't planning to get one with Molly. When I'd asked him about it, he'd told me that if he needed to worry about a prenup with his fiancée, he wouldn't have fallen in love with her to begin with.

I believed my brother. There were plenty of women in his life before Molly. He'd learned a lot from his first marriage. And he'd finally found a woman up to the challenge of him.

"Dillon, are you okay?" Vera asked, breaking me out of deep thought. She fidgeted nervously and I realized I'd basically been glaring at her as my mind spun in a hundred different directions.

Thank you resting bitch face for making my friends feel so loved.

Also, thank you Vera for getting married and making me question everything in my entire life.

I smiled and brushed at strange, stray tears. "You're gorgeous," I whispered. "I'm sorry, you're like this total vision of perfection and it just... got me thinking." I waved a hand in the air. "Sorry, my thoughts are scattered today. I have got to stop letting Wyatt talk me into shots every time we go out."

"Maybe we should start a petition," Kaya grumbled.

"You're stunning, Vera, seriously. Killian is going to die when he sees you," I assured her.

"I'd settle for shocked silence," she said, holding back tears. "Maybe a tear or two."

The room filled up after that, the flower girls and ring bearer arrived and all the other attendants. Chefs and waiters were everywhere in the kitchen, preparing for the elegant reception. Champagne glasses were passed around and we toasted our friend and the nuptials about to take place. And then we toasted our friendship and love for Vera. And as the toasts went on, I let the liquid courage kill some of the strange butterflies flapping around inside me.

Not that it could kill everything. I realized I would have to go through Molly and Ezra's wedding too. And probably Kaya and Wyatt's before I even found a consistent date for the receptions.

I had basically army-crawled out of Vann's apartment this morning because a lasting relationship was the last thing I wanted. The career, remember? The goals? And accomplishments? All that travel? And the general feeling of just needing to get my life together before I added anyone else to it.

But now I felt shockingly alone—glaringly single. Like everyone else in the world had this wonderful, beautiful, perfect relationship and I had... a lonely apartment and an uncertain future at Bianca.

Tears filled my eyes as I realized this wasn't a new feeling. This wasn't something I had just recently stumbled into now that my friends were all settling down.

This emptiness... this utterly depressing feeling of total isolation was something I had carried with me since I could remember.

This was why I'd gotten pulled along with the prep school crowd, trying whatever was put in front of me, sleeping with whoever was interested. This was why I'd hated going to my dad's house where the lonely feelings I struggled with were only amplified. This was why it had been hard to be at home with my mom when the same feelings were reflected in her.

This was why I'd chased a culinary career—because I could see the sense of community there, because I wanted the friendships and relationships my brother had with his people.

And it was why I'd hooked up with Vann last night. He'd felt like part of that impossible dream I just wanted to taste. I wanted to hold and immerse myself in it for only a few minutes.

Only when I'd woken up there this morning, those romantic feelings of belonging and companionship were gone.

It was cold in his bed where I'd been drenched with reality. It was even lonelier there than in my own bed.

Because he didn't want anything real or long term. He'd wanted to hook up.

We had wanted to hook up.

And once that was over, there was just him. And there was just me—same girl, same problems, same life.

I squeezed out of the office—it was getting hot in there with all the people—and escaped down the hallway toward the bathroom. If anyone asked where I was going, I planned to tell them I needed to freshen up, but no one stopped me.

Out of the corner of my eye I could see black tuxes interspersed between endless bouquets and floral decorations. The air smelled like honey and lavender and an early summer evening.

The bathroom door couldn't have shut fast enough. I braced myself against the sink, everything new, gleaming and still smelling like fresh paint. I wanted to cry, but I refused to mess up my perfect makeup. Besides, I tried to reason, this wasn't worth crying about.

Just because everyone in my orbit had found their happily ever after didn't mean I wasn't going to find mine. This wasn't a competition to see who could be the happiest. This was life and it didn't make sense—would never make sense. That didn't mean it couldn't be beautiful.

Or that I couldn't be happy without a man.

I couldn't control the timing of things. Life happened in its own sequence. And I would just have to wait for the right time and for the stars to align and for Mercury to get out of retrograde.

Or was I waiting for Mercury to go into retrograde?

"You don't even believe in that stuff," I told my reflection.

"Believe in what?"

I whirled around, bumping my hip against the thick concrete counter. "I don't think you're supposed to be in here," I told Vann, completely shocked to see that he'd followed me in the women's bathroom.

He leaned over, looking cool as a cucumber checking for feet beneath the stall. He didn't bother arguing my point. His raised eyebrows said everything. *We're alone. What does it matter?* When he was upright again, he folded his forearms over his chest, wrinkling his crisp white shirt and tuxedo jacket. "What are you, like the one-night stand fairy? I didn't hear you leave this morning."

Oh, so he was just going to lay it out. Like all of it. My cheeks instantly flushed, the blush so strong it spread across my chest to my shoulders like wildfire.

This wasn't how I did things. I came from a world that turned passive aggressiveness into an artform. We didn't say what we thought. We said what you wanted to hear. And I would never bring up something like a one-night stand and put them on the spot.

God, Vann. What the hell?

I cleared my throat of the frogs that had taken up residence there and tilted my chin in the hopes that I looked as calm and collected as he did. "I, uh, have a hard time sleeping in any bed but my own."

Lie.

And he knew it.

His eyebrows scrunched together over his nose, bringing attention to the perfect proportions of his face. God, he looked amazing in that tux with his hair styled back. An image flashed—his cut biceps caging me in, his broad, bare torso slick with sweat and rippled with muscle, his hips pressed against mine. *I'm going to save you from those blind dates, Dillon.*

I shivered, wondering if that was a real memory from last night or my horny imagination.

It was at that point I tripped over nothing.

Vann canted his head to the side and regarded me in my bridesmaid regalia. "I would have walked you out."

I mimicked his pose, wrapping my arms around my body. But where he looked like a testosterone tightened tiger about to spring, I was the picture of hollowed out insecurity and self-doubt.

I struggled to swallow, contemplating how to explain my actions. "I knew we had a big day ahead of us, I didn't want to bother you."

"Is that what you think you would have done? Bother me?"

His words were wrapped in warmth and an intimacy he'd earned last night, but it was intimacy I didn't feel since I could barely remember a damn thing. I shrugged, trying to play this cool. "You know what I mean."

"No. I don't."

Laughing to break the tension, I said, "Listen, I realize we had a lot to drink last night and I just didn't want you to... to feel awkward. It was a mistake and I was trying to save—"

"Last night was a mistake? You're telling me you regret what happened?"

Obviously, yes. This was awkward as hell and I would have done anything to not have this conversation. So yes, I regretted sleeping with him, especially now that I realized he was going to give me the third degree about it.

But also no. No, I didn't.

Another partial memory. This time he was positioned over me

and I was clawing at his chest, my back arched in perfect submission as his magic rocked through me like a tidal wave.

Sharp and real, and oh my god, I needed to hit the pause button on these unwanted memories before I orgasmed right here on the spot.

Holy shit, I was in over my head.

"I don't regret what happened," I rushed to tell him. "Not at all." I cleared my throat again. "What I'm trying to say is that we barely know each other. And you're Vera's brother, which complicates things. And basically, I had a great time last night, but I didn't want to... prolong the inevitable."

His chin jerked back a notch. "The inevitable?"

"We hooked up," I explained, my shoulder lifting in that weak shrug again. "The end."

His expression shuttered, a hard, impenetrable wall slamming over his eyes, tightening his jaw and locking his lips in place. After he'd stared at me so long and hard, I started to fidget, he shrugged too. "The end."

Relief drilled through me, opening up entire springs of hope that this conversation was also coming to a close. I loosed a small smile. "Right. You get it. The end."

His jaw ticked. My relief dried up with my sense of safety. He looked like a shiny new bullet, waiting in the chamber for the trigger to be pulled.

I shivered again, that same climax-filled memory pinging through my head. I was nervous. But I was also hella turned on.

He took a step forward, his lips twisting in a sideways smile. Only it wasn't a pleasant smile. It was the equivalent of the safety being clicked off that gun. "Let me get this straight..." Another step forward. "We had a little too much to drink last night and hooked up."

I bobbed my head back and forth. "I would say we had a little more than a little too much. My judgment was definitely impaired." I tried to laugh again, but the sound hit the atmosphere like dust being sprinkled on the ground.

Taking another step forward, he nodded again. "What you're saying is we made a reckless decision last night."

"Reckless. That's a good word for it." My butt bumped against the counter. I'd started to retreat, but he wasn't picking up the stay-away-from-me vibes.

Maybe because they were mixed up with the take-me-now ones?

He moved forward. "And because we didn't use our most... sober thinking, we've now reached The End of whatever was between us."

I tried laughing again, but it got me nowhere. "Isn't that what you're saying?"

He was in front of me now, close and warm and smelling like freaking heaven. His hands landed on either side of my waist. The smooth silk of his tuxedo brushed over my bare arms, sending shivers and tingles abuzz inside me.

"No," he admitted openly—although that emotionless mask was still in place. "That is not at all what I'm saying."

I couldn't breathe. I couldn't swallow. I was totally paralyzed by his words and what they could mean. Did he want to do it again? Sober this time? Drunk again? Did he just want a hookup? Did he want to run away together?

What the hell did any of this mean?

Instead of asking any of those questions, I managed a weak, strained, barely audible, "Oh."

He nodded as if he expected that kind of response from me. "Yeah, oh." He stood straight, putting inches between us, making me instantly cold. He turned and when he was at the door to the bathroom, he added, "There's something about you, Baptiste." His gray eyes turned silvery with heat, pinning me in place and stealing whatever response I was trying to spit out. "I don't know what it is yet, but it's enough that I know this isn't The End. This is just the beginning."

It took me a full five minutes after he'd left to collect myself. I leaned against the counter, hoping I wasn't somehow ruining my dress, but not strong enough to care.

When I could finally trust my shaky legs to walk back to the office, my blush had turned to a ghostly whiteness that made me look like a corpse.

I could handle a one-night stand like a pro. He was right about me. I really was the one-night stand fairy. I took no prisoners. I left no witnesses. I got in. I got out. I got what I wanted. And I moved on with my life.

Or at least I used to. And I was determined to do that now.

That was what men liked anyway. At least all the men I had known. And not only the men I'd personally experienced in these situations.

My dad was the same way. My brother, until recently had been the same way. Every man I'd ever known had preferred one-night stands to the drama of bad relationships.

Tony, my mom's husband, isn't like that, my mind whispered to my battered, barely-beating heart. *Killian isn't like that. Wyatt's not like that.*

True, I had to admit. But they were the small minority compared to the rest of the male population I'd experienced.

And I hardly doubted—no offense Vera—that Vann was in the one percent of decent guys after last night's shenanigans.

We'd had a good time. We'd had too much to drink. And then we'd had each other in a number of debauched and delicious ways.

But now it was time to go our separate directions. Besides, tonight was the last night I had open in all the foreseeable future and beyond. I was married to my restaurant after this.

And Vann... Vann had his life to return to.

He would always be a good, but fuzzy memory to me. And I would be the same to him. And hopefully, one day, in the future, I would settle into being okay with adding another fuzzy night with a man to my list.

The. End.

FOURTEEN

DESPITE MY PEP talk and firm resolve, I still had to walk down the aisle with Vann. If I thought it was going to be awkward before our little bathroom chat, I had no idea what was in store for me after.

In hindsight, I probably should have ditched the whole affair completely.

Was there such thing as a runaway bridesmaid?

I could be the first. I liked to blaze my own trail.

But instead of following that instinct, I'd gotten into line next to Vann and slipped my arm through his. He hadn't held me especially close, but he hadn't stood cumbersomely away either. I could feel the warmth of his body and the smooth tux fabric that did silly things to my head. And my resolve.

I caught another whiff of him—he smelled so amazing. And considering he likely didn't use an arsenal of skin care products and army of makeup magicians to freshen his face, he managed to look the opposite of hungover.

God, he was a good-looking man.

Congrats to those Delane kids. They had good genes.

We were first up, having places on the outside of the bridal train.

I liked to think of myself as closer to Vera than Kaya, but it also made sense for Kaya to walk down the aisle with her boyfriend and for the only two single people in the bridal party to walk next to each other.

Killian sat Jo in place of his mother, and I tried not to sniffle. It was easier to ignore Vann when I realized I would have to fight all my emotions to survive this wedding without sobbing uncontrollably.

Vann leaned in while I pretended to scratch the corner of my eye and ignored the wetness my fingertip came away with. "You ready for this?"

"We have the easy job," I whispered back.

He turned his head, pulling my attention toward him. His eyes drifted over my formal attire. "No, you just make it look easy." He leaned in, his lips brushing my earlobe. "You're too beautiful, Dillon. I'm finding it hard to look directly at you."

Before I could reply, the bluegrass quartet began the prelude music, and he was pulling me down the aisle. I struggled for a few seconds as his words seemed to trip up my feet and make me forget how to do simple things like walk... and breathe... and blink. But I recovered quickly.

We walked passed packed rows of people, all watching expectantly for the blushing bride. I probably knew a lot of people here, but they were all a blur as the beauty of the moment consumed me. Starting at my feet, fizzing up my legs and through my chest, reaching my fingertips and the very top of my head.

White and pink peonies interspersed with the prettiest greenery was draped from the ceiling and along the walls and decorated the aisle chairs in elegant wreaths. There was a wrought iron arch at the end of the aisle, backdropped by the open patio and the late afternoon sun and the hum of Durham just beyond.

That was where Vann and I parted ways. But not before his fingers brushed mine in the sweetest goodbye.

Or maybe his fingers brushed on accident.

God, this whole wedding haze was clouding my judgment.

I waited for my fellow bridesmaids to join me. And then it was the flower girls' and ring bearer's turn. They were adorably off course and mischievous. The pastor gestured for the room to stand, the hired band changed their music and Vera entered the room on her dad's arm. Killian made a choked sound and I glanced over just in time to see a single tear roll down his cheek.

That's when the tears started flowing for everyone. I was a strong woman and all that, but even I couldn't hold it together when Killian, a man that was basically my brother and one of the smartest, strongest, most resilient guys I had ever known, was staring so completely enamored at his bride.

They didn't stop either. Not when the pastor started talking about the sanctity of marriage and the sanctity of the lifelong promises the happy couple was about to speak to each other. Not when Molly's mom read a verse about love from the Bible. Not when one of Vera's second cousin's sang a song by the Lumineers while they lit a unity candle. Not when they whispered choked vows and Vera sniffled her I do's. Not when they were pronounced man and wife. And certainly not when they shared their first kiss as newlyweds.

The wedding erupted into a true celebration after that.

Vera and Killian danced down the aisle, freshly dubbed Mr. and Mrs. Quinn. We followed, cheering and wiping tears and loving these people more than any of us knew was possible.

My loneliness disappeared, reminded of how happy I was for my friends—how special this day and night were for them. How completely wonderful they were for each other.

The wedding guests were asked to mingle in the bar area, while the staff reset the restaurant to accommodate for the meal and the bridal party scurried outside to take advantage of the late sunlight.

For an hour and a half, the photographer snapped pictures of the happy couple and their coordinating wedding party. Vann and I were continuously put next to each other, forced to touch, forced to be close. And I'd like to think we weathered it like pros.

I mean, there was the lingering brush of his hand along my spine.

And the extra close posturing as his chest pressed against my back or his arm wrapped around my shoulders, tugging me into him.

But that was the point of pictures—that we all looked like we knew each other. And liked each other. And like Vann and I had totally slept together the night before.

Oh wait, not that last one.

I would be surprised if Vera got her pictures back and I wasn't face-palming through half of them.

What made it worse were the tingles and snapshots of the night before running through my thoughts whenever Vann touched me.

By the time we reentered the reception, I needed a drink. And fast. The rest of the guests had been reseated at tables around the room and Vera and Killian were making their way through the crowd to the head table.

I veered off course and slid onto a barstool. I'd seen the guy behind the bar a few times before, but I didn't think he worked here. After giving me a surprised look, he walked over with a smile on his face.

"What can I get you?"

"Something strong," I responded immediately. Then of course, I thought about last night and the questionable decisions I'd made and changed my mind. "Just kidding, something mild. Barely alcoholic. A virgin daiquiri if you have it."

He laughed at my insane answer. "Is that really what you want? A virgin daiquiri?"

I plopped the side of my head in my hand. "No, I want an Old Fashioned." I scanned the shelves of liquor. "With that Bulleit Rye."

His grin kicked up a notch, giving him the most devilish look I had ever seen on a man before. This guy was trouble. And he knew it. "Atta girl."

"Don't make me regret this decision," I told his back as he searched for the right bottle.

"Good whiskey isn't a drink people should regret." He found what he was looking for and then started searching for something else. With an apologetic look over his shoulder, he said, "Sorry, this isn't my bar."

"I didn't think so. You look familiar, but I don't think I've seen you here before."

After he'd gathered everything he needed, he shook his head and said, "I own Craft." He paused to look at me, searching for recognition.

"I was just there!" I told him. "Friday night. It was amazing."

"That's good to hear. We haven't been open for very long. But since Killian has convinced half my staff to leave their good employment to take a chance working with me, I offered to work his wedding."

"You know that was his game plan from the beginning, right?"

He laughed, but his eyes stayed focused on the drink in his hands. "I'm realizing that. I think the whole kitchen staff is here for the same reason."

"They are," I said seriously. "It's why the wedding took so long to plan. They had to line up a quality catering staff that could please two very good, very picky chefs."

"And their guests," he added—another sly look.

I smiled. "And their guests. Who are mostly chefs."

He grimaced. "Not an easy task. I think they ended up flying someone in from California."

"Probably safe to outsource."

A body slid onto the bar seat next to me. It was Vann. He didn't bother looking at the bartender. He only had eyes for me.

"They're looking for you," he said, his voice pitched low and direct.

I licked my lips and tried not to look at his. Maybe I should forego the drink altogether. "Who?"

"The girls," he said, not needing to give them names. "I think they want you to sit down before they bring the food in."

"Ah. Okay. Sorry, I was just grabbing a drink first."

At just that moment, the bartender slid my Old Fashioned across the counter. I could already tell it was a good one. The orange peel was curled perfectly, and he'd given me two cherries.

"How much do I owe you?" I asked, suddenly realizing I didn't have my purse on me.

He winked at me. "Bridal party drinks for free."

Had more beautiful words ever been spoken? "You probably shouldn't have told me that."

His laugh was deep and genuine. "Remember what I said about whiskey."

That people shouldn't regret drinking it. Maybe there was truth to that. Last night's bad decision had been brought to you by tequila. Maybe whiskey would appeal to my more rational drunk side.

Not that I intended to get drunk three nights in a row. I wasn't that girl anymore.

Still, a little something to steady the nerves was in order. Especially with Vann boring a hole into the side of my head.

"Thanks again..."

"Will," he supplied. "Will English."

"Thanks again, Will English. It was a pleasure to meet you."

Vann was full on glaring by the time I stood up. He was apparently my escort in all ways tonight and stuck by my side as we skirted the outside of the room trying to get to the head table. "Who was that?"

"Will English." Giving him a perplexed look, I added, "He just told us."

"I meant, who is he? How do you know him?"

I shrugged, not understanding where the attitude was coming from. "I don't. We just met. He made my drink." I held up the cut crystal tumbler so he could see for himself.

"Huh."

"What does that mean?" I didn't like his tone is what I meant.

"It means, I thought you were a nice girl."

Now that sounded like an insult. "Excuse me?"

"I used to date nice girls. They didn't work out for me. So, I stopped dating them."

"Okay."

"And then I met you. I assumed you were a nice girl. I thought I would make an exception. Just for you. And you're telling me we're at The End. I was wrong about you being a nice girl."

I stopped, whirling around and planting my free hand on my hip. "I am a nice girl. I'm a very nice girl. I'm the nicest girl you'll ever meet."

He leaned in, a surprising smirk tilting one side of his mouth. "No, Dillon, you're not." Just when I contemplated smacking him, he added, "But don't worry, I think I'm into it."

He turned away and made his way back to his seat. I mumbled, "You think?" to his back, but he was already gone. What did that mean? He thinks he's into it? Into me?

I took a long sip of my Old Fashioned, even though I usually preferred to wait until the ice melted. I tried to decide if last night was a fluke or if Vann Delane was going to drive me to drink. Er, all the time.

THREE HOURS LATER, I was full of all kinds of amazing food, the best drinks I had ever had, an insanely delicious honey, vanilla, and lavender wedding cake, and so much laughter.

The dinner had been one of the best I'd ever had. The toasts from Ezra and Molly had been heartwarming and moving, the cutting of the cake adorable, and Kaya happened to catch the bouquet—when Vera tossed it directly to her while she was sitting down.

Dancing had started an hour ago and I was having the time of my life moving around the floor with my friends and a string of single guys that never let me stop. I'd only had one other drink so I was also pleasantly sober.

This was a night for the books.

And I was so happy that Vera and Killian would have these perfectly beautiful memories for the rest of their lives.

I had just escaped the dance floor to take a break and sit with my brother for a few minutes—who had two left feet and hated anything but slow dancing where he could just sway back and forth—when I nearly bumped into another girl practically throwing herself at Vann.

The moment surprised me so much that I had to take a step back and regroup.

To be honest, I'd had my eye on him the whole night. Not that I was being a creepy stalker or anything. But after last night, and then today, there was just this awareness of his presence. I couldn't help it! I was female after all.

It was in our DNA to know where available, attractive, mysterious men were at all times.

Er, at least I'd found that to be true in the last twenty-four hours. When it specifically applied to Vann Delane.

But let's not analyze that too closely.

Okay, so maybe I'd picked this side of the dance floor to walk off because he happened to be standing nearby. And maybe I'd totally nailed my aloof exit with a laughing conversation with Molly so that I could pretend that I had no idea he was over here. And maybe, just maybe, but probably not likely, I had been hoping he would stop to talk to me.

He hadn't said anything to me since before dinner and I found that I didn't like that he was also playing the aloof game.

It was okay when I did it. But frankly, he was annoying me.

Also, since when had I turned into this girl that was all, "Pay attention to meeeee?" I wasn't that girl. I was levelheaded. I was unattached. I was perfectly confident in my single status.

Where were all these emotions coming from and what did I do with them? Because keeping them and dealing with them was not a viable option.

And now there was this female in front of me, who had deliberately blocked my path so she could have all of Vann's attention and I was contemplating murder in the first degree. Basically, it was time for another drink and a scavenger hunt for my sanity.

"Excuse me," I managed to bite out politely. Okay, politely-ish.

She barely turned her head to acknowledge my presence and just kept talking to Vann with enthusiastic hand gestures. I tried to step around her when one of her flailing arms nearly clotheslined me.

I took a step back and glanced at Vann. The damnable man was trying to bite back a smile. Those gray eyes shifted to mine, full of humor.

He was enjoying this.

"Excuse me," I said louder.

The woman turned to finally give me her attention, an ugly sneer twisting her otherwise pretty face. "What?"

Okay, that was it. I tried to be nice. At least polite. And I could even admit, at least to myself, that I was playing a game with Vann, but she didn't know that. Now she was just on my nerves.

Leaning around her, I grabbed Vann's hand and tugged him toward me. "I just need him," I told the snotty woman. "For a sec," I promised.

Vann let me pull him onto the dance floor, ignoring the evil woman and her demonic glaring from behind him.

"She is awful," I told him as we naturally started to move with the upbeat music.

He finally let go of his smile. "She barely said anything to you."

I growled, thankful he couldn't hear me over the bass. "She didn't need to," I told him. "It was her attitude."

His eyes lit with pretend understanding. "Ah. I get it now."

"Thank you."

He leaned in, brushing a stray hair over my shoulder. "Told you."

My eyes naturally narrowed. "Told me what?"

"You're not a nice girl."

I continued to stare at him, wondering what this meant. He sounded like he was gloating, like he'd uncovered some great secret about me. But I didn't get it.

I was nice. Most of the time. To the people I loved anyway.

And I had always been nice to him.

Nice-ish.

"I'm super nice," I argued. "That biotch had it coming." I realized something awful way too late. "Oh no, I'm so sorry, she wasn't your wedding date or anything was she?"

His eyes bugged in a satisfying way. "Her? No. No. No."

Three no's was good confirmation he wasn't into her. That shouldn't have made me as happy as it did.

"If you'd rather dance with her..."

He rolled his eyes and wrapped his arm around my waist, tugging me against him. "I'm dancing with the girl I want to be dancing with."

He was always so straightforward with everything, so completely direct and unflinching. It was strange. Or at least different than the other guys I had spent time with. Even my brother had a tendency to dance around sensitive issues with me. Ezra was always afraid the truth would break me. Like I was this delicate flower that was at risk of losing her petals.

To be honest, Vann's way was jarring. Like actual punches to my gut. But it was growing on me. I found I didn't like to be treated as though I were fragile. Vann's way seemed to convey more... respect for me. He trusted me to be a grown-up woman with her own mind.

And that was validating in a way I didn't expect.

My jealousy was also appeased.

The music changed, slowing way down. The DJ said something about fulfilling a request, but all I could hear was the frantic beating of my heart as Vann wrapped his hands around my waist and I found my arms curling around his neck.

He looked at me from beneath hooded eyelids and thick lashes. "You don't remember much about last night, do you?"

I shook my head, another blush creeping over my face, painting it in red with the admission of truth. "There were too many shots. It's coming back to me, but it's all jumbled and messy."

His lips kicked with a smile. "I remember some messy parts too."

Dropping my head, I pressed my cheek against his chest to hide. "Oh, my god."

His laugh rumbled beneath me and I had to close my eyes against the rapid beating of my heart. Oh hell, I liked that feeling too much.

His head dipped, so he could press his cheek against my forehead. "It was a good night, Dillon. I'm disappointed you don't remember. It's making me insecure."

I clutched him tighter, unable to look him in the eyes. It was making me question everything. But that wasn't something I could admit to him. I tugged my tried and true *fine* personality tightly around myself. I was fine. Last night was fine. Everything was fine. "It's not you. Seriously, I can usually hold my liquor better than that."

"I didn't realize you were too drunk to remember." His voice had lost the teasing edge and was replaced with concern.

Shrugging, I stayed under cover. "It's one of my superpowers. I'm usually more careful though."

We danced in silence for a while, both of us lost in thought. Honestly, I could barely untangle mine to make them out. I couldn't even guess at his.

There was a lot to think about. A lot to be embarrassed about. Just all around a lot.

"I'm not planning to take you home tonight," he announced.

I pulled back, unable to not look at his face and gauge whether he was serious. "Are you for real right now?"

His gray eyes turned silver with emotion I couldn't read. "I don't want you to get the wrong idea about me. I'm not usually so... easy."

My mouth dropped open. Was that a dig at me? I honestly couldn't tell. Forget what I'd just decided about this man. He wasn't open and honest. He was an enigma. A total and complete mystery. Who was he? "Are you insulting me?"

He laughed and pulled me tighter against him. His lips dropped to my ear. "No, not insulting."

We danced in silence again. I was hypnotized by his body so

close to mine and his lips at my ear, his breath floating over my bare skin. I was glad he didn't think he was going to get laid two nights in a row. That wasn't a thing I did.

Mostly because I didn't sleep with anyone anymore. Mostly because I was basically a monk.

Nor did he need to know how disappointed I was at the same time I was utterly relieved. How did that even make sense?

And yet there was a part of me that wanted to go back to his place and remember everything this time.

I needed to know if he was as good as all my drunk memories popping up uninvited.

Picking my head up off his chest, I finally found the right thing to say. "I have to work tomorrow anyway."

His furrowed brow was enough of a question.

"You got this random snapshot of me being totally irresponsible and reckless this weekend. But I promise, I'm usually way more settled down and focused than this. Tomorrow it's back to work and my schedule becomes total insanity. So... what I'm trying to say is..."

"Yes, please tell me what you're trying to say."

His impatience made my heart skip. Was I doing the right thing? I was doing the only thing. "I'm trying to say thanks for hanging with me this weekend and making sure I always had someone, so I didn't feel like a total loser for being single." There, that should do it. I was complimentary, direct, and to the point. He should get the point.

And he did. Only it didn't feel like the right thing. It felt awful.

His chin jerked back, and his eyes widened in surprise. "Am I being dismissed?"

That was a yucky way of putting it. "No! No, it's not like that."

"Then what's it like?"

I nibbled my bottom lip and tried to figure out the right way to explain what I meant. This would be a super good time for an uprising, by the way. Or an apocalypse of some kind? An alien invasion? I wasn't picky. Any world-ending scenario was fine with me.

"I work an impossible schedule," I explained more carefully. "I'm just saying, I have no time in my life for commitments or obligations. I have to get Bianca back on her feet. I have to figure out how to run a kitchen by myself. I'm just trying to be good at my job, pay bills, and find time to go to the gym. It's not you, Vann. I think you're amazing and so funny. You've helped me in so many ways. I just don't want to... get your hopes up."

I wanted to snatch all those words out of the air and shove them back in my mouth. God, could I be a bigger idiot?

Wasn't I the same girl that couldn't keep her shit together all weekend? And now I was turning down the only good guy I'd been around in years, maybe even my entire life, just because my work schedule was busy?

I wanted to slap my hand over my face, but I resisted the urge.

Besides, my heart knew the truth. It was currently calling me a liar.

It wasn't my schedule that was making me take a step back from Vann—it was fear.

I was terrified of him and what kind of relationship he wanted. It obviously wasn't the one-night stand variety. Or the slip me a roofie and take advantage of me kind. That launched us firmly into uncharted territory and I just wasn't ready to tackle another new thing.

He smiled, but it was forced and shadowed. "I get that. I'm busy too. I wasn't... I hope you didn't think we were like a thing. Obviously, it was one night. I'm just saying, it was a good night. If you ever have the night off, we should do it again."

My heart squeezed painfully. This was what I wanted, I reminded myself. This was how I was with dates now. I tried them once and then I ran—usually before the check arrived. And I was okay with that.

So why did it feel so awful now?

And why was I such a fucking psycho who couldn't make up her damn mind?

He leaned in and kissed my cheek. "Have a good night, Dillon. Good luck tomorrow."

Now he was brushing me off? But isn't this what I'd asked for? I had made this bed. Now I needed to lie in it. "You too, Vann."

He stepped away from me mid-song and I wanted to cry at the loss of his body heat. Why had I said all of that? Why couldn't I just recognize a good thing when I had it and shut up for once?

He started dancing with the mouthy girl that had bumped into me before. He might not have wanted to dance with her earlier, but now he seemed to be having a great time.

I tried to make the best of the night after that, but the magic of the wedding had been crushed beneath my frightened foot. I danced with friends and stayed until Vera and Killian said their goodbyes and then snuck out the kitchen entrance, so I didn't have to talk to anyone else.

By the time I stumbled inside my apartment, exhausted and frayed, I was glad it was all over. Vann wasn't close enough to be in Ezra's wedding, although he might go. But other than that, I wouldn't have to see him anymore.

We would officially go our separate ways, which would completely uncomplicate my life and give him the freedom to do whatever he wanted.

I could finally relax.

I could finally focus on my job and stop obsessing over him.

Which was exactly what I did as soon as I laid down in bed.

Just kidding. I tossed and turned all night and eventually fell asleep out of sheer, battered exhaustion.

FIFTEEN

"HOW DID THE WEEKEND GO?" I asked Blaze as soon as he walked through the door to Bianca Monday morning.

His eyes widened and he took a step back as if I'd scared him. I was too tightly wound to pull back. I had spent the morning on the treadmill at my apartment, going over the weekend numbers and his notes.

He wasn't the most verbose person out there and so there wasn't a lot of detail about the weekend. The numbers had been within the recent averages—which wasn't the best news ever, but they weren't worse. So, there was that.

"Morning, Chef," he greeted, being polite where I clearly failed. "It's good to have you back."

I tried not to roll my eyes. "Details, Blaze. I need weekend details."

He shrugged and looked around. "We're still standing. I think that's a good thing?"

His dry sense of humor was growing on me, but I wanted more than that. "Did things go smoothly? Were there any big complaints? Or did y'all run things like usual? Did you run out of anything?"

"We did run out of the scallops on both nights. I think the way you've changed up the recipe has been a huge hit. We might need to figure that out."

I was pleased to hear that. Extremely pleased, actually. "Coffee?" I held up the French press I'd brought from my house just for these Monday meetings.

He looked visibly relieved to see caffeine. "Yes, please."

And I was happy to have a somewhat comfortable and normal conversation with him. After I'd poured us both a mug, I continued to interrogate him for the better part of the hour on everything that happened while I'd been at the wedding.

From what he said, everything seemed pretty normal. Which wasn't necessarily a good thing for Bianca, but I was happy things didn't totally implode while I was gone.

"Sales are still down," he said at the end. "I know we're way in the red."

I nodded, having a hard time admitting the truth of our circumstances. "Ezra doesn't want this restaurant to fail," I promised. "That's why he brought me in."

"I realize that, I'm just... hesitant to believe that you can help." When he realized what he said, he added a quick, but insincere, "No offense."

"None taken." Lie. "I get your point." Truth. "But I have a game plan. Starting with updating this menu. It's so outdated and run of the mill. I'm disappointed in my brother for letting it stay as long as it has."

"Ashlynn and I came up with it," he admitted.

"Oh." I had the strongest urge to murmur no offense, but that wasn't necessarily the truth. Instead, I looked him in the eye and said, "You're a better chef than that menu. This whole kitchen is better than this."

"Well, I, uh—"

"Did Ezra ever come in and help you out?"

The tips of his ears turned red. "Every once in a while."

"Blaze, for real, if Ezra can cook it, it's too easy." At Blaze's half smile, I added, "He thinks he's an amazing chef, but we both know he's barely competent. I get that we have to indulge him every once in a while, but my goal is to make the menu complex enough that he can't come back here and mess things up."

Blaze folded his arms over his chest and nodded. "Okay, I can get on board with that."

"I have this vision..." I'd been working on it all weekend. Strangely enough, the night at Vann's that I could barely remember sparked the concept.

"I want to simplify everything."

His brows furrowed together. "I thought you said you wanted to make things more complex?"

I waved a hand in the air, swiping away the opposing ideas. "I want both to be honest. Complex in the way that we're making the best food possible. But I want it to be clean, simple and stand out. Right now, Ezra has the menu swamped with fussy French dishes that most people can recognize. I want to go in the opposite direction and make the ingredients the superstars, not French tradition."

"Okay, I think I'm tracking with you..."

"Our motto will be casual French. We'll get rid of the beef Bourguignon and foie gras and coq au vin. I don't want escargot anywhere near this place. And we'll replace the heavy, typical, pedestrian dishes with savory crepes and perfectly seared hanger steak with a tarragon crème sauce, the best charcuterie in the city with wine pairings and scallop croquettes." I thought about how our scallops were doing recently. "Or maybe we keep the scallops the way they are and do a white fish croquette. I don't know, these are just some ideas I've been playing around with."

"What about a cassoulet? We could use pork belly or duck confit or something trendy and interesting?"

"Yes! That! Simple flavor profiles cooked to perfection. I want this to be the most elegant and least intimidating meal Durham has ever seen. Does that make sense?"

He took a minute to think over my vision. I started to worry that it didn't make sense, when he took a deep breath and nodded eagerly. "You're making French food accessible to anyone. Giving it a casual atmosphere. Taking the stuffiness out of it."

I could have sworn my grin reached both ears. "Exactly! I'm taking the stuffiness out of it. Out of Bianca."

"I think it's brilliant. And the perfect way to get the public interested in eating here again." He snapped his fingers, a thought just occurring to him. "We could do half-price board and wine nights. Maybe only for happy hour or do it the whole night or whatever. People would come in by the droves for good charcuterie and cheap wine."

"Blaze, that's an amazing idea!" I grabbed his bicep and shook it like a crazy person. "You're getting me more and more excited by the minute."

"This is a great idea, Chef. Seriously, it's exactly what we need."

Now that he was on board with this idea, I had to sell him on the actually crazy thought I'd had after all of my bridal brunches over the weekend.

"Okay, there's something else. And this might be off the rails, so feel free to tell me I'm totally bonkers. I mean, I might still make you do it. But you have permission to tell me I'm straight up crazy."

"You're making me nervous."

I laughed, but it was slightly hysterical. "Right now, we're only open for supper. But we're open for supper every day of the week. I'm thinking about closing on Mondays, making the supper hours more exclusive."

"Have you talked to your brother about that?" He didn't look convinced at all.

"Annnnnd." I tried not to laugh at the nervous look on his face. "What if we closed for supper on Saturday and Sunday nights. And instead opened up those mornings to brunch."

"Wait, what?"

I explained again, slower this time. "We do a French brunch

instead of supper on the weekends. We could do more varieties of crepes and quiche and Austrian pancakes and a wide selection of pastries. We could offer some fruity, breakfast-y cocktails. And bring back a breakfast charcuterie with a cold meat, baguette and brie plate."

"It's different..."

"And there's nothing like it in this section of the city. I did some research and drove around this morning. There are no dine-in breakfast spots around. We'd be the only one."

"Do you think it could supplement losing Saturday and Sunday night?"

"We're within walking distance of three churches and a strip mall. Okay, the strip mall is a bit of a drive, but not much. Plus, they're building that apartment complex and movie theater not far from here. We make money on the weekends, but not enough. I think a brunch would amplify our presence and bring in a new set of consumers. It would be up to us to make the dinner option good enough for people to want to spend their money here all week long and to make the brunch option good enough that we could make up for the loss of Saturday night. But I think we can do it."

He still didn't look convinced. And I couldn't blame him. Changing up a menu was infinitely easier than going from supper to brunch two days of the week. But I had the best feeling about it. And as it stood right now, Bianca was drowning.

If I didn't do something drastic, we might lose her completely. And then what would I do? I didn't think anyone would hire a head chef right after she bombed her last restaurant. Honestly, outside of my brother, there wasn't a restaurant on the planet that would hire me for another EC job. I just wasn't qualified for the position.

I could go back to sous chef somewhere. But I had the itchy feeling, now that I'd accepted this job, I had officially overqualified myself for the rest of the positions I was actually qualified for.

Which made me highly motivated to get Bianca back on her feet.

"Have you talked to Ezra about any of this?" Blaze asked, hesitation loud and clear in his tone.

Showing some teeth in my smile, I said, "I'm not Wyatt. Ezra gives me whatever I want. If I decide to take Bianca in this direction, it's only a matter of when." He flinched at the truth in my words and I knew I had to soften the news before I lost him completely. "But I can't accomplish any of this without you and the rest of the staff. If you're not on board with any of this, speak now or forever hold your peace. I can't do this without you, Blaze."

His expression softened as he looked around the kitchen he'd worked in way longer than me. "If you really think it will work, I'm willing to try anything." When he turned back to look at me, his eyes were full of hope and gravity and concern. "What happens if it doesn't work?"

"We could call it a trial run," I suggested, wanting to give him a tangible solution. "And we could switch back to dinner any time we wanted." He nodded slowly. "Or we could just work our asses off and make our own success."

A small, confident smile broke free on his face. "I like that second option the most."

I threw my hands in the air. "You are the actual best, Blaze!"

His smile grew. "You know you're not like any other EC out there right?"

It was my turn to smile and be filled with something like hope and gravity and fear. "Is that a good thing?"

"I guess we'll find out."

He was right about that. But by the time the rest of the staff had filtered in and I'd pitched my vision to everyone, it felt like more than a dream. It felt like a possibility.

I brought in the white board I'd picked up at Walmart on the way into work and turned the morning meeting into a brainstorming session, letting everyone from sous chef to dishwasher give me their ideas.

Granted, they weren't all amazing ideas. But there were plenty of good ones.

I had been concerned most about switching hours from evening to morning, but the general consensus was excitement that they might get a night off every once in a while. To be honest, I was excited about the same thing.

From a competing business standpoint, I believed our take on brunch would give Bianca something special, something that Ezra's other restaurants didn't have. Something that no restaurant nearby had.

After the weekend, I was hyper-focused on making Bianca succeed. My personal life felt like a failure at this point. I wouldn't let Bianca self-destruct too. I was working at taping my heart back together after the wedding, but in the meantime, I was wholly throwing myself into this restaurant and her success.

For selfish reasons, my conversation with Vann had really done a number on me. True, I still needed to figure out what I wanted. And I wasn't sure that was necessarily Vann. But I also wasn't Kaya who accidentally fell in love, but would have ignored relationships forever as long as she had her job.

This job, Bianca, was important to me. But I couldn't let it be everything. If I wanted a relationship, or at least a steady dating life, then I had to make space for it. I had to have courage for it.

But first I needed to put out the dumpster fire that was this restaurant. Then I would tackle my love life mess.

Another drunken memory from my night with Vann popped into my head, followed quickly by a sultry shiver down my spine.

"You fucked that up," I whispered to myself when I was alone in my kitchen. "Time to move on."

There were other guys out there.

Liar, my heart argued.

Not like Vann, my brain agreed.

THE NEXT MORNING, I met Molly at her gym. She had a guest pass waiting and a scowl on her face.

"You better love this class," she growled at me.

I'd never known her to be a grumpy person. But then again, I'd never interacted with her before coffee. "I love you. Does that count?"

Her glare turned dangerous.

I smiled wider.

She led the way to the women's locker room. "I don't know what spawned this evil desire to get sweaty first thing in the morning, but Vera always buys me McDonalds afterwards." I started to gag at the very thought of eating that cheap, greasy trash when she spun around and pointed a stern finger at me. "And don't you dare talk bad about the greatest breakfast place in the land or I will leave you here to die on your own!"

"The dramatics are truly outstanding this morning."

I glanced up to see Vann standing outside the girls' locker room dressed in running shorts and a sweaty gray t-shirt.

It was a straight up miracle I didn't trip over my own feet and faceplant. What was he doing here?

Molly groaned and rubbed her face, "I'm sorry, Dillon. Honestly, I think I'm still hungover from the wedding."

Vann gave her a look. "I didn't realize you were bringing a guest."

Molly blinked at him. "Is Dillon considered a guest?"

"I gained like four pounds this weekend," I rushed to explain and then resisted the urge to slap a hand over my mouth. Why had I admitted that? Why couldn't I have said something about getting in shape? Or wanting to try a new gym? Or anything that didn't involve my flab-ifying midsection?

"Ugh, me too," Molly agreed. "Which is why I'm here. Now it's my turn to fit into a wedding dress and I don't have the excuse of being pregnant."

"Although if you really wanted to, you could." I grinned at her, warming up to the idea of having a niece or nephew. Sure, I was excited for Vera and Killian, but Molly's baby would be related to me. "I mean I don't think it's hard."

She tilted her head, not looking amused. "But then who would you drag to spin class at the butt crack of dawn?"

Vann and I accidentally looked at each other and then quickly looked anywhere else. "Oh, I'm sure I could find somebody..."

"You wouldn't," she assured me. "Vann is the only person crazy enough to want to go to spin class, but he doesn't do nice things for anybody."

"That's not true." My defense for him was out of my mouth before I could think better of it. I accidentally looked at him again, but this time he didn't look away, so I had to first. "I mean, that's not a nice thing to say, Molls. Surely, he's nice to people. Other people. At least his sister."

"No, she's right," he said. "He's not nice to anyone. Not even his sister. Or her annoying best friend." He started to walk past us, shooting an indecipherable look my way. "Or her best friend's friends either."

I couldn't help but stare at his back, and okay, his toned butt, as he walked away, a towel slung over his straight, proud shoulders.

And we were back to the beginning. Where he found me annoying again. That was fun.

"Sorry, about him," Molly said, leading me all the way into the locker room this time. "He won't admit that he's a bear before coffee, but he can be really grumpy."

"I get that. No worries."

She turned to face me while I took off my sweatshirt and threw my hair in a ponytail. "I thought you guys were getting pretty close though. I saw you dancing at the wedding."

I stood up from tying my shoe. I figured I could level with her. "We did dance at the wedding. And we kind of got to know each other." And slept together. "But I don't know... he's a tough cookie."

She frowned and looked at the door as if he would reappear and give us all the answers. "True. But... I don't know, he seemed to open up with you."

"Not really," I assured her. "I feel like I barely know him at all."

"He danced with you in front of his dad and sister, so that means something. He hasn't even brought a girl home to meet Vera or their dad in years. He's like super weird about getting girls' hopes up or letting them meet his family."

That was all news to me. Hope bloomed inside me and I wasn't quite sure what to do with it. Did I want to be the girl that got special treatment from Vann? Did I want to be the girl he was willing to introduce to his dad.

Not that he did. But we did dance in front of all our family and friends. That could mean something.

All I managed to say to Molly was, "Huh."

"If you like him, don't give up on him, okay?"

"What do you mean?"

She stopped for a second to look me in the eyes and grip my hands. "He's a good guy, Dillon. A great guy. And he deserves someone wonderful. He might be prickly around the edges, but once you get to know him, you'll see that he's like the most generous person you'll ever meet. And he's secretly funny and kind and super loyal. I'm just saying, even if he's giving you the stay away vibes right now, clearly there was something there over the weekend. Don't give up."

I opened my mouth. And then I shut it. Then I opened it again, hoping something neutral would come out. I tried blinking, but that didn't help either. Finally, after she'd started to look at me funny, I came up with a profound, "Duly noted."

Her smile was still sleepy, but it was also knowing. She saw way too much for not having a cup of coffee. "Okay," she said, grabbing her towel. "Are you ready to die?"

Twenty minutes later, I kind of wished I could die. Vann had gotten to class before us. Actually, everyone had gotten to class before us since we'd chatted for so long in the locker room. The only two bikes left were the ones in the front row. Apparently, no one in this class was an overachiever.

Molly had gripped my bicep with two hands when we'd stepped inside the cycle studio. "Don't make me do it," she'd pleaded, her voice high-pitched and hysterical.

Bailing totally crossed my mind and I was tempted to give in to that panicked urge. This was dumb. I wasn't here to impress Vann. I just wanted to burn off some of the alcohol and wedding cake from last weekend. And I thought it would be cool to hang with Molly a few mornings a week.

I didn't sign up for front row in an exercise class I'd never been to before.

Not to mention Vann would be directly behind me—watching me inevitably fail at basically spinning my feet on spikey pedals. It was humiliation I did not welcome. Nor did I need. Nor did I have to go through with.

But just when I'd been ready to grab Molly's quivering hand and flee, Vann had turned around and raised a single, challenging eyebrow.

It was like he could sense my flight reaction kicking in. He didn't think I'd go through with this. He didn't think I was serious about cycling. He probably thought I was here to see him.

I would show him.

Only now that we were well into the class, I realized it wasn't slipping off the pedals into a puddle of my own sweat and tears that I had to worry about. It was the super slimming workout tights I'd chosen to wear this morning and my ultra-formfitting halter top.

And, because I hated underwear lines, I wasn't wearing any. My butt crack was potentially the sweatiest it had ever been, and Vann was here to freaking witness it. And not just see it but have a front row ticket to the sweaty ass show. Literally.

I had been trying to get Molly's attention for the better part of the last ten minutes, but she had this technique where she stared at the ground the whole time. Probably so she didn't fall off the bike, but still. I needed her to wake up and pay attention to me.

Also, there was a good possibility she'd actually fallen asleep and was somehow managing to pedal unconsciously.

Not a bad plan, Molly Maverick. Not a bad plan at all.

Another side note—this class was complete and utter hell. This was how I imagined boot camp. Forty-five minutes of a straight incline up the world's steepest mountain. Maybe minus the techno version of Taylor Swift in the background.

And I worked out. I wasn't like Molly who could consume seventy-five percent of the planet's fast food in one day and wake up the next morning somehow thinner than the day before. I was starting to suspect she had a pet tapeworm.

She complained about her lack of curves and Gumby-like body, but she had no idea how good she had it.

I couldn't eat half of what she did and even hope to be marginally thin. My body type was brought to you by weekend drinking, six days a week workout and dinners consisting of cocktail cherries and bleu cheese stuffed olives.

To be fair though, most of my dinners happened at two in the morning, after I'd been cooking all night, so I was never in the mood to cook for myself. Especially when there was only me.

I usually just grabbed what was available. Which meant cocktail accoutrements. And sometimes good cheese I nicked from the restaurant kitchen.

The instructor looked at me and smiled sadistically—er, at least that was how it appeared from my angle. Like he was possessed with a workout demon intent on enslaving the entire world with cycling. "All right," he shouted into his headset, "who's ready to kick it up a notch?"

I shook my head rapidly. Not me. I was so not ready to kick it up a notch. No notches should be kicked.

Molly groaned next to me. I turned to see if she was okay and she mouthed, "I hate you." Well, okay then.

It was easy to stop obsessing over Vann after that, since I was convinced I was about to pedal my legs right off my body.

By the end of the class, I was gasping for breath and sweating every last drop of liquid in my body. I stumbled off my stationary bike and grabbed for my towel with shaky hands to wipe it down. I wasn't always diligent about this step of community workout protocol, but the amount of sweat I'd drenched this bike seat in was unnatural. I'd straight up desecrated the poor thing.

"Oh, my god," Molly groaned. "That was hell."

"That was pure insanity," I huffed. "Why didn't you warn me?"

Her laser glare was answer enough. "Are you serious?"

I managed a weak smile. "You said it was hard. You didn't say I wouldn't be able to walk straight for a week after."

She threw her hand in the air. "That's exactly what I said! Those were my exact words!" She turned to the person standing behind me. "Can you believe this, Vann?"

My throat dried out and it had nothing to do with the workout. "My memory is a little fuzzy about what you said."

"At least she didn't run out of here to puke," he said, standing closer than I thought he would have at this point in our estranged relationship.

"Who did that?" I had to ask.

"Vera," Molly said seriously. "She claimed it had something to do with the pregnancy, but it sounds like an excuse to me."

"Obviously." I snapped my fingers. "Maybe I should get knocked up too. That would get me out of a couple of jams."

Molly laughed, but Vann stilled beside me. I was afraid to look at him, realizing what my comment must have sounded like to him after our one-night stand.

"I think there's a few steps you have to take first," Molly suggested. "Like finding a guy willing to knock you up. And I don't think you're going to have any luck in your current pool of losers."

The sound that came out of my mouth was supposed to be a

laugh, but it was more like the sputtering sound of mortification. "You never know..."

She gave me a knowing look, but she had no idea the hornet's nest she was poking right now.

Vann leaned in and nudged me with his elbow. "They're all losers then?"

Was he fishing for a compliment? Or just trying to make me melt into a blushing puddle of embarrassment. Seriously, what was I supposed to say to that. "No one interested in being my baby daddy at least."

"Have you asked any of them?"

"What?"

His glare cut through me, tearing my insides to shreds. "Have you asked any of them? Maybe they aren't all the losers you think they are."

I used the towel to pat my sweaty face and stall for time. "I guess that's true. Some have been more memorable than others."

He flinched, catching the punch I'd subtly delivered him. "And some are just forgettable?"

"Completely."

Molly blinked at us. "You guys want to fess up to something?"

I smiled brightly and took a step back from Vann, lest I do something crazy like actually punch him—or climb him like a spider monkey and shut him up the old-fashioned way. "What? No. I think this is a classic case of boy power." I held up my fist. "You know, those poor men have to stick together."

"I'm going to leave now," Vann announced. "Have a good day, Molly."

He stalked off, his gray t-shirt drenched in sweat, clinging to all those cut muscles on his biceps and back. My eyes drifted to his ass—I mean, staring there was inevitable—and then to his tight calves. God, had a man's calves ever looked so delicious before?

"You're staring at him," Molly pointed out.

"He didn't say goodbye to me."

She snorted a laugh. "Unbelievable! You're into him."

Officially grabbing my attention again, I swung around to glare at her, trying to play innocent. "Hardly."

She rolled her eyes and headed for the locker room. "Yeah, that looked like you *hardly* noticed him. You're drooling by the way."

I touched the towel to the corner of my mouth on instinct. "I am not."

She turned, grinning over her shoulder. "You didn't have to play dumb this morning. You can tell me if you like Vann."

"Ugh." I winced, dreading the upcoming conversation. "It's complicated."

"Men are always complicated," she agreed. "They like to blame us for the games and being high maintenance. But they're the real trouble."

It felt good to hear her say that. And it prompted me to spit out the truth. "We slept together after the rehearsal dinner."

She dropped her towel and tripped over her feet. After she'd managed to collect herself and stand upright again, she gaped at me. "You did what?"

I dropped my face into my hands. "We slept together. And it wasn't... my finest moment."

"What do you mean?"

"I mean, I'd had a lot to drink at dinner. And that whole weekend. And there are some fuzzy spots that I might not totally, completely, wholly... remember."

She dragged me into the locker room and plopped me down on a bench. "Wait a minute, you're telling me you slept with Vann, but don't remember sleeping with him?"

"I remember parts of it," I clarified. "And the parts I remember are good parts." Staring at my hands, I felt myself blush. I must have been the color of a ripe tomato. "Really good parts."

"Wait, does he know you don't remember?"

I nodded, letting the full weight of her judgment descend. "I woke up in the middle of the night and realized what I'd done. So I escaped before he woke up."

"Oh, no."

"I didn't realize he'd be so pissed. I thought, I don't know, I didn't take it very seriously I guess. I thought we were just having fun. But he's all like, I don't even know how to have fun. And then I said some stupid things at the wedding. And the whole weekend is a blur of messing up! Molly, fix it for me please."

She immediately pulled me into a hug, wrapping her arms around my shoulders. "Okay. I will. How do you want me to fix it? Do you want things better with Vann because you're second guessing brushing him off? Or because you don't want bad blood between you, but you want to move on?"

"I don't know how to answer that either. Can you also decide that for me too?"

She laughed at me. Seriously, laughed at me. "You must really like him."

Her words seemed to grab whatever air was in the room and suck it straight from my lungs. "What?"

"You're so worried about him. I've never seen you like this with a guy before. Usually you're happy to use and lose them."

If by use, she meant get them to buy me dinner. And by lose, she meant fake a text before the check came, then she'd hit the nail on the head. "That's true, but only because they're usually Tinder randoms that aren't exactly the bring home to mom kind of gentlemen. Vann is just... more complicated than my usual blind date."

"By complicated, do you mean he has his life together?"

"Yes. Yes, that's exactly what I mean."

She released me and stood up. "What if you tried to be friends with him first? I know this might be a foreign concept, and please take no disrespect from this, you know I love you and everything about you. But... what if you, oh, I don't know, tried dating without sleeping with him? See what happens then?"

I rolled my eyes and wrapped my arms around my chilling torso.

Dang, my body was freezing now that it was starting to cool down. "Sounds risky."

Her smile softened. "He's not going to leave you just because he gets to know you."

I resented her words. Not because she had meant them maliciously, but because she knew me and had the right to call me out on my bullshit. Only there was more to my story than just the fear of being known by someone who could potentially hurt me. I mean, there was definitely that. But there was also more. "You don't know that," I said instead, it was easier than the truth. "Isn't that why couples breakup? They get to know each other and decide they don't like what they know?"

"It didn't happen with Ezra and me."

"You guys are different though." She gave me an annoyed look. "Besides, I don't want my only options to be to get hurt badly or get married. Is there a third option?"

Now her smile turned into a frown. "I think you're doing the third option."

I threw my hands in the air because the third option wasn't working either. "See? This is why I'm keeping my distance from now on. I need space from Vann so all of these volatile emotions and freak outs can end. We spent too much time together over the weekend and we were the only single people in the bridal party. Basically, it was bound to happen. I'm just glad it's out of my system now."

"So, you're choosing the moving on option?" But she didn't sound like she believed me.

"It's better for everyone this way."

"Whatever you say." She walked over to her locker and opened it. "You want to meet here on Thursday for another class? Or are you over getting your butt kicked?"

"Are you seriously willing to do this with me?"

"I hate it," she admitted. "But I do want to look amazing in my wedding dress. I need a partner though. One that sticks this out longer than the three guest passes I have. So, you need to join the gym and help me."

"Is Vann going to be here every time."

She shrugged and it was a little too casual for my Spidey senses not to kick in. "Not every time. But you're moving on so what does it matter?"

She had a point. And it seemed like he was moving on too. What did I have to lose? I could join this gym and have a workout partner that I loved. Win-win.

I'd have to avoid Vann in the process. I could do that. Easy. Like taking over Bianca had been easy. Or like climbing Everest in a bikini would be easy.

SIXTEEN

BY THE END of the week, I was frazzled as hell.

Bianca had not been going smoothly. There were moments of pure genius with my staff. But the majority of my days and evenings were struggling through tough conversations and trying to steer them in the right direction.

The food was, frankly, not up to par. The majority of it was mediocre at best. And as I tried to gently remind people what I was looking for in each dish, meals were taking longer and longer to get out to diners.

Plus, service was slow anyway. Which should have meant we had plenty of time to perfect each plate. But the opposite was true. The more free time we had, the more difficult getting them to focus became.

I was anxious to implement my ideas and switch Bianca's focus, but I also needed a killer marketing plan to coincide with the changes. Which meant getting Molly on board. Which meant, coming clean to Ezra about my vision shift.

I had been telling the truth when I told Blaze I wasn't scared of Ezra. He didn't intimidate me like he did most of the people that worked under the umbrella of EFB Enterprises. But he did have the power to say no.

What I really wanted, was a good week of service and profit under my belt before I explained all the reasons he needed to change everything. But it didn't look like that was going to happen anytime soon.

I needed to hard sell this thing. And fast. Before the major change that happened was a closed sign in the front window.

I still had no idea why he thought I could be the one to save this place. Surely, he knew more talented and experienced chefs... Surely, there had been more prominent people interested in the position.

Bottom line, I didn't know what the hell I was doing.

He walked into the kitchen looking all kinds of business. I smoothed my hair back in the wild messy bun that seemed like the best option this morning but I was now regretting, and adjusted the bandana I'd tied around the front.

"Hey, big brother," I said to him, nerves already fluttering in my stomach.

His hard gaze relaxed some and he smiled at me. "How's it going?"

I swallowed the oversized lump of fear in my throat and shrugged. "I'm still alive."

"Have I told you lately that I'm beyond grateful for you?"

"Once or twice." His words soothed some of the pain in my chest. "You know I'd do literally anything for you right? Like actually anything. A kidney. Half my liver. Seriously, running this restaurant for you is easy-peasy."

His smile wobbled. "That's good news, because I have another favor to ask of you."

My eyes narrowed on instinct. This didn't sound promising. And now he was fidgeting! Ezra never fidgeted. Like ever. He was always one hundred percent comfortable with who he was and what he wanted. "I'm nervous," I admitted—because he looked nervous.

"Molly wants to host a brunch. At our place."

"Okay..."

"This Sunday."

"Okay..."

"She'd like you to come."

"That sounds fun. I'd love to come."

His hand swiped over his mouth, the telltale gesture that he was second-guessing himself. "The thing is, she's invited a few other people."

"Vera and Killian?"

"They're on their honeymoon."

"Oh, right. So, Wyatt and Kaya?"

He nodded. "And Vann Delane."

Ezra's anxiety made sense now. "Ah."

"She told me not to make it a big deal. But she wanted you to have all the facts." His hands dropped to his hips and he suddenly looked like our dad. "Is there something I need to know about you and Vann Delane?"

Oh lord, not this. I blinked at him innocently. "What do you mean?"

"Why did Molly want me to warn you about Vann Delane coming over?"

There were about three hundred things I'd rather do than talk to my brother about my effed up dating life. One was getting a Brazilian. Another was getting audited by an anal IRS agent. "Who knows. Molly gets stressed about weird stuff all the time."

"That's true."

"And stop calling him Vann Delane. You know him by now. Surely you're on a first name basis."

He shrugged, staring at the dish I'd been experimenting with in front of me—a croque monsieur that I'd made with heirloom tomatoes, jalapeno jam, and gruyere cheese. I couldn't decide whether to add thinly sliced prosciutto or thick slices of peppered bacon.

"I don't know," Ezra admitted. "I thought we were too, but now Molly is going to all these lengths to put on the perfect brunch and make sure you're there and he's there… It feels right to move back to when things were formal and unfamiliar."

I laughed at his silly overprotectiveness. "You're ridiculous, you know that, right?"

He nodded. He did know that. "So, should I tell her you'll be there?"

"Let's trade favors," I suggested. Sucking in a shaky breath, I set my knife down and planted my hands on the counter. "I want to change things up here."

His eyebrows furrowed over his nose. "What do you mean? Like the menu?"

"I mean, like a lot of things." I launched into a pitch about the menu change, honing in on my casual French philosophy and then adding in the brunch idea and a couple different happy hour suggestions the staff had helped me come up with.

"You don't want to change the menu, you want to restructure the entire restaurant from top to bottom."

Nibbling my bottom lip, I decided honesty was better than blowing smoke up his ass. "This place is failing, Ezra. You know that. You probably know that more than anybody. You hired me to fix that for you. I've only been here a little while, but it's been long enough to understand that what we're doing now isn't working. Not even a little bit. This place needs an overhaul or it's going to fail. And I would really, really like for my first time as captain to not be of a sinking ship."

He smiled, his eyes flashing with awe. "I would like that for you too."

"Will you sign off on the changes?"

"You want to change a lot, Dillon. And those changes sound pricey," he argued, shifting back into the frugal, domineering business genius I knew him to be.

"But if the changes bring in more clientele, they'll pay for themselves. Right now, not changing isn't an option. I don't know how much longer you can go on bleeding money like this, but if I were you and there were other options available, I would at least explore them." He appeared to be listening intently, so I pushed on. "And the brunch thing doesn't have to be permanent. We have the freedom to explore it and then pull back if we're doing better in the evenings. But I've done my research in this area, Ez, and there aren't upscale brunch or breakfast spots in this area. But there are a lot of churches. Which means a lot of people out and about during the breakfast hours on Sunday. This could work."

He stared at me. "I hate when you call me Ez."

I smiled, I couldn't help it. "Or it could fail," I answered honestly. "Friendly reminder that I don't know what the heck I'm doing. I'm just trying to save your restaurant."

"Hey, this is your restaurant now too."

Ignoring him, I added, "I think Molly could sell this on social media. She'll weave her promo web like the killer spider she is, and we'll give Bianca a renewed look. A younger, fresher, more hipster image. And we'll catch everyone. The entire freaking city."

"I'm impressed," he said. My insides beamed from his praise. I would never let him know, but his praise meant the absolute world to me. It always would. "I mean, you have no real numbers or figures. But you seem to have thought about it a lot."

The feeling of impressing him shriveled inside me. "You can't keep the restaurant the way she is. You have to do something."

His hand was back to his face, rubbing his jawline. "I'm inclined to believe you."

"Yes, do it," I pushed. "If we don't turn things around or make money, we'll go back to this way. This... outdated, geriatric, sad way."

A surprised laugh burst out of him and he shook his head at me. "All right. Tit for tat. Call Molly. Figure it out." He pointed a finger at me. "Just don't rub my face in it when you're wildly successful and make me millions."

He already had millions, but I decided now wasn't the time to mention that. Instead, I placed a delicate hand on my heart and promised, "I would never."

"Yeah, yeah." Taking a step back, he added, "I'm working out of Lilou today. See you Sunday. Molly said don't come before ten."

"I'll bring mimosas."

"Don't you have to work later that day?"

I shrugged. "I'm at my best when I'm a little tipsy."

Dad voice was back. "Dillon..."

"I kid, I kid." He shot me his most parental scowl but left me to it. He knew me better than that. Although if Vann was going to be there, then maybe I wasn't kidding after all.

Blaze walked in the kitchen a few minutes later, arms full of a delivery he must have met outside. "Morning, Chef."

"We got the okay!" I told him, as excited as I had ever been.

He set his crates on the counter and looked at me quizzically. "The okay for what?"

"The menu changes. Goodbye outdated French fare. Hello casual and chic! Ezra's even on board with the brunch switch up. You and I are going to have to sit down at the computer today and figure out the schedule later. And nobody is going to be happy at first. This is going to take an adjustment. But in time I think it will be better for everyone."

"Seriously?" He blinked at me. "He okayed all of it?"

I couldn't tell if he was excited or pissed. True, he hadn't been super on board with the brunch idea in the first place, but I thought it was because he didn't believe that Ezra would let me do it over any negative feelings he had for the concept. Maybe I had read the room wrong...

My smile dropped. "All of it. I'm going to set up a meeting with his social media guru next week to develop an online plan. I want to launch this thing like the opening of a brand-new restaurant." I thought about it for a second and then added, "Basically, I want to erase Bianca entirely and start new."

His face looked pained for a second. Confusion and remorse and fear flashed in alternating shades. I started to worry he was about to tell me what an idiot I was and how stupid this idea was. When he finally spoke, the words rushed out of his mouth in a raw confession. "I got an offer."

My bubbling excitement screeched to a halt. "What?"

"Another job offer," he explained. "After Ashlynn quit, I guess word got out that things were not, er, great here. Not that anyone has ever believed that we had our house in order. But... anyway, one of my buddies mentioned to his boss that I might be looking for something and they called with a position on Sunday."

He'd been sitting on this for days. Which meant he was seriously considering it. Damn.

"Where?" He didn't have to tell me, but if I was losing the one chef in this kitchen I could count on, I felt like I had a right to know.

"Sunday House."

Okay, that was a legitimately wonderful restaurant. Quite frankly, a full step up from flailing Bianca. "Oh."

"Listen, I don't know what I'm going to do yet. I just... I wanted you to know."

The elation I'd felt moments ago turned sour in my stomach. "I can't offer you more as far as salary goes. I wish that I could, but—"

He held up his hand, quick to stop me. "I'm not leveraging, Chef. I swear. I just... I wanted you to know what was going on."

He meant he wanted me to know what was going on because he was leaving. If he knew I couldn't leverage a better offer and he'd been thinking about it since Sunday, the logical conclusion was that this was his resignation.

Still, I was going to make him say it, because somehow this was worse than firing Ashlynn. Somehow, taking the control out of my hand and having someone willingly walk away, was infinitely worse. "So is this like your two weeks or..."

"Not yet," he promised.

"When do you have to give them an answer?"

He held my gaze. "They didn't give me a date. It was kind of an open-ended proposal."

Which meant they really, really wanted him. "And if I decide to let you go first?" It was a catty and unrealistic response.

He saw through me immediately. "You can't afford to let me go."

"But you might leave anyway."

His mouth pressed into a deeper frown. "This isn't personal."

Letting out a trembling breath, I nodded my head. He was right. I knew he was right. He knew he was right. This wasn't personal. He was doing the best thing for his career. Had Wyatt thrown a huge hissy fit when I left Lilou to pursue better things for myself? Nope. He'd wished me well and offered to help whenever I needed him.

The problem was that Blaze had more experience than me. I couldn't exactly send him off by telling him to call me day or night if he needed anything. He'd probably block my number afraid I'd be the one calling him at all hours of the night, drunkenly begging him to come back.

"I know," I told him. And it was sincere. "I know this isn't personal. You have to do what's best for you and your career. And honestly, Sunday House is that." I held up my hands, gesturing around at the recently gleaming kitchen. "I wish it was Bianca. I wish I had more to offer you as far as career path or head chef or whatever, all of it. But I'm glad Sunday House recognized your incredible talent. And I wish you the best."

"I haven't quit yet," he reminded me, his frown somehow even more pronounced.

I waved him off. Yeah, he hadn't quit yet, but he was going to. Saying goodbye now would save me the pain and heartache later.

And the existential crisis when Bianca started to circle the drain.

"Okay. You're right." I smiled, but it was watery and thin. "Think about it. Let me know what you decide. I'd love it if you stayed on at least through the menu transition to brunch. But think about that too and let me know what you decide."

His expression softened and I couldn't stand the look of pity staring back at me. "Okay, I will."

Mustering all the false bravado I could gather on such short notice, I widened my smile and brushed loose hair away from my face. "Until then, we have an entire menu to overhaul. We need to get working."

He nodded. "Yes, Chef. Where do you want me to start?"

"I want to change the menu tonight, Blaze. Like a few hours from now. We'll use the office printer and make a temporary menu until we settle on a permanent lineup. I may need you to run to the store, depending on what we have and don't have around here. There should be some change-ups to our regular order in the delivery. I had been planning to test different things. But I'm feeling in the mood to mix things up tonight."

"You want to change the menu tonight?" The panic in his voice resonated through the kitchen, but it was the look of utter disbelief that made me truly question my decision.

If I had been hoping to charm him with my adorable ignorance, I'd already failed. Blaze didn't want to start a new menu tonight. He wanted to tweak the old one. Which was the smart business decision to make.

But I was in a mood for chaos. I wanted to make a statement. I wanted to announce to the city that I would no longer tolerate business per usual. Bianca was officially under new management. And if I was going down with the ship, we were going to make as big of a splash as possible in the process.

I must have smiled, because Blaze's expression only became more concerned. "Are you okay, Chef?"

"I'm great," I told him. I wasn't sure if I meant it or not, but I was currently adopting the fake it till you make it philosophy I knew and loved so well. "Let's get to work."

To be honest, by the end of the day, I barely survived crawling into my bed. And I didn't even bother taking off my shoes.

It had been fourteen hours of pure insanity. Scrambling all morning to figure out five dishes we could serve tonight that did not resemble slop. Plus, three appetizers, two salads and four side dishes.

I rolled over and stared at my ceiling, my arms too heavy to lift and my legs sore and overworked thanks to the combination of spin class and hard day. But the pain felt good.

I'd worked hard today. Blaze had worked hard today. It was like he felt guilty for threatening to leave, so he was trying to make it up to me. Which I was absolutely okay with. I would suck every single ounce of go-getter out of him. And then go up in flames as soon as he left.

Regardless of the impending doom, I couldn't help but feel amazing about service tonight. We had more meal compliments sent back to the kitchen than ever. In the history of cooking. Or at least in the history of Bianca.

Our diners loved tonight's menu. And while it was far from pretty or perfect back in the kitchen, we were able to serve plates that had been executed to hit our diners straight in the taste buds.

Granted, each plate we served was tweaked a little differently than the last one, but they all tasted great. And in a yelling, sweaty, chaotic kind of way, it was fine.

I needed a shower. At the very least, I needed to kick off my greasy shoes. But I couldn't summon the energy. I closed my eyes and drifted to sleep where I had dreams of beautiful food and a bustling restaurant and a man that told me I was too beautiful before he gave me the best sex of my entire life.

SEVENTEEN

"YOU'RE EARLY!" Molly complained. "I told Ezra to tell you not before ten."

I smiled at her efforts to slide a coffee cake ring onto a decorative plate. "I can't help it." I stuck a finger under the front of the pastry and helped her unstick it from the butcher paper beneath it. "Just like you can't help always running late."

She rolled her eyes and sucked on her thumb. "You can help it," she mumbled around frosting. "Turn on Netflix or something. It's simple."

"I don't even know where to start on that thing. Some of us don't have the luxury of binge watching anything but our bank account getting bigger."

She laughed at my trophy wife dig. "Some of us get to binge watch Netflix and our bank account. You just have to marry money, honey."

"Ezra!" I called out. "Your gold-digging girlfriend is making fun of me."

He popped his head over the balcony where their bedroom was located. "I told you not to come early."

I shrugged again and repeated, "I can't help it."

He disappeared upstairs, and I pulled my organic orange juice and bottle of cheap champagne from the tote at my feet. Waving one in each hand, I smiled at Molly and asked, "Forgive me?"

She reached for the ten-dollar champagne. "You brought the good stuff!"

From Vera that would have been sarcasm, but I had Molly's number. She blended into Ezra's life effortlessly, but the girl preferred Taco Bell and bargain bin wine. She had no palate for the good stuff.

Just another reason to love her to pieces.

"Who all is coming?" I asked, taking a look around at egg bake and quiche and piles of donuts. This was enough to feed an army. Or to put six people into a seventy-year carb coma.

"Uh, you and me."

I looked at her. "Okay, I figured that much."

"And Ezra."

"This is a lot of food for the three of us."

She tried to hide her smile but failed. "I just wasn't sure. The menu got away from me. I ordered one quiche, but then I wasn't sure if everyone liked spinach. So, I ordered a second. And then that egg bake looked amazing. And I couldn't decide about the donuts and here we are."

"Babe, we're all foodies. We'll literally eat anything just to try it."

"Not anything," she aptly pointed out.

"As long as you didn't make it yourself, we'll literally eat anything."

She slapped me with the kitchen towel that had been over her shoulder. "Now you're going to have to eat all of this. So, I hope you're happy." She moved quickly around the kitchen, gathering all the packaging and tell-tale signs she wasn't the chef behind this breakfast feast.

Not that the guests wouldn't figure that out within seconds of stepping in this place.

Unless she invited people we didn't know to breakfast. Leave it up to Molly to gather strangers in her home just so the food didn't go to waste.

"Kaya and Wyatt," she added.

"Is that everyone?"

"And Vann." The doorbell rang before I could interrogate her further. "Better get that," she told me.

"Ezra already told me you invited him." She threw a huge, pacifying grin over her shoulder. "I think you misunderstood me the other morning. I wasn't asking you to play matchmaker."

Ignoring me, she pulled open the door and greeted Wyatt and Kaya. "Good morning!"

I leaned over from where I stood in the kitchen and waved. "What up, bitches."

Wyatt waved back and Kaya did a little dance. "Goooood, morning," she sang out.

Joining me in the kitchen, they surveyed the spread with wide eyes. "Did you invite everybody in Durham?" Wyatt asked.

"Har, har," Molly returned. "I don't feed large quantities of people on a regular basis, so I'm new to these things."

Wyatt picked up a donut. "We'll find a way to manage somehow." He grabbed a second donut and a took a bite out of each. "I mean, an excessive number of donuts is hardly a crisis."

"We can host next time," Kaya added.

"Next time?"

"It should be monthly, don't you think? Otherwise we're never going to see each other."

That was true. We were all at different restaurants now and basically had zero free time. If we didn't plan something like this on the regular, I would be destined to a solitary life of cats and constantly throwing away leftovers that were too much for one person.

Not exactly the life I hoped to lead.

"I'm in," I volunteered immediately. Although my stomach

dropped a bit at the realization that if I started brunch at Bianca, I couldn't actually be in. I would have to be out. Very, very out.

"Me too!" Molly agreed.

"You're in charge of the pastries," Kaya told her. "You'll probably be able to freeze everything we don't eat and bring it over."

Wyatt grabbed a third donut. "We probably have enough here for the next... thirty to forty brunches."

Molly threw a donut hole at him, but he ducked and caught it in his mouth. "Not if we keep inviting you, Wyatt. You're like the donut version of Cookie Monster."

Ezra bounded down the stairs and joined us. "Stop giving Molly a hard time," he ordered, wrapping his arms around her immediately. "She orchestrated this all by herself. I'm proud of her."

And then he kissed her on the top of her head, painting them as the most perfect couple of all time.

My stomach dropped further, like it had been trapped in a faulty elevator shaft right before it plummeted eighty stories to its death.

She looked up at him, gazing at my brother like he had hung the stars in the sky. "I told you when you first met me that ordering takeout was one of my top life skills."

He nudged her nose with his. "That you did."

Moved by the romance in the room, Kaya leaned on Wyatt. He wrapped his arm around her, his hand still clutching a half-eaten donut.

Good thing I hadn't eaten anything yet. Or I would have puked it up all over.

Ugh, what was it about couples that made me simultaneously want to be in one and swear on all that was holy that I would never be ooey gooey like these mushy love birds?

Thankfully, there was a knock on the door, and I didn't have to dry-heave my loneliness all over Ezra's kitchen floor.

"I'll get it!" I moved before anyone could talk me out of it. Conversation continued in the kitchen, but I tuned it out, assuming they were all declaring their undying love for each other and blah, blah, blah.

I ripped open the door. Vann stood on the other side. The temperature instantly dropped, and goosebumps rose all over my arms.

We stood there for a prolonged moment, time and space and all the universe ceasing to exist as we tried to figure out what to do next.

"Brunch?" he eventually said, holding up a netted bag of Clementine's.

He hadn't shaved this morning. There was stubble roughing up his usually smooth jawline. And he had ditched his preppy look for a navy-blue Cycle Life t-shirt, a pair of gray sweatpants and a loose stocking cap. God, it was unfair how sexy he looked.

And this should not be a sexy look, by the way. I had only ever been exposed to the buttoned-up, I-have-a-trust-fund-and-private-plane gentleman attire. And because those were the kind of men I had previously dated, they were the only ones I had experience with. I imagined a man that could take me to a five-star dinner and be able to afford the tip. I thought I wanted the nice car and country club membership and standing golf outings with his college buddies.

Vann, like this, was the opposite of everything I knew about men.

And yet...

I licked dry lips and tried to keep my breathing steady. "This way." I gestured toward the kitchen.

He stepped inside the door but didn't move beyond the entryway. "I didn't know you were going to be here," he confessed in a low murmur.

I leaned in, accidentally inhaling his freshly showered smell. "I did know you were going to be here," I whispered. All I could smell now was crisp soap, men's deodorant, and citrus. It had completely stolen my ability to lie.

Or think clearly.

He flinched, my words sparking curiosity. "Thought we were

going separate directions, Baptiste. But you keep finding ways to run into me."

Some of my senses came back at his accusation. I stood straighter, realizing I had been totally crowding him. "The gym was an accident." It was an accident. "And it wasn't like I could tell Ezra no when he invited me to brunch. Although, be on guard, Molly's trying to set us up."

Something flashed across his face, but it happened so fast, I couldn't grab the emotion and put a name to it. "Seems about right. I think we're the only single people she knows."

"We'll just have to make it clear we're not interested in each other," I told him. "So, she doesn't keep trying."

Leaning in, his chest bumped my shoulder and it was all I could do to remain completely still. Lest I do something ridiculous like shiver. Or swoon. Or tackle him to the ground and start dry-humping him. "You're not interested in me," he murmured, quietly enough that the kitchen couples couldn't hear him. "If I remember correctly. I was totally up for a more memorable round two."

The devil was all over his mischievous face when he backed away, a snarky challenge sparking in his eyes.

My cheeks flamed red, embarrassment burned like a wildfire in my blood. "Were you now?"

"You're the one that put on the brakes, Dillon. Not me."

I gaped at him as he pranced into the kitchen all high and mighty.

Okay, he didn't prance.

But he might as well have. Cocky bastard.

Everyone cheered for Vann's oranges, like he'd managed something spectacular. But hello? I brought the cheap champagne.

I filled my plate with quiche and a Bavarian crème and a kruller —because I wanted to make Molly feel better for buying all these pastries, obvi.

And fine, I grabbed an orange too. But that was more to ward off the very real and present threat of scurvy than because I wanted to make Vann feel like people actually wanted what he brought.

We gathered around Ezra's table, our plates laden with good food and carbs and love. Mimosas and hot mugs of coffee were passed around and great conversation commenced.

I could tell Vann was a little nervous, except around Molly. These weren't his regular people apparently. And we were a little short-staffed without Vera and Killian present.

He'd ended up in the seat directly across from me and so every once in a while, I would catch his eye and we would look away quickly, pretending we didn't notice each other.

What was I supposed to do with this guy?

He was right. I had put on the brakes. Immediately.

But now I wasn't so sure that was the best idea. I was clearly attracted to him. I liked to flirt with him. I liked to look at him. I would like to know if I liked to do other things with him...

That same drunken image of his naked body over mine flashed in my head.

I shook my head and took a sip of coffee. "Dillon's thinking about switching up the weekend at Bianca and doing brunch instead of supper."

Everyone looked at me, eyebrows raised in surprise.

"Bianca needs a new approach," I explained with a shrug. "What we're doing right now isn't working. I need to make some big changes. And fast."

"When are you thinking of changing things up?" Kaya asked.

"Soon." I looked at Molly. "I'd like to jumpstart the change with a social media campaign."

She nodded excitedly. "Of course. I love the idea. It would be such a good location for breakfast. And all that natural light and white décor. That place was built for Saturday mornings on Instagram."

I smiled at her praise. She wasn't exactly the food expert in the group, but she was exactly my target market. Her enthusiasm was encouraging.

"That's a good call, Dillon," Wyatt put in. "It might be a hard adjustment for your staff though."

"We've been talking about it quite a bit. I have some strategies we're going to try. Worst case, I hire a few additional servers and line cooks. It should be a pretty simple menu. I want uncomplicated elegance."

"Casual French is how she pitched it to me," Ezra added. Then shrugged, his expression melting into admiration. "The concept is impossible not to love. Hopefully execution is as easily embraced."

I felt Vann's stare all over my skin, making me hot and hyper aware of him and stupidly nervous. "Hopefully," I said meekly.

"Thinking like a real head chef now, huh?" Vann's voice held this note of gloating that made me immediately furious.

And overly warm.

Leaning forward, I toyed with my empty champagne glass. "You know, since I am one."

His smirk was unsurprising, but just as smug. "I'm impressed, Dillon."

"That makes me feel so much better. Now that you're impressed, Vann."

He rested his elbows on the table, dipping his head so we were exactly eye level. "I assumed that was your goal. Impressing me."

My jaw snapped shut, my teeth clacking together in frustration. I shot him a tight-lipped smile. He hid his grin behind a sip of coffee.

I narrowed my eyes at him. He opened his, all wide-eyed innocence.

The rest of the table watched us like a tennis match, their heads bouncing back and forth.

I turned to Ezra and smiled sweetly. "I guess I have you to thank."

"For what?" he asked smoothly, trying to smother a laugh at my expense.

"For making me a real head chef."

Ezra shrugged. "I don't think you can credit me with any of what you're doing at the restaurant. That's all you."

I shoved a bite of abandoned donut in my mouth and tried to act normal. Between all the compliments and support and Vann's teasing and gloating and just all-around presence, I was completely frazzled. If I was a bird all my feathers would be ruffled right now. All of them. Every last one.

"There was a time I would have thought this was impossible," Ezra continued. Fresh embarrassment descended like a tsunami. "Now here you are, telling *me* how you're going to run *my* restaurant."

I knew he meant well. I knew this was a moment of genuine love and affection coming from my older brother. But did it need to happen right now? With Vann here? And all these other people?

Of course, Vann didn't take the polite, socially acceptable way out. Oh, no. He had to poke the hornet's nest. "Why do you say that?"

Ezra had no embarrassment meter. I didn't even think he knew how to feel embarrassed. There was not a gauge inside him warning him when to slow down or stop. He just plowed onward, ticking up quite the body count behind him.

Today was the first time I'd been considered a real-life casualty. But that didn't make it easier.

"Because Dillon used to be wild. She couldn't hold a job, let alone manage a restaurant." His voice sobered, losing the humorous edge he'd had seconds ago. "Honestly, there was a time, I thought I was going to lose her." I glared at him and he flinched, realizing he'd said too much. "But now look at you, sis." His tone was peppy with renewed energy, hoping to cover for his unwanted trip down memory lane. "You pulled it together."

"Thanks, Ez." I only used his nickname to irritate the bejesus out of him. "But we don't have to rehash any of that today. Or any day. Or ever..."

Vann's ears perked up like a hunting dog on the scent. "Must have been a pretty scary time though. I mean, especially as her brother."

Ezra nodded.

I was going to murder Vann.

"It killed me when Vera was with Derrek the Dick," Vann spit out. "I felt totally helpless."

I noticed Molly throwing shade from down the line and was thankful for my one ally. Even if she didn't say anything. Ezra didn't even notice Vann's backhanded tactics.

"Sisters, man," Ezra sighed.

"All right, I think that's enough of the big brother support group," I said, standing up to clear plates. It was officially time to get the hell out of dodge. "You two can meet next month. Ezra, it's your turn to supply the shitty lemonade."

Vann looked straight at me and I swear there was a twinkle in his gray, gray eyes. "Whoa, I'm sorry if I offended you. I can just relate to Ezra. That's all I was saying. I know what it's like to care for somebody, watching them struggle and not be able to do anything about it."

"Especially when they don't want help," Ezra added.

"I didn't need help," I argued, hating that we were having this discussion even after I'd tried so hard to get away from it. "I was fine."

"Now you're fine," Ezra called after me as I stomped toward the kitchen. "You know what you were like six years ago. You know that wasn't fine. Not even fucking close."

There was a weighted silence as his words hung in the air, effectively piquing everyone's curiosity and ripping me wide open.

I heard Molly whisper a forced, "Ezra, drop it." But other than that, nobody spoke for a long time.

Shoving my dishes beneath the faucet and letting them clatter in the sink, I wrenched the faucet on and wished Ezra's apartment had more privacy.

Taking a deep breath, I knew I had to say something. I couldn't just let the morning end like this. Besides, it was six years ago.

Six whole years.

I should be better at this by now.

Why wasn't I better at this?

Popping back into the open dining room, I plastered on a fake smile and looked at my friends sitting in tense silence.

"I used to be wild," I told them in an obvious sort of way. "I know that surprises all of you, but I lived out my college years... well, like I was in college. I drank too much. I partied too much. I did a lot of things that were too much. But I'm better now. I grew out of it. There's nothing to worry about anymore."

It was clear that Ezra didn't fully believe my quick attitude change and pacifying smile, but after the hell I'd put him through during my early-twenties, I knew he might never truly trust that I was all the way okay ever again.

And he didn't even know the worst of it.

Kaya waved me off. "I had no idea you liked to drink. I guess we can finally be best friends. I was waiting for you to become a borderline alcoholic. And now I have the final piece of the puzzle."

I smiled at her candidness, feeling marginally better.

Molly laughed too and said, "The first time I ever met Dillon, she told me 'parties were like her thing.' It's important to know your strengths."

I smiled a little wider, but the pressure in my chest was still suffocating. Sweat broke out on the back of my neck and I felt unwanted hands crawl up my legs.

"I'm going to go," I nearly shouted, desperate for some peace and quiet. "Thanks for brunch, Molls. I'll, uh, call you later." I took three steps backward. "You too, Kaya. Bye, Wyatt. Ezra." I reluctantly looked at the big old elephant in the room and briefly met his eyes before grabbing my purse off a stool and pretending to search for my keys. "Vann. Bye, everyone."

I escaped their calls of goodbye and practically sprinted from the building. I wasn't usually this jumpy when someone brought up my past, but the combined presence of Ezra and Vann made shit too real for ten a.m.

"Dillon!"

Apparently, my quick exit, Wile E. Coyote style, wasn't enough of a message for Vann. I glanced over my shoulder to find him chasing after me. And damn, his eyebrows were scrunched together. He had something to say too.

I waved at him, my keys gripped tightly in my hands. "Oh, hey. Sorry, I need to get to work. We haven't switched over to brunch yet, so I have a lot of prep that still has to happen."

He jogged faster. "Hey, stop for a minute."

My door unlocked and if I wouldn't have hesitated like a fool, I could have totally thrown my body across the driver's seat and locked the doors before he caught up to me.

But he was running. In that t-shirt and sweatpants. And damn it, I got distracted.

His fingers wrapped around the top of my doorframe, holding it open. "Hey, would you slow down?"

I shook my head. No. No, I would not. "I really have to go."

"So, you're like a runner?"

I blinked at him, trying to make sense of his words. "Usually, I'm a yoga-er. But I've been looking to get a little more in shape. Hence the spin class."

He smiled. It was blinding in the morning light. Breathtaking. Nerve-racking. Life changing. "That's not what I meant. You run. You have one-night stands because you don't want commitment."

I frowned. He was not going to figure me out this morning. Especially when he was only working with partial information. Not after the shit he'd just put me through upstairs. "No, I don't have time for commitment. I work every night. And all day. And basically, all of the minutes of my life. I have time for one-night stands." Those violent hands started to inch up over my bare legs again. I kicked one foot out, shaking my leg just to get the haunting sensation to stop. "And I just don't... I don't have one-night stands either. Like ever." Remembering Ezra's tell-all novel upstairs, I was forced to amend. "Anymore anyway. Once upon a time maybe, but that stopped."

"Six years ago?"

"Excuse me?"

His look gentled, but his smile warmed, and I hated that it made me want to open up to him. Nobody should have that kind of power in a smile. "Listen, I feel like I misjudged you."

"You've actually misjudged me since you met me."

He ignored my snark. "And I'd like to start over. Or try again. Or... I don't know what I want to do. But I feel bad for what just happened."

He felt sorry for me is what he meant. "I grew up, Vann. That's all that happened. I lived this kind of wild, party girl life and then I woke up one day and I realized I couldn't keep living my life like that. I couldn't keep... going with zero responsibility and zero commitment and zero anything to live for. I needed goals and a purpose and..." I ran a hand over my hair, trying to smooth it down as the wind ruffled it. "My dad had just died. I didn't know how to cope. And my mom was a mess. And I never had any boundaries growing up. So I just... I did things I'm not proud of. But that phase of my life is over now. And even if Ezra doesn't believe me, I've spent the last six years trying to prove it to him."

His smile disappeared. Along with that warm and melty look in his eyes. Now he just looked concerned. Damn, I really messed this up.

"Sounds like there was a lot going on," he noted.

"There was," I agreed, unable to meet his eyes. "A lot going on."

His hand shot out and grabbed mine, holding it gently in his. He bent his knees so that we were eye level. His gentle grasp and the thumb rubbing over my knuckles coaxed me to look at him. "I'm sorry you had to go through a rough time, Dillon. I'm sorrier you thought you had to cope that way."

I found that I couldn't swallow. Or retract my hand. Or do anything but sway closer to him. "I-it-it's not your fault. I didn't even know you then."

He held my gaze. "Regardless. I'm sorry life was so awful for you. I'm sorry your dad died. I'm sorry that you felt the only way to fix any of it was to drink or party or whatever. I'm sorry for all of it."

What I really wanted to do was throw my arms around him and cry into his neck. I wanted him to hold me for the next seven years while my heart healed and my mind unfragmented and all the memories of that lifestyle died.

Instead of acknowledging his kindness or how much his words had affected me, I took a step back and tossed my purse to the passenger side. "I need to go."

"Runner," he whispered, and I knew he was smiling before I even looked at him.

"So what if I am?" I asked, finally understanding what he meant.

He shrugged, shoving his hands into his pockets and looking too adorable for his own good. "I'm just glad to know it's not my skills in bed."

I leaned back toward him, relishing the flirty space we'd found again. "It might be though. You don't really know, do you?"

His smile died and his signature frown took its place. "No, I guess I don't."

I stepped back, getting as close to the car as possible. "I'm saying... Maybe you shouldn't say no to free advice."

His concerned gaze turned into a very serious frown. "Are you saying you remember?"

I shook my head, not wanting to admit that it didn't matter if I did. He'd broken my celibacy streak but that didn't mean I was ready to make it a regular thing. "Sorry." I shrugged and inched closer to my car. "Good thing you're not looking for a nice girl."

He followed me, leaning into the car door—the only thing between us. "You're not a nice girl, Dillon."

That shiver was back, rolling down my spine and bringing heat with it. "That's not what you said before."

"I was wrong."

I sucked in a deep breath and dropped to my driver's seat, afraid of what would happen if we kept talking. "Bye, Vann."

"Bye, Dillon."

I drove away from Ezra's apartment feeling completely unsettled. My emotions warred inside my chest. And in my head.

This wasn't fair. He wasn't playing fair.

He'd told me I was a nice girl and he wasn't interested in nice girls. He'd said that. Not me.

So, when I dropped my guard, it was under that assumption—that he wasn't interested in me. And now what was he saying? That he did like me?

My hands tightened around the steering wheel until my knuckles turned white. "I like him too," I told the empty car.

Duh.

Sometimes I had to say the most obvious things out loud before I believed them. But the truth was, I liked Vann. I really liked him.

But so, what? I'd had crushes since... since I stopped dating. They'd never pursued me like this though. They'd never gotten me to sleep with them.

They'd never crawled so completely beneath my skin all I could think about was them.

Was it worth trying something with Vann?

What if I just... went for it?

I used to be spontaneous. I used to be wild and reckless and devil-may-care.

And it had gotten me into trouble. When I'd walked away from that lifestyle, I promised myself I would never do anything haphazardly again. I would never jump into something without gauging how deep the water was. I would never walk out on a limb without knowing if it could hold me. I would never just act and hope it worked out.

Never again.

Bianca was the closest thing I'd done in the last six years to an uncalculated risk, but I'd been weighing my options for almost the same amount of time. Even if the final decision was sort of thrust on me, it had been an internal conversation for years.

And what about Vann? Surely I didn't need another six years to decide if I wanted to take a chance on him or not.

He was a risk—the biggest kind.

But was he worth it?

My mind said no. My mind remembered the consequences from my life before. My mind knew how badly men could hurt, how easily they could destroy.

My heart argued a different story.

There was just something about him that I wanted more of. I couldn't help it. Vann Delane was different. And I wanted to get to know everything about him.

Including what he was really like in bed.

EIGHTEEN

VANN WAS EVERYWHERE AFTER THAT. Or maybe I hadn't noticed him before. Maybe he'd been in my life for a while, but I'd been so focused on surviving that I hadn't paid attention to him.

Regardless, he was here now.

When Vera and Killian got back from their honeymoon, he was at the airport to greet them. When I joined Molly for spin class three mornings a week, he was there. When I went to the organic grocery store near my house, he was there. Picking up more oranges.

And the worst part? It was impossible to ignore the man. Not when he looked so adorably happy to see his sister. Or so deliciously sweaty after an hour of medieval-leg-and-butt-torture. And especially not when he carefully picked out his oranges, bringing each one to his nose and smelling them to make sure he was getting a good one.

Trust me, I tried to ignore him. And pretend I didn't see him. But it was impossible. He was everywhere.

But most especially he was in my bones, in my very blood.

Because even when I didn't see him, I thought about him.

I thought about him in the morning, when I woke up way earlier than I wanted to. I thought about him during prep, when I would have to get tough with an employee or make a hard decision. I thought about him when I went home to a lonely bed and empty apartment. I thought about him when I got a hit on my online dating app that Kaya had set me up with a year ago and I never used, and it wasn't him.

I couldn't stop thinking about him.

The only time I managed to think about anything else was when I was planning the dishes for our soon-to-open brunch menu. Then, and only then, could I wrap my head around grilled asparagus wrapped in paper thin slices of heirloom tomatoes and rich prosciutto. He couldn't infiltrate my poached egg in sourdough with sriracha hollandaise and everything bagel seasoning. Nor could he come close to my version of a croque madame with grapefruit jelly, crispy pork belly, creamy comté, and an over easy egg on brioche.

Casual French food was the only thing saving my life right now. Both personally and professionally.

I glanced at Cycle Life as I crossed the street in front of it. Lilou was currently having some work done to the parking lot, so I'd been forced to park my car closer to Vann's shop than the restaurant I needed to borrow lettuce from.

All romaine lettuce was currently confiscated as nationwide outbreaks of E. Coli rocked the food industry. People were getting sick like crazy and all romaine had gone through an emergency recall.

Since we'd quickly thrown all our lettuce away, I was currently on the hunt for substitutes. Thankfully, due to a clerical error and Wyatt's hunt for a better sous chef than Benny who made the clerical error, they had ordered an obscene amount of butter lettuce. Which he graciously offered to share with me at the low, low price of my eternal soul.

When I had refused to sell my non-physical body parts to him, he'd said, "Okay, then just come back and be my sous chef again so I'm not stuck with so much fucking butter lettuce. I'm contemplating lighting it all on fire."

When I'd said, "That much, huh?"

He'd replied with a casual, "Maybe I'll light Benny on fire instead."

Which led me to rushing over in hopes that I could take some of the dreaded butter lettuce off Wyatt's hands and save Benny from being burned at the stake.

I was also checking out Cycle Life to see if Vann was anywhere to be seen, while keeping a low profile and working the totally aloof angle.

Basically, I was looking anywhere but where I was going. And that was a tragedy. Because one second, I was playing the role of super spy while I walked casually down the sidewalk in Louboutin Mary Janes I would never usually wear to work and a sun dress that flared in all the best spots. And the next second, my arms flew wildly in the air as I totally biffed it.

I was pretty sure I screamed too.

Because one could not fall the way I just had, my dress going up over my head, my knees meeting the pavement with a hard thwack and my palms following shortly after, without screaming bloody murder.

This was Molly's fault. Because of my crazy schedule, we'd met for breakfast to go over our marketing plan. And then news of the romaine had come in the form of a panicked text from Blaze, causing me to swing into Bianca instead of going home to change first. Now I was at Lilou—well, almost to Lilou—and my timeline was shrinking.

And I twisted my ankle.

Damn, that hurt!

I gingerly picked myself up from my sprawled position and attempted to untangle my ankle. It didn't budge.

"What the hell?"

Attempt number two of standing up, didn't go any better. I looked back to see the stupidly pointy heel of my shoe trapped in a cut out on the manhole cover I'd just walked over.

Pulling my leg harder proved futile. I was well and truly stuck.

I would have to unstrap my shoe to get it out. But I'd have to stand up to do that. Argh! This was what I got for dressing up before work.

If I didn't get this butter lettuce situation taken care of soon, I was going to have to cook in these bad boys.

Which might have been fine, if they weren't currently pissing me the hell off!

"Son of a bitch," I hissed at the ground as I slowly pulled myself to standing on my free foot. "Son of a bitch!" I snarled, when I started to tip over again.

What was with this manhole cover? And how had I found the one hole to stick my shoe into on the entire city block?

"Dillon?"

Slamming my eyes shut, I turned away from the voice that belonged to the man jogging my way. This was not the way I wanted to capture his attention. Or anyone's attention.

There was only one way to play this—like I wasn't totally trapped in the manhole. Where was my I'm fine personality that everyone knew and loved?

"H-hey, Vann."

He was in front of me a second later. "Are you okay? I saw you fall."

My cheeks burned red. Of course, he had.

"I-I'm fine."

He gave me a look, showing that he didn't believe me. Not even a little bit. And he was right. My palms and knees burned and by the trickling liquid feel running down my leg, I had an awful suspicion I was bleeding. Plus, there was my shoe—still stuck.

He took a step back, his eyes roaming over my body, finally landing on my stupid, expensive shoe. "Are you stuck?"

I casually tried to twist the heel out. Maybe if I relaxed, the hole would loosen its grip.

Nope.

If anything, I managed to make it more stuck.

"A little," I confessed.

Vann's lips twitched with the urge to laugh. "Can I help?"

A frustrated sigh escaped my lips before I could temper it. "Sure. I guess."

That look was there—the one that called me on my bullshit. But he didn't say anything. Instead he dropped to his knees, his warm hands wrapping around my calf and ankle.

My core clenched as warmth spread where his hands moved over me. I cleared my throat, hoping he didn't notice how his touch was making me react.

He tugged on my leg and my ego was somewhat soothed when it didn't immediately release. His hand moved up to the back of my thigh, the other one sliding down toward my ankle. I held my breath, trying to ignore the contrast of his gentle touch and rough, calloused palms.

He looked up at me and smiled. "It's really stuck."

I blinked at him, taking in the way the sun caressed his dark hair, and sharp angles of his face. I wanted to reach down and brush my fingers over his cheekbone. "I'm aware," I said instead.

"Hold on to me."

"What?"

"I'm going to tug it out, but I don't want you to lose your balance again. So, hold onto me."

"O-okay."

I did as he commanded, resting my hands on the tops of his broad shoulders. He did some magic with my shoe and leveraging my leg and this time when he tugged, my heel popped free.

The momentum of it propelled me forward, despite my loose grasp on Vann and I started to flail again. He managed to catch me by grabbing a tighter hold on the backs of my thighs and steadying me.

And there we stood for several long moments. Me standing above him, my hands now gripping his muscular shoulders. Him, on his knees, his arms hidden beneath the skirt of my dress, his hands clutching the backs of my thighs, just below my bum.

My mouth dried out and my entire body flushed. But it wasn't from embarrassment.

This man and his touch and the intimate way he looked at me, did things to my resolve. Things that hadn't been done in a long time.

"You're bleeding," he murmured.

"What?"

"Your knees are bleeding."

I shook my head, coming back to my senses. "Oh."

"I can help with that."

Our gazes had locked, the heat from his licking its way over my body, erasing my embarrassment and building a fire within me. "What?"

"I can help with the bleeding," he repeated. His hands squeezed my thighs for the briefest moment before he stood up and took a step back. "I have a kit in my office."

"A bleeding kit?"

His lips twitched again. And it was absolutely devastating this close. "A first aid kit."

That made more sense. "I'm sure I'm fine. I'll just, er, walk it off." I tried to take a step and wobbled. "Owie," I whimpered like a total weenie.

"How about you let me help you. It's what I'm good at." He wrapped his arm around my waist and took my arm in his other hand, helping me hobble across the parking lot toward his storefront.

"You're good at helping people?" I asked, letting the sarcasm and disbelief seep into my tone. I wasn't trying to torture him, but to be honest, I was so far out of my comfort zone, that I didn't know how to talk to him without being defensively sarcastic. I just needed for this embarrassing moment to end.

This was by far the worst he'd seen me to date.

"Helping you specifically," he clarified. "It's becoming my super power."

I shot him a side look. "Is that so?"

"You should start hiring me to spot you from now on. I'll just follow you around all day, waiting for you to get yourself into trouble."

I nearly choked on my spit, totally embarrassed all over again. "What would that solve?"

"Then I'd already be there, and you wouldn't have to call me."

He held open the door to his store and I limped inside, the air conditioning instantly cooling my skin and forcing goosebumps to appear. "But why can't you save me before I get into trouble? That seems like something I would actually pay for."

"Good point," he laughed. "I'll spot you and save you before you need saving. I'm going to be really busy."

He walked me through the open space of his store, dodging expensive bike displays and power bar stands and a circular rack of spandex. I tried to memorize every detail. He'd managed this cool vibe that I didn't expect in a sports equipment store. But somehow it was all raw and urban while also smart and intuitive. Vann's shop was completely badass. It immediately made me want to take home a bike for myself.

Which was totally insane because I could barely manage spin class.

Clearly, he knew what he was doing in the store.

"You know, I managed just fine before you came along. Somehow I lasted all twenty-seven years of my life without needing someone to save me." Okay, that wasn't entirely true, but I'd survived, hadn't I?

He shot me a look, but it was ruined by his wide smile. "It's no fun to save yourself though. It honestly sounds exhausting."

He was joking. But he was right.

It was exhausting to save myself. And worse when I failed. There were a lot of moments in my past that I didn't regret. They weren't the brightest spots in my journey, but they had helped shape me into the person I was today.

But the big thing. The one that made all other moments small in comparison, was crippling in heaviness. It wore me down to my bones. It pushed me into bed and made me want to stay there forever.

And then it followed me in my dreams and woke me up at the earliest promise of daylight.

My hands shook and my knees knocked whenever I thought about it and all I wanted to do was pull into myself and forget that it happened. Forget that I had needed someone to save me that night and had no one. Forget that this was the person I was now, distrusting, scared, vulnerable.

There was the Dillon before the event.

And there was the Dillon after.

What I hated most, was that the people I knew preferred the Dillon after. She was more responsible. She kept a steady job. She had goals and aspirations and the beginning stages of a marketing plan.

They didn't know how much I'd given up to be this person. They didn't know the price I paid to realize the need for a new Dillon.

Vann noticed the shift in my mood. His eyebrows drew down in concern. "Hey, where did you go?"

I closed my eyes at the sensation of his fingers brushing hair back from my cheek and tucking it behind my ear. "I was thinking."

"About what?"

I opened my eyes and held his gaze. "Thank you for saving me today," I whispered to him. "Thank you for all the times you've saved me. You're right. It's exhausting when I try to do it on my own."

Instead of saying something cocky, like I expected, he smiled gently and leaned in close. "Always, Dillon. I'll always save you."

My damsel in distress heart fluttered with new, fresh promise while my mind spun in every direction. Could I trust him? Did he mean that? How could he? He had only recently gotten to know me.

Turning away, he cleared off his desk and coaxed me into sitting on top of it. I glanced around at the tidy space, enjoying the personal touches that seemed so Vann.

Behind his desk was a giant picture of the front half of a bike, driving through a puddle of water. The painting made it seem that water and mud were being splashed everywhere. And since the front tire was the focal point, it took me a second to notice the smaller image of the cyclist in the background, leaning over the handlebars, sporting an intense, wholly focused look on his face.

"That looks like you," I told him while he dug around for his first aid kit.

"Molly did that for me," he said, still distracted in his pursuit of antiseptic wipes. "When she and Ezra first started hooking up, I managed to guilt her into it."

"How's that?"

He met my eyes briefly, a guilty look in his. "She paints whatever Vera wants and then she started painting for Ezra. I was like, it's my turn, woman." He tipped his chin toward the incredibly vibrant and gorgeous masterpiece. "She painted that. And then made me swear I wouldn't hang it in the store proper. Because she's crazy." He said that, but the affection he held for her was obvious in his tone.

"You and Molly are close?"

After finally gathering the supplies he wanted, he knelt in front of me and brandished some alcohol and cotton swabs. "We are. We used to be closer before your brother came into the picture. But she's still like a sister to me. Always will be. We grew up together." He blew out a breath and it breezed over the scrapes on my knees. "I mean, it's always been Vera and Molly. I have barely any memories without those two together." He looked up at me, a strange expression crossing his face. "Except for when Vera was with Derrek, I guess."

I frowned at the name I recognized easily by now. Having been friends with Vera for two years, I knew her story pretty well, including how her mom had died and how her dad had fought a serious battle with cancer. Derrek was the asshole that had abused her for years. She'd finally broken up with him and escaped, eventually finding Killian. And now Derrek was ancient history. Thank the Lord.

Vann pulled the thoughts from my head and said, "You know all that though. Since you're friends with her."

I nodded, trying not to flinch as his hands moved over my knees and he started administering first aid on my vaguely gruesome injuries. "I mean, I know Vera's story. I don't know yours."

Our gazes met again, crashing into each other from where he knelt in front of me. I sucked in a sharp breath at the thoughtful look that pulled his lips into a frown and drew his eyebrows together.

"It's mostly the same," he said, shrugging.

"You had an abusive boyfriend too?" I gasped. "Was his name also Derrek?"

The thoughtful look disappeared, replaced with that smile I was slowly becoming obsessed with. "Don't joke around, Dillon. That was a hard time in my life."

I dug my foot into his side. "Now who's making a joke?"

He laughed, the low rumble filling the room and making my heart flutter. "If we're not making jokes, then I have to be honest. There was no abusive boyfriend. Or even non-abusive boyfriend. I've been into girls my whole life. Still am, actually."

It was my turn to laugh. Leaning forward, I whispered, "You don't have to prove to me that you're straight. We slept together, remember?"

One of those dark eyebrows jumped. "I remember. Do you remember?"

"I'm working on it," I admitted.

His gaze darkened, heated, warmed in a way that had me squirming on his desk. His focus dropped back to my knees. "Be still," he ordered. After a few silent moments, he asked, "So what about you?"

"What about me?"

"What was foster care like?"

His words were so excessively gentle, I couldn't help the melted chocolate feeling in my chest. But it wasn't my story. "I wasn't raised in foster care. Ezra and I are half-siblings. Same dad. Different moms."

He looked up again, an adorably perplexed look pulling out the wrinkles in his eyes. "Oh."

I smiled, easing the tension. "I got the better end of the stick. Ezra's story is much more tragic than mine." The confusion on his face deepened. "I'm kidding. It's a joke between us. He's better at being a grown up because he had a harder childhood. He always tells me he'd rather be him than poor, spoiled me."

"You lived with your dad growing up?"

I shrugged. "Sometimes. My mom and dad were married, but not always together. It didn't make sense to me as a kid. And to be honest, I still haven't put all the pieces together."

"How so?"

I blushed like usual. Remembering my dad typically brought out my worst emotions. "He was a serial cheater. Like, in the worst way. But he liked being married. Or rather, once he married my mom, he decided he was never going to get married again. Like that was it for him. He wasn't going to mess with that again. And he never wanted a divorce. So, my parents stayed together. Even though sometimes they weren't together. Does that make sense?"

"Did he take care of her when they weren't together?"

I shrugged. "I don't know. She doesn't talk about it much. There were times when I was at her house and she was so poor. Like barely able to keep the lights on. But then I would find out that he'd managed to get her fired from her last job so she would want to come back to his house. Or he would stop paying child support, so she'd be forced to call him. He was crazy abusive like that."

Vann sat back on his heels. "Was he trying to work it out with her?"

A laugh bubbled out of me and I hated how bitter it sounded. "No. That was the thing, he was never willing to change. He just wanted her to put up with him." I swallowed around a lump of unwanted emotions. "By the time he got sick, my mom was exhausted from his games. She moved back in and took care of him until he died. It worked out for her though because he left her some money." I rolled my shoulders, trying to banish the cold memories of my dead dad. "She actually ended up marrying one of his business partners a few years back. Tony is the nicest guy ever and totally adores her. They're really happy. They're spending the summer in Paris."

He smiled and it felt like he was happy for my mom, even though he'd never met her before. "Are you two close?"

"Me and my mom? Yeah, super. She's my favorite human."

He laughed at me and stood up, holding out his palms. "Hands."

I blinked at his. "Yes, they are. Very good, Vann. Now, where's your nose…?"

He rolled his eyes, but he laughed too. Because I was hilarious. "No, I want your hands. They're bleeding. I'm going to finish cleaning you up."

I did as he asked, holding out my hands for him. His touch was so tender and careful and commanding and he was always this dichotomy of soft and hard. Gentle and rough. Sweet and salty. It was driving me crazy. And messing with my more rational thoughts.

"Thank you," I whispered, my voice low and hoarse.

"You're welcome."

He was surprisingly good at this, I realized. He knew exactly what he was doing. "Do you do this for all the women that biff it in front of your store?"

His grin was wicked. "Technically, you're the only woman that's face-planted in my parking lot, that I've noticed." I dug my toe into his kidneys again and loved watching him squirm. "Hey!"

"A gentleman should always tell a lady that women fall all the time. That you spend half your day fixing bloody knees and scraped palms."

He looked up at me and shook his head. "How about I tell you I deal with my fair share of injuries, but usually on our Taco Tuesday bike rides. Everyone gets drunk and then wipes out and I'm usually the only one in the right mind to deal with them."

I was strangely moved by how sweet that was. "Doctor Delane, medicine cyclist."

He snorted a laugh at my corny joke. "Yeah, something like that. Also, my dad was sick for a long time and I learned some tricks while he was in care."

The amusement died on my lips, my heart squeezing for him. My heart ached as I remembered he lost his mom too. "It sucks to watch someone you care about suffer."

Our gazes crashed together once more and I suddenly realized how close he was, standing between my legs, cradling my palm in his. "It truly does."

"He's better though, yeah? Your dad, I mean?"

His head bob was cautious. "Remission for now. He still has to get scans."

"Still, that's good news."

"Did you care for your dad?" At my look, he quickly added, "I wasn't sure... By the way you've talked about him, I didn't know what kind of relationship you guys had."

Oh. Me neither. To Vann, I admitted, "Complicated, strained. Stilted. But he was my dad. I still loved him. No matter how much of an asshole he was." There was a heavy pause while Vann ingested that information. The mood felt too heavy now. Too serious. "Plus, he left me a crazy inheritance. You have to love someone that makes you rich, right?"

His surprised laughter made me smile. I watched twenty expressions flicker over his face as he decided how to feel about my candid response.

"I'm just kidding," I told him quickly. Lest he think of me as a gold-digging, ungrateful biotch. "The money was kind of awful after everything."

"Is that what prompted you to go to culinary school? And work so hard?"

I wished I could say yes. This would be the right opportunity to paint a new picture of my past. Nobody really knew that story—except for Ezra and he would never share any details. Not even to Molly. Even if he had no qualms with general headlines at brunch.

"Actually no. Inheriting that kind of money turned me into a spoiled brat. I didn't know how to handle losing my dad. Or even how to uncomplicate how I loved and hated a person that was dead. I kind of went off the deep end. I made all kinds of awful decisions and mistakes and totally messed up my life. And then... after that, I went to culinary school." He'd stilled. Totally froze. He was looking at me so intensely I thought I would burst into flames. "I had to live for something," I told him in a strangled voice. "I needed a purpose. And I found it cooking."

There was more silence as he let my words, my confession, my truth, settle into the air between us. I hadn't told anyone that much in a long time. And hearing it out loud I realized what a small portion of the story I'd given up. But still, for me, it was a lot.

Too much.

He leaned closer, dropping his voice. We were so close I felt his breath on my lips and the warmth of his skin. "I think you're amazing," he whispered, raw honesty making his voice rough. "No matter how you got here, you have so much to be proud of. You're not a spoiled brat anymore. You're strong and resilient. You're... breathtaking."

I wasn't totally sure who moved first or why that was the moment that ignited the fire between us . But as soon as he'd stopped talking, maybe even before, my lips were on his and my freshly bandaged hands were wrapped around his neck.

His mouth moved over mine with a voracious hunger, a man desperate and greedy for something he'd been deprived of.

God, he felt so good. So intensely right.

Our bodies mashed together as he kissed and kissed and kissed me. Our tongues tangled and our lips moved in a sexy rhythm, finding the perfect cadence of teeth and tongue and desire.

His hands landed on my hips tugging me more fully against him. We were lined up just perfectly. His waist to the apex of my thighs. I groaned at the sensation of him there, at the stark contrast of his masculine to my feminine.

I tightened my grip around his neck as he deepened the kiss. There was nothing tentative about his touch. Nothing nervous or timid. Memories of the night we slept together swam in my head with more clarity.

It wasn't so much the exact detail I remembered, but his body over mine, his hands on my skin, the delicious way he tasted.

His hand moved up my rib cage and over my breast. His thumb brushed over my nipple and I shivered. He did it a second time, adding pressure and I broke the kiss as I gasped for breath.

He trailed kisses along my jawline, down my throat and over my collarbone. I arched my back, pushing my breast into his hand, needing more of that wicked magic.

He laughed against the curve of my neck and tightened his hold on my nipple.

"You're driving me crazy," I panted, barely coherent. Barely stopping myself from ripping off my clothes and letting him take me on his desk.

"I know." His voice was rough sandpaper, heavy with desire.

"I don't make the best decisions when you—" He pinched my nipple again and I lost the ability to form sentences.

He tugged the strap of my dress off my shoulder, and then the top of my bra beneath my breast. His lips clamped around the same peak and I made a sound I had never made before. "I think you should go to dinner with me," he said around a mouthful.

"Wh-what?"

He lifted his head, his eyelids heavy and low. Sex was written all over his face. Sex and seduction and passion.

And it was working.

It had been a ridiculously long time since I'd been with a guy outside the rehearsal dinner with this particular guy. I'd had a lot of bad dates. I danced at parties and weddings and went out with my friends, but no guy ever came home with me. I put on this big show so nobody would realize I was totally celibate.

But now, with the air cooling the place where Vann's mouth had just been, I realized how alone I'd been. How incredibly lonely.

How isolated I'd made myself.

"Dinner," he repeated. "Or brunch. Or whenever you have time. I think we should try it."

"You're not into good girls anymore, remember?"

"And you're not into anything serious, remember?" He leaned forward and stole a quick kiss. I didn't pull away. In fact, I followed after him hoping for more. His head dipped so that his lips were at my ear. "Go out with me, Dillon. Let's see how good this is."

"What if it goes badly?"

More of that rumbly laughter. "What if it's the best thing that has ever happened to either of us?"

I pulled back so that he was forced to look me in the eyes again. "I don't do this," I told him, gesturing between us. "I don't sleep with guys or make out with them in the middle of the day. I know I seem happy go lucky, but I'm careful about who I let in."

The frown lines appeared by his eyes. "Why is that?"

There was a lot I could say here. Or I could lie. But I didn't want to do either. At least not today. Instead, I shrugged and looked away. "I don't want you to get your hopes up that I would be as easy as the rehearsal dinner night."

He growled something I couldn't hear. When I turned back to meet his gaze, his eyes were on fire. The silver in them was molten and bright. "I'm not that easy either," he argued. "And I wasn't expecting anything from you now. I just..."

"I wasn't saying you were! I don't want you to have false expectations."

"I don't have any expectations at this point. I like you. That's it. And yeah, I had a lot of fun that night with you, but you don't even remember it so trust me when I say it's not an experience I ever want to repeat. I prefer to be remembered. And I prefer that the woman I'm sleeping with has the ability to remember me." He flicked the cup of my bra so that it covered my nipple again and then adjusted the strap of my dress. "Sorry, that was distracting me."

I pressed my lips together to keep from smiling. He'd somehow managed to separate my last two experiences with sex in a candid way that made me not feel guilt or shame for sleeping with him.

It was kind of mind-boggling how he'd accomplished it so effortlessly. It also helped that I was starting to remember our night together. In fragmented, blurry bits and pieces, but they were coming back to me in bursts of intense passion. And that was a good thing. It separated what Vann and I did consensually, with that horrific night six years ago.

Vann hadn't realized I was as drunk as I had been. And after knowing him better now, I realized he never would have slept with me had he known I wouldn't be able to remember in the morning.

He was a decent guy. A good guy.

"I'm going to have to look at my schedule," I told him. "I'm not sure when I'll have time."

He reached into his pocket and pulled out his phone. "Can I give you my number? Then you can just text me. I'll make it work."

"What if it's five in the morning and I make you miss spin class?"

Half his mouth lifted in a sweet, patient smile. "Then I'll miss spin class." He cleared his throat and added, "Or we'll go to the later class together."

I laughed. I couldn't help it.

"Okay. Vann Delane. Yes."

His smile actually stopped my heart.

Okay, not quite. But it was a close call. I could lose myself in that smile. I could say yes to a lot of things just to see that smile again.

Damn.

He kissed me again and I did lose sense of time and reason and where I was. Again. Finally, we exchanged numbers and I told him I had to pick up butter lettuce, but that we would definitely find time to go on a date.

I walked, er, sort of hobbled to Lilou with a ridiculous smile on my face and a lightness in my clunky shoes. For the first time in my entire life, I felt seen. And I felt cared for.

It wasn't just the first aid he'd so sweetly administered, it was the way he protected my heart and my priorities, and me. Vann had rescued me several times, most of the time to my own embarrassment.

But I was starting to wonder if the biggest thing Vann was going to rescue me from was myself.

NINETEEN

IT TURNED out that I didn't have a break in my schedule for another two weeks. So in between our busy and opposite schedules, we barely had time to chat on the phone, let alone see each other. Our relationship, or whatever you wanted to call what we were doing, was reduced to flirtatious texting and five a.m. spin class. During which, I could hardly be called flirty.

Although Vann had taken to riding the bike behind mine. He enjoyed the view apparently.

I continued wearing the tightest leggings I had. And no underwear.

We grew more comfortable with each other in the absence though. The late-night texting and early morning, sleepy-selfies made me lower my guard. Having sex with Vann, even while I was drunk, had opened this door to a possibility of a relationship with him. But now that we were talking about a date and not seeing each other, texting was opening the possibility of getting to know him without the pressure of sex.

It didn't make sense to my logical concept of how relationships worked. Sleeping with the guy and then getting to know him? That wasn't normal. But it was working for me. It had removed the crushing fear I had been living with for years.

By the morning of our date, I was ready to get some face-to-gorgeous-handsome-clean-cut-face time in.

I wrapped my hair up in a meticulous messy bun and checked out my outfit in the mirror on my bathroom door. In tune with our unconventional relationship, for our first date Vann was taking me on a bike ride.

Frowning at my reflection, I contemplated changing. This was not how I liked to look on first dates. I was always glam to the max. Sassy shoes. Big hair. All the makeup. Something that made the guy think WOW. Or DAMN. Or anything along those lines.

Today's outfit said, "I tried a little harder than morning spin class."

Not my best look. Still, I knew Vann would appreciate comfort over va-va-voom. And I could appreciate that about him.

My hair was twisted and tied in a complicated network of pieced out layers. My makeup was the waterproof variety. And my sports bra and halter workout top were supportive and not sexy in any way.

I did stick with the tight, light gray leggings and no underwear though. I might regret my decisions later, but I'd cross that bridge when I got to it. For now, I was shooting for "Don't forget I'm a girl when I totally kick your ass on the trails today."

My phone buzzed on my unmade bed. I forced myself to stop fiddling with my hair and read the text.

I'm here. Can I come up?

I smiled at my phone and shot him a quick text back with the apartment number and directions to my front door. Then I walked to the entryway and buzzed him in.

There was this giddiness to my day. And it was strange and wonderful and at war with a hundred different emotions inside me. I had never had this with a boy before. I had never been so completely head over heels. I had never felt this safe. I had never known a relationship could be this fun.

Which sounded ridiculously pathetic. Especially for someone who was already twenty-seven. I had given up on men being worthy and upright and kind.

Other than Ezra and Killian and Wyatt, I didn't even know men could be this... likeable.

All the men in my life, from high school till now, had wanted something from me. My dad had wanted a trophy he could show off at parties. The guys I'd dated before culinary school had wanted sex. Or my money. Or my connections. But mainly sex. And they wanted it so badly, they would do anything to get it from me.

Or they would just take it from me. Whether I wanted to give it up or not.

Okay, to be honest, that only happened the one time. But I would never go through that again.

Never.

I waited for the stubborn resolve to push Vann away, to get him out of my life. It was how I coped. It was how I protected myself. Instead of opening myself up to being hurt like that again, I pushed people away.

And then I made sure they stayed away.

How was it that Vann was on his way up to my apartment now?

The knock at the door shook me out of my thoughts, but even as I opened it, I couldn't make myself sabotage this morning. I wanted to hang out with Vann. I wanted to spend time with him. I wanted to kiss him. I wanted to ride bikes and enjoy the outdoors with him. Which in itself seemed crazy.

Whatever it was about Vann, made me want to try. And as strange and unlike me as that seemed, I was just going to go with it.

My therapist might even call this a breakthrough.

He was clad in spandex head to toe and if he wasn't so adorable I would have laughed. Okay, I did laugh. But not hard enough that he ran away.

"What?" he asked, a smile playing at the corners of his lips.

"It's just that..." I giggled again and slapped a hand over my mouth. "I wasn't expecting Lance Armstrong this morning."

He took three menacing steps toward me, trapping me against the wall. His lips descended on my throat, kissing and nibbling while he growled something about how Lance Armstrong was a traitor to the sport.

Obviously, I laughed harder. Also, he was now tickling me!

"I'm sorry!" I gasped for breath. "You're not Lance Armstrong!"

He lifted his head, but his hands stayed planted on my ribcage, dangerously close to my breasts. "I appreciate that."

Letting my eyes drift over him again, I had a change of heart toward the whole ensemble. His legs were thick and strong and muscled like none I'd ever seen before. And his chest and arms were no different. He wasn't bulky like body builders. But there was a thickness to his muscles that showed they had seen lots of exercise.

This man took care of his body. God, had that ever been sexier?

Or maybe it was just that working in the food industry had significantly lowered my expectations of the male form. Sure, there were guys like Wyatt, Killian, and Blaze that took care of themselves. But there were also the other kind of men—the ones that didn't find time to work out and succumbed to the endless beer and carbs.

Not that I was judging them.

I'd gained like three pounds since taking over Bianca. Between the overworked schedule and stress, my coping mechanism consisted of cheese and red meat. Hence my fresh commitment to spin class.

I wasn't out of shape. I took care of myself for the most part if you ignored the part about the cheese and red meat. But I had nothing on Vann. He was like a perfect specimen of the male body. And I wanted to get to know him inch by delicious inch.

His gaze warmed and one of his hands moved its way up my body to cradle my face. "Hey."

It was too easy to get lost in those gray eyes. "Hey."

"It's good to see you this morning," he murmured, his head dipping with intent.

"It's been a while," I agreed.

"We should probably do this more often."

My belly flipped with the way he sounded so into me. I wasn't used to this. I couldn't remember a time when someone had been so interested in spending time with me. Like it was the only thing he wanted to do. "Oh yeah?" I laughed.

"Then I might be able to keep my hands to myself," he explained. "I'm just thinking about you. I'm trying to be nice."

I pitched forward, bringing our bodies flush against each other. "Maybe I like when your hands are all over me."

He smiled and it was everything bright and beautiful. Like the sunlight hovering just below his thunderstorm gray eyes. "Then maybe we should compromise. I see you more. And you get to have my hands all over you. Fair?"

I nodded, feeling breathless and totally swept away. "Fair."

Then we kissed. And kissed. And kissed. I got more of his hands. And more of his mouth. And forget cycling and spandex and nature trails.

This was what I wanted all day and all night.

But he apparently didn't. Because despite my best efforts at seduction, he pulled away. Our foreheads touched while he stood there trying to catch his breath.

"Woman," he growled. "You are some kind of magic."

My heart burst. Just like that. It exploded.

Okay, maybe not literally. But holy hell, there was something about him I just couldn't resist.

I slumped against him, loving the feel of our frantic hearts beating against each other and the way his silky spandex felt against my exposed skin. But he wouldn't even let that last forever.

Apparently, he was playing hard to get.

He kissed my forehead and stepped back. "I came all the way up here," he teased. "I might as well snoop."

"What?"

He started walking around my apartment, picking up random things from my kitchen counters and inspecting them.

I had a gigantic kitchen. It was why I'd picked this place. And the island was the centerpiece of the entire open space. It arced in a long line of gleaming quartz, set against the backdrop of my navy blue cabinets. My vintage appliances and metal stools made it picture worthy.

The only regret I had was that I didn't get to spend more time in it.

But now that the schedule at Bianca was about to change... that might change too.

He whistled when he opened my double oven and peered inside. Turning around he took in the inset living room with a wide-open view of downtown Durham. There was a pretty terrace outside the long wall of picture windows, covered in green plants that my house-cleaner kept alive for me.

I was suddenly embarrassed of my extravagant pad. I knew Vann was self-employed and I also knew that was hard. Running a small business was one of the hardest things on the planet. Success was only managed with grit and grind and endless amounts of tenacity.

There was always that combination of hard work, the right opportunity and just enough good luck that could launch a small business owner into happy success and autonomy. But at the same time, it wasn't easily-earned success. Or easily kept. You would always have to work. There would never be a break. You could never just take it easy and breathe a little. Or have weekends and major holidays off. Or even sick days. And just as often as things could be great and busy, they could be slow and stretched.

Watching Vera and Killian open their own restaurant from the front row had been incredibly eye-opening. Owning their restaurant had added a heavy layer of stress. Even Vera felt it, and she had been the sole proprietor of Foodie the food truck. A restaurant was an entirely different beast. Especially when it was the caliber they were shooting for.

When I met Vann's intense gaze, his eyebrows were raised expectantly. "Quite the place, Baptiste."

I wrapped my arms around my waist protectively and shrugged. "Did I forget to mention that I'm an heiress?"

His mouth broke into a huge grin. "I picked the wrong first date."

Nerves dropped in my stomach like a boulder off a mountain. I hated, loathed, detested when guys thought they had to prove themselves to me. It was the fastest way on the planet to turn me off.

I took a step back, feeling my skin turn white. "Oh?" I managed weakly.

"I should have made you take us to Cancun or something," he said, laughing.

The tightly wound tension I'd managed to work up in thirty seconds disappeared just like that. He wasn't going to try to compete with my accidental wealth. Whew.

It was my turn to raise an eyebrow. "Didn't I tell you? I only take the guys I really like to Cancun for our first date."

He folded his arms, a challenge flickering over his face. "So, we *are* going." I tilted my head in confusion and he added, "You said, you only take the guys you really like to Cancun. So... when does our plane leave exactly? I should probably pack a few things."

I shook my head at him, but couldn't help but walk toward him, pulled in by that invisible gravity that kept me trapped in his orbit. "You think I like you a lot?"

He nodded. "It's obvious."

"You're so full of yourself."

His straight-face was in danger of becoming one of those huge grins I loved so much. "It's okay though. I like you too, Dillon."

My heart did a herkie in my chest, arms up in the air, cheerleader-style and everything. I practically tripped down the living room stair into his arms and straight into another kiss. How did he keep doing this? Every time I questioned what I was doing or when I would run or what if I didn't run, he would do something like this that totally reinforced why I was willing to take this chance with him.

It was like he was showing all these layers that promised I could trust him, promised I could trust my heart with him... promised I could trust my bed with him. He laid layer after layer, careful to make each one perfectly reliable.

And now we were standing on this steadfast foundation that felt firm... strong... safe.

It was me that broke our kiss this time, afraid I'd start crying. "Should we go?"

"Are you ready for this?"

"I mean, no," I told him honestly. "I don't even own a helmet, let alone a bike. I'm the least ready person on the planet."

His laugh rippled through me, pulling shivers with it. "I got you a bike. And a helmet." He eyed the messy bun that had taken me the better part of the morning to construct. "Although, you might have to change up your hairstyle. Sorry if that's a problem."

I shook my head. "It's no problem." Apparently, I was willing to do anything for this guy.

How did one recognize true love? By the female's willingness to redo her hair.

Just kidding. This wasn't true love. It was way too early for that!

I ignored the protests from all the different emotions and organs inside me. This wasn't love. Not that it wouldn't be soon. But we weren't there yet.

Ahem.

"I'll be right back," I told him.

"I packed a picnic too," he said to my back. "I know this cool spot by a lake. I thought we could take a break for lunch there."

His suggestion had me turning around again. "You cooked?"

He shrugged, self-conscious. "Don't get your expectations up. I just thought... I don't know, I'm already making you go on a ride with me. I didn't want you to go hungry."

The puddle on the ground? Yeah, that was where I just melted.

Out loud I managed a cool, "O-okay. That sounds good."

TWO HOURS LATER, I collapsed on the blanket he'd laid out at a serene spot near the lake he'd mentioned. It was every perfect thing he'd promised it would be. This was maybe the most tranquil place I had ever been in my life. I didn't even know it existed this close to Durham. Or on planet earth in general.

We'd been riding for a long time. Vann was a total expert on a bicycle, while I trailed behind him and tried not to crash into a tree.

I had wrongly assumed that because I could survive spin class, I could ride a bike. Through a forest. Also, there was that saying, "Like riding a bike," which implied that once you learned how to ride a bike, you never forgot.

What a bunch of bullshit!

First of all, I didn't ever remember bike riding being this hard. Ever. Especially not when I was a kid. And I used to ride my bike everywhere. Like all over. I was a total pro between the ages of six and thirteen.

Fast forward fifteen years and I learned the hard way how advanced brakes had gotten. Also, how sharp pedals were.

And not to be crass, but this seat wasn't nearly as nice as the design I'd rocked in elementary. My vintage childhood banana-seat beauty was an entirely different species than what Vann had me on today.

It was like the difference between a shark and a minnow.

And I was learning the hard way how to ride a shark.

But we'd had fun. He'd pulled over a few times to show me some pretty spots in the dense forest or help me figure out things on my bike. Like the gear shifts. And how not to kill myself every time I tapped on the handlebar brakes.

And that didn't even touch how hard of a workout this was. I was just over here huffing and puffing while he casually pulled out our lunch and spread it over the blanket.

I discreetly checked out his head and body, looking for any signs of sweat. There weren't any. This man was officially an alien.

Oh, good Lord, I didn't even want to know what I looked like to him. My hair had been matted down by the helmet I'd abandoned as soon as we'd stopped riding. My makeup was testing the limits of waterproof and physics and the general rules of the universe. And I was very concerned I smelled bad.

I knew what I looked like after spin class. It was amazing he hadn't assumed I was a grizzly bear come to take his lunch.

Or did that only happen in Yogi Bear cartoons?

"This place is breathtaking," I panted, pretending not to pant and that I wasn't out of breath at all.

He nodded, but his attention stayed fixed on what his hands were doing. "I found it a few years ago. I come back often."

"By yourself?" Fishing much, Dillon? I resisted the urge to slap my hand over my eyes.

He laughed at my lame attempt to get former dating information out of him. "Mostly. I find I do my best thinking here." He nodded toward where we'd parked our bikes. "And on one of those."

"How'd you get into cycling? Or was it something you've always done?"

He handed me a plate that was so healthy and organized I couldn't help but smile.

"Don't judge me," he added quickly.

"For what?"

He heard the strained tone of my voice and laughed. "You chefs have a serious chip on your shoulder when it comes to eating healthy."

"Not true!"

"Kale chips are delicious. I promise."

"And the sandwich? Or... sandwich-like-thing?"

"It's a chicken salad lettuce wrap. I used Greek yogurt and sriracha. I promise it's good."

He also had orange slices—because this was Vann after all.

Oranges were obviously his favorite. And a salad with stone fruit and nuts on it.

He went to a lot of work to get this all together. I was truly impressed. "This looks amazing. Seriously."

He smiled and I could see him visibly relax. "Uh... the cycling? I started working in a bike shop when I was in high school. The guy I worked for was obsessed with bikes. I mean, he was also this gruff asshole. But he taught me how to respect the ride and take care of my equipment. He showed me how it could be an escape. And a therapist. And a friend."

I liked the way he talked about bikes. It was exactly how I felt about food. An escape and a therapist and a friend. It was there to take me away from my thoughts and life and the humdrum reality I'd boxed myself into. And it also listened to all my problems, let me pour into it my frustration and fear and the thousand other emotions I felt on a daily basis. And it was definitely a friend. The constant listener in my life. The always understanding, never judgmental, unconditional love I wanted so desperately.

"I get that," I told him, real emotion lowering my tone. "You just knew you wanted to own a shop then? Like from that moment?"

He shook his head. "Not quite. I thought about college for a bit. Took some business classes and what not. But I don't know, it just wasn't for me. I'm not a... traditional learner. I hate school. I hate tests. I hate homework. I wanted to do something that I could see results in immediately. Opening my own business eventually became that thing. As I got more and more responsibility at the bike shop, I saw that it could be profitable if it was managed right. I decided to open something and be the successful owner I wanted to be."

"That's so cool."

He smiled around a bite of his chicken salad lettuce wrap. "Cool. Also, hard. It's been a long road to get where I am today."

"You mean, doing well?"

"I mean, climbing out of the red." His gaze grew distant, thoughtful. "It's taken a minute to get where I'm at. I didn't always know what I was doing."

I hummed in agreement. "Being a grown-up is hard."

He looked at me, a plate of food on his lap, completely clad in spandex, his cheeks a little red from the exertion of riding and sun and wind. He was all testosterone and chiseled masculinity. There was nothing struggling about him now. He had it all figured out.

He was all that was man.

And looking at me now, the way he was, made me feel completely, one-hundred-percent, female.

I wiggled a little at his open assessment, shoving my mouth full of kale chips and following it with a long chug of water. "I mean, there's a lot going on," I added, trying to pull myself out of this hole I'd unwillingly walked into. "Bills and business. And... making your own dental appointments."

He finally smiled, erasing the building tension with that one expression. "I've always had to make my own dental appointments."

"Oh?"

Nodding, he set his plate to the side and laid down on his side, with his head propped in his hand. "Yup. My dad couldn't remember stuff like that. He also didn't care about any of it. I realized quickly that if I wanted good teeth, I was going to have to solve that problem myself."

"How old were you when you made your first dental appointment?"

He thought about it for a minute and then said. "Uh, seven maybe? And I've been on a strict every six months schedule ever since."

"You're kidding."

He smiled, flashing perfectly straight and white teeth. "I never joke about the dentist."

I threw a kale chip at him. He caught it in his gleaming chompers. "I never had to do that kind of stuff for myself. I mean, I wasn't always rich. I don't want you to get that idea. When my mom wasn't with my dad, we were super poor. Like showering in truck stop bathrooms and splitting Top Ramen for every meal. But my dad was in charge of my healthcare, so I never had to worry about braces or checkups or anything."

"I can't decide which childhood I'd rather have," he murmured, a frown replacing that blinding smile. "Sounds like we both had it kind of rough."

I laid down on my side next to him. "I think that's how most childhoods are. You know? If your parents didn't totally mess you up, were you even a kid?"

He laughed and I loved the way it made me feel bubbly and happy and so totally removed from those dark memories.

"Maybe it's not always your parents though. Sometimes it's your circumstances," he suggested.

"And sometimes it's other kids. What I'm saying is there isn't a way to get out of it unscathed. The only path to adulthood is trial by fire."

"And then it's just more fire."

We reclined on the blanket at the same time, as if we'd had the same thought. Our shoulders bumped into each other as we watched the clouds drift across a bright blue sky. The summer breeze cooled my skin and lifted the rogue hairs across my forehead.

I turned my head and looked at him. He did the same thing. The sky was in his eyes. "Something happened to me." The words were out of my mouth before I'd fully decided to say them. "It's what turned me into a runner. Or, uh, the person I am today. It made me want to run. I just... I get scared. And I run away before things can get real."

His fingertips drifted down my forearm until he found my hand. He wove our fingers together as he searched my face.

My body had stiffened, the itch in my feet that was, even now, whispering to run.

"Is that why the night of the rehearsal dinner was not okay?"

I nodded. "It bothered me that I couldn't remember. That I

would put myself in a situation like that when I was so far gone. And then I just assumed that you were the kind of guy that would..." I shook my head, unable to even say words about Vann that would suggest he was anything but incredible. And trustworthy.

"Do you want to talk about it?" His hand squeezed mine and I knew this was a safe space. I knew he would take my confession and treat me with grace and kindness. I knew I could tell Vann anything. At this moment, I knew that. But I still couldn't get the words out.

They had lodged themselves in my throat and calcified over time. They were fossils by now. Still real. Still damaging. Still slicing my trachea wide open. But I could not speak them.

"I find that I can't actually say the words yet," I whispered, finding it hard to even get that much of a confession out.

His brows drew down in a deeper frown. "I'm here for you, Dillon. Whenever you want to say them, I'm here to listen. You won't shock me. You won't scare me off. Whatever happened, I am here to help you carry the burden."

I realized then that he hadn't put all of the pieces together. And I shouldn't have expected him to. Just because the answer was so clear to me, didn't mean anyone else would assume it about me. But I felt hope in his promises.

He'd stayed this long. Maybe he could hear the truth and trust me like I was learning to trust him.

"Thank you," I told him, tears wetting my eyes.

"Come here." He pulled me into a hug right there on the blanket, in our sideways position. Our legs intertwined automatically, and we wrapped each other up in the tightest hug—spandex to spandex.

We stayed like that for an hour. Just hugging. Just feeling warmth from each other and reassurance and the promise of something yet to come.

It was the most perfect afternoon of my life.

TWENTY

REOPENING WEEKEND! And it felt so good.

Bianca was officially launched with our new vibe. Molly had helped come up with a gorgeous tagline—casual French for the modern American. And we'd run a ridiculously successful internet campaign thanks to her freaking genius marketing super skills.

We'd even revamped the interior of the dining room to reflect a brighter, sunnier, more brunch-like mood. Flowers were refreshed. Dishes were replaced. I'd even convinced Ezra to go with a lighter, smaller-pronged set of silverware.

I'd reached out to Killian's bartender friend, Will English at Craft, for some French breakfast cocktails and was super impressed with his help. This morning we were serving our version of a French 75, champagne and gin and a splash of orange juice. We'd added a toothpick with a strawberry, lime wedge, and agave syrup drizzle. We were calling it the Breakfast 75. We also had a pomegranate and champagne sparkling thingy that was perfectly refreshing. They were both delicious. I'd had ample samples this week.

Just to be sure—obviously.

We also had traditional mimosas and Bloody Marys.

Because now wasn't the time to get snobby. We were trying to get people inside the restaurant. If they wanted tomato juice and vodka with whole strips of bacon and a cheeseburger slider on a stick, who was I to turn them down?

If they were willing to pay $17.99 a pop, more power to them.

Our final menu was something I considered a work of art. The whole kitchen staff had pitched in to make this brunch a shining star in a section of Durham that had no breakfast options.

Of course, my dreams included total and complete world domination. But I would start with this neighborhood and work my way out.

We had an eggs benedict station, that included protein and vegetarian options like smoked salmon, fried green tomatoes, and crispy, peppered pork belly. Our croque madame had been perfected with jalapeno raspberry jam, hickory smoked bacon, rich and creamy camembert and crispy kale chips—that idea I'd gotten from Vann's picnic.

But hey, those crunchy little suckers really worked. And I loved the salty component they brought.

There were so many other mouthwatering items on the list as well. Enough that we hoped nobody would be able to decide their first time sitting down and then they'd note at least three other things they wanted to try. They'd mark this restaurant in their heads with a gold star and the memory that they wanted to come back and try x, y and z.

And maybe, if we were super lucky, they'd give us a glowing review on Yelp.

Or Google.

That was possibly wishful thinking. But after being here for months, I hoped for something other than the demise of my very short-lived career.

"Three tables so far," Julia, one of my most reliable servers, said as she breezed into the kitchen. "But they seem excited about the menu change."

My stomach squeezed with nerves. Three? That was hardly enough to justify the time change. "That's good." Because it was, I reminded myself. "We have to start somewhere. At least there are people out there."

She nodded with a tight-lipped smile. "Good point, Chef."

I tried not to smile at her. Clearly this girl was terrified of me. Which meant I was doing part of my job right!

My impulse was to rip off my toque, throw it on the ground and do a happy dance right on top of it. But I kept my cool.

At least for now.

"Good work out there, Jules. We can save the sign-spinning for later in the morning." Her jaw unhinged and I couldn't help but laugh. "I'm kidding."

She hurried from the kitchen.

"You're in a good mood this morning," Blaze noted while we all watched the printer, waiting for the first order to appear.

Shrugging off the giddiness that had followed me all week, I told him, "I'm excited to see how this goes. I've got a good feeling."

"I do too," he agreed. "I think this is going to change Bianca's reputation for good."

I beamed at his unexpected compliment and then remembered he would be giving me a final answer later today if he was going to leave Bianca or stay as sous.

He'd told me he'd get me through opening weekend before he moved on. But now it was opening weekend and my hopes that he would change his mind were slowly dwindling. He hadn't said anything since our initial conversation.

And there had been a day he had mysteriously asked off last week. I'd tried to casually pry, but he'd been a locked box. And when I had asked the rest of the staff in his absence, they hadn't given me any useful information.

So here we were. Hours away from his final decision. And I was a tight ball of nerves.

This was terrible planning on my part. I should have scheduled the meeting a year from now. But definitely not on the day we launched Bianca's new menu. During our first brunch.

One day I would get my life together. Probably not any day soon. But one day.

One. Day.

"We should talk," I blurted, unable to hold back my morbid curiosity any longer. And honestly, I was starting to question my mental sanity and if I could even make it that long. I was basically bubbling over, waiting to see how today went, waiting to see if this would work or if we'd fail before we ever really started... waiting for him to give me his answer.

Honestly, I was about three seconds away from just firing him, so I didn't have to try to survive when he quit. Also I needed to get rid of some of this intense adrenaline. We were at critical levels.

"We should," he agreed.

"Let's go to my office."

Surprise jumped all over his face. "Now?"

"Listen, I'm over here just assuming the worst. Let's talk about it and I'll adjust accordingly. And I'll also work better today. This is important to me." I turned to Eduardo and Caden. "Can you all hold down the fort for five minutes?"

Their eyes bugged and it made me seriously question my example of leadership in this place. Why did no one want the sous chef job?

Was I as bad as Wyatt?

"You'll be fine," I told them gruffly. "All you have to do is follow the ticket. You got this."

"That's not necessary," Blaze cut in, sounding as surprised as Eduardo and Caden looked. "We can talk later, Chef."

I hated that he was bossing me around right now. He was totally messing with my power trip. And my authority in the kitchen. Leaning forward, I forgot all the advice Vann had imparted on me and lashed out with my emotions. "We'll do it now, Chef. If you don't mind."

His gaze flashed to mine. "It's really not *necessary*, Chef."

Something in his tone caught my attention. "What are you saying?"

He shrugged and turned back to his task. "I'm not leaving."

"Say that again?"

His grumpy glare was somehow endearing after all this time with him. "I'm not going anywhere. So, can we move on?"

"Wait, like this weekend? Or ever?"

I could tell he was really starting to lose his patience with me, and I couldn't help but relish torturing him after he'd put me through such hell the last few weeks.

"Ever. I'm not going anywhere ever."

"You're serious?"

His cheeks burned red. I grinned. "I'm serious. I thought I would be happier in a more established kitchen, but to be honest... you've grown on me. I've been impressed with how you've handled yourself and this restaurant. You can cook your ass off. And I can't help it. I'm curious to see what happens."

Arching an eyebrow, I waited for the truth. When he didn't volunteer it, I was forced to pry. "Seems a little risky to stake your reputation on curiosity." His frown deepened. "I'm just saying... you could always follow us on Twitter."

"You've earned my respect, okay? Is that what you want to hear? I expected you to be this entitled egomaniac that thought she knew everything, but you've turned out to be the opposite. And on top of that, I am impressed with the changes you're making. You've somehow managed to make me excited for this place. And since I figured that was a miracle, it might be good to stick around with a woman that can work miracles."

I smiled and it was genuine and full of emotion and all the gratitude that could possibly pool inside me. "Hey, those are some nice things you just said."

His lips lifted in what I could barely call a smile. But there was a hint of something that wasn't a frown. "They are nice things. That I just said. I like you, Chef. I guess I'm hitching my horse to your wagon."

"Well, yeehaw then."

He completely ignored me after that. Apparently, he liked my cooking style. Not so much my jokes. Which was fine with me since he was staying.

I was a walking, talking praise hands emoji.

To be honest, if push came to shove and Blaze had wanted to walk away from Bianca, I could have managed. I would never have gotten a break and I wouldn't have had anyone I could have relied on as much as I relied on him. But the rest of the kitchen I could have figured out.

It would have been painful. I might have gone entirely gray and developed a cluster of ulcers. But we could have done it.

I was ultra-thankful we didn't have to do it. Blaze had decided I was worthy. That this kitchen was worthy. That for now, he'd rather be here than anywhere else.

And that was enough for me.

Basically, our first attempt at brunch was already a success. Who even cared about the rest of the day?

Oh wait, I did.

And it was a good thing because the kitchen got busy after that. More praise hands emojis.

Seriously, I had not worked this hard at Bianca until this morning, our first brunch service. I didn't think anyone had worked that hard until today. We managed to keep up, but our kitchen muscles were atrophied, and we didn't have the sharp orchestration other kitchens like Lilou operated with.

After we sent out three wrong orders in a row, I knew I needed to do something to get our heads back in the game. I played basketball in high school and this was the point of the game the head coach made key substitutions—second half, down by ten, three starters with four fouls, it was time to shake things up. Only I didn't have bench players to sub in. So, I needed to be spectacularly creative. Or at least very stern.

"Hey, everyone, can I have your attention please?" Yelling was a good option. Also throwing things. Once, in culinary school, I'd shadowed one of the best chefs in Charlotte and watched him punch his fist into a brick wall over and over. He'd gotten his point across very effectively. His sous chef had also had to give him six stitches. Something she was apparently used to.

Every chef had their own, unique way of dealing with stress. I'd seen Wyatt smash plates and dump just-shy-of-perfect filets in the trash. Most chefs I knew of subscribed to the might is right philosophy. To be fair, we were passionate creatures on a schedule.

And while it was easy to get irritated and scream at all the people that should be working as hard and perfectly as you, it was also dumb. I wasn't a yeller by nature. I certainly wasn't going to start yelling now just because I got a promotion.

And today, I was in a particularly good mood now that Blaze was staying, and brunch was going so well. That didn't mean I would continue to send out subpar plates.

People paused what they were doing and looked over at me. When I was sure I had the attention of the room, I cleared my throat and said, "I appreciate what you all have done here. The change in schedule. The change in vision. The change in leadership. Y'all have managed to weather me like champs. And a part of me wishes that I could stop asking you to do impossible things. A part of me would love to tell you we're just going to coast from here on out. That what you're doing right now is good enough. That who you are right now is good enough. But it's not. And you're not. And I will never, ever settle for good enough." They were staring at me. Not smiling or scowling or showing a single emotion with their faces. They were just staring at me and I wasn't sure if that was a good sign or if they were ten seconds from staging a walkout. "I have audacious dreams for this place. I have giant, larger than life aspirations for this kitchen. I have huge, career-changing goals for all of you. And if you stick with me and help bring this vision to life, I know you'll be proud of your work and your career. It's not going to be easy. To be honest, it's going to be hell most days. But that doesn't mean it won't also be good and worthy and the best fucking ride of your entire life." A chef named Bryan smiled from the back and I found courage in that one encouraging expression to push on. "So, stop sending out wrong dishes. Stop doing half-assed work. Stop assuming that what you're doing is good enough. Because it's not. It's time to strive for utter perfection. Let's be better than the competition. Let's be better than we are right now." I paused for dramatic effect, and to catch my breath. I could hardly believe I was the person demanding excellence from my kitchen like this. I had never considered myself a leader before, never even wanted to be one. But here I was, rallying the troops and digging deep to inspire excellence. "Let's be the best we've ever been!"

A cheer rose up around me, men and a few women clapping, a few of them drying their eyes. I felt like a general, inspiring my troops to win the war.

I nodded, once—a proud, proficient chin bob—and the kitchen burst to life again as my chefs poured over their work and did the best they could possibly do.

Adrenaline coursed through my veins, my blood bubbling with the rush of victory. For the first time since I'd stepped inside Bianca as executive chef, she felt like mine. And I finally felt up to the task of running her.

What I'd said to my staff applied to me as well. I needed to get better. Be better. Do better. Always. I could never sit back on my haunches and coast. If I was going to do this well, then I would have to try hard at it every single day.

I took a steadying breath, accepting the challenge.

Okay, Bianca. I'm all the way in this.

"Chef?" a nervous server wrung her hands in front of me.

Oh great. What now? "There's a table out front demanding to speak with you."

Nerves plunged my stomach to my toes. This was never a good

sign. And right after I'd given the speech of my lifetime no less. To the server, I went about looking busy and asked, "Did they say what it was about?"

She shook her head. "No, just that they needed to speak with you about what you were doing back here."

To Blaze, I said, "You got this?"

He nodded. No problem. He was my second in command. For real now. Of course, he could handle this.

I wiped my hands on my apron and followed her from the kitchen. Bianca's dining room wasn't especially large, and it was totally open so I spotted the demanding table immediately.

I tapped the server on the shoulder and pointed toward it. "Is that it?"

"Yes," she answered.

"Okay, I got this. Thanks, Chrissy." I marched past her toward the rowdy patrons at least two cocktails deep. "What is going on here?"

Molly grinned at me, waving her Breakfast 75. "We're supporting you!"

I smiled at my friends. They'd taken up the largest booth in the restaurant, a circular monstrosity that barely held them all. Molly and Ezra. Vera and Killian. Kaya and Wyatt. Vann.

Butterflies jumped off cliffs in my stomach, plummeting toward my knees before soaring toward my chest. Everything fluttered in me at the sight of Vann. He smiled at me from where he was only half on the edge of the bench. "Hey."

"Hey," I whispered back.

"We're not here for you," Killian announced while he stabbed a piece of potato cassoulet, gesturing at his wife. "We're scoping out the competition." His chin jerked toward everyone else. "But they wanted to support a friend or whatever. We figured two birds."

I rolled my eyes, laughing at his teasing. "Now that Salt's open, make sure everyone knows who started brunch first."

"Okay, I'll make sure they know it was us."

Kaya leaned forward, giving both of us the evil eye. "It was me. I did brunch first."

Killian and I shared a guilty smile. That was true. She did. But Sarita wasn't even in the same zip code as Bianca so surely, she meant over there, in her specific area. Just like I meant here, in this specific area.

Or something like that.

"This is something else, Dillon," Molly announced, her voice filled with awe. "This is the busiest I've ever seen Bianca!"

I looked around at the full tables and hot dishes being brought out of the kitchen. The bar was packed with people. Outside, clusters of waiting diners dotted the sidewalk in front of the patio.

"I'm so impressed," Vera added. "You've done the most incredible thing with this place."

"And the food..." Wyatt kissed his fingertips. "It's like you had a really amazing mentor or something, because, Dillon, you're killing it."

My eyes misted with their thoughtfulness and super kind words, but I bossed the tears back. I didn't want to scare off customers by breaking down into obnoxious sobs in the middle of Saturday morning breakfast. "You guys! Stop! Before this all goes to my head."

Vann reached out and grabbed my hand, holding it gently in his. "It should go to your head, Baptiste. Be proud of what you've done. You're wonderful."

No, he was wonderful. And it was currently taking all my willpower not to jump on his lap and attack his mouth with my own.

"Do you want a tour?" I asked instead. I could attack him in private at least.

His eyebrows jumped. "You can do that?"

"Sure. It's my restaurant."

My brother leaned forward and butted in. "Technically it's my restaurant."

Obviously, I ignored him. "Come on," I told Vann. "I'll show you around."

"Can we come?" Killian asked.

Tuning to the people around us, I couldn't help but laugh. "You don't need to come. You know what the inside of a kitchen looks like."

"This kitchen, specifically," Vera added. To the table, she said, "We've all helped here at one time or another."

"Hey, thanks for stopping by," I told them as Vann stood up next to me. "You can go ahead and tell me it was the best meal of your life. You're supposed to lie to your friends."

"It's up there," Kaya insisted. "Like for real. No lies necessary."

My cheeks flushed at her compliment. Kaya wouldn't lie to me, even if I asked her to. She was too much of a straight shooter. Besides, she'd want me to get better if I was doing something wrong and telling a chef exactly what they wanted wasn't the way to do that.

"Y'all are seriously the best." I felt the tears threatening again, so it was time to leave. "I'll tell Chrissy this meal's on me."

"Not happening," Killian ordered, his mouth full of a croissant.

Vera gave me an apologetic look. "We're here to support you, friend. Which means we're paying for this meal."

Ezra's face became a little less mottled. "That's a good idea."

Everyone ignored him.

"We should make Ezra get it," Wyatt murmured as he took another sip of his water and avoided everyone's eyes.

"That's a great idea!" Molly agreed, slapping Ezra on the back. "We'll take the check."

The purple color was back, painting Ezra's expression. I smiled at my big brother, so thankful for everything he'd done for me and all his support. He was seriously the most amazing person I knew. And he believed in me from the very beginning. I'd never had to prove myself to him. He just automatically thought I was the perfect person to help his restaurant.

Still, I couldn't not tease him. What kind of little sister let her brother out of stuff like this?

"I'll let Chrissy know. See you guys later."

Vann and I left them to bicker over the check. I could hear them all the way to the kitchen, but it only made me smile.

This was my vision for Bianca—this right here. I wanted a loud, busy dining room. I wanted friends and family meeting here, celebrating, laughing, spending some of the the most important moments of their lives together here. I wanted first dates and anniversary dates and lunch dates. I wanted business meetings and girl nights out and small business pitches. I wanted this dining room to be a revolving door of the chaos of life.

Because the food would be an afterthought. The good food would be a perk of knowing the perfect spot to handle all of your unique and individual needs.

I wanted the answer to the question, "Where do you want to go tonight?" to always be, "Bianca."

But more than anything, right now, I wanted to share this victory with Vann.

"This is the dining room," I told him as we passed through it. "And that's the bar." I pushed through the in and out doors, introducing him to the other half of the restaurant.

The noise paused for only a moment as the scurrying chefs acknowledged the stranger in their midst. And then they turned back to their work and ignored us.

"This is where the magic happens," I told him.

He was silent, thoughtful, as he followed me through. We hurried past the varying stations and all the food being prepared. Not because I was anxious to be alone with him, because he hadn't washed his hands and I was super conscious about food safety.

Mm-hmm.

The hallway was marginally quieter, but it wasn't until we were inside my office that I finally felt as though we had some privacy. He closed the door behind him, grinning at me.

"Are we in a hurry?"

I launched my body at his, wrapping my arms around his neck

and clinging to him like this embrace was the only thing holding me together.

His hands landed on my back, rubbing, soothing, putting the scattered, nervous pieces of me back together. "That's quite the operation you got out there. I had no idea you were so official."

I looked up at him, taking in the short stubble along his jaw. He hadn't shaved this morning and there was something so sexy about that and Saturday morning Vann and the way his body wrapped around mine so naturally.

Curiosity sparked inside me and I couldn't help but ask. "What did you imagine I did?"

"I mean, I don't want to diminish your accomplishments or anything, but I kind of pictured like a McDonald's fry cook or something."

I slapped his chest with my hand, laughing at him. "You're a brat."

He caught my face in his hands, the callouses from riding his bike so often rubbing along my jaw. "And you are beautiful, Dillon Baptiste. I knew you were talented, but I didn't even know someone could be this talented. You've blown my mind."

I rolled my eyes, loving his words of affirmation, but knowing they weren't entirely true. "Your sister's a chef, remember? And light years ahead of me. Thanks, though."

He wouldn't let me walk away. Instead, he held me tighter, dropping the sweetest kiss to my lips. "You're light years ahead of Vera. Are you serious?" He dropped his voice. "It's not even a competition."

It wasn't a competition. And Vann's opinion wasn't super informed because he wasn't a chef. But I loved the tummy flutters and light head his compliments brought.

I smiled at him, drinking him in and this moment and how close our bodies were. "Thanks for coming this morning. It means a lot to me."

"You mean a lot to me," he murmured, dipping his head to trail kisses along my jawline. "I'm so proud of you, Dillon. You did what you set out to do. You rescued the restaurant. You became a chef that can handle all this. You're amazing."

I held him tighter and turned my head to intercept his kisses. My lips were jealous for his mouth.

He didn't hesitate. He kissed me with a wild passion that quickly caught in my blood, burning through me with wicked heat.

Our mouths moved against each other, kissing, biting, tasting. When I gasped for breath, his tongue invaded my mouth, taking command in the very best way. I ran my hands over his broad chest beneath his light blue oxford and shivered as my fingers traced over each tight muscle.

He did the same to me, trying to make sense of the body hidden beneath my chef's coat. Eventually he gave up and flicked open the buttons, His hands delving beneath to do all those things I loved so much.

My breasts in his hands, he walked me back to my desk. I bumped against it and slid to a sitting position, perfectly aligned with his body as I wrapped my legs around his waist and tugged him against me.

"Don't you have to get back out there?" he asked between kisses and moans of pleasure.

"I have a few minutes," I whispered. "As long as we're quiet.

I snapped open the button to his jeans and wiggled the zipper down. Something had come over me. Something like the spirit of a total hussy.

But God, it felt good to be this free. I couldn't remember the last time I'd been so bold with a man. Maybe I never had been. Maybe I'd spent so much of my late teens and early twenties dodging unwanted advances that I hadn't gotten to have fun with it.

I shook my head, kicking those thoughts out of my mind. I ran a finger under the waistband of his boxer briefs and enjoyed the quiver that pulsed through his body. "I probably should have locked the door," he murmured as he leaned over me, pulling the cup of my bra down so he could close his mouth around the peak of my breast. His tongue swirled around my nipple and I had to close my eyes against the sensation.

I plunged my hand into his boxer briefs, wrapping my hand around him. It was my turn.

"Holy shit, Dillon," he groaned. He kissed me in a way I had never been kissed before. In a way that took everything from me, as if he was consuming my very soul as his lips moved over mine in the most delicious way. But he also gave everything in return—like he wasn't just taking my soul, he was exchanging ours. And now he would hold mine. And I would hold his. And they would remain safe and cherished forever within.

He made a rumbly noise in the back of his throat before standing up and knocking my hand away. I looked up at him, desperately trying to catch my breath, assuming that our office tryst was over. His gaze was dark, a thunderstorm rolling through those gray eyes of his. Emotion and desire flickered over his face. And then all at once, he gripped the sides of my black leggings and tugged them down.

I made a sound that was somewhere between a panicked yelp and a desperate moan. He stared at my sex for only a moment, before bringing his mouth back to mine and plunging two fingers inside me.

"My turn," he rasped against my lips.

I couldn't kiss him after that. All I could do was close my eyes and let sensation take over.

He moved his long, rough fingers in and out, filling me only to deny me seconds later. And then fill me again.

Clutching his shoulders for balance, I held on as he drove me closer and closer toward fireworks.

"God, you're so fucking beautiful," he whispered in my hair. "You move me, Dillon. In every way."

His thumb pressed down on just the right spot and I lost the ability to think completely as every muscle in my body tensed and contracted. Lights exploded behind my closed lids and I gasped his name as I tumbled over the edge.

He hummed his approval against my temple and then held me as I pieced myself back together.

Holy hell.

When I had finally collected myself and was able to open my eyes and meet his heated gaze, I couldn't stop the self-conscious blush that stained my entire body.

"Like I said," he teased with a smile lifting the edges of that beautiful mouth of his. "This was, by far, the best brunch I've ever had."

My heart pounded in the fragile cage of my chest, threatening to jump out and run away with this man. "That was..." I pressed the back of my hand to my cheek and tried to shake the glazed, sated look off my face. "That was..."

He smiled. "Will you remember it this time?"

I nibbled on my bottom lip, knowing I could never forget this time. "You're so full of yourself," I said instead of admitting the truth.

His smile kicked up a notch, calling my lie. "And you're so full of it."

Leaning forward, I caught his lips with mine and nearly kissed him into more fun. When I pulled back, I enjoyed the dazed look on his face. "I have to get back to work."

He nodded. "I want to see you again. Soon."

"Okay."

"Is it going to be difficult getting away?"

"I'll figure it out," I promised. "I want to see you again too."

He nodded and kissed me again. Suddenly, I hated work and Bianca and brunch. All I wanted to do was kiss this man and see what other fun things he could do with those very dexterous fingers.

"Walk me out?" he said when we were able to calm down and some of the blush had disappeared from my cheeks.

Of course, my hair was a mess and I was still trying to unrumple my clothes.

We said goodbye without kisses and promised to text later.

If anyone in the kitchen noticed the sexed-up look painting my expression, they didn't say anything. Seamlessly, I jumped back into head chef territory.

There was something about Vann that swept me away, that took over me completely. He was the first man I'd ever been willing to take a chance on. The first relationship that had demanded my attention, that compelled me to dive in deeper.

Vann was becoming so much more than I knew how to explain. He had saved me over and over. But now, he was saving me from something so much bigger than adulting.

He was saving my heart.

TWENTY-ONE

"YOU'RE SURE YOU GOT THIS?"

Blaze laughed on the other end of the phone. I held it away from my face for a second and checked the number just to be sure I'd called the right person. I'd made Blaze laugh. Boom!

"Yeah, I'm sure," he returned confidently. "You know, you've left me in charge before. I can make it through a night without burning anything down." He paused and then added, "Or burning anything for that matter. I'm very proficient at not burning things in general."

I rushed to assure him I had faith in him. "No, I know. I realize you're good at what you do. It's just, you know, your first time with the new menu and we have that new hire and—"

"Chef, seriously, we're good! Have fun on your date."

"Doctor's appointment," I clarified, but then couldn't remember if I'd said doctor's appointment or dentist appointment earlier.

"Mm-hmm."

"What are you saying?"

"Hey, it's cool. You've been working twenty-four-seven. If you need the night off, take the night off. You're the boss."

I was the boss. I was the boss of a kitchen that was starting to act like a kitchen. And it felt amazing. So when Vann had texted to see if I could get the night off and do the Taco Tuesday ride he did with his cyclist friends every week, I'd jumped at the chance.

"You're a good guy," I told Blaze, genuinely meaning it. "And a great sous chef. Thanks for covering for me."

"Anytime," he promised.

God, that felt so good. Sunday House was officially off the menu for him. He was fully committed to Bianca and me. This was loyalty. This was trust. And I was so grateful it went both ways.

I clicked off with Blaze and smiled at Vann. "Everything good?" he asked.

Stepping closer to him, I nodded my head and pressed a kiss to his jawline. "Everything's good."

"Mmm," he rumbled, pulling me into a deeper, longer, more satisfactory kiss. We were tucked away in his office, making the most of our privacy—something we were getting really good at.

Since our first date by the lake, we'd seen each other as much as we could over the last month. But to be honest, between our opposite work schedules and individual busy days and nights, our offices had been our most consistent meeting place.

I would pop over to his shop for lunch during the week. And he would swing over to mine after hours while I worked on paperwork and closed Bianca. On Sundays, he would hang out for brunch. And now I was here, with him, waiting for the rest of his bike gang to show up so we could ride twenty miles for "the best tacos in the Carolinas."

I doubted that, but I was willing to check it out.

Cycling still wasn't my thing, but I had fun with Vann, and he promised me this trip involved beer. I just hoped he wouldn't have to bust out his first aid skills on me a second time. Me, plus cycling and drinking beer all night, did not sound like the safest combination.

But I was willing to try anything once.

Okay, that was a lie. But I was willing to try at least some things as long as Vann was involved.

His hands dipped beneath my tight workout tank and squeezed

my sides. I slid back on his desk and wrapped my legs around his waist. Our mouths moved against each other with increasing hunger.

I loved the scrape of his five o'clock shadow on my face tonight. Wrapping my arms around his neck, I arched my back and pressed more tightly against him.

He made another rumbly sound when I caught his bottom lip between my teeth at the same time I scraped my nails against the back of his neck. "You're something else," he murmured against my lips.

"You're one to talk."

His smile broke the kiss, both of us gasping for air with the reprieve. He took a step back, running a hand through his unkempt hair while I pressed mine to my swollen lips and tried to figure out how we'd gotten to this place where we kissed whenever we wanted and neither of us felt the need to ask permission.

The permission was already given. He had consent to kiss me as much as he wanted.

Praise hands emojis all day every day.

He pulled back and our gazes crashed together. There was something so deep in his gray eyes, something hidden but surfacing, open but not yet exposed.

"I like you a lot, Baptiste."

His words were said in the richest, warmest tone. They shot straight to my heart and spiraled all the way down to my toes.

"I like you a lot too, Delane."

"It's different though, isn't it?"

"What?"

"Us," he said simply.

I held his gaze, but didn't know what to make of his thoughts. "What do you mean?"

"Has it ever been like this for you? I mean, in a relationship?"

I hadn't ever really been in a relationship before, so I wasn't sure what to say. "No," seemed like an honest-enough answer. "I've never felt like this about anybody before."

One side of his mouth kicked up in a half-smile. "There's something here," he murmured, his eyes a stormy tempest of truth and raw honesty. "There's something between us."

My heart kicked in my chest, a jolt of surprise rocketing through me. "What do you mean?"

His head dipped and the other side of his mouth joined in a blinding, breathtaking smile. "I'm just saying I'm glad we're together."

If I thought my heartbeat was fast before, it tripled with those sweet words. My entire body felt like it was rushing and speeding and twirling out of control. I had so many emotions I didn't know how to pick one as the most dominant. God, it felt good for him to say that, to say we were a couple. Like way, way good.

In a way I had never expected it to.

This man, that had been so completely annoying at first and then cocky and then just everywhere, had somehow turned into home for me. He'd gone from stranger, to friend, to my everything. And I wasn't even sure how it had happened?

I certainly wasn't looking for a serious relationship when Vann walked into my life. I wasn't even looking for a non-serious relationship. I had just wanted to survive the day. And Bianca. And this life of mine that felt too much for me.

And yet, his careful approach had been exactly what I'd needed. All the different times he saved me and cared for me had taught me to trust him before we were even friends. Vann had proven what kind of man he was before he ever asked me out or kissed me or even slept with me—not that I had let us go all the way since that drunken rehearsal night... but it didn't matter because apparently some subconscious part of my brain had already trusted him.

That was huge for someone like me. Someone whose trust had been so totally and wholly shattered. Someone who didn't think she would ever get naked with a man again, let alone sleep with him... let alone give him all of her heart.

My past was separated from my present one day at a time. It was like tearing off wallpaper with a plastic fork. Slow, frustrating and time-consuming. But I was starting to see some progress. I was starting to differentiate between what happened one night at a party at some guy named Justin's house, and the care and devotion of a committed relationship.

Even without considering the rape—which was nearly impossible to do—my dating back then had been random hookups and one-night stands. I would never, ever, ever, in a hundred million years, believe that I had somehow asked for that to happen to me. But I wasn't dating the caliber of man I needed in general. I had been settling for second and third and fourth best.

I had been scared to be who I was. And because I couldn't come to terms with the person I was, I let other people define me. I let them tell me who I was and what I wanted.

And in the middle of that sticky, ugly, broken mess, I'd been drugged. And raped.

This thing between Vann and me could not have been more different. He cared about me. He was committed to me. He went out of his way for me. And he was apparently going to be damn sure I could remember him if he ever decided to sleep with me again.

I loved the way he'd said it too. Because, yes, good grief, there was something about him I could not ignore. I was drawn to him, pulled in. I thought everything he said was funny and that he was maybe the most wonderful human on the planet.

It was sappy and mushy, and I'd totally sold out for love.

Yuck.

Er, wait. Love? I didn't mean that. I couldn't meant that.

"What was that?" I teased, too afraid of the direction of my thoughts to stay serious. "We're a couple? Are you sure, because this is the first time I'm hearing about it."

He smiled, in that self-deprecating way that told me he knew he'd slipped that profound declaration in a little too casually.

"Is that all right?" he asked, and it was the sweetest question I had ever heard in my entire life.

"Hmm, that depends," I teased. "What exactly are you asking?"

Now his lips pursed into a frown, not nearly as happy with my question as I had been with his. "This is awkward as grown-ups," he admitted. "If we were seventeen, I'd ask you to be my girlfriend."

My smile was probably blinding him, but I couldn't help it. "You could still ask me."

Surprise flashed in his eyes, but it settled into that same mysterious affection I noticed earlier. God, I wanted to know what it was. I wanted him to open his mouth and spill all his secrets. I wanted to know every last thought in Vann Delane's head because I was positive, I would love them all.

"Will you be my girlfriend, Dillon Baptiste? Exclusively?"

I nodded while I tried to find the ability to speak. It was a juvenile request of me to ask. And probably obsolete as most people our age didn't sit down and ask each other to go steady with them. But I had never been formally asked to be anybody's girlfriend before, so to me, it was everything. Everything I had been waiting for and wanting and needing.

And he wanted to be exclusive. Not that he ever had anything to worry about on my side, but dang, it was good to hear him say exactly what he wanted.

Sorry, but there was nothing wrong with a little define the relationship talk, especially when it led to such happy results.

"Yes," I breathed, pushing the word past my lips. "Yes, I'd love to be your girlfriend, Vann Delane. I'm exclusively yours."

Stepping closer to me, he wrapped me up in his arms and held me there for a long time. My cheek pressed against his chest, his heart beating steadily inside him. It was incredibly comfortable and wonderful and... safe.

I realized with Vann I felt nothing but safe.

"Are you ready for this?" he asked after a few minutes. "It's going to be fun."

"You say that like you're convincing yourself."

He took my hand and pulled me with him out of his office. "It is fun," he insisted.

"See? You're kind of backing up my point here."

"There are tacos. And margaritas."

"If I'm reading between the lines accurately," I looked at him, suppressing a smile, "and I do believe that I am, this whole bike ride thing is going to suck but you're reminding me that there will be food and libations if I persevere through the sucky parts of it."

His smile and rumble of laughter was enough to send tingles racing through my body. "What? That's crazy."

I couldn't help but smile in return, even if I knew I was exactly right. "Uh-huh."

"I bought you something," he murmured, the smile never dimming. "I mean, you know I own the shop and everything. But I promise I picked this out just for you."

I repeated the words echoing through my head. "Wait, what?"

We stepped outside into the hot early August heat and I nearly melted right then and there, next to the prettiest Tiffany Blue bike with a comfy white banana seat and a basket between the handlebars. There was even a pretty pink bow tied around the front.

The realization of what was happening hit me like a ton of bricks and for a second time, I said, "Wait. What? Are you serious?" He wore the most beautiful smile yet. It was his biggest, his brightest, his most blinding. This was, hands down, the most stunning creature I had ever laid eyes on. "Vann, did you buy me this bike?"

He tucked his hands into his pocket and grinned away.

"Vann, for real, is this for me?"

He shrugged. And shuffled his foot. "You're always complaining about how uncomfortable bike seats are."

I turned to face him, readying to throw my arms around his neck and kiss him senseless when a voice called out from the ugly recesses of my past.

"Dillon? No way!"

Dread curdled through me, tightening around my bones until

they felt crushed beneath the pressure. I froze. Actually froze in place. My limbs refused to move. My heart stopped mid-beat. My brain turned to an unusable icicle in my head. I stood there, half turned toward Vann, half sucked into the vortex of my hellish nightmare.

"Dillon!" the voice called for a second time. "No fucking way!"

I could feel Vann's curious gaze crawl over my skin. I could hear the questions bouncing around in his head, filling the air with my worst fears. I could sense my past, that night six years ago, springing from the grave to zombie the shit out of my present life.

"What the hell are you doing here?" Not being able to respond, did not deter Justin from carrying on a conversation. He was exactly like I remembered him. Stoner meets ungodly amount of family money meets only ever interested in a good time. He was one of those people you could never be good friends with because he was all shallow end and no substance. "Do you know the bike shop guy? Are you buying this bike?" There was a pause before he tried a different tactic. "Is she buying this bike?"

"It's a gift," Vann answered, his voice taut, strained. "Dillon, are you okay?"

"You do know each other! How crazy is that?" Justin just kept babbling like my behavior wasn't totally off, like I clearly didn't want to be anywhere near here.

"How do you know her?" Vann demanded. His hand landed on my back in what was meant to be a protective gesture. I flinched at the contact and pulled away, finally breaking the paralysis that had taken over.

"Dillon and I go way back," Justin explained. He folded his arms over his long-sleeved shirt and grinned at me. "We grew up getting in trouble together."

God, that sounded way more salacious than it was. But then again, wasn't that the whole point? We would party together. We would drink and experiment with drugs together. And we would apparently let each other get drugged and raped.

Those fuzzy memories tripped through my mind again. The ones I couldn't quite grasp. The ones that whispered the awful truth but never let me examine it closely.

"Is that so?" Vann asked, reaching for me again.

I stepped away, wrapping my arms around my middle and wishing for a getaway car. I just wanted to run away. And then I wanted to crawl into a steaming hot shower and never leave.

"God, I haven't seen you in fucking forever, DB. It's been at least..."

"Six years."

He grinned at me, not understanding the significance at all. "Has it really been six years? What the hell happened to you? You just..." he made an explosion sound with his mouth and gestured with both fists, "disappeared."

Courage slithered between my breastbone and heart, forcing a path where fear and pain and my past threatened to crush and destroy. "Do you remember the last time we saw each other, Justin? Do you remember that party?"

His blank look said everything. To be fair, I didn't think he was the guy that had drugged me. He liked to have a good time, but he also liked for it to be mutual.

"It was at your house. Right after you got home from Ibiza."

His face lit with recognition. "I brought back the good gummies."

I didn't know about that. Gummies. My party had ended after a cocktail.

"You were wasted that night." His head tipped back as he laughed at the memory. My stomach turned and my mouth watered with the nauseous threat. "Good times, good times."

"Are you here for a reason?" Vann demanded. He was practically vibrating with fury, but all I could do was stand there and tremble.

"The taco and beer ride?" Justin turned back to me. "What happened to you, Baptiste? Nobody's seen you in forever. Scotty heard that you died."

"I didn't die." But there were nights there at the beginning that I thought I might want to. Not for any other reason than to get the disgusting feeling of a stranger's unwanted hands all over my body out of my head.

"You should come out with us again," he insisted. "We're going to Bendi's tonight. And next weekend, we're going up to Leyla's lodge. You should come. Remember her fucking hot tub?" He laughed at his own phrasing. "Remember the time we—"

"No." The word was a sterling silver bullet blasted from my mouth.

Justin's manicured eyebrows lifted. "What?"

"I don't do that stuff anymore. I have a job."

"A what?"

"A job."

He looked around at the bike shop, trying to figure out how I fit. "Here?"

"Er, no." I let my answer hang in the air for a few minutes while Justin tried to process everything. "At a restaurant called Bianca."

"Oh." Justin squinted at me and dropped his voice. "Wait a job? Are you like... poor now or something?"

I rolled my eyes. Some of the crippling fear receded in light of this guy's lunacy. "No, dummy, I'm not poor. I just... I needed purpose. I didn't want to waste my entire life at Leyla's lodge. I went back to school and got my culinary arts degree. I just took over as the executive chef."

He ran a hand through his floppy dishwater blonde hair. "That's cool." The interest in catching up with me had already diminished. I was a different girl than the one he knew six years ago. "Oh. Sweet."

Said in the flattest voice ever.

"I want to go." I heard the words as they left my mouth, but even I was surprised I'd said them.

Justin looked at me funny. "What?"

I realized he thought I meant to Leyla's. Turning to Vann so there was no confusion this time, I held back tears and whispered. "I want to go home."

Vann took a step closer to me and grabbed my biceps with supportive hands. "Are you okay?"

I ripped my body away from his touch, not able to disconnect his comfort with my unwanted past. Wrapping my arms tighter around my waist, I shook my head and hiccupped a choked sob. "No. I need to go."

"What's wrong with her?" Justin asked Vann.

Tears blurred my vision so I couldn't read the look Vann gave Justin. "How about you back off and let me take care of her?"

"Dude, something's got her fucked up."

"Yeah, dude," Vann snarled. "I'm starting to think that fucked up something is you. So back up."

Justin finally stepped out of the way, arms raised in surrender. "It's not me. I haven't even seen her in forever."

A guttural cry escaped the prison of my chest and I nearly collapsed right there in front of Vann's shop and the crowd of cyclists gathering near the curb. Vann reached for me out of instinct, but drew his hand up short when he saw me flinch again.

"Fuck," he muttered to himself. "Let me... put this inside. Do you want to walk with me?" He grabbed the pretty blue bicycle that he'd surprised me with by the handlebars. I cried harder, realizing I had just totally screwed up our night.

Maybe our entire relationship.

Justin's face was all over my mind now and with it, memory after bad memory of all the terrible mistakes I'd made. But most prominently the horrific mistake that wasn't mine to claim, but mine to bear. Forever and ever.

Vann managed to get the bike inside his shop and lock the door while I huddled near him without touching him. He kept shooting furtive glances my way. Every single time those stormy gray eyes filled with concern it made me cry harder.

Hadn't I been praising my breakthrough with this man not minutes ago? And now I was trapped in my nightmare, a mental loop of the events of that night spinning around in my head without stopping.

Somehow, I ended up in Vann's Jeep. And somehow he drove me home while I curled into the fetal position in his passenger seat.

He kept saying, "It's going to be okay, Dillon. I've got you." Over and over those words were like a blanket on my ice-cold skin.

I've got you. I've got you. I've got you.

He parked at my apartment building in a visitor's spot and turned off the car. I had expected him to drop me off at the front and drive off into the sunset, anxious to get away from the psycho in the middle of a nervous breakdown.

"I'm going to walk you upstairs," he told me firmly. "I don't think you can do it on your own."

I nodded numbly, not knowing what else to do. I was afraid he was right. I was also afraid of what my doorman, Teddy, would say if I stumbled through the front door looking like this.

There was a huge chance Vann was right too—I couldn't make it upstairs on my own.

"Just... please, don't touch me." My voice was ragged and small, barely audible.

His voice broke too. "Dillon, you're killing me."

Fresh tears poured out of my eyes. "I'm sorry."

"Don't. Please don't apologize."

He shoved his door open and hurried around the front of his Jeep to open my door. I wished I was strong enough to ask him to carry me upstairs. I wished I could find the courage to touch him. To remember that he wasn't the one that had hurt me.

But my body had locked down. When confronted with fight or flight, I'd chosen to freeze. My teeth chattered as my body surged with adrenaline and those groping, clawing, intrusive hands.

He ripped my dress off and tore my underwear away from me. He shoved my legs open and thrust inside me. Then he held my arms down as I weakly tried to fight back.

I gasped for breath and tried to sink to my knees. Vann scooped me up even while I cried out.

Minutes past as I fought for clarity, as I beat the demons back and tried to reemerge in the present.

When Vann was finally able to take my keys from me and open my apartment door, he deposited me on my sofa and hurried to the kitchen. I heard water running as I pulled my knees to my chest and rocked myself back and forth.

"Should I call someone?" he asked, hovering over me with a glass of water in one hand and a throw blanket in the other. "Ezra? Your mom? Vera?"

I shook my head. This was bad enough. I didn't want to introduce anyone else to my secret shame.

"No," I sniffled between sobs. "I'm fine."

He was silent for a minute before saying. "No, you're not, Dillon. You're not fine. Something is seriously wrong."

I cried harder. His words had hit with such precision, it was like they'd punctured my heart and ripped it open.

Tipping over on the couch, I stayed there sobbing, with my knees pulled up to my chest for a long time. Vann covered me with a blanket and took a seat at the other end of the couch.

"I'm here for you, Dillon. I'll be right here. If you need anything let me know."

I couldn't find the words to thank him, but his presence was enough. It was soothing to know he wasn't going to leave.

His presence was like a guard against the evil thoughts and memories from six years ago. He sat still and silent at the end of the couch, respecting my wish for him not to touch me, and slowly the broken pieces of my soul started to piece themselves back together again. My sobs became silent as the tears continued to fall, but my body shook and trembled less, and my heartbeat began to steady.

I hadn't had a crying jag like that in a couple years. Not since my senior year of school.

My therapist would call this a relapse. And that was exactly what it felt like. All the careful work I'd trudged through to make the small steps toward healing undone and erased.

Two small steps forward, six hundred steps back. Right to that memory of that bedroom. Right to that drug-blurred night.

Eventually there were no tears left to cry. My eyes dried and my soul shriveled. I sat up and I turned toward Vann, tucking myself into the farthest corner of the couch.

He looked at me, eyes red and strained. There was despair there, fear I had never seen except when looking in the mirror.

"I was raped." The words fell out of my mouth as an apology and an explanation. "Drugged. And then raped."

TWENTY-TWO

VANN DIDN'T EVEN FLINCH. I realized my reaction to Justin told more than my words ever could have. "Was it by that fucking asshole? I will go back and kill him if he touched you, Dillon. Say the fucking word."

He was serious. The truth of his threat rang through the room. Another piece of my soul clicked back into place. I didn't condone murder by any means, but Vann's willingness to go that far for me helped restore some of my faith in humanity in a messed up kind of way.

"It wasn't Justin," I told him, fighting through the sick feeling curdling in my stomach. "It happened at his party though."

"You're sure?" Vann asked. "Because that smug motherfucker rubbed me the wrong way."

My lips twitched at his zeal. It had been six years after all. Six. I had survived the aftermath for six whole years. I wasn't a victim anymore. I was a survivor. Even if the pain of what happened still threatened to suck out my soul and shatter it into a million unfixable pieces.

"It was a guy I didn't know. I don't even remember his name. I'm not sure I ever knew it to begin with."

"What did you tell the cops then?"

I pressed my lips together, ashamed to admit the truth. And maybe this was what killed me the most—that at the end of the day I was a coward. I was a fucking coward that hadn't even been able to stand up for myself.

These words had never left my mouth before. Not all of them. My therapist had heard broken, battered bits of the story, but never all at once. She had been the only person I'd been able to tell. And only because it had felt like life or death, only because the secret couldn't stay trapped inside only me. I needed someone else to share the burden, to understand the depth of my pain.

"I didn't," I whispered, feeling like I would choke on the truth.

"What do you mean?"

"I didn't tell the cops."

His lips pressed into a straight line, his eyes filling with sorrow, frustration, and anger. So much anger.

The words came in a rush. Confessing my personal sin opened the floodgate and my secrets spilled from my soul. "I was drugged. I remember taking a cocktail from someone at Justin's, but I don't remember who. Someone had been passing them around. Mine was drugged. Or maybe they were all drugged. I'm not sure..." I turned my head, staring out the window at the city. I couldn't look at Vann. I couldn't bear his judgment. "I have memories of what happened, but they're blurry. Foggy. Sometimes I wonder if I've made them up completely." I took a steadying breath and let the words settle in the air. The truth, in all its messed-up-ness was like getting thrown off a bridge. The falling sensation rocked through me like a cannon.

"I can't remember what he looked like," I whispered. "I don't have a name. Or a description. Or even clarity of what exactly happened that night."

Vann ground his teeth together. I could feel his anger, his outrage. I felt sick, too afraid to ask if it was directed at me.

And then, as if I needed to prove myself to this man that had trusted me until now, the events of the night came tumbling out of me. "I used to be wild," I told him. "A total mess. My dad was sick and then dying and then dead... It started in high school though. We were rich assholes with too much money and not enough parental supervision. I was at a party every weekend and nothing was off limits. Alcohol, sex, drugs... When my dad died, I just... I just lost the ability to care about consequences. He'd been absent my entire life. Even when I lived at his house, he wasn't there. Even when he spent time with me, he was never there. Never truly present. I grew up being the thing he used to manipulate my mom. Or the party trick he would prance around social clubs with. I wasn't his daughter. I was his weapon. By the time I got to high school and he could no longer use me anymore, I didn't even know what my purpose was anymore. I mean, how fucked up is that? That's when the drinking started. And then the drugs. And I was out of control. When he died... I don't know, something snapped inside me. By the time I showed up to Justin's party, I thought I didn't care about anything. I thought nothing could make me feel again. Nothing could make me care. And then I accepted a drink I shouldn't have. The memories are blurry at best. I woke up to hands all over me. They were rough... painful. I remember trying to swat them away, but I was so damn weak." Tears leaked from my eyes again and I was surprised there was any moisture left in my body. My chest shuddered as I tried to breathe through the lancing pain across my rib cage. "He pulled off my clothes and I could not stop him. I was in and out of it, waking up in the worst of the pain. He would shove my face with his hand, shutting me up when I tried to make a protest. He smelled like too strong cologne and cheap beer." I glanced at Vann, my voice breaking when I saw tears reflected in his eyes. "I woke up naked and sore and sick the next morning. Justin's place was mostly empty. But I didn't stick around to see if anyone was there or had seen anything. I fled. I ran away. And I never went back."

"You didn't tell anyone?"

I shook my head, loose strands of hair getting caught on my wet cheeks. "I didn't know what to say. I was too ashamed to tell Ezra. I should have gone to the police, I realize that now. But I was twenty-one and terrified. I had no hard evidence. I had no memory of what the guy looked like. I had nothing. Plus, at the time, I was afraid that if they called in character witnesses, they would find out that drugs were... I wasn't like this upstanding citizen, okay? And the thought of them using a rape kit on me..." I hiccupped through another sob, wishing I could shrug off the shame that had followed me since that day. "I would do things over if I could. I would do anything to go back to that morning after and make different decisions."

"Dillon..."

"I did finally get tested for disease and pregnancy though. About a month later. I couldn't stomach the idea of having to live with something venereal forever. And I was worried about a baby."

My heart hammered at those awful memories. The thing about being violated was that it didn't end after the act was over. The actual act, the actual rape, had been the quickest part. It was the rest that would follow me around for my entire life. It was the pain and sorrow, the grief, the shame and embarrassment, the stupid guilt that shouldn't even be mine. It was the tests that happened later. The continued exposure as I tried to make sure my body had survived in ways my soul hadn't. And for those women that were brave enough to tell law enforcement... they had more tests and testimony, they had court cases and lawyers and opportunity after opportunity to relive their horror. The rapist walked away free as a fucking bird, while we had to suffer it over and over and over.

"I'm clean," I quickly added. "And there was no pregnancy caused by it." The words tasted like ash in my mouth, but I still managed to spit them out. "In those ways, I got lucky, I guess."

Vann moved so quickly I barely caught my breath before he was kneeling in front of me, his hands tentatively on my knees, his eyes dark and intense. "Not lucky. Nothing about that is lucky." His fingertips dug into my knees and I found that I didn't want to push him away now that the story was out in the open, no longer hiding inside only me. "Dillon, I am sorry that happened to you. It's not okay. Nothing about it is okay. I am wrecked that you had to survive that violence."

I shook my head, tears falling freely. "I feel like a coward for never telling anyone. He could still be out there. He could still be doing that to other women."

He lunged forward, wrapping me up in his arms, cradling me against him. "You're not a coward," he whispered against my temple. "You're the bravest woman I have ever known."

"Vann..."

"Stop," he ordered, his gravelly voice sounding as though it had been dragged over hot coals. "I refuse to let you blame yourself for any part of that night. That should never have happened to you. You should never have been put in a position where you would have to question your decisions every damn day. That fucking asshole should never have touched you. That's what should have happened. He's the goddamn coward. Not you." He pulled back, cradling my face as gently as humanly possible with both hands. "I have never met anyone more beautiful than you, Dillon Baptiste. I have never met anyone as kind or as giving or as funny. You are everything that is beautiful and lovely. Everything that is sweet. You are the opposite of all that happened. And if I ever find out who it was, I promise, we will make him pay. I promise, he will suffer like you have. He fucking dared to hurt something I love so much, I would be happy to put him away forever."

My wounded heart tripped over his words, finding more pieces of itself at the same time it grew in my dormant chest. "Love?"

He seemed to realize what he'd said and that it had been the first time that word had been whispered between us. It only took him a moment to nod with conviction. "Yes, love. I love you, Dillon. I've been falling slowly for you since you walked into the Bianca kitchen when you wanted to turn down the job. I had never seen anyone as beautiful and confused and frustrated as you. I nearly dropped the stack of plates I was holding that night. Since then it's been a downward spiral into wholeness. I love you. I want to keep loving you."

I threw my arms around his neck and pressed my heart against his chest, needing the comfort of his solid body. "I love you too," I cried, fresh tears wetting my lashes. "I didn't know I'd be able to feel this way. Not after what had happened. And not after confessing it. I didn't even know if I was... loveable. Or if I had the ability to love back. I thought I would be empty forever. Forever broken. And yet you've made me feel like a can be whole again. Complete. Anything but empty. I love you, Vann Delane. I hope I always do."

He held me like that for a long time. Our hearts beating against each other, our arms wrapped securely around one another.

He held me until I stopped crying. He held me until I could smile again. He held me until I was brave enough to face the world again.

I STEPPED out of the shower the next morning and wrapped myself up in a towel. Blinking at my reflection in the steamed-up mirror, I reached out and wiped my hand over the cool glass, making a window for my face.

My eyes were still puffy from yesterday's crying and my fresh face had seen better days. My long, wet hair dripped at my shoulders, water droplets rolling into the gray towel I'd secured tightly. But there was a light inside me that hadn't been there in a long time—maybe ever. I looked stronger today. I looked resilient. I looked... confident.

This was me, I realized. No fake personality to make other people feel comfortable. No dark, twisted secrets to stash away in the recesses of my soul. No pretense. This girl in the mirror had bared it all to someone she loved last night, and she had lived to tell about it.

That was the definition of surviving for me. This was the goal in living. Opening up to Vann and sharing all the dirty details of that night six years ago, had changed me. But this time, in a good way.

There were women out there that could tell their stories boldly. Loudly. Despite their fear and shame, they sought justice above all. I applauded those women.

I truly did.

To me, they were heroes. Not just victims. Not just survivors. But real-life warriors waging war against one of the worst kinds of injustice.

But there were so many more women like me. Women not brave enough to share their stories with the world. Women not able to even speak the words to people that were close to them. Women not even able to utter them aloud and let them live in the open air.

The pain was too personal. The memories too close. The horror and trauma of the constant nightmare we had to live with. It wasn't just fear that held us back from speaking out. It was grief too. And pain and shame and a million other things. Every victim of sexual assault was doing their best just to live through the days that followed. Just survive the fucking day and the torrent of blame and awful thoughts spinning through our heads at all hours.

Maybe one day I would speak out. Maybe one day, I could stand up and share my story beyond the walls of my therapist's office and this apartment. But today, telling Vann had been enough. Telling one person that understood me and believed me and supported me was... life.

Maybe that seemed cowardly to the outside world, but I was learning that bravery looked different for everyone. But most of all, healing took time. Years. Sometimes an entire lifetime.

And right now, today, this morning, pieces of me that had been broken for a long time felt... mended.

That was enough for me. At least for now.

I didn't know what could be done at this point anyway, so much time had passed from the night everything happened. I had a specific date, a specific location and too many fuzzy memories. No DNA testing could be done. No likeness could be drawn. No names could be given.

Vann was insistent that we try. Neither of us liked the idea of that monster prowling around free, looking for other women to victimize. But he also refused to let me take the blame for that. He refused to let me share any of the rapist's guilt. It was the rapist. Not me.

Never me.

I found that I was starting to believe him. That I believed him more than I didn't believe him. Which was a strange feeling after being unable to trust nearly the entire male species as a whole for so long.

But I did trust Vann. And I wouldn't have been able to had I not fallen so hard and so completely for him.

He was waiting in my room when I walked out of the bathroom. He was tucked into a chair against the wall, flipping through Netflix options without settling on anything. His eyes found my still wet body immediately.

They eventually made it to my eyes but not before taking their time moving up from toes to nose.

"Feel better?" he asked in that sweet, careful voice he'd been using with me all day.

I nodded. The hot shower had felt amazing after yesterday, cleansing and soothing and like it had washed away the ickiness that lingered.

Vann had spent the night after we'd fallen asleep in each other's arms on the couch, talking and talking and talking. We talked through more of my past. And he shared his with me. We talked about what it was like to have a parent die, my dad and his mom, and how that left grief marks so deeply etched in our hearts that it was easy to want to fill those lines with something else. We talked about my years in culinary school and how food had started my healing process. We talked about his years with Cycle Life and how lonely that had been for him. At some point our eyes had closed, even as we continued to talk. And heal. And fall deeper and deeper in love.

It was in those hours that I knew I trusted this man completely. He had my heart. He had my soul. And he could have my body whenever he wanted because he would never be the man from six years ago. He would never disrespect me or hurt me in that way.

The rapist six years ago was a monster.

Vann Delane was the man I loved.

I woke up to him carrying me to my room, cradled in his arms. He'd attempted to settle me in bed and walk away, but I'd caught his fingers before he could go anywhere and pulled him down with me.

We'd woken up, tangled in each other's arms. He'd ordered breakfast from Uber Eats and we'd enjoyed veggie egg-white omelets and protein shakes from his favorite nearby food truck. It had been a little too healthy for me, but I loved spending time with him and enjoyed the meal despite the lackluster components. And I could admit that Vann was going to be good for my diet.

I was sure he needed to go to work soon, as did I. But I couldn't bring myself to suggest that he leave.

When our gazes finally found each other, his was burning with heat, liquid silver with desire. A tingle followed the same path as his look, starting in my toes and rocketing through me. My heart kicked against my breastbone and my core thrummed with anticipation.

We had been through something devastating and emotional last night. I had cried for hours. And he had shed tears with me. Then he'd held me the entire night, wrapped securely in his strong, safe arms. And helped me start picking up my shattered pieces.

The connection between us was stronger than ever. As was this building attraction.

I loved him.

He loved me.

And yet we'd only been fully intimate one time and I could barely remember it.

I found myself desperate to separate that experience from the one six years ago. I wanted to put as much space between Vann and the faceless rapist as possible.

Not only that... I wanted Vann.

Wanted his body and the experience. I wanted his hands all over me and his mouth everywhere and for his body to touch mine in ways that would leave me forever branded by him.

Vann looked away, rubbing his hands on his athletic pants. He'd taken a shower first thing this morning and borrowed my toothbrush, but he only had his clothes from yesterday. They were rumpled and adorable, and God, I wanted to rip them off him.

"Hey," I murmured, desperate to have his gaze on me again.

He looked up. I dropped my towel. His eyes bugged and his lips parted. That was probably the last thing he had expected me to do.

"Dillon, I..."

I could see him struggling for words and it only made me more comfortable. I walked toward him, surprised at how confident I felt in the full light of day.

He licked dry lips and tried to speak again. "We don't have to... I know you're still upset... I don't want to rush you..."

I climbed onto his lap, straddling his hips with zero protest from him. His inability to function properly made me smile.

"I want to," I told him. His gaze searched for mine again, needing full permission. "I want you, Vann. You're nothing like... that night. This is what I want. You are what I want. And not just in this way. I want you in every way. I love you." His Adam's apple bobbed up and down in a sign of emotion. "I trust you."

His hands landed tentatively on my waist, careful, gentle... hopeful. "I love you too," he promised.

Our mouths crashed together with that final permission, hungry, greedy, and desperate for more. His teeth scraped over my bottom lip and his tongue invaded my mouth, tasting me, devouring me.

I let him take over, coaxing me deeper and deeper into desire. Tugging at the hem of his t-shirt, I was tired of being the only one not clothed. He pulled at it, helping me yank it over his head.

Our bodies crashed back together, my bare breasts against his solid chest. I moaned at the sensation. His hands landed on my hips and tugged me more fully against him.

"You are the most beautiful thing I have ever seen," he murmured between kisses. "God, woman, I am so fucking lucky."

My heartbeat tripled at his sweet words, letting them sink into my blood, deep into the center of my bones. "I need more," I gasped, running my hands over all that warm, glorious skin of his chest and biceps.

"Mmm," he agreed.

One of his hands held my breast, rubbing his thumb over my nipple the way I liked. His other pulled the back of my knee, spreading my legs wider, seating me tightly against his hard body.

My hips started writhing on their own and he pinched my nipple until my back arched in pleasure.

"I want you, Dillon," he whispered. "More than I've ever wanted anyone or anything."

"Take me then," I ordered, ready for all that he had to offer.

He smiled against my mouth. "Better make it memorable though, yeah?"

A squeak escaped me as he scooped me into his arms before tossing me on the edge of the bed. I raised my hands above my head, expecting him to follow me, when suddenly he was gone.

I leaned up on my elbows to find that he'd dropped to his knees so his head could disappear between my legs. I gasped, clawing at the down comforter on my bed while he drove me toward madness.

"Vann," I panted as he did wicked things with his tongue and teeth.

"So fucking lovely," he murmured against my most sensitive place.

Two of his fingers joined his mouth, reaching so deep inside me I thought I would faint. I made sounds I had never made before. And writhed like a woman who had lost her mind to sex.

His thumb found the place I needed him most at the same time he whispered, "I could watch you all day."

Lights exploded behind my closed eyelids as every muscle in my body tightened in pleasure. The orgasm rocked through me, curling in my core before stretching to every limb. My back lifted off the bed as my knees closed around Vann's head tight enough to crush the poor man.

When I finally came down from the experience, he was standing over me with a satisfied smile on his handsome face. "God, I love you."

I bit my bottom lip and nodded my head. "I love you too."

He started to pull down his athletic pants but stopped before he got to the good part. "Shit, I don't have a condom."

And that opened up a conversation we needed to have. "I'm on birth control. Especially since, uh, it happened. I just... it's important to me, even though I've been celibate for six years."

A dark emotion crossed over his expression at the memory.

Wanting to push past it, I asked, "But have you been tested recently?"

The darkness faded into an affectionate smile. "We went over this the last time. I've been tested recently and I'm totally clean. You're also clean. You assured me like ten times the first time."

Hazy memories flickered through my mind of going above and beyond the call of duty to assure him I was good to go.

Oh, good grief. That was embarrassing. I slapped a hand over my eyes and groaned. "Now I remember."

The sound of his pants sliding off his body and dropping to the floor had me peeling my hand away to admire the glory that was Vann Delane's toned, gorgeous body.

Holy hell. This man was perfect.

And he was mine.

He started to move over me. I wiggled back on the bed, so we had room to... move. He followed, nipping at my breast as we went.

"You're sure you're okay with no condom?"

"I promise," I whispered, anticipation and heat flooding me all over again. Hadn't I just had an orgasm? Was I going to be greedy today?

Yes, yes I was.

He kissed me again until I couldn't help but clamp my legs around his waist and lift my hips to meet his. I wanted this man.

I had never wanted anything more.

He slid inside me slowly, taking his time, enjoying every freaking second. We both gasped when he was fully seated, my entire body awakening to the feel and pleasure of him.

Just when I didn't think it could feel any better, he began to move. And move. And move. We gasped for breath as he took turns with my nipple in his mouth or kissing me. My fingernails dug into his lower back as he filled me completely, pulled out and then thrust inside me again until all I could feel was him in every inch of my body.

Before I knew it, I was at the edge again, chasing that fireworks explosion he was so very good at giving me.

And then I was falling. Falling over the edge of sensation and feeling. Falling in love with him deeper and deeper and deeper. And falling right into his safe and wonderful arms.

He chased after me and I watched as his eyes slammed shut and he became the sexiest thing I had ever seen in my entire life. I knew exactly what he meant when he said he could watch me all day.

I wanted to watch him again. And again. And for the rest of my life.

We held each other for a long time, wrapped naked together beneath my heavy comforter, whispering sweet nothings and declarations of love and making this the most beautiful memory I had of sex.

He was everything my past was not. He was trustworthy and loyal and beautiful. He was funny and sweet and kind. And he was mine.

"I'm going to be so late for work," I groaned, after talking myself into checking the clock. "And I just got them to get there on time."

He smiled and kissed my shoulder. "I think we should call in."

I blinked at him, surprised he'd even suggested the idea. "What?"

"Why not?" he asked, a wicked smile lifting his lips. "We're the bosses after all."

That was true. We were the bosses. And we were damn good ones too.

So that's what we did. We both called in and left our businesses to the staff we'd worked so hard to train. And then we stayed in bed for the rest of the day, talking about our future, talking through our pasts and falling more and more in love.

Vann Delane had been the most surprising thing to ever happen to me. And the best thing. He'd saved me when I didn't know I needed saving. He'd led me to healing I didn't know was possible. And now he would be the future I never expected.

I loved this man that was so good at helping me fix all that was broken in my life. This man that had reached inside of me and helped mend the broken pieces of me too.

TWENTY-THREE

"DID YOU SEE?"

I looked up from my paperwork to find Blaze grinning. The sight was so startling I didn't know what to say. Or do. So I just blinked at him and waited for more words.

"Chef, did you see?" he asked slower, enunciating every word carefully.

"See what?" I shook my head. "Why are you smiling?"

He shook the newspaper at me. I hadn't noticed he was holding it. Seeing him happy was too distracting. And slightly disturbing.

"Check out the living section," he ordered.

Not understanding where any of this was going, I took the paper from him and noticed it was only the living section.

Then I noticed a picture of Bianca front and center.

"What is this?" I gasped, standing up and jumping to the balls of my feet.

Blaze's smile disappeared, tired with my confusion. "Just read it."

The headline read, *New Chef in Town* and I realized slowly, painfully slowly, that the article, by Durham's premier food critic, was about me. Oh, my god!

"Dillon Baptiste might have family connections but her innovative ideas are all her own," I read aloud. I looked up at Blaze with the widest eyes ever. "Is she serious?"

"Keep reading," he encouraged.

This time I listened to him. Reading as quickly as possible, I picked out the parts I couldn't believe were actually there. "She might be young, but she's proving to be a force to be reckoned with... Her makeover ideas were the facelift the struggling restaurant needed... now known for its mouth-watering brunch and trendy décor, Bianca is quickly becoming a must for this city's foodie culture... I visited three separate times and was only more impressed with each visit... Looks like little sister has a few things to teach her restaurateur brother." I gasped and then laughed and then read the article all over again. "Ezra is going to kill me!" I screamed. "Blaze!"

He smiled again, an ear-to-ear grin. "I know."

"This is us!"

He nodded. "I know."

"We made the paper!"

He laughed at me. "I know."

I launched myself around the desk and threw my arms around his neck. "Thank you for sticking with me," I sniffled against him. "I couldn't have done any of this without you."

He hugged me back. "I know."

I couldn't stop smiling. And now I had to tell Vann. And Ezra. Plus, there were so many chefs to gloat to.

Good thing they were all out in my dining room.

We were celebrating again. Kaya and Wyatt's engagement this time. He'd asked her last night, surprising her by showing up at Sarita and sending one of her dishes back to the kitchen. She'd been so upset at the arrogant customer that thought he knew more than she did, she nearly threw the plate in the garbage without looking at it. He'd shouted at her from the doorway where he'd snuck in to watch her open the ring box.

They'd had a magical moment. She'd said yes of course.

Vann and I were now officially still on the outside of our couple friends. Only dating. Not married or engaged.

Yet.

I smiled to myself, because I knew it was coming. Not today. Probably not this year. But this man was the man I wanted to spend the rest of my life with. This was the man I wanted saving me from myself forever and ever amen.

Congratulating staff members along the way, I left them to prep for the day and burst from the kitchen to my waiting friends. I'd offered to host a celebratory lunch for my bestie and her new fiancé at Bianca. I had just been finishing up in my office and was getting ready to come out here when Blaze walked in with the paper.

"My first review!" I shouted at them forgetting about the happy reason they were here.

"What?" was the collective response from them.

I held the paper up so they could see. "I'm a force to be reckoned with!"

Throwing myself into Vann's arms, I felt lucky he was ready to catch me. He took the paper from me and quickly read the article. "New chef in town indeed," he laughed, squeezing me in a tight hug.

He passed the paper on to his sister, who had to read it over the sweetest, tiniest, most adorable newborn swaddled in her arms. Cecily Violet, or Cece for short, was the most precious baby that had ever been. We were all in love and taking turns doting on her.

Vann had turned out to be an incredible uncle that loved to buy her presents and ingeniously passed her off whenever there was a threat of a dirty diaper.

And Vera and Killian were an inspiration as far as busy parents went. Vera was still on maternity leave from their now busy restaurant. She was exhausted and alone a lot as Killian carried the burden by himself. But they were making it work and still working hard for their dreams. And their marriage.

They gave me hope that there could be kids in my future as well.

Even with a crazy, intense job. Even with Vann working as much as I did.

He wrapped his arms around me as my friends passed the newspaper around. "Is this the real reason we're here?" Wyatt asked. "The engagement lunch was just a front, wasn't it?"

Laughing, I shook my head. "Blaze just brought me the article. I had no idea."

"Uh, I'm not surprised," Kaya gloated. "I told you, babe."

"Congratulations!" Molly squealed when she finally got the paper. "Oh, my gosh, how exciting!"

"I can't take all the credit," I told her. "I do have a pretty kick ass PR squad."

She smiled at me. "I can only get them here. It's your food that makes them stay and write amazing articles about you."

"Proud of you, sis," Ezra announced, one of his rare smiles big on his face as well. "I hate to say I told you so, but..."

I stuck my tongue out at him.

"Come on, we were all right," Killian added. "We all knew you'd flip this place around. I mean, Ezra seriously did his best to run it into the ground, but you handled it like a pro."

Ezra's smile died and he glared at Killian.

"It feels good, doesn't it?" Vera asked. "There's nothing like a good review to solidify your purpose."

I nodded. She was right.

"It's not the reason we do this," she added. "But damn, it feels good."

"As if there was any question," Vann whispered in my ear. Then planted a sweet kiss on my cheek.

"This all feels right," I said to the group, admiring my friends as they sat with the ones they loved. I'd grown up alone and lonely. When Ezra first showed up in my life I could never have anticipated how big my family would become.

But now, here they were, surrounding me, supporting me, loving me.

Most of all, this man by my side. He'd saved me countless times. And then the most important time. And he was walking with me as I healed. He'd encouraged me to go to the police and give a statement, which I had. With him by my side of course.

They had been kind and understanding, but were honest when they said there probably wasn't anything they could do now. Vann had even reached out to Justin a few weeks back and asked him questions about my attacker.

It hadn't gotten us anywhere, but we were working on closure without all the facts and hard truths anyway.

I was learning to let the past go as my present became more beautiful. And I'd started group therapy with other victims of sexual assault. I hadn't shared my story yet, but I'd cried with everyone who had each week I'd been.

My confidence was growing as my heart and soul were healing. I wasn't ready to share with other people just yet, but I knew one day I would be. And when that day came, I would use my story to help others get through the worst of theirs.

This world was so ugly, so very broken. And there were victims everywhere. My group was showing me that. Women I would never have suspected. Women in jobs of every kind or stay at home moms. Women of every age and color and income. Women attacked by people they knew and thought they loved, by family members, by total strangers.

So many stories, all in varying degrees of sick and awful. My heart broke and would always break for women that had to suffer like I did. Women who had to carry their attack with them for the rest of their life.

But if anything beautiful could come out of such tragedy and devastation, it was the sisterhood I was finding among the victims. We had each other. We were learning to lean on and trust each other. And we would always, always stand up and fight for each other.

This group of people would do the same for me too. Especially the man at my side.

He helped me serve lunch while my staff prepared for dinner service. And then we sat down with our closest friends and laughed and toasted to love and life and this beautiful joy we'd found in each other.

Wyatt and Kaya shared details of the engagement and even though it was the second time I'd heard the story, since Kaya had called me late last night to fill me in, I enjoyed every word all over again.

I didn't know it was possible to be this happy. Or this complete. Or this hopeful for the future.

I didn't know it was possible to love this much or laugh this much.

I didn't know it was possible to heal.

Vann had come into my life at the perfect time and he'd swept me away in grumpy helpfulness. He was the thing I didn't know I needed. He was the man I didn't know existed.

And he was the love I'd hoped for my entire life.

When our friends had left and it was just the two of us in the dining room, he wrapped me up in his arms and kissed me until my lips were swollen and my heartbeat thrummed beneath my fragile breastbone.

"I hate that we have jobs," he groaned.

I laughed, because before there was an us, we only had our jobs. "I know," I sympathized. "I do too."

Only we didn't hate our jobs. We loved our jobs. We'd just recently found something to love more.

"Come over tonight after?" he asked, his lips trailing sweet kisses along my throat.

"You'll be asleep," I reminded him.

He sunk his teeth into my collarbone. "Wake me up."

I shivered. It was my favorite thing to do. "Okay."

Satisfied that we would see each other soon, he took a step back and hit me with those warm, bright gray eyes. "I love you, Dillon Baptiste."

I smiled and it felt as though it came from my very soul. “I love you, too, Vann Delane.”

UNTITLED

Thank you so very much for reading The Something about Her! The entire Opposites Attract series has been one of my most favorite things to write ever. I have loved weaving romance and some comedy and all the delicious food with real issues women face every day.

Dillon and Vann have been a joy to write. They've also been extremely difficult as I tackled some heavy issues with Dillon's past. Even with incredible movements like #metoo, and women gaining more and more courage to speak out against their attackers, I want to acknowledge those women that have not yet found their voice. If you have been attacked and have held it tightly to your chest, unable to find the words to verbalize what happened, I just want to encourage you. What happened to you is horrific and not acceptable. But the guilt is not yours to bear. You are innocent, dear friend. You are the victim.

But you are also a survivor.

Seek help if you are ready and speak out when your trauma finds its voice. And please know, that even in your silence, you have support. You have a tribe of women that stand with you and stand up for you. You are seen. And you are loved.

And to those that read simply to be entertained, thank you for spending your time with Dillon and Vann and all the other foodie couples of Durham! I have adored taking this journey with you.

Stay tuned for an upcoming series featuring Will English and his adventures at Craft coming this fall! And look out for my next second chance romance, Never Fall in Love with a Rockstar, coming June 25th, 2019!

NEVER FALL IN LOVE WITH A ROCKSTAR BLURB

Never Fall in Love with a Rockstar, 2019!

My name is Clover Calloway and I've lived two separate lives.
The first, I like to call "my past." I never talk about it. I try not to think about it. My rockstar days of playing in one of the hottest bands on the planet are over. Along with the most volatile, beautiful, tragic love story of all time.

Over the past five years, I've settled into my second life. My "normal life." The one where I work a normal job, hang out with normal people and fall in love with a normal, but wonderful guy. The life where I'm admittedly a little bored, but also safe.

My past wasn't boring. But my past broke my heart into a million, unfixable pieces. So, I'm determined to keep it where it belongs—behind me.

And the man responsible for the shattering of me? Malachi Porter, lead singer and mastermind of Bright Tragedy, should stay there too. Far away from me and this idyllic life I've carved out for myself.

But what happens when my two lives collide?

When Malachi comes crashing into my perfectly normal world, he threatens to destroy it, promises to annihilate everything I've replaced him with.

He upends everything I thought I wanted and forces me to question the reasons I left Bright Tragedy all those years ago.

But I didn't walk away five years ago, I ran. As fast as I could go. And while my heart is whispering that it's different this time—that he's different—my brain is screaming for me to run again.

Malachi Porter isn't a normal guy. And he doesn't belong in my "normal life." But, nevertheless, he's bound and determined to make a place for himself here.

I just hope my heart can survive him, that we don't burn into another bright tragedy.

Keep reading for an excerpt of Never Fall in Love with a Rockstar!

Preorder HERE

ACKNOWLEDGMENTS

In the busiest season of life thus far, we decided to buy a house, move, launch Pierce and Ivy's spring line and release a book. These last few months have been nothing but madness. So first and foremost, I want to thank my God, who is a God of miracles, who always puts me in this posture of needing Him so that He can do miraculous things right in front of me. Thank you, Zach, for thriving on this chaos, for getting the details right when I forget them all and for cheerleading me through every day when I just want to panic. Thank you to my kiddos who are so understanding when I abandon life to shut myself away and write. Thank you to my mom and mother-in-law who have gone above and beyond with sleepovers and babysitting hours. To Amy Bartol, who is waiting on the next chapter of our super exciting project while I get my life together. To my friends and Bible study who have gotten the worst of me lately and still love me. To my editor, Amy Donnelly, who works so hard around my never-on-time deadlines and to Lenore, my beta reader, who puts up with all of my chaos. Especially when I got the flu in those last few hours and put all of us behind schedule! Thank you to my assistant, Holly, who has learned to just do what needs to be done and manages my mess.

Thank you especially to the entire OPTS team at my bank, who fell in love with my stories while asking for every last financial document on the planet and made buying a house in the middle of releasing a book so very worth it. Seriously, you all are the very best. And thank you to my bloggers and readers, who continually and consistently show up for me. I could not do this without you. You give this job joy. And you somehow manage to top every single release. Thank you for your support and your time and for falling in love with these love stories as much as I have.

ABOUT THE AUTHOR

Rachel Higginson was born and raised in Nebraska but spent her college years traveling the world. She fell in love with Eastern Europe, Paris, Indian Food and the beautiful beaches of Sri Lanka, but came back home to marry her high school sweetheart. Now she spends her days raising their growing family. She is obsessed with reruns of *The Office* and Cherry Coke.

Rachel's next second chance romance, Never Fall in Love with a Rockstar is coming June 25th, 2019!

Other Books Out Now by Rachel Higginson:

Love and Decay, Season One

Volume One

Volume Two

Love and Decay, Season Two

Volume Three

Volume Four

Volume Five

Love and Decay, Season Three

Volume Six

Volume Seven

Volume Eight

Love and Decay: Revolution, Season One

Volume One

Volume Two

The Star-Crossed Series

Reckless Magic (The Star-Crossed Series, Book 1)
Hopeless Magic (The Star-Crossed Series, Book 2)
Fearless Magic (The Star-Crossed Series, Book 3)
Endless Magic (The Star-Crossed Series, Book 4)
The Reluctant King (The Star-Crossed Series, Book 5)
The Relentless Warrior (The Star-Crossed Series, Book 6)
Breathless Magic (The Star-Crossed Series, Book 6.5)
Fateful Magic (The Star-Crossed Series, Book 6.75)
The Redeemable Prince (The Star-Crossed Series, Book 7)

The Starbright Series

Heir of Skies (The Starbright Series, Book 1)
Heir of Darkness (The Starbright Series, Book 2)
Heir of Secrets (The Starbright Series, Book 3)

The Siren Series

The Rush (The Siren Series, Book 1)
The Fall (The Siren Series, Book 2)
The Heart (The Siren Series, Book 3)

Bet on Love Series

Bet on Us (An NA Contemporary Romance)
Bet on Me (An NA Contemporary Romance)

Every Wrong Reason

The Five Stages of Falling in Love

Trailer Park Heart

The Opposite of You (Opposites Attract Series)

The Difference Between Us (Opposites Attract Series)
The Problem with Him (Opposites Attract Series)
The Something about Her (Opposites Attract Series)

Constant (The Confidence Game Duet)
Consequence (The Confidence Game Duet)

Connect with Rachel on her blog at:
http://www.rachelhigginson.com/

Or on Twitter:
@mywritesdntbite

Or on her Facebook page:
Rachel Higginson

Keep reading for an excerpt from one of Rachel's upcoming second chance love story, Never Fall in Love with a Rockstary, coming June 25th, 2019

Preorder HERE Never Fall in Love with a Rockstar

NEVER FALL IN LOVE WITH A ROCKSTAR CHAPTER ONE

My fingers flew over the keys. Up and down. Black and white. Sharp and natural and sharp, sharp, sharp. The damper pedal lifted with my momentum. I pressed down again, elongating the notes, pulling the best of the melody out of the song and letting it hang in the air, notes dancing and twirling and singing in the emotional symphony. Beethoven had never sounded so good.

I took a breath. Closing my eyes at the final, heart-stopping crescendo, I lifted my fingers and let the last notes resonate through the vaulted ceilings in perfect harmony.

When the sound died and the song drifted from the building, I couldn't help but wait for applause. It was ingrained in my nature. My entire life I'd played to crowds much bigger than this one. And so, I sat there, my breath trapped inside my chest, my eyes closed in anticipation and... nothing.

There was no eruption of cheering and wild clapping. There was no demand for an encore. There was no stadium filled with rabid fans, blissed out at the end of the best show of their lives.

Only one person was clapping for this performance and it was Maya from the MAC makeup counter. And she only did it because she knew it made me happy. I grinned at her over my shoulder. She clapped louder, jumping up and down in a pure attempt to feed my ego.

A cluster of teenage girls moved between us, laughing and chatting, eyes glued on all the pretty things around them. I quickly turned away, ducking my head and focusing on the gorgeous grand piano that filled the center of the glistening lobby.

Nobody recognized me these days, but better safe than sorry.

When the shoppers had moved on, I gathered my music and slipped it inside a folder. Maya was still slow clapping by the time I reached the counter that was covered with tubes of lipstick.

"Woman, you were on fire today," she cheered. "I was seriously moved by that last piece. Tears, Clover. Actual tears." She pointed at the corner of her eye where her electric blue eyeliner was smudged.

"Moonlight Sonata." I took a steadying breath, banishing the lingering emotions that clung to the edges of me. Beethoven's masterful piece was one of my favorites too. And I rarely played it. But today I'd been in the mood for melancholy and memories. And that song, above all others, despite what the tabloids and bloggers said about me once upon a time, weighed the heaviest with my past. "It's a good one."

She leaned forward on her elbows. "You're stupid good, you know that?"

I tilted my head, letting my long, fiery red curls fall over my shoulder and partially hide my face. "What you really mean is I'm good for Macy's standards, right?" I looked behind me as Walter arrived and started to set up for his three-hour block. Macy's hired us for elegant entertainment. We were the background music for the high-end department stores evening and weekend shoppers. There was a rotating total of six pianists and each of us were happy for the work. It was a relatively easy way to make a hundred bucks.

This was all part of my new normal. Trying to live and eat and sleep off the grind of regular employment.

Once upon a time, my piano-playing skills made me lots and lots of money. Not that I put in fewer hours. But it seemed easier to make money as a headline band dropping platinum albums.

It seemed easier, I realized. But it hadn't been.

I breathed deeply of this normal life I lived now and smiled at the simplicity of it. Sorrow and heartache tugged at the corners of my thoughts, desperate to get my attention and claim some space in this adjusted life of mine, but I refused to give them room.

They were banished, along with everything else that used to be.

"Girl, I mean you're good period. Stop playin'."

"You're really sweet. Thank you."

She winked at me. "You're welcome."

"What is all this?" I asked, picking up a random tube of lipstick and turning it over. Russian Red. "Wow, this is bright."

"Restocking," she sighed. "It's a pain in the ass. But also, better than giving tweens makeovers all day."

"What about former tweens? Do you have time for one of those?"

She laughed her deep, throaty laugh that always made me smile. Maya and I had gotten to know each other slowly over the last few years after I'd first started playing at Macy's. She'd been one of my most favorite parts of slowing down and finding normal.

She was a real friend. And a real person. There was nothing shallow about her. She jumped right into a deep friendship and demanded raw honesty. There were still parts of my life I kept a secret from her, but that wasn't because I didn't want to tell her the whole sordid history of how I'd ended up in Kansas City, Missouri. It was for her safety. And mine. And to honor all those pesky nondisclosures I'd signed.

Her big brown eyes widened. "Oh, my gosh, is tonight the night? The big night?"

I nibbled my bottom lip and nodded. "Yes." My stomach flipped with anticipation for the surprise that waited for me just hours from now.

She leaned forward, bouncing on her toes with shared excitement. "What do you think it is? Oh, my gosh, what if he proposes?"

I lifted a shoulder and felt my stomach drop to my toes. Equal parts dread and hope spiraled through me, chasing each other, racing to see which emotion would win. "I have no idea what it is. He's so excited though. He can barely contain himself. Yesterday, he had outfits spread out on his bed like he was deciding which one to wear."

"Oh my god, Clover! This has to be it."

I shrugged again. "It could honestly be anything, but a proposal, Maya? For real, that would be crazy."

"Would you say yes?"

I took too long to think about my answer. Maya wanted an easy, breezy yes. She wanted to know that my relationship with Adam Shepherd was a whirlwind romance that had totally and completely swept me off my feet. She wanted a real-life romantic comedy and epic love story wrapped in one. She wanted me to be happy. And it was so sweet of her. But it was also unrealistic.

I'd already had all of that. And it had ended in the worst kind of tragedy.

Her question was supposed to have an easy answer. Even if I wasn't ready for the proposal now, I was supposed to want it sometime, right?

Meet a normal guy. Fall in love with a normal guy. Marry a normal guy. Live a very normal happily ever after.

Every girl's dream. Except mine.

"We've only been dating for six months," I told her, laughing, playing it off, shining light on her absolutely ridiculous idea. "He hasn't even told me he loves me yet." A sick feeling rolled through my stomach, my body wholly rejecting the idea of saying those words to anyone.

She blinked, her fake lashes fanning over high cheekbones. "Oh." Maya was a romantic to her bones. She wanted everyone to fall in love. If a man so much as knelt to tie his shoe in front of the makeup counter, she assumed it was some elaborate proposal stunt. "Well, maybe tonight's the night for I love yous!"

My heart thrummed with the idea, bossing my nerves back in

line. This was an easier question to answer, although she hadn't asked it. Would I tell Adam I loved him if he said the words first? Yes. Yes, I would.

At least, I hoped I would.

Sometimes my mouth had a mind of its own.

I bat my lashes at her. "Better make me look pretty just in case."

She grinned and grabbed the tube of Russian Red. "The good news is, if he doesn't love you yet, he will after I'm done with you!"

Jumping up onto one of the high back stools, I set my messenger bag full of sheet music at my feet and waited patiently for Maya to make me gorgeous. The woman was a magician when it came to makeup. Seriously, she could make anything look beautiful.

Not that she had to try very hard. She was truly one of the most stunning women I had ever seen. Her dark skin was absolute perfection. Her natural hair, wild and curly and edgy, so perfectly fitting to her larger than life personality. And her curves the kind that every woman wanted, dreamed of, spent hours in the gym to get. She was one of MAC's bestsellers consistently because everybody wanted to look like her.

Hell, most women wanted to be her.

Also, because she could transform anyone from blah to banging with a few mystical strokes of her brushes.

Thirty minutes later, I barely recognized myself in the small circular mirror on the counter. She'd given me smoky eyes, highlighted cheekbones, and dang that Russian Red if it didn't look amazing on my lips next to my natural red hair.

"No way," I whispered as she grinned over my shoulder. She'd highlight the dusting of freckles over my nose and under my eyes and given me perfectly porcelain skin that seemed to have no blemishes. Although, I knew that to be a lie. I looked better than I ever had.

I looked even better than when I'd had an actual makeup team.

"You're going home with this lipstick," she ordered. "You need to own it and wear it every damn day."

"It makes my hair look so red." I groaned. My hair and I had been at odds since I could remember. There was a time I did anything to hide the crimson curls. I straightened, I tied it back and hid it under stocking caps and finally, when the PR team got involved, I colored it in crazy vibrant colors like neon pink or bold purple. I loved the fun shades, even if I looked like a Barbie.

But, I'd given all that up five years ago and went back to my natural shade. The curls were more manageable than trying to straighten this mess every day. Eventually, my new hair stylist had found the perfect red to match my roots. I didn't even get it dyed anymore. This was just me. Clover Callaway, completely natural. Completely anonymous.

Nobody expected the red curls. They were my new signature. And I was slowly learning to love them.

Like I was slowly learning to love this life.

"You're welcome," Maya repeated, laughing. "Tell you what. If I had your hair, I would rock the shit out of it."

Now that I believed. "M, if I had your hair, I would never worry about my hair again."

She bugged her eyes out at me. "You think this is easy? You have no idea how long this takes me every day."

"Same," I sighed.

Shaking her head, she murmured, "I guess the grass is always greener."

"Now isn't that the truth."

An older woman and a thirty-something younger version of her stepped up to the counter, pointing out eye shadows. "That's my cue," Maya whispered, totaling up the lipstick with her employee discount.

I gave her my credit card. Honestly, whenever she picked out makeup for me, I gave her my money. Maya knew best. "Thanks for this."

She grinned at me. "Good luck! I want all the details tomorrow."

To be honest, I wasn't expecting anything as grand as I love yous. Adam and I had met at one of my other jobs—local photographer. He had been a groomsman at a wedding I helped shoot. We'd hit it off when he'd gotten socked in the face with a wayward basketball.

The groomsmen and groom, while waiting for the bride and her attendants to get ready, had been messing around in the church's gym. My photographer friend, River, and I had been shooting fun photos of the pickup game in their tuxes when Adam had gotten distracted and taken a ball to the face. Blood had gushed everywhere, spurting out his swollen nose all over his tux.

His excuse? He'd been staring at me and hadn't seen it coming. I'd rushed to his aid and helped nurse his poor nose back to semi-normal, so he wouldn't look like a cartoon for the wedding pictures.

He'd asked me out before the night was over, and now we were dating.

Adam was one of those guys that always made things easy. He was laid-back, responsible, and adorable. The last six months had been a surprising whirlwind of romantic dates and constant butterflies. And tonight, he'd planned something epic for our six-month anniversary.

I had never celebrated relationship anniversaries with anyone before, so my expectations were low. But I was also ridiculously excited. It made me feel special. I loved the idea of celebrating small milestones with this simmering anticipation for more to come.

And it just fit Adam in every way. Of course, he would make a sweet thing out of our six-month. Of course, he would make me feel cherished. Of course, he would make this about us. And not about himself.

I left Macy's in my cool blue Mini Cooper, my favorite of all the cars in the world, and drove directly to his house. We lived across town from each other, so I didn't have time to go all the way home after my shift before I was supposed to be at Adam's house in Kansas City suburbia.

He was thirty-one with a stable job as an IT guy at a tech company, which seemed redundant to me. But he assured me even tech companies have tech problems.

His house was bigger than what he needed as a single guy. It seemed huge for him alone. When he'd first moved in, he'd shared it with three roommates. They'd all gotten married in the meantime and moved out. Over the last two years, he'd been slowly remodeling and updating. Making it his.

I didn't know why I found that attractive, but I did. It showed me how stable he was. How reliable. How invested he was in his life.

And for those reasons, I loved his house. It was this symbol of responsible adulthood and trustworthiness.

It was an older one and a half story home with the master bedroom on the main floor and three bedrooms and an adorable terrace that looked out over his sprawling backyard. He'd let me plant a flower garden on the terrace last spring complete with pallet planters he'd built for me and hanging pots. It was my favorite place in the entire world.

The hot summer air stuck to my skin as I got out of my car and hurried toward his front door. I didn't want to start sweating and ruin all of Maya's hard work.

Pushing through the open door, I stepped inside, feeling a little extra ownership in Adam's place. Six months was a milestone.

Six months meant something special.

"Hello?" I called out, feeling brave that I hadn't even texted to let him know I was on my way.

I'd earned the right to show up unannounced, right?

He stepped out of his bedroom, tugging a t-shirt down at his waist. My eyes lingered on the smooth, stretch of skin across his midsection and I felt a burst of warmth bloom through me. This was going to be a fun night. It had to be.

"Hey," he grinned at me. "You're here."

He was so happy to see me. It was written all over his handsome face. My heart swelled in my chest as I realized this was what a normal, healthy relationship felt like. This was what it felt like to be happy.

"Hey," I repeated. "I'm here."

We moved together across the living room, sidestepping furniture and the big, clunky coffee table he'd built himself on his first try at furniture making. Our arms wrapped around each other and he dipped me into a long, satisfying kiss. Butterflies buzzed beneath my skin at the sensation of his tongue tangling with mine. The scruff of his jaw wasn't typical, and I shivered at the sensation.

Maybe we didn't have plans tonight. Maybe we were going to hang out here instead and find other ways to celebrate six months.

"Are you ready for this?" he asked when he'd pulled away.

"Depends," I laughed. "Are you ready to tell me what we're doing?"

He took a step back, barely able to contain his excitement. No offense to my bedroom skills, but any hopes of staying in tonight were dashed in that one uncharacteristic skip in his step.

Reaching into his back pocket, he pulled out printer paper with barcodes in black ink. "I have tickets to Bright Tragedy! They're playing at the Uptown Theater tonight."

His words were a bullet to my good mood, killing whatever happiness and anticipation had been inside me. My heart dropped like a stone to my stomach, calcifying and fossilizing and drying up all at once. "The Uptown Theater is too small for them," I heard myself say, my brain relying on logistics to make this not true. To change what he'd said into something different, something that didn't make me want to run away from his house, from this city... from this country.

"It's a more intimate show," he explained, his grin ticking wider. "This tour they're doing is all about small shows and private meet and greets. I missed the tickets for the meet and greet, but I managed to grab the main event tonight."

His grin stayed in place, waiting for my reaction. I did breathe a small sigh of relief that he'd missed the intimate photo op. God, I couldn't even imagine the shit show that would have been.

You wouldn't have gone, my brain whispered honestly. And it was true. If Adam had tried to drag me to a private event where I would have been forced to interact with the members of his and the entire world's favorite rock band and take pictures with them and shake their hands... I would have run screaming from his house. That was the worst-case scenario for me.

But a concert was a different story. Not because I had any interest in watching Bright Tragedy live or seeing them in person ever again. But because I wanted to preserve what I had with Adam.

I refused to let Bright Tragedy steal any more of my happiness. I refused to let them take anything more from me than they already had.

But this wasn't a celebration for me. This was one of the hardest things I would ever have to do.

And the worst part... I couldn't even tell Adam why.

He didn't need to know that I used to be a member of his favorite band. Or that I had grown up with the guys. Or that the lead singer, Malachi Porter, had been my first boyfriend. My first everything. My only everything until Adam. I had loved him with all that I had in me. I had thought we would get married. That our entire lives would be each other and our band.

And that Malachi, or Kai as his adoring fans knew him, had hurt me in the worst way possible—that he had let our love burn into the brightest tragedy and left me ashes and dust and wisps of nothing.

He'd left me barely breathing.

He'd left me hurting more than I knew was humanly possible.

With no other choice, I'd fled. I'd disappeared. I'd carved out my normal, safe, happy existence without him. And without the world-famous band I'd helped build.

But now, my wonderfully normal boyfriend was asking me to go back to that dark place and I didn't know how to tell him no without exposing all my shadowy secrets. Secrets he would never forgive me for.

Secrets I could hardly explain fully or reconcile with the girl I was now.

"Are you okay?" he asked, concern drawing his eyebrows

together. His strong hands landed on my shoulders, rubbing soothingly. "Do you not want to go?"

I tried to smile, but it wobbled. And then it died completely. "I'm sorry, I just don't love their music like you do." Panic seized hold of my heart, squeezing it in an iron fist.

His face fell, crumbling with disappointment. The grip on my heart tightened. "Oh, but it could still be fun? We're in the balcony. We'll get drinks..."

I couldn't stomach the way he was looking at me. I couldn't be responsible for ruining this for him. I knew I had to face this. I knew I had to go. It was the only way to save my past from totally screwing up my future.

If I told Adam the whole truth, he would never look at me the same. He would never treat me the same. He would never... want me the same.

I would become an idol. And my past would become a badge of honor. And his feelings for me would become plastic.

But the band... if they saw me. If Malachi saw me...

They wouldn't, I decided. They won't. They can't. How many fans did I recognize at any of our concerts? Zero. The stage lights were too bright. The crush of the crowd was too big. The adrenaline of the performance was too intense.

And besides, Malachi wouldn't be in the right state of mind anyway. He wouldn't even notice me.

I ignored the despair that colored everything inside me black. Death seeped inside my new life, turning everything cold and corpse-like. My bones grew stiff and my muscles weakened. My heartbeat slowed to a crawl. My lungs shook with the effort to draw breath.

"It's fine," I heard myself say, desperation to save this easy new life of mine setting in. I wanted to shake my limbs loose of the rigor mortis. "It will be fun."

He squinted at me, trying to make sense of the hollow sound of my voice. "I promise, you're going to love it. Love them," he said, overly enthusiastic. "You'll see why I think they're amazing. You'll be a super fan by the end of the night."

I smiled, it was paper thin and fake, but it held. He was wrong. I had already been a super fan. I had been their biggest fan. I had wanted them to have the most success. To be the greatest thing that had ever graced the stage.

Now I knew better. I had loved a broken thing because I wanted to fix it. Instead, it had broken me too.

"Maybe," I told Adam, knowing the truth would be the opposite.

His answering smile restored some of my faith in life. I wasn't the same girl I was five years ago. I wasn't a part of Bright Tragedy. And I wasn't in love with Malachi Porter.

But I did like Adam. And I could support him this one night. I would slip inside the theater, be a good girlfriend and hang out on the balcony. And then we would leave at the end of the night and life would go on.

Malachi and the guys would move on to the next city.

And I would move on with my new normal.

Easy.

Read the rest of Clover Calloway's story when Never Fall in Love with a Rockstar releases June 25th, 2019!!! Preorder HERE